THE FINAL
COORDINATE

THE COORDINATE BOOK 3

MARC JACOBS

By Marc Jacobs © 2022

The Final Coordinate
(Book 3 in *The Coordinate Series*)

It has been three months since Logan and Emma escaped the battle in the Hidden City, but the fight for survival has just begun. Supay has destroyed Vanirya, and Earth is next, unless they can find the Leyandermál, the most powerful weapon in the universe, before Supay, or anyone else, does.

They will first need to find Isa, who holds the key to locating the Leyandermál, but she is lost in time with Annika. Logan and Emma will have to search throughout history to find her, unraveling the clues left behind in humanity's past, but their search will not be easy. Not everyone wants them to succeed, while others are sinisterly counting on it.

Join Emma and Logan as they race against time to save humanity, and each other, in *The Final Coordinate*, the thrilling conclusion to *The Coordinate* series, where failure may be the only option…

Copyright

The Final Coordinate

Copyright © 2022 by Marc Jacobs

Printed in the United States of America

First Printing, 2022

Paperback ISBN: 9798404537956

Publisher: Marc Jacobs

marc@marcjacobsauthor.com
www.marcjacobsauthor.com

Dedication

To My Loving Family, Friends, and Editors:
This book is dedicated with love and appreciation to my family, my
friends, and all my incredible editors – who have inspired me and
helped me to make this series a reality.

Contents

Chapter 1 – Flight

Isa and Annika carefully navigated down an icy hill, heading for the partially snow-covered, partially grass-covered Icelandic highlands nestled in between two mountain ranges. There was a 50' deep river gorge ahead of them that jaggedly wove through the highlands as far as the eye could see in either direction. Spanning the river gorge was a path of ice forming a natural bridge suitable for crossing. A gust of wind whipped ice and snow off the ground, smacking their faces and reddening their already frigid cheeks.

"It is the cold winds of the North Atlantic battling the subarctic winds of the Norwegian Sea," commented Annika in Russian to her young Vaniryan friend, Isa, with whom she was lost in time in a foreign land.

Isa, using her Vaniryan telepathic abilities to comprehend Annika's words and communicate back in Russian, replied, "Isa does not know who is winning the battle of winds, but Isa knows who is not." Isa raised her forearm to shield her face from another prickly gust.

Fortunately, both their bodies remained warm in the thick brown outfits they'd been wearing since they escaped through the portal in Qelios' compound amid the battle in the Hidden City. That seemed like forever ago, now. They worried about the outcome of that battle and what might have become of their friends.

"The strong winds blowing off the ocean is actually a good sign. It means we are close," said Annika.

"Close to a way home for Isa?" asked the young Vaniryan, who looked barely 11-years old. Although given how long Vaniryans lived, Annika knew it was possible she was considerably older than that.

"No, but we're near the western coastline," answered Annika, turning sideways to side-step down the icy slope as it got steeper to avoid falling.

Following suit, Isa turned sideways and asked again, "And then Isa and Annika will find a way home there?"

Annika shook her head. "To be honest, I don't know what we'll find when we get there."

"Will Annika's kind be there?"

Annika chuckled. "You are just full of questions today. Iceland's biggest cities like Reykjavik, at least in the time I come from, are on the country's southern and western coasts. I'm just hoping someone lives there, an early settlement, a small village, something."

"If people are there, will they be able to help Isa and Annika go home?" asked Isa, enduringly hopeful and unaware that her home had been destroyed by Supay shortly after their escape.

"No." Annika knew they had been lost *at least* 800-years in the past based on when the Vaniryan star – TYC 129-75-1 - went supernova, long before an inkling of the technology needed to generate a portal back to Vanirya existed.

Confused, Isa replied, "Isa does not understand. If people cannot help, why does Annika want to find people?"

"It is just an idea I have. Maybe there is still a way they can help us, some way we can get a message back to—"

Annika was interrupted by the sound of horse hooves clopping on ice and approaching footsteps.

"Someone is coming," said Annika.

"Has the Hunt found Isa and Annika already?"

"No, I don't think that's it," replied Annika. Gazing at Isa's circular alien face, golden-white hair, silver-white skin, six-fingered hands, tiny mouth, missing nose and two perfectly round white eyes with radiating blue pupils, Annika was worried about how those approaching might react to Isa. "You have to hide!" she urged as the sounds drew nearer. Annika spotted some large boulders off in the distance. "Hurry, quick, hide over there!"

"It is too far," responded Isa, as the sound of horses and footsteps approaching were getting closer. "There is no time, and Isa will not leave Annika alone."

"But Isa—"

Isa closed her eyes and focused. In a flash, the energy inside her started swirling, quickly consuming her in a swath of bright light while her energy rapidly reconstituted itself to replicate the energy signature of another human Isa had once touched: Emma. It was over quickly. Annika could hardly believe her eyes, but suddenly standing before her was a sweet looking 11-year-old version of Emma, green eyes, slightly pudgy youthful face, and long-blond hair.

"How in the world? You look like—"

Annika didn't have time to finish marveling over Isa's transformation as a horde of marauders came crashing over the hill's peak and down the slope to investigate the strangers traversing their lands. The rugged marauders, wearing tattered skins, rough-fitted boots and carrying medieval weapons, ran up to them. A few rode on horseback.

The men gathered behind their chieftain, a bushy, blond-bearded man clad in chain mail armor and wearing a helmet. The chieftain sat atop a majestic fjord horse, light tan in color, with a long thick white mane, a strong, arched neck, sturdy legs, and a compact, muscular body. The clan banged their weapons together to intimidate Isa and Annika.

With one hand on the hilt of his large sword, the chieftain stared down at Annika and asked her in an unfamiliar language, "Hverjir eru þeir sem brjóta á jörðum okkar?" ["*Who are the trespassers upon our land?*"]

Annika, who did not speak the language, didn't understand what he was asking, although Isa, with her Vaniryan abilities, did. Annika remained silent, unsure how to respond, while Isa said nothing.

Angered by Annika's silence, the chieftain yelled at her. "Kona, þú ert óskynsamur að hunsa mig. Hafa þeir þegar klippt tunguna út eins og ég ætla að gera ef þú talar ekki?" ["*Woman, you are unwise to ignore me! Have they already cut out your tongue like I will do if you do so again?*"] Annika continued to hesitate, so the chieftain drew his sword.

Isa stepped in front of Annika, standing nose to nose with the fjord horse, sort of, since the horse towered over her. She addressed the chieftain, "Mor er forvirret og lider av den kalde isen og snøen. Vær så snill, ikke skad henne, hun er uvel.' ["*Mother is confused, suffering from the cold, ice and snow. Please do not hurt her, she is unwell.*"]

The chieftain cackled out-loud, followed by his men. "Þá er móðir þín veik og heimskuleg að láta barn tala fyrir hana." ["*Your mother is weak and foolish to let a child speak for her.*"] His men banged their weapons together approvingly.

Isa replied, "Fyrirgefðu móður. Móðir þýðir ekki að móðga." ["*Please forgive mother. Mother does not mean to offend.*"] Isa took Annika's hand and began telepathically explaining to her what was going on.

The chieftain was not sympathetic. "Það getur engin fyrirgefning verið fyrir móður sem myndi yfirgefa heimili sitt með barni og flýja inn á láglendi þrátt fyrir að vera ekki nógu vel til að sjá

10

barnið á öruggan hátt í gegnum ferðina. Móðir þín er grimm og ótrú, og við refsum grimmt og ótrú." [*"We cannot forgive a mother who abandons her home with her master's child and escapes into the highlands despite not being well enough to see the child safely through the journey. Your mother is cruel and disloyal, and we punish the cruel and disloyal."*]

Isa began tugging urgently at Annika's hand to suggest that it was about time to run.

Seeing Isa's urging, and somewhat amused by it, the chieftain dismounted his fjord horse. He was a big man, heavy enough that his landing on the ice made a crunching boom. He took a commanding step forward and aggressively clutched Isa's hair, pulling her head toward him. Annika tried grabbing his arm to pull it away but the chieftain swiftly swung his free, iron-knuckle-covered right fist at Annika. He dealt a harsh blow to the left side of her face that drove her down into the snow, breaking her nose and fracturing her cheekbone. Her nose immediately started gushing blood.

"Nei!" [*"No!"*] cried Isa.

The chieftain screamed, "Heimsk kona!" [*"Stupid woman!"*] and threw Isa to the ground in Annika's direction. Isa helped Annika get back to her feet.

The chieftain raised his sword for all to see and announced, "Stúlkan hefur stríðsanda. Við munum taka barnið aftur og gera hana að okkar eigin. Drepa konuna!" [*"The girl has a warrior spirit! We will take the child back and make her our own. Kill the woman!"*]

The chieftain reached out to grab Isa again, but this time, Isa did not stand idly by. She looked at the fjord horse and caused her alien eyes to flare a bright blue color, spooking the horse. The horse neighed and reared up, knocking the chieftain over and causing his men to jump backwards. Startled, all the other horses reared up, too, and together with the fjord horse, started running wild among the men, knocking them over or forcing them to scramble out of the way, before the horses eventually galloped away uphill. Meanwhile, during the commotion, Isa and Annika had taken off downhill.

"Náðu þeim! Dreptu þá báða!" ["*Get them! Kill them both!*"] hollered the chieftain, prompting his men to chase after them.

"To the river, over the ice bridge!" screamed Annika, blood flowing out of her nose.

The chieftain's men pursued them but Isa and Annika reached the river gorge and ice bridge first. The bridge, which was nothing more than a build-up of ice rising 50' above the water's surface, did not entirely stop the river's flow. It had several breaks in it that allowed water from upriver to squeeze through downriver. As they crossed the natural bridge, the horde continued to gain ground.

"We have to do something, we cannot run forever," uttered Annika after they reached the far end of the bridge, worried that the men would pursue unrelentingly until catching them. Annika, for one, was not sure how much longer she could keep it up. To her dismay, Isa stopped dead in her tracks near the end of the bridge. Stunned, Annika shouted, "What are you doing? Come on, we have to go!"

Isa fixed her stance in the middle of the ice pass, glaring at the rushing mob. For a moment, she hesitated, wondering if she should, but then, she just exploded, unleashing a blast of blue energy from her fingertips directed at the ice pass, obliterating the ice in front of her. The ice bridge blew apart!

Some ice chunks flew toward the chieftain and his men, striking several. Other chunks plunged into the river below. The break in the bridge extended 100 feet out from Isa's toes. Two of the chieftain's men caught near the end of the broken ice fell helplessly into the fast-flowing waters. Given the weight of their armor, they quickly sank below the surface and the river whisked them away.

Isa stood there, resolute in her decision. They had deserved it, she told herself. The chieftain slowly stepped up to the other end of the shattered ice pass, not wanting to inadvertently fall over the unstable edge. If the loss of his men bothered him, it didn't show. Rather, he stared at Isa, bewildered, angry and intrigued by what he had just witnessed. Isa stared back at him with a defiant gaze that conveyed a clear message: *do not ever try to hurt Annika or Isa again.*

Isa turned around and walked toward Annika, who had a relieved smile on her face even though her left eye was already swollen shut and her cheek black and blue. Isa grinned back.

"Come on, let's get out of here before they find another way around," said Annika.

Chapter 2 – Nightmares

Emma sat in a chair on an apartment balcony overlooking a jagged river gorge. She could see her breath in the early morning air of Borgarnes, a coastal town an hour north of Iceland's capital, Reykjavik. Even though it was 7 a.m., in the late winter, sunlight was still scarce with only a few beams peeking over the horizon. Emma had come to enjoy the early morning serenity over the last few months that they had been there. It gave her a chance to think, and lately, she found herself out on the balcony before dawn more often than not.

Logan, who had just woken up, joined her outside in the chilly morning air. "Good morning," he said, squeezing through the sticky sliding glass door.

"Hi," responded Emma without turning around.

"Aren't you cold?" he asked, himself wearing a sweatshirt and jeans but still feeling the chill.

Emma shrugged her shoulders. "A little."

Logan sat down in a chair beside her. "How long have you been out here?"

"A few hours."

"A few hours?"

"I couldn't sleep."

"You had another nightmare, didn't you?" asked Logan, worried about her.

"Logan, I saw him again."

"Was it the same dream?"

"Mostly, but this time, I saw the end…"

"What do you mean?"

Her voice quivering, Emma whispered, "I saw it…"

ΔΔΔΔΔΔΔΔΔΔΔΔ

Supay, his hulking form dressed in all black and his radiating blue eyes staring at Emma, slowly approached her. She stood her ground among the shattered ruins of the Hidden City just after the battle, surrounded by lifeless Vaniryan bodies, broken ice structures, and a few surviving Remnants. Supay glared at her, gestured to the dead and screamed in a booming voice, "See what you have done?!"

"You did this, not me!" Emma yelled back.

Supay sneered at her. "Naïve of you to discount the role you've played in their fate, and soon, of the entire planet."

"You do not have to destroy Vanirya!" pleaded Emma.

"If only you had come with me, I would have spared them."

"You still can. Please, don't—"

"What is done cannot be undone."

"Then I will travel to the past to stop you!" retorted Emma.

Supay cackled at her conviction. "You are too late. It is already your future."

He snapped his fingers and vanished. Immediately, the partially broken ice ceiling that covered the Hidden City completely collapsed around Emma, revealing the pale-purple Vaniryan sky in its entirety. Emma could see Supay's massive starship hovering in low orbit. Next, she watched in horror as it fired its fusion cannon at the Vaniryan sun before disappearing into the stars.

"No!!!!!!" she screamed, but there was nothing she could do. She witnessed the blast strike the star, resulting in a terrifying explosion followed by a haunting boom. Remnants started screaming and running for their lives when they saw it, but there was nowhere for them to run, nowhere to hide. In seconds, the exploding star engulfed the entire planet, obliterating Vanirya, Emma and all the remaining Vaniryans along with it…

ΔΔΔΔΔΔΔΔΔΔΔΔ

A tear rolled down Emma's check. "And that's when I woke up. It seemed so real. After that, I couldn't shut my brain off. I couldn't stop thinking about it, or him, or about how things might've gone differently if I'd just gone with him…"

"Em, you have to stop doing this to yourself," urged Logan, blowing into his hands to keep warm.

"That's easy for you to say. I'm the one that made the choice, not you. And when I did, they all died." The guilt Emma was feeling from what happened to Vanirya after she, Logan and the others escaped the battle in the Hidden City was getting worse.

Logan shook his head. "You had no way of knowing what Supay would do."

"He told me exactly what he would do and I didn't listen. I chose to save myself."

"Em, he would have done it regardless."

Emma snapped back, "You don't know that!"

"I know that you shouldn't keep blaming yourself!"

"I'm sorry. You're right, I know. It's just... I can't shake the feeling that I made the wrong choice."

Logan took a deep breath and replied, "You can't keep second-guessing yourself... you can't stop making decisions."

"And what if my next decision gets *you* killed, or all of us?" countered Emma.

"Em, even good decisions have consequences. That's life, and we have to live it." Before Emma could respond, Logan's text-message chime went off on his phone inside the apartment. Logan didn't move.

"Don't you want to see who it is?" asked Emma, using the text message as an excuse to end the conversation. Logan knew it, too, but he didn't want to keep pushing her. She was having a hard time right now, and he knew the demons she was fighting weren't going to be defeated overnight or in one conversation.

"Yeah," he replied, standing up and heading back inside.

After he disappeared, Emma got up and approached the balcony railing. Leaning against it and looking out at the horizon with the tip of the sun now visible, she reprimanded herself, "Come on, Emma, snap out of it." She knew she had to before her emotions ate Logan alive. She'd been hard on him the last few months and she could tell it was taking a toll on him. A few seconds later, he came back.

"Who texted you?"

"Dr. Arenot... they're on the way over."

"When?"

They heard a knock at the apartment door.

"Now," answered Logan.

"Already? I thought we weren't leaving for another half hour," blurted Emma.

"I guess they're anxious to get to Reykholt," replied Logan, walking back inside to get the door.

Emma followed him in and before he could open it, insisted, "At least let me get out of my PJ's!"

Once she disappeared into the bedroom, Logan opened the door to greet Professor Jill Quimbey and Dr. Jonas Arenot. The former Harvard professors, now Pegasus mission specialists, came in.

"Where's Emma?" asked Professor Quimbey.

"Still getting ready. You guys are early."

"Yeah, well, your coffee machine works better than ours," responded Dr. Arenot, heading right for it.

That morning, they had planned to drive to Snorri Sturluson's former home in Reykholt, located in a mountain valley about an hour east. There, Sturluson had built a fort-like farm compound. It was one of a handful of properties owned by the Icelandic poet, historian, and politician in the 13th century, but the best known because it was where Sturluson wrote his famous *Prose Edda* and where Hákon IV, King of Norway, had seventy men ambush and assassinate him.

They were researching Sturluson because he had authored the *Final Journey of the Vanir* poem that contained the clues which, several months earlier, had enabled Logan and Dr. Arenot to find Emma and Professor Quimbey in the Hidden City on Vanirya. He had also written about the 'Vanir gods' in his *Prose Edda*. Needless to say, they had a lot of questions for Sturluson, including about the message he left behind for them to find, and what had become of Isa and Annika, who presumably met Sturluson after going through the portal and being lost in Iceland 800+ years ago. And if they were

18

going to find Isa, assuming she was still alive, they had to start with Sturluson.

Thus, while in Iceland, they had spent the last few months scouring national museums, libraries and archives in Reykholt, Bessastaðir, Reykjavík, Stafholt and Borgarnes, studying documents written by or discussing Sturluson. They had also spent time at the Snorrastofa Research Center in Reykholt which focused on the medieval period in general, but Sturluson in particular. Although they had turned over every stone and examined every word of Sturluson's writings looking for clues, along with the help of think-tank experts back in the States, they were no closer to finding an answer than when they first arrived in Iceland.

After a few minutes, Emma emerged from the bedroom dressed in a long black coat, jeans and black boots. "Ready to go find some answers?" she asked, sounding more upbeat than a few minutes earlier.

"Optimism… brilliant," replied Professor Quimbey.

"At least someone is," said Dr. Arenot, now armed with a cup of caffeine.

"Why wouldn't I be?" questioned Emma. "Going back to the underground tunnel where the king's men murdered Snorri Sturluson, to investigate a historical crime scene? I wouldn't miss it."

Logan was amused. "You and your love for crime scenes."

"You know me," replied Emma, grinning.

"You really think that innkeeper where we had dinner the other night was on to something?" questioned Dr. Arenot.

Emma replied, "You heard him. He said there's a marking on a fieldstone in that tunnel which we obviously missed the first time around… a small doodle."

"Doodling that might've been left behind by a kid on a field trip," said Dr. Arenot.

Professor Quimbey rolled her eyes. "Jonas, sack your pessimism, will you?"

"But don't you think we'd already know if there was something significant in there?" responded Dr. Arenot. "Since we got to Iceland, we've read everything there is to know about Sturluson. Surely *someone* would have written about it if it was important."

"*If* there was something *significant* in there, sure, but maybe not if there was something more subtle, like doodles on rocks," countered Emma.

"For there to be something there no one has written about, and for us to have missed it the first time around, it would have to be *really* subtle," replied Dr. Arenot.

"Well, subtle is what we do best," said Emma, glancing over and smiling at Logan, her partner-in-crime and love, even if she wasn't doing a very good job of showing it lately.

Dr. Arenot cracked a smile of his own and replied, "I would be a fool to disagree. I guess we'll find out soon enough. Captain Evans and the others should be ready with the cars in a few minutes."

Chapter 3 – Theories

President Andrew Barrett listened intently to his staff's morning briefing from behind his Oval Office desk, anxious for them to finish. He had another meeting scheduled after this one, and his staff's highly detailed reports were taking longer than normal, partly because the president had been out of town for two days.

Chief of Staff, Miles Garrison, could tell the president was getting antsy, so he spoke up. "Gaby, can you prepare a draft of the State Dinner press release by this afternoon?" he asked White House Press Secretary, Gabriella Flores.

"Yes, of course," she replied. "I just want to make sure we coordinate the announcement with the British Ambassador before news of the Queen's upcoming visit hits the British tabloids. Remember, they're six hours ahead of us, so the sooner we get something out the better."

"Why don't you come by my office in an hour and we'll see if we can speed things up," suggested Mr. Garrison. Gaby nodded.

The president pressed a button on his desk to let his Executive Secretary, Ms. Woulette, know he was ready for his next meeting. He then said, "And Gaby, be sure to check with the First Lady, too. Her staff is working up something quite special and may already have some details for the announcement. I haven't seen the First Lady this excited about a State Dinner since I took office. It's safe to say she's looking forward to having dinner with the Queen far more than she ever does with me."

Mr. Garrison replied, "Can you blame her, Mr. President? Talking work over every meal for the last thirty years, it's probably quite exhilarating having dinner with you."

Mr. Garrison's casual relationship with the president, his lifelong friend, always confused the staff who never knew how to respond to the banter. But not the president. He knew exactly how… "Coming from someone who hasn't had a meal without cable news on in the background since college, I'm quite sure–"

"I'm quite sure you are both peaches to dine with," interjected Ms. Woulette, who had just opened the Oval Office door. "You two are like two peas in a pod. Mr. President, General Covington and Director Orson are ready and we've got General Nemond on video."

"Alright everybody, we'll finish this up in our afternoon briefing. If something comes up before then, let Miles know," said the president.

The president's entire staff exited the Oval Office except for Mr. Garrison. In came the venerable General Warren Thomas Covington, and intensely wired National Security Agency Director, Sue Orson. Ms. Woulette closed the doors behind them.

The president got up from behind his desk to relocate to the couches in front of the Oval Office fireplace, which were separated by an elongated glass coffee table. The Seal of the President of the United States was visible below the coffee table on the carpet. General Covington and Director Orson sat down on one couch, and the president and Mr. Garrison sat on the other. The president pressed a button on a remote and the video screen above the fireplace turned on, showing the commanding officer of Pegasus West and Area 51, General Bernard Nemond, from his office in Nevada. The Pegasus Project's leadership was fully assembled.

"Good morning everyone," said the president. Looking at General Nemond in the video screen, he added, "Although quite a bit earlier for you, General."

"Yes, sir," replied General Nemond with an amused smirk. Located in Nevada, he was used to the three-hour time difference and pre-dawn meetings.

Getting right to it, the president asked, "Any progress in Iceland?"

"No sir, the team hasn't found anything new," replied General Covington. "They continue to run through academic and archival options, and still have a few more places to visit."

"When are they going back to the Sturluson property to investigate the marking in the tunnel the local told them about?" asked the president.

"As a matter of fact, they're doing that today," answered General Covington.

"Good," said the president. "How about our group in Arlington, have they turned up anything new?"

"Nothing," said Covington.

Frustrated, the president uttered, "We're running out of time."

"Mr. President, I recommend bringing the team home in two weeks if they don't find something new by then," advised NSA Director Orson.

"Why?" asked the president. "I thought Iceland was the key to this whole thing. Is there a concern?"

"No sir, I just thought with Supay still out there—"

"We haven't seen any sign of Supay, have we?" inquired General Nemond through the video screen.

"No," replied Director Orson, "but it's just a matter of time…"

"Or not," interjected the president.

"True, sir, but we know Supay can change his appearance, so we can't say for sure whether he's here or not," Orson responded.

"If he is, then why hasn't he done something?" asked General Nemond.

"Because the timing isn't right," conjectured Director Orson.

"I'm not following," said General Nemond.

"That makes two of us," chimed in the president.

Director Orson tried to explain. "It's just a working theory, but we believe Supay won't risk upsetting the timeline of events that led to his discovery of Emma and Earth."

The president thought about it. "But Supay would not be going into the past to change something that has already happened. Any actions he takes today would only change the present."

"For all Supay knows, what needs to happen hasn't happened yet, Mr. President," said Director Orson. "The only reason Supay knows what he does is because Mr. West and Dr. Arenot solved the clues left behind in Snorri Sturluson's *Final Journey of the Vanir* poem. If they don't do that and find their way to Supay's home planet, Supay never learns about Ms. James or Earth, and until Supay knows for sure how and when those clues got into the *Final Journey of the Vanir* and how and when West and Arenot discovered them, he's not going to risk altering the time continuum for any of those events."

"So...he can't change the past without risking changing his present?"

"That's right, Mr. President," replied Director Orson. "If he changes even one small thing anywhere along the timeline, that could change everything."

"So, he'll only attack from this point in our timeline, then," surmised the president.

"Or at some point in the future, but yes, that's what our best minds think," Orson responded. "At least, that's the theory, that until he's absolutely certain how and when all of the events that led to his discovery occurred, he won't make a move."

"But isn't it clear to all of us that the alien Issor and Russian scientist Annika are the ones who left those clues behind?" asked the president, continuing, "Ms. James told us that those two escaped the ambush inside Qelios' compound by going through a portal to Iceland."

General Covington nodded. "Yes, Mr. President, that is the assumption we're all operating under, but it is also our understanding from Captain Evans, Ms. James and Professor Quimbey that Supay doesn't know about Isa and Annika because they disappeared into the portal before Supay arrived."

The president thought about it and said, "Then once Supay learns about Isa and Annika, and discovers how West and Arenot solved the *Final Journey of the Vanir —*"

"Time's up," declared the general.

"That's why we have to use the technology underneath Area 51 to go back in time and take out Supay preemptively!" declared Director Orson. "We can't be reactive on this one, waiting for Supay to bring the fight to us. We can go back to the battle in the Hidden City better prepared this time, or go back in time to Chersky before the explosion occurs, and we can save American soldiers in the process!"

"We are not playing god, Sue," chastised the president. "We have no idea what could happen if we do that. Using the Vaniryan technology to change the past is not an option for all the reasons we just talked about. We could change our own history, cause Supay to attack Earth 800-years earlier when the world is hardly capable of defending itself, or who knows what else. It's too risky."

"Mr. President, with all due respect, everything we do is risky at this point," replied Director Orson. "We're all just assuming that because Issor is a Vaniryan trapped on Earth, that she's the Missing Remnant or that she's on our side. But how do we know Issor isn't one of Supay's spies and that she didn't pose as a cute little alien to infiltrate that tree village on Vanirya where Evans, James and Quimbey found her?"

"Do you really think that this Issor is our enemy?" questioned the president.

"I'm just saying we have a whole team out there right now looking for her, when none of us knows for sure who she is or what will happen when they find her, Mr. President. If it's true that Supay can change shape, then for all we know, Issor could actually be Supay lying-in wait."

"You could be right, Sue," said President Barrett, "but, I think we have to trust our team's instincts on this one. I don't know about anyone else, but if this Issor is still alive, I'd feel a lot better finding her before Supay does and taking our chances."

"And the second we find her, that might just be the moment it becomes too late for all of us," lamented Director Orson.

Moderately frustrated with Director Orson, but also cognizant of her concerns, the president replied, "Are you suggesting we stop looking for her?"

"No, of course not."

"Then exactly what are you suggesting?"

"If you don't want to go back in time, sir, I understand, but let's at least use the Vaniryan pyramid and send a strike team through the portal to Supay's home world. We still have an opportunity to defeat Supay before it's too late!"

The president shook his head. "And risk starting a galactic war we can't possibly win? It's a suicide mission, Sue."

"The men are prepared for that," insisted Director Orson. "This could be our only shot to stop Supay before it's too late."

"No, it's too dangerous, and the implications too unpredictable," replied the president to Orson, who continued to push back...

"Let's at least consider sending in a reconnaissance team to gather as much intel as we can on Supay, to perform a visual observation of his ground and air activities, resources, technology, troop preparation, and report back. I know this is not a typical recon mission, sir, and we don't know exactly what they'll find, but *any* intel a recon team can glean from Supay's home world could be useful. We don't know our enemy, sir. I think we owe it to ourselves to learn all we can, if possible."

After thinking about it, the president responded, "Okay Sue, prepare a plan for a mission to Supay's home planet. Surveillance only, nothing more. Have the team combat ready, but only if engaged, understood?"

"Yes sir," replied Director Orson, pleased with the president's decision. "Sir, I'd also like to recommend bringing Captain Velasquez back from Iceland to lead the recon team. He's seen Supay, his soldiers, fighter ships and weapons in action during the rescue mission to Vanirya. He already knows what he's dealing with. Every little advantage might help keep the team safe on the mission."

The president agreed. "Call him back. Speaking of combat, Warren, what's the status of the new weapons we've been working on using the weapons the team brought back with them from Vanirya?"

General Covington replied, "Mr. President, I will let General Nemond answer that since he's closer to the research taking place at Area 51."

General Nemond jumped in. "Mr. President, we're definitely making progress. We have two oversized laser cannon prototypes in testing on the USS Roosevelt. We're having a harder time replicating the hand-held weapons the team brought back with them, but we're close to testing."

"Intel is reporting that the Russians already started testing their hand-helds yesterday, and that they're using our own weapon prototype," said Director Orson.

"Damn it!" snapped the president. "How is that possible? We need to figure out where the information leak is coming from and fast! Is that clear?"

"Yes, sir," said everyone.

"What about the Russian science team, what do they have to say about it?" asked the president.

"They've stopped communicating with us," replied General Nemond. "Minister Menputyn has severed communications."

"Menputyn's angry about the Chersky incident and doesn't believe our team's story about what happened to the three Russian scientists who ended up on Vanirya with Evans, James and Quimbey," added Director Orson.

"What does he think happened, that we executed them all on Vanirya?" questioned the president.

"He certainly believes Captain Evans was capable of that, sir," responded General Covington. "It's pretty clear that Menputyn intends to do everything in his power to find the Missing Remnant, who supposedly knows the location of the most powerful weapon in the universe, the Leyandermál, on his own. And after he finds the Leyandermál, he plans to use it to defeat Supay, and then—"

"—to take over the rest of the world," interrupted the president. "Menputyn can't do this by himself. Supay is bigger than his geopolitical aspirations. He knows that, right?" asked the president rhetorically.

"You've told him multiple times, sir," responded General Covington.

"Not enough, it seems. Find the leak, and in the meantime, let's hope the team in Iceland gets somewhere," said the president. "Finding the Leyandermál before Supay, and apparently, before Menputyn, is our best hope, and when we do, let's pray Ms. James or her alien friend Issor can make some sense of it, whatever *it* is. Right now, it seems like they are the only ones who can."

Everyone nodded in agreement.

The president concluded, "Alright everyone, that's it for now. Sue, get me the reconnaissance plan by the end of the day."

"Yes, sir."

Chapter 4 – A Better Truth

Isa and Annika navigated a grass-covered rolling hill with interspersed patches of snow, the fifth such hill they had come across in the last hour alone. They were following a path that led down a slope into a mountain valley. Several days had passed since their hostile encounter with the chieftain and his men. The entire left side of Annika's face was battered, swollen, and black and blue, from her left eye down to her mouth. Annika's face looked every bit as bad as she felt. Feeling horrible for her friend, Isa leaned over to pick up some snow from a snowy patch and handed it to her. The two sat down for a moment.

"Thank you," replied Annika, holding the snow up to her face to soothe the pain. She needed medical attention, although what that looked like in whatever century they were in was entirely unclear to her. Looking downhill with her one good eye, Annika spotted several structures up ahead, along with grazing fields, horses, cattle, pens filled with smaller animals, and people walking about. An outer wall enclosed the entire property, but it's gates were presently wide open. "Do you see that?" asked Annika.

Isa glanced where Annika was looking and saw it also. "What is that place?"

Annika replied, "It looks like a farm, but a whole lot bigger."

"Maybe farm can help Annika," said Isa.

Annika held the snow up to her puffy face. "Let's hope so. Maybe we can rest there, too."

"And eat? Isa is also hungry. Is it a place for such things?"

"I don't know what that place is, but we have to get help somewhere," said Annika, just then noticing that there were even more structures located at the back of the property. The additional structures were made of wooden columns and planks supporting a high pointed wood roof, perhaps living quarters for those working the land, and were built in a bowed manner giving them the shape of upside-down boats.

Isa helped Annika up and they resumed walking. As they approached the farm at the valley's bottom, they left the patches of ice and snow behind in favor of long grass. Their approach did not attract much attention at first, not even when they walked through the outer gates. After all, the arrival of an unarmed woman and her young child did not concern anyone. Encountering no resistance, they continued down the middle of the property, passing grazing fields and fence enclosures, pens and cages, cattle, horses, pigs, sheep, goats, hens, geese and ducks.

As they neared the main house, a groundskeeper finally intercepted them and asked, "Hvers vegna nálgast þú lögmanninn? Ertu með viðskipti hérna?" ["*What business do you have here at the Lawspeaker's home?*"]

Isa responded, "Móðir þarfnast hjálpar. Móðir er sár." ["*Mother needs help. Mother is hurt.*"]

The groundskeeper, although taking note of the brutal blow to Annika's face, didn't seem interested in helping them. "Þetta er ekki staður lyfja." ["*This is not a place of medicine.*"]

A loud voice came from behind the groundskeeper, "Ó bull, Jorgg! Við munum aðstoða þeim sem þurfa hjálp." ["*Oh nonsense, Jorgg! We shall assist those who require help.*"] A large, tall and round man with a broad gray beard that matched his full head of long, unkempt graying hair, approached them. He immediately noticed Annika's bludgeoned face.

Jorgg the groundskeeper stepped back. "Yes, Lawspeaker, my apologies," he said in Old Icelandic.

"Please, Isa and Annika need a place to rest," pleaded Isa, continuing to speak in the Lawspeaker's language. "And food and care for mother's injury, please."

Annika looked badly hurt and Isa, a child, appeared harmless. Spurred by sympathy rather than suspicion, the Lawspeaker instructed Jorgg, "Bring them inside and escort them to the guest hall. Hallveig will know what to do." The Lawspeaker turned around and walked off to the side of the main house, presumably to look for Hallveig.

Jorgg started guiding them toward the main house.

Isa quietly said to Annika, "The Lawspeaker-man means to help."

Jorgg guided them through an arched bronze doorway into the main house, and into a hall with elaborately carved wooden benches.

"Wait here," he said.

Isa and Annika sat on the benches, and studied their new surroundings. A row of wood posts ran the length of the hall in order to support a pointed roof. There was an unlit fire pit in the middle. Oil lamps illuminated the hall and decorative weapons and animal skins covered the walls. The hall's design and décor suggested it might be a place for meetings and gatherings.

"I'm no expert in Icelandic history, but whoever this Lawspeaker is, he is no commoner," remarked Annika.

After a short wait, the Lawspeaker entered the hall with a woman. They walked right up to their guests.

"Oh dear," said the woman in Old Icelandic upon seeing Annika's face. She reached out to touch it. Annika flinched since even the slightest touch hurt.

The Lawspeaker reprimanded the woman. "Hallveig, be gentle." Now addressing Annika and Isa, he added, "Please forgive my wife, she lacks the touch of Iceland's finest healers."

In real-time, Isa telepathically relayed translations to Annika so she could understand what was being said.

"Rubbish, Snorri! I have healed every wound of yours that you have ever presented me. Be kind with your words, or I shall turn your next wound sour," snapped Hallveig.

Proud of his wife's feistiness, and with a bellowing laugh, he said, "Hallveig is a strong woman. She has an entire country and this Lawspeaker afraid of her words."

"Respect for my words is not fear," replied Hallveig, who continued to examine Annika's face.

"Aye, this is so," conceded Snorri.

Into the hall wandered a white goose with a long neck and legs. It had clearly escaped its enclosure. After seeing them all, the goose extended its neck and let out a nasal honking sound, talking to the humans.

"You do not belong here, feathered friend, unless you wish to become dinner," responded Snorri. As if the goose understood him, it quickly turned around and waddled out of the hall.

"There is always a strong-willed one no enclosure can contain," remarked the Lawspeaker. He returned his attention to his guests and studied Annika's battered face. "Who did this to you?" he asked.

At this point, Isa helped Annika answer in Icelandic. With poor pronunciation and slowly, Annika responded, "I do not speak your language well, but men two days north from here attacked us... near the jagged river."

"Ah, Kurgandur," said Snorri, familiar with the chieftain's violent claim of rule over that part of the highlands. "Kurgandur had agreed to leave those lands."

"Kurgandur has not," uttered the 11-year-old voice of Isa.

"And who are you, child?" asked the Lawspeaker.

"Manners, Lawspeaker," criticized Hallveig.

"Yes, my apology. Manners are always to be true and first. I am Snorri Sturluson of the Sturlungar family and this is my wife, Hallveig of Ormsdottir. And now, I should like to have your names."

"Isa," piped up the Vaniryan.

"Annika," replied the Russian scientist, intuiting the question.

"Of what surname? Of what family?" questioned Sturluson.

Isa thought about it and came up with the first names that popped into her head. "Isa and Annika of the Jaans family from Jaannos."

"I have not heard of such a family. Where is this Jaannos?" questioned the Lawspeaker.

Isa fed the words to Annika so she could respond, "It is very far away, in a place called Vanirya… Russia." Annika had ad-libbed the word 'Russia,' trying to add a measure of credibility to her response, but forgetting that, at that time in history, her homeland was not yet called Russia. Rather, it was called Kievan Rus' from the 9th to mid-13th centuries and Grand Duchy of Vladimir for several centuries after that.

"The Jaans family from Jaannos of Vanirya, Russia? It is all unknown to me," replied Sturluson, skeptical and suspicious. He did not like being lied to.

Hallveig saved them, for the time being. "Snorri, there will be time enough later to educate your geography. It is time now to help our guests with their injuries and provide them with clean clothes and a place to rest. We can discuss the remainder over dinner, which I will invite them to if you do not. Manners are always to be true and first."

"Yes, of course. My Hallveig is wise and truthful in speaking up to me at times. Few are. She will take you to a guest room, help you clean up, give you fresh clothes and tend to your wounds. You are welcome to stay here tonight, and I shall enjoy your company as my guests at dinner."

"Thank you, Lawspeaker," said Annika with the help of Isa.

The Lawspeaker nodded and turned to depart the hall, hurrying off to attend to another matter. He left the two of them alone with Hallveig.

"Follow me," instructed Hallveig.

They left the hall and Hallveig briefly spoke to a woman who appeared to be a servant. Hallveig then led them to another room with wooden shelves, a wood table, and animal-skin covered benches. There were bottles of liquids and ointments on the shelves, torn rags, blades, rudimentary scissors, and a jug of water on the table. She sat Annika down on the bench and Isa sat beside her. Hallveig grabbed a cloth, poured some water on it, and began cleaning Annika's face, trying not to hurt her.

"You are not the first to run afoul of Kurgandur, for he himself is foul. And when one is foul, it is hard to expect a fair result," said Hallveig, continuing to wipe down Annika's skin. A silver necklace with a dangling cross-hatched symbol made of gold, hung around Hallveig's neck.

Hallveig stood back up and turned to fetch a bottle on an upper shelf. She appeared to know what she was doing.

"Hallveig's necklace is very pretty," commented Isa, who had a liking for necklaces.

"Thank you, Lady Isa," replied Hallveig. "Do you like jewelry?"

"Yes," Isa replied.

"Do they have much jewelry where you come from?" inquired Hallveig, surprised, knowing that jewelry was reserved for the elite, and the two of them looked anything but that.

"Some," replied Isa, even though the only jewelry she had ever seen before was the heart shaped pendant necklace Emma wore on Vanirya.

"Perhaps we can make some jewelry for you," suggested Hallveig. "You can tell me what you like, and we can forge it together." Isa smiled while Hallveig reached for a blade and cloth.

Annika squirmed, concerned Hallveig was about to use the blade on her face, and worried about the risk of infection from an unsterilized medieval blade. But Hallveig instead used it to cut off a small piece of cloth only. Subsequently, she dipped the smaller cloth into a bottle of liquid.

Relieved, and with Isa's help, Annika asked, "What is that liquid?"

"It is the Haförn ointment made from angel root, thyme, powdered nettle root and ground Haförn claw. I obtained it from an apothecary in Álftanes."

"What is Haförn?" asked Isa.

"The Haförn is a white-tailed eagle," replied Hallveig.

"What does Haförn ointment do?" wondered Isa on Annika's behalf, and curious herself.

"It will chase away the bad blood to reduce swelling and draw the body's good blood to the surface for healing," answered Hallveig.

At that point, Annika just nodded. She was willing to try anything. Her face was killing her. She had no idea how many broken bones she had, so whatever Hallveig was proposing to do, she was up for it. She closed her eyes and allowed Hallveig to apply the ointment.

Hallveig dipped her cloth into the bottle and generously applied the ointment to Annika's face. At first, the liquid burned profusely, but soon the burn turned into a pulsating cool. Annika could feel her swollen skin tighten, as if the ointment itself was sucking the blood out of her skin. Hallveig applied multiple layers of the ointment.

"There, that should be enough for now. We will apply more later. Let's go to your room and get you both changed. Then, you can rest until dinner."

"Thank you," replied Annika with the utmost sincerity, already starting to feel better.

Hallveig led them to a guest room. The simple space had two thatch-covered benches built into the wall, a wood table, clean clothes, rags to wash up, and a jug of water.

"Hallveig, we do not know how to thank you. You have been so kind," said Annika with Isa's assistance.

Hallveig responded, "Only because it was the will of the Lawspeaker, but at dinner tonight, you will tell the Lawspeaker who you really are and where you are from. I have traveled Iceland and over the sea to the Norwegian Realm. I have never heard of your family or the places you claim to come from. Snorri was right to question your words, especially with the clan feuds worsening, and spies infiltrating our lands. I rescued you from his questions earlier, but I will not do so again. You would be wise not to trifle with

Snorri or he will return you to Kurgandur for your reckoning, or I will ask him to."

Hallveig abruptly turned and left. Annika and Isa fell back into their thatched beds for rest, although they doubted they would get much. They had until dinner to come up with a better truth.

Chapter 5 – Where the Geese Don't Fly

A loud explosion woke Isa up. She heard screaming. She crawled out of bed to see what was happening. When she stepped outside, she saw laser fire raining down from above and invaders swarming her village on the ground and in ships, picking off Remnants left and right. One blast from a hovering craft severed her forest village's largest tree at the base. Isa watched in horror as the multi-hundred-foot-tall tree toppled over, taking out other trees and branches along the way before crashing on top of fleeing Remnants, crushing them.

Panicked, Isa scanned the scene for her parents, but all she saw was the Hunt—which consisted of Supay's Dokalfar warriors wearing all-black metallic suits with faceless, spiked helmets—rounding up Remnants, throwing them face down on the ground beside one another and pointing laser guns at their backs. That's when she spotted her parents, Mae and Andu, lying on their stomachs near the middle of the captive group.

She screamed and broke forward to help them. One stride in, a large Vaniryan man snatched her up and covered her mouth to keep her quiet. Isa, being but a small toddler, didn't have the strength to fight back. Not yet, anyway. The man dragged her behind a tree.

Isa tried to wriggle free. The man squeezed her and said, "What are you trying to do, get yourself killed?"

Isa, frightened and desperate to help her parents, again tried to break free from the man's grasp. She let loose a small blast of blue energy from her hands. The man fell backward, shocked by the power of the tiny girl who barely looked old enough to walk. Isa began to run but the man grabbed her ankle and pulled her back in.

"Child, there is nothing you can do! I am Lassar, a friend of your village. You sprinting into that fray will help no one. We need to get you out of here."

Suddenly, a ship with bright lights dropped through the overhead tree cover, breaking branches on its way down. It landed on the forest floor. A ramp lowered and out of the ship walked a tall, threatening-looking Vaniryan with a crooked face dressed in all black, looking menacing.

"Are there any others?" asked the black-clad Vaniryan while surveying the prisoners.

"Yes, Supay. We are rounding them up," responded one of his Dokalfar.

"Good," Supay replied. Looking at the prisoners lying face down, Supay demanded, "Tell me, where is the Missing Remnant who legend says will one day defeat me? Tell me and we can all find out together if it is true."

No one responded because they didn't know. Supay pointed at one of the prisoners and searched his mind with his advanced telepathic abilities. After finding nothing, he shot a blast of energy from his fingertip, blowing a wide hole clear through the prisoner's back, instantly killing him. The prisoner's back kept disintegrating even after he was dead, as Supay's destructive energy continued to eat through his lifeless body.

Isa started to cry but Lassar again covered her mouth to prevent her from giving away their cover.

"Still, no one talks?" asked Supay. He turned over another Remnant, this time a woman, so he could look into her frightened gaze.

"The Missing Remnant will kill you someday," the woman uttered, her voice quivering in anger and fear.

Supay cocked his head, seemingly pitying her, a momentary pause that gave her a split second of hope before he pointed his finger at her stomach and shot her in the midsection with his energy beam, killing her just like the first prisoner.

"Why do all Remnants believe in an empty legend?" shouted Supay.

"If it is an empty legend, why do you search for it?" questioned another captured Remnant. It was Isa's mother, Mae. "You search for it because it frightens you!"

Supay scoffed. He spun Mae over so he could see her face. When Isa realized who Supay was talking to, she cried, "Mother," and began shaking uncontrollably.

Supay replied to Mae, "Your faith in stories foretold by the stars exposes you all for the fools that you are. I search for the Leyandermál whose secret the Missing Remnant guards, nothing more. I will find it with or without your help and spare all who aid me."

"You will find no help here," uttered Mae.

"So be it." Supay pointed his finger and shot her in the chest, killing her.

Isa wanted to scream but couldn't, not just because Lassar was still covering her mouth, but because, in that moment, Isa's voice died with her mother. Isa's father, Andu, lunged for Supay but Supay's henchmen gunned him down before he got close. Andu fell lifeless next to Mae. Supay was done. "Gather the rest and bring them up to the ship for interrogation and extermination. If anyone tries to escape, disintegrate them."

"Yes, Supay," replied his Dokalfar warriors.

Supay's Dokalfar began loading prisoners onto transports and searching for any uncaptured Remnants. Lassar grabbed Isa's hand and took off. Three of Supay's Dokalfar spotted and pursued them. Lassar and Isa raced for a Tree Gate a hundred paces away. It was how Lassar had come to Isa's village from Jaannos to deliver a message. Now, it was how he planned to escape with Isa back into the forest on Vanirya.

When they reached the Tree Gate, Lassar turned his laser gun to maximum power and set it to self-destruct. He laid it down just outside the tree's entrance, and ushered Isa into the tree. Isa could hear Lassar's weapon revving up to detonation and Supay's Hunt getting closer. Fortunately, just before the gun exploded, the green energy of the tree flared and absorbed them, sending them elsewhere in the forest. Supay's Dokalfar reached the tree right when the gun detonated, obliterating the base of the tree, destroying the Tree Gate and killing Supay's Dokalfar in the process.

ΔΔΔΔΔΔΔΔΔΔΔΔ

"Wake up," said Annika, nudging a whimpering Isa. "You fell fast asleep. It's time to go."

Isa sat up, still shaken by her nightmare. It was one that haunted her regularly. Brushing it off, she responded, "It is dinner already?"

"Yes, Hallveig is waiting for us in the hallway. Are you okay? It sounded like you were having a bad dream."

"Yes, Isa have bad night story." She pulled herself together, got up and followed Annika out of the room. Hallveig was waiting for them, and she brought them into the dining hall.

Meat, fowl, berries, wild greens, nuts and grains were sprawled out over a long, wooden communal table, along with jugs of ale. Oil lamps and a lit fire pit similar to the one in the guest hall, brightened the room. Servants were busy cooking meat over the fire pit's open flames and bringing the cooked food to the table. The

Lawspeaker was already eating and drinking when his guests arrived.

Isa and Annika sat on the bench across the table from Snorri, and Hallveig sat beside him. At first, the Lawspeaker kept eating, ignoring their arrival, but that soon changed after a few additional mouthfuls.

"Welcome to our nightly feast," said Snorri, while Isa continued translating for Annika in real-time. Proud of his robustly packed table, Snorri bragged, "Looks like nothing you see on your slabs back home, eh?"

Annika hesitated after Isa translated for her, sensing there was a more nuanced question in Sturluson's words. She shook her head.

"It is beautiful food," complimented Isa.

"What is the food like back home?" asked Snorri, subtly trying to find out where they were from just as Hallveig suggested he would.

Annika responded with Isa's assistance, "Meats, fish, potatoes, carrots, eggs, salted herring…"

The Lawspeaker picked up one large chunk of red meat and hand-tossed it in front of Annika. It made a thud when it landed. She queasily eyed its undercooked, bloody appearance.

"It is the back meat of the powerful ísbjörn, a rare treat in Iceland when it comes, drifting the oceans aboard ice floes from the northern seas," explained Snorri.

A white bear, Isa conveyed to Annika telepathically. *A polar bear*, Annika realized.

Snorri stared at Annika and explained further, "It is a powerful beast. It took four men to conquer this champion. Often, it takes more as men do not always win the battle hunting this formidable prize."

"Oh," replied Annika, saddened more for the polar bear than for the men who lost.

"You must taste," Snorri urged her.

His words had the sound of a test. Not wanting to offend her host, Annika picked up the ísbjörn with her bare hands and bit into the least rare section of meat she could find. Still, a healthy amount of meat juice sprayed out of it, at least, that's what she hoped it was. The meat was incredibly tough and chewy.

"You can still feel the raw power of the beast when you eat it, fighting you to the bitter end all the way down," remarked Snorri. "Much like the rumor the winds of Njǫrd have carried to my ears of the raw power in the highlands two days ago that fought off Kurgandur's men to the bitter end." Annika and Isa froze. The Lawspeaker appeared to know what had happened in the highlands.

The Lawspeaker looked at Annika's bruised face, which already appeared less swollen due to the Haförn ointment, and asked her, "You said it was Kurgandur who did that to you?"

Annika apprehensively replied, "Of what power do you refer—"

"The power of two witches roaming the highlands capable of breaking the ice, freeing the dark spirits of Helheim to rise up through the breakage and conquer Midgard. Are you the women Njǫrd's winds refer to? Answer me!"

Snorri snapped his fingers and a half-dozen farmhands armed with swords and axes rushed into the dining hall. The Lawspeaker stood up, impatiently awaiting a response.

After Isa and Annika telepathically consulted, Annika replied with Isa's help, pausing after each sentence, "Lawspeaker, there is as much truth in that rumor as fantasy... It is expected Kurgandur would exaggerate the cause of his defeat, for that is the true rumor he fears the winds of Njǫrd carrying throughout the land... We do not deny we are the women of the embellished rumor but we are no witches... My broken face is not the face of a powerful witch."

Snorri thought about it and responded, "We shall see. Innocents do not lie when asked who they are and where they come from."

The Lawspeaker motioned and two of his men stepped forward and grabbed Annika's left arm. A third shoved an oil-lamp with a large opening at the top in front of her. Snorri's men forced Annika's left hand into the lamp's burning flame. Annika screamed as her fingers burned but Snorri's men held her still.

"Enough," ordered Snorri after a few more seconds, satisfied with the pain he saw on Annika's face and the scorching of her fingers that she wasn't a witch.

One of Snorri's other men brought Annika a small box filled with snow collected from the hills. Annika, fighting tears, immediately thrust her burned fingers into the icebox.

Following another discreet signal, Snorri's men next grabbed Isa's left arm and brought the oil lamp close. Isa did everything she could not to use her powers because she knew that would only worsen their situation. She screamed when Snorri's men shoved her fingers into the flames.

"Snorri, stop this!" shouted Hallveig.

"Stop!" instructed Snorri, and his men immediately pulled Isa's hand out a split second after exposing her fingers to the flames. Isa buried her hand in the icebox next to Annika's.

"Snorri, enough of this nonsense. They are not witches. They never are!" snapped Hallveig, tired of the ritualistic test that had never once confirmed a witch.

"Lawspeaker, we are friends, I assure you," insisted Annika, wincing from the pain of burnt flesh even with her hand buried in ice. "We ask only for your help. Please."

Snorri remained unconvinced. "Whether Kurgandur's rumor is embellished or not, you have lied to me."

"Isa and Annika wish privacy," said Isa, looking around at Snorri's men.

Snorri, who was not used to negotiating with children, even his own, thought about it. There was something unusual about Isa, although he couldn't quite put his finger on it. He agreed to Isa's request and told his men and the cooks around the fire pit to leave.

Once the room was clear, the Lawspeaker, still worried about what portion of the Kurgandur rumor *was* true, walked over to a wall and removed a battle axe which had been hung there for decoration. He returned to the table. He had no intention of sitting with the two strangers unarmed, not until he was absolutely sure what the truth was.

"You have your wish, girl, and now I shall have mine. Tell me where you are from or you shall know Odin's wrath."

Isa explained. "The Hunt sought to capture Isa and Annika in a battle in the Hidden City for the one who would bring death to all. Isa and Annika escaped to this land, but now, are lost with no way home."

"And where is this Hidden City?" asked Snorri.

"Far away on Vanirya," replied Isa.

Snorri grumbled and his face turned red in frustration. "Our Viking ancestors have sailed the oceans of this world, to all the lands where geese can fly, and I know of no place called Vanirya. I questioned you of this when you first said it and yet you persist."

"That is because Vanirya is far away where Lawspeaker's ships cannot sail and geese cannot fly," replied Isa.

Snorri seemed irked but slightly more intrigued. "You continue to confound with riddles to protect your secret, but you would be wise to trust me."

"Isa and Annika have been running from death too long," said Isa, again proving to be more self-assured than any child Snorri had ever dealt with before. She continued, "Isa and Annika wish to stop running, but can only trust Snorri if Snorri will trust Isa and Annika."

"Now you challenge my honor, child? Do you know who I am? I am the twice elected Lawspeaker of all of Iceland. I have the ear of kings in Norway, Sweden and Denmark and am the chieftain of these lands from Reykjavik to Reykholt. I do not see that you have a choice but to trust me." He tightened his grip around his battle axe.

"Neither honor nor axe will stop the Hunt or the death that Supay brings," said Isa.

All of a sudden, Annika realized something after hearing Isa's concerns about Supay coming for them. She recalled the myth she had learned on Vanirya about how the Missing Remnant hides in the stars, in the past, or in the future. And she recalled their conclusion in the tree sanctuary of Jaannos that the Missing Remnant hid on Earth according to the Scroll of the Va, which showed where the Missing Remnant had fled. Annika, knowing Isa was a Remnant from Vanirya, suddenly made the connection: Isa might be the Missing Remnant that Supay was after.

With Isa's help, Annika explained, "Lawspeaker, our secret does not just protect our own lives; it protects the lives of many worlds... of the entire known universe."

"If secret escapes, the monsters will come," interjected Isa. Whether it was coincidental or not, the flames in the fire pit surged to new heights when she said it.

"Hel must be listening," remarked Snorri, referring to the god of the underworld. For all of Snorri's rise to power as Lawspeaker of Iceland, as ambassador to the kings of Norway, Sweden and Denmark, and as a feared chieftain, Sturluson was also a poet and historian who deeply believed in mythology. And at that moment, he was right in the middle of his greatest historical achievement of all, an epic writing that incorporated mythology, called the *Prose Edda*. If ever there was a believing ear for Isa's and Annika's stories about monsters and powerful beings capable of causing death, Snorri Sturluson's was it. He believed in such things, just like he believed in witches.

"If you will swear to protect our secret and help us, we will show you where we come from," said Annika, silently agreeing with Isa that if they were going to trust anyone and stop running, Sturluson seemed as good a choice as any to guard their secret and keep them safe from harm given his powerful status. Plus, Annika thought he might be able to help them in other ways.

"Show me? How?" asked a cynical Sturluson.

"You must pledge to do this, please," said Annika.

Sturluson, who was also a lawyer, understood the art of making deals and the importance of doing so if he wanted to get something in return, so he agreed, "Aye, this I will do, and Hallveig, too."

Annika stood up and pulled her hand out of the icebox. After doing so, her burnt hand began feeling like it was on fire again. With her voice cracking in discomfort, she said to Snorri, "We must go outdoors," and to Isa, she said in her mind, '*and you must be prepared to show him.*'

Snorri, unsure what he was getting into, led them outside. He pushed open the door and walked out, followed by Isa, Annika and Hallveig. Hallveig said to Annika when she passed her, "I hope you know what you are doing. I warned you not to trifle with the Lawspeaker. He will not hesitate."

The four of them stood alone under a starry night, staring up at the brilliance of the heavens in 13th century Iceland. Annika looked for the constellation Orion the Hunter, and specifically, for the star Betelgeuse which served as the back right shoulder of Orion.

Annika, an astronomer who had been working on the Roscosmos space program's top-secret project using the U.S.'s stolen Pegasus technology before the Chersky accident, knew the location of TYC 129-75-1 well: slightly below and to the left of Betelgeuse. While Supay had already blown up the star at the end of the Battle in the Hidden City, that event would not be seen on Earth for another 800 years. Thus, in the middle ages, TYC 129-75-1 remained as visible as ever.

Annika spotted Betelgeuse and then, the faint light of TYC 129-75-1. Now, it was time for her to explain it to Sturluson. Although she was not a historian, while studying astronomy at Russia's top space university, M. V. Lomonosov Moscow, Annika had studied constellations and knew that Orion the Hunter was a Greek constellation that did not exist in Scandinavian lore. But Orion's Belt – consisting of Alnitak, Alnilam and Mintaka - did, and it was referred to as "Friggerock" or "Frigg's Distaff."

Alnitak was the star associated with the bottom left of Orion's Belt, and there was a direct constellation line that connected Alnitak with Betelgeuse at the back right shoulder of Orion:

While Annika did not know what the Norse called Alnitak, she knew how to direct Sturluson to it. With Isa feeding her words, Annika explained, "Locate the bottom left star of Friggerock." Once he did, from there, she guided him up to Betelgeuse which wasn't difficult because it was the brightest star in that section of the night sky.

"Now, just below and to the left of the bright star is Vanirya," said Annika, having done all she could to convince him. The rest was up to Isa.

At first, Sturluson remained skeptical, saying, "I see the star, but not the truth," but then he looked down and saw Isa's glowing blue eyes. He swept Hallveig behind him using his left arm, and held up his battle axe in his right hand. "You are a witch, after all!" shouted Snorri.

"Isa is a child, Lawspeaker. She is no witch," replied Annika.

"What is she then, a creature of Aurvandil's making?" he asked, referring to the Nordic god of stars.

"Isa will not harm Snorri," said Isa, and in that moment, she changed form. A bright white light consumed her body until she finished changing back to her beautiful Vaniryan appearance.

As the aura of light dissipated, and Isa's golden-white form stood before him, Snorri uttered, "Oh, the god of stars, Aurvandil! You are a light-being from another heaven above our own!"

"As I said before, we are friends, Lawspeaker," assured Annika, "and can protect you from your enemies, if you will help us." Annika got down on her knees to ensure Sturluson understood the magnitude of the commitment they were willing to make, and Isa did the same, looking up at the Lawspeaker with her oversized, round radiating blue eyes on her nose-less face. "We beg of you to take us in. We do not want to run anymore," said Annika.

"So is the Kurgandur rumor true, little girl, that you have the power to melt and destroy the ice on command?" Sturluson asked Isa.

"Yes. Isa promises to protect Snorri and Hallveig from enemies if Snorri will help protect Isa and Annika's secret."

Looking into Isa's hopeful eyes, Sturluson finally saw a truth he could trust, a sincerity in the girl's alien gaze that brought him calm. "I will do what I can as the winds of the highlands already carry the rumor throughout the land." Looking at Annika, Snorri was curious, "And you, are you of true form or are you also of the heavens?"

With Isa's assistance, Annika replied, "I am human just like you, born somewhere far away from here where your ships have not yet traveled."

Sturluson appeared regretful. "Please forgive me for burning your hands," he said to Isa and Annika. "I did not know, and what we do not know drives fear in these lands. I am sorry to have given in to it. Hallveig, can you please bring the snigill ointment for their burns?"

Hallveig nodded and departed to retrieve the snail gel, which reduced blistering and eased pain from burns due to the unique combination of antioxidants, antiseptic, anesthetic, anti-irritant and anti-inflammatory properties in snail slime.

Isa slowly rose and approached the Lawspeaker. She touched his gray, bushy beard and replied, "It is fair. Lawspeaker did not know. And Isa and Annika did not know to trust, either."

Snorri gently took Isa's hand, bewildered and relieved to see that none of the six fingers on her alien hand showed evidence of burns. Where once he was afraid of her, now he was in awe of the light-being. "You are a unique creature of light and magic from a world high above our eight worlds, from a new realm I did not know existed. You are a unicorn from the heavens."

"What is a unicorn?" asked Isa.

Sturluson replied, "We shall go back inside, and I will draw you one."

Isa smiled and responded, "And Isa and Annika will explain the rest of the story to Lawspeaker, because the monsters will come."

Chapter 6 – Just Scratching the Surface

The early morning drive from Borgarnes to Snorri Sturluson's 800+ year-old farmhouse in Reykholt took over an hour. Captain Carrie Evans drove their large SUV through the winding roads of Iceland's highlands and lowlands, passed snowfields, green pastures, streams, waterfalls, and wayward sheep, with the same fearlessness that she used to tackle mountains and enemy forces. A second SUV carrying additional security struggled to keep up with her.

Emma, who was seated upfront beside Captain Evans, held her breath around one of the sharper turns and commented, "It's a good thing I didn't eat before we left."

"Am I driving too fast for you, James?" asked Captain Evans, mildly amused.

"Umm, I'll be okay, I think…," replied Emma, feeling queasy.

"Sorry. I'm just used to driving SEALs around. The boys usually like my fast-paced turns."

"I bet they do. I'm also willing to bet that baby-sitting us on field trips to libraries, museums and old farmhouses isn't exactly what you had in mind when joining the Navy SEALs."

"That's true, this definitely *isn't* what I thought I'd be doing," responded Captain Evans with a chuckle, "but I volunteered for this, so…"

Emma was curious. "A year ago, you were climbing mountains around the world, leading search and rescue missions, commanding recon ops. Isn't this like—"

"Getting demoted from beat cop to desk cop?" answered Evans, anticipating Emma's question.

"Well, yeah, kind of," replied Emma.

"You don't think me driving you all through Iceland is what I signed up for?"

Emma shook her head. "Seriously, you're one of the first women to ever join the Navy SEALS... you've climbed the tallest mountains on every continent..."

"James, after seeing what we saw on Vanirya, the mountains here on Earth don't seem so tall or important anymore, if you know what I mean."

"Uh-huh, but Covington could have assigned a lot of other soldiers to protect us. Why'd you volunteer?"

"I guess I just don't like leaving things to chance, not with something as critical as what we're doing here. I lost my entire team on Peak Pobeda during the Chersky Mission..."

"I know. I'm really sorry."

"Don't apologize. It wasn't your fault, and hey, I got you and Quimbey out of there alive, by dumb luck really. But those boys were my friends, maybe my only friends... they were family. I owe it to them to see this through. Otherwise, what'd they all die for?"

"I get that. But you know, they're not your only friends," assured Emma, gesturing to herself, Logan and the professors.

"I appreciate that, and that's why I'm here, to make sure nothing bad happens to you."

"Hey, let's not think like that, okay?"

"James, I've seen what's out there. So have you. I'm just being realistic, and I'm done losing people I care about. Until Supay goes down, boring backroads of Iceland or not, this is where I need to be. You're my mission now."

"In that case, let's pick up the pace around these turns," insisted Emma, suddenly ready to embrace Captain Evans' daredevil driving.

Captain Evans laughed. "I've always liked that about you, James... once you get wound up, there's no stopping you. Alright, here we go. Buckle up!" Captain Evans stepped on the gas and off they went.

When they reached Reykholt, a village in the Reykjadalsá valley of Western Iceland's Borgarfirði region, the temperate conditions were a welcome change from the coastal cold of Borgarnes. There was a sign on the side of the road, visible as they were driving in, which indicated that Reykholt had a population of 60. The sign immediately after that one provided directions to the local school, church, Sturluson's home and the Snorrastofa research center. The small town also had some stores, restaurants, farm homes, guesthouses, inns, and plenty of grass fields. Most people who worked in Reykholt commuted in from elsewhere.

They parked in the Snorrastofa's public lot located directly across the street from Sturluson's home. The second SUV arrived shortly after and pulled up next to them. Captain Evans got out and walked over to tell the second group to hang back in the SUV. After all, everything seemed quiet from where Evans stood, and their destination - Sturluson's farm home – was just a few feet away in case they needed help.

Unlike most tourist landmarks, the grounds around Sturluson's home were freely accessible. Meaning, visitors could walk right onto the property and up to the house, no tickets needed, no security lines. The only expectation was for visitors to treat the landmark with care and respect.

Emma, Logan, Professor Quimbey, Dr. Arenot and Captain Evans entered the farm property, which spanned several sprawling grass hills, and proceeded to their destination: a small geothermal pool far from the main residence, down a hill at the back of the property. As famous as Sturluson was for literary, historical and political reasons, he was also famous for his circular, stone pool dating back to the 10th century. The pool was fed by natural hot springs and was the earliest known geothermal pool in the country.

Early in the morning, steam rose off the pool's hot water. On the other side of the geo-pool was a wooden doorway, with an iron-ring door handle, built into the side of a grassy hill. The door was locked by a chain and padlock. Logan smiled when he looked at the door in the hill because it reminded him of a hobbit-hole in the Shire, and for good reason.

While studying Sturluson over the last couple months, Logan had learned just how much the Icelander's works influenced J.R.R. Tolkien's *The Hobbit* and *Lord of the Rings* books, and how Tolkien had even once said in a debate with close friend C.S. Lewis, author of *The Chronicles of Narnia* books, that he'd rather his English students at Oxford read Sturluson than Shakespeare. Logan was fairly confident that Tolkien conceived his hobbit-holes made famous in his novels right here staring at the very same door in the hill that they were now trying to get into.

Ironically, on the other side of the peaceful door was something quite the opposite: the site of Sturluson's gruesome murder in an underground tunnel that led from the geo-pool all the way back to Sturluson's farmhouse.

"Where is he?" asked Logan, looking at his watch.

"Patience… he'll be here," said Dr. Arenot.

Logan still had his doubts. "Are you sure he said to meet him at the pool?"

"Yes, Gunnar said right here," replied Dr. Arenot, referring to the property's conservator, who also doubled as the head research fellow at Snorrastofa.

Seconds later, Gunnar popped up over the top of the grassy hill, arriving from a different direction. He steadily edged down the slope.

"Good morning to you all… my apologies for making you wait, but a young lamb stood his ground in the middle of the road," said Gunnar.

Dr. Arenot, who had befriended Gunnar during their time researching Sturluson at the Snorrastofa, quickly reminded him that he was not late, at all. "You are right on time, my friend," replied Dr. Arenot.

Gunnar wouldn't have it. "Nonsense. If I don't arrive before my guests, then I am late." He pulled a key ring out of his jacket pocket and walked up to the door to unlock the padlock. He inserted a key, turned it and they all heard a solid click. He removed the padlock and the chain fell away, opening the doorway to the past. Stale air from inside the tunnel rushed out, among other things...

"Alright, now that we've let Sturluson's ghost out for his morning stroll, you best get inside and conduct your business. I wouldn't want to be in that tunnel when Sturluson returns... Some say at night, you can still hear him shouting as he flees up the tunnel trying to escape the ambush, screaming at the foot of the stones where he was murdered."

"It's a good thing it's not nighttime, then," responded Evans, forging ahead into the tunnel, followed by the others. Gunnar turned on his flashlight, while everyone else used their cellphones.

They entered the tunnel excavated by Sturluson over 800 years ago as an underground short-cut between his house and the geo-thermal pool, a definite luxury during Iceland's winter months. Horizontally laid wooden planks with vertical wood beams reinforced the walls, and cross-beams overhead supported the triangular-shaped wood ceiling. Along the walls on both sides were waist-high walls of fieldstones continuing the length of the tunnel. The stones, which were not worked, smoothed or carved, reminded Logan of the fieldstones used to construct terraces at Machu Picchu where stones were cleverly fit together based on their original shape and size. Dirt and gravel formed the floor of the tunnel which, while lengthy, eventually ran into a dead-end wood barricade. Instability in the earth had led the property to close off the remaining passage to Sturluson's residence years earlier.

"With all the wood beams in here, it reminds me of a cedarwood sauna," observed Dr. Arenot.

Emma walked up to the section of the wall where King Hákon's men murdered Sturluson for disloyalty, denoted by a small cross etched into the face of one of the rocks. The lower-level stones in the wall were darker in color. Some theorized it was the permanent staining of Sturluson's blood spilled during his murder.

"So, you have come to see the doodle, the professor tells me," said Gunnar.

"Yes. You know it?" replied Emma.

"Aye. It is not much of anything but follow me." Gunnar led them about 2/3 of the way down the tunnel, studying the fieldstones until he found what he was looking for: a gray fieldstone set about shin-high on the right side of the tunnel. "Here you go," announced Gunnar, squatting down to point it out.

Logan looked where Gunnar was indicating, but didn't see anything. Admittedly, he hadn't lowered himself down yet to get a closer look, but still, he couldn't see what Gunnar was pointing at.

"Hmm, that's strange," muttered Gunnar, looking around at the surrounding stones to make sure he had the right one.

"What's strange?" asked Dr. Arenot.

Gunnar appeared perplexed. "It's just that… it should be right here, on this stone. But it looks like someone's defaced the etching. See for yourselves…"

Although hard to see, with the benefit of Gunnar's flashlight, after closing in for a better look, they could see that the surface of the fieldstone had been disturbed. There were scratches, chisel marks and broken stone, as if someone had used a chisel and mallet to break away the stone's top layer to remove the doodle.

"Are you sure this is the right one?" asked Emma in a concerned tone of voice. She and Logan exchanged a worried glance.

"I am. I don't know how or when this could have happened. There's been no signs of a break-in or a trespassing incident reported that I know of, but someone has definitely defaced this stone."

"Are there any cameras that might've captured the incident?" inquired Logan.

"No. We don't have security like that here. Never needed it before. Who would do something like this?" questioned Gunnar, both astounded and irritated.

"When was the last time you remember seeing the etching undisturbed?" asked Captain Evans.

"It has been a few weeks, maybe a month or more since I last recall taking note of it."

"Has anyone asked about it recently?" followed up Evans.

"Not that I know of."

"Is it possible someone else at the Snorrastofa research center received a call about it?" asked Dr. Arenot.

"Possible, but you must remember, we are a small facility. A call like that would have been routed to me or Katrín. We are the only research fellows at the institute, and I would have heard about it. When I get back to the Snorrastofa, I must report this."

"We are so sorry this happened, but if you don't mind me asking, what did the etching look like?" asked Emma.

"I don't mind. It resembled a two-dimensional stick figure of an animal with a flat back angled slightly up to the right, two parallel legs slanted forward like forward-slashes, and a triangle-shaped head with a line extending out of it at a 45-degree angle, resembling a horn."

Emma could not picture it in her mind, so she asked Gunnar, "Can you draw a picture of it in the dirt?"

"I suppose so." Gunnar, who was already in a squatting position, drew a picture in the dirt floor using his index finger:

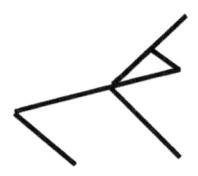

When Gunnar was done, he stood up. "There, my drawing is not perfect, but it is close. It is as I tried to describe: a stick-figure animal with a horn."

"Maybe it's a bull," suggested Professor Quimbey.

"Or a deer," speculated Dr. Arenot.

"I think it looks like a unicorn," said Emma.

"Yeah, that could make sense, too," agreed Logan. "Snorri Sturluson did write about unicorns in his *Prose Edda*."

"Those are all possibilities, but unfortunately, we will never know," said Gunnar. "My apologies, but I have to cut our time short. I must return to the Snorrastofa to report the vandalism. Please follow me."

"Of course," said Dr. Arenot. "Gunnar, we really appreciate your time this morning." Dr. Arenot took a second to snap a photograph of Gunnar's drawing with his phone.

"You are welcome. Most people do appreciate my time and the history that lives here. Regretfully, not the vandals who did this." Gunnar turned to walk outside and they followed. Once they exited the tunnel, Gunnar locked the door back up with the chain and padlock and said goodbye. "Best of luck with your research," he said. "And please, let me know if you need anything else. You are welcome to linger about the property as long as you wish."

"Thank you," replied Dr. Arenot. One by one, they shook Gunnar's hand, whereafter the property's conservator took off to go report the incident.

Once Gunnar was far enough away, Emma spoke first. "This is not good. Someone is on to us, tapping our communications or something. This feels like Italy all over again."

"How's that possible? I thought all our devices were completely encrypted," said Professor Quimbey.

"Let's not jump to any conclusions," replied Dr. Arenot. "It could have been a totally unrelated act of vandalism, we don't know for sure."

Emma wasn't buying it. "Or maybe Supay."

"I think it's highly unlikely Supay is sneaking around with a chisel and a mallet," replied Dr. Arenot.

"You don't know that," countered Emma. "You have to admit, the timing is odd."

"Yes, the timing is odd," conceded the professor.

"It could've been the Russians," suggested Captain Evans. "Covington said we might have company."

"We should let him know," said Professor Quimbey. "Covington said to report anything out of the ordinary, and this qualifies."

"Quimbey's right," agreed Captain Evans. "If we're done here, let's return to the car and call Covington from the road."

They began walking back up the grass hill, passing several gravesites on a pasture shared with a neighboring church. Emma and Logan veered off toward one of the graves. When Professor Quimbey saw where they were headed, she told the others to slow down for a second. She knew what they were going to look at.

Emma and Logan stopped at a long, rectangular gravesite covered in small round stones with a marker on it that read "Sturlungareitur (1179-1241)." Snorri Sturluson was buried there. They stood over his grave looking at his final resting place and wondered, did he have the answers? Did he meet Isa and Annika in the past or know what happened to them? Did he know the Vaniryans or the Norwegian Albo?

"I sure wish he could talk," said Emma. She looked at the grave a few feet away from Snorri's. The headstone read: "Hallveig of Ormsdottir (1199–1241), Ljós lífs míns mun aldrei slokkna." For tourists, there was a plaque beside Hallveig's grave, stating in multiple languages:

"Hallveig of Ormsdottir, the wife of Snorri Sturluson, was born in 1199 and died of natural causes in 1241. Married for nearly 20 years, it is widely believed that their relationship was full of love because Snorri was heartbroken when she died. One need look no further than the touching epitaph Snorri wrote on his late wife's headstone: 'The light of my life shall never extinguish.' Sturluson's love for Hallveig is a rare window into the heart and soul of Iceland's best-known poet, historian, and politician."

"She died the same year he was assassinated," remarked Emma. "Sounds like her death devastated him. So sad." After staring at Snorri's and Hallveig's graves for a few more seconds, Emma wondered, "So, what do we do now? We've looked everywhere, read everything. I have no idea where we are supposed to go next."

Logan thought about it for a moment and replied, "Maybe we're going about this all wrong."

"All wrong? The clues in the *Final Journey of the Vanir*, Sturluson's reference to the Vanir in the *Prose Edda*, his Nine Worlds of the *Yggdrasil* tree with one of his realms being Vanaheimr, home of the Vanir gods... it *all* points to Sturluson. *Everything*."

"I know, and perhaps that's exactly why we can't find anything."

"I'm not following."

"What I mean is, maybe Sturluson took steps to cover up the very clues we are looking for."

"Okay, so maybe we need to start looking deeper into Sturluson's extended family, then," proposed Emma.

"Or, *yours*," suggested Logan.

"What do you mean?"

"I mean, we should start focusing on your family, again, instead of Sturluson."

"Logan, we spent a lot of time on those genealogy reports the president gave us, everyone did. They didn't go back far enough in time and weren't helpful. And we already talked to my family and got nowhere."

"I know, but maybe that was because we were so focused on Iceland and Sturluson that we rushed through it or missed something. Most of your family is from Florence, right?"

"Yeah…"

"Em, if your family name Rossi really was meant to mirror Issor in reverse, and if you really are related to her somehow, then maybe it's time we start taking a deeper look at your family in Florence and work backwards to find Isa."

"And what, interview my relatives again?"

"I don't know, but we have to do something different. Maybe this time we can visit some of the places your relatives used to live rather than just talk to them on the phone. Can you call your cousin Enyo and see if he's around this week? If it's a bust, we'll be back in a few days. What do we have to lose?"

"Nothing, I suppose. Should we all go to Florence?"

"No, just you, me, and Captain Evans for protection, of course. The professors can stay behind with the other security detail and keep researching Sturluson. No reason for them to stop doing what they're doing while we check out Florence, especially if it's going to be a waste of time. What do you think?"

"Sounds good. When we get back to Borgarnes, I'll call Enyo, and then we can talk to Covington about going to Florence."

Chapter 7 – Homecoming

After Logan and Emma spoke with her cousin Enyo Rossi and discussed their proposal with General Covington, the general arranged to fly them to Florence with Captain Evans. The plan was for Captain Evans, along with some U.S. soldiers from the nearby Pisa-Darby Military Complex, to stay in an apartment directly across the street from Enyo's apartment where Logan and Emma would be staying, so that they could be available on a moment's notice.

Upon landing in Florence, they traveled to Enyo's in a van arranged by the Consulate. After fighting afternoon traffic on Florence's cobblestone streets, they reached a five-story apartment building just outside the city center where Enyo lived with his wife Mimi, son Lorenzo, now 10 years old, and six-year-old Gia. The apartment's ground floor had a café on one side of the entry door and a small market on the other. They all got out of the van and grabbed their bags.

"Okay guys," said Evans. "Remember, I'll be right across the street hanging with the Darby boys. Let me know if we're going somewhere, and use your panic buttons if you need to. Got it?"

"Yep," responded Logan.

Evans crossed the street while Emma and Logan turned toward Enyo's apartment building. Before they even reached the entryway, the door between the café and market burst open. Bounding out of it ran an excited Lorenzo followed by Gia. Enyo was right behind them.

"Emmy!" shouted Lorenzo, throwing himself into her body, while Gia crashed into her leg.

"Oh my!" blurted Emma, hugging her adorable cousins. "I've missed you guys!"

While she greeted them, Logan walked up to shake Enyo's hand. "Mr. Rossi, it's very nice to finally meet you. Thank you so much for letting us stay with you."

"Please, call me Enyo. I was wondering when Emma was finally going to visit again. She hasn't been here since she stayed with us many summers ago."

"She talks about that summer a lot," said Logan.

"So do we. We've really missed her. Zoom just isn't the same. Do I have you to thank for bringing her back to us?"

Logan started to say 'no,' but before he could, Emma said to her young cousins, "Hey you two, I want you to meet Logan."

"Hi!" blurted Gia enthusiastically. Lorenzo waived and Logan said "hello" back.

"Let's go upstairs," suggested Enyo. "Mimi's been cooking for you both ever since we got your call yesterday that you were coming to Florence. Kids, do you want to help them with their bags?"

Lorenzo beat his sister to Emma's bag, so Gia went for Logan's. She couldn't lift it. She grunted as she tried but it was too heavy. Logan chuckled. "I got it." He lifted it up out of Gia's struggling arms. "You should save your strength for Emma."

Emma grinned appreciatively. "You see guys, I told you he was sweet."

"Upstairs we go!" announced Enyo, leading the way into the apartment building and up a multi-hundred-year-old staircase to the top floor. Every step creaked, echoing the same sounds heard by the building's residents for centuries. When they reached Enyo and Mimi's apartment, the door was wide open. Mimi, along with the aroma of her cooking, were waiting inside to greet them.

"Emma!" shouted Mimi when they walked in. Mimi hurried over and hugged Emma tightly. Logan extended his hand to shake hers, but Mimi wouldn't have it. She kissed him on both cheeks and embraced him, too. "So nice to meet you Logan!"

"Lorenzo, can you take their bags to their room?" asked Enyo. Lorenzo, who was bigger and stronger than Gia, managed to pick up both bags. Gia insisted on helping and so, she followed along, putting her small hands on the underside of one of the bags even though Lorenzo was carrying all the weight. They disappeared down the hallway.

Not long after, Gia screamed in a shrill tone usually reserved for when Lorenzo was doing something wrong, "Stop it! Mama!"

Irritated and embarrassed, Mimi charged down the hallway with a full head of steam. On her way, she said to her guests over her shoulder, "I'm sorry, I'll be right back."

Enyo laughed. "Kids."

Emma inhaled a whiff of dinner simmering on the stove. "Yum! Whatever Mimi's cooking smells delicious!"

"It is every night for us," chirped Enyo.

"God, I've missed it here so much," said Emma.

"Wow, look at that balcony!" uttered Logan, just now seeing the outdoor space overlooking the Florentine rooftops.

"I know, it's beautiful, right?" replied Emma, grabbing his hand and leading him outside.

The balcony spanned the entire length of the apartment and was accessible from every bedroom. The Rossis had turned it into a

68

rooftop garden with outdoor tables, perfect for a meal, morning coffee or early evening drink. It offered stunning views of Florence's medieval architecture and iconic red tile roof skyline, including the 376-foot-tall Duomo of Florence.

"It's quite a view," remarked Logan, finding unexpected peace in the breathtaking sea of red tile roofs. "For a second, I almost forgot why we're here."

Emma leaned her head on his shoulder. "I know. Isn't it nice?" replied Emma, sharing Logan's sentiment and enjoying the momentary respite from their worries.

Enyo joined them outside. While they were soaking in the view, Enyo asked Logan, "Have you ever been to Florence before?"

"No, I haven't."

"Well, then you are in for a most wonderful treat." He walked up to the balcony railing and, for Logan's benefit, pointed to the Duomo, part of Florence Cathedral. "That is the Cattedrale di Santa Maria del Fiore, and to the left..." Enyo moved his index finger, hoping Logan's eyes could follow. "...over there is the Galleria dell'Accademia where Michelangelo's *David* sits. Maybe you can see top of museum. If you plan to visit museum or cathedral, let me know. I will get tickets and provide my famous personal tour."

"We really appreciate that," replied Emma, pretending to be interested.

"I must ask, what brings you to Florence? It was most unexpected to get your call yesterday, and when I spoke to your mom, she had no idea you were even coming."

Sheepishly, Emma replied, "I haven't spoken to her in a while... or to my dad, either."

"Why? Is everything alright?"

"They don't approve of me taking the semester off to tour Europe with Logan. They're really unhappy about it, actually." Emma hadn't told Logan that her parents blamed him for her 'irresponsible' decision to take the semester off from Georgetown for an 'extended backpacking vacation,' when they could have just waited until after graduation. Her dad had never really embraced Logan, always believing he was an underachiever in high school and distraction from the career goals he had set for her. And while he had grown to like Logan more once Logan showed drive in pursuing a degree at Georgetown, his doubts about Logan returned when Emma decided to take the spring semester off with him. Of course, they didn't know what Emma and Logan were actually doing in Europe, and unfortunately, Emma couldn't tell him.

Enyo responded, "They may not understand, but you must know, they love you no matter what. They just want what's best for you."

"I'm not sure that's true," mumbled Emma, even more angry at her dad for asking her to break up with Logan and return to school. She hadn't told Logan that part.

What Logan hadn't told Emma was that her dad had also called him, angry and rescinding his blessing for Logan to marry her. That last part hurt Logan, and while he wasn't necessarily dissuaded by her father's actions, they certainly gave him pause. What kind of family was he marrying into? One that disapproved of him? He grew up in a broken family with no relationship with his dad, and the last thing he wanted was to marry into another one, or worse, to be the cause of a rift between Emma and her parents that left her in the same place he was. He knew he didn't need Mr. James' blessing, but didn't he want it? What once seemed like a perfect love story between him and Emma now seemed complicated. Maybe that made it more real, Logan thought, but for the first time since they started dating, he wasn't sure what his perfect love story looked like anymore, or if this was it.

"You should call them," urged Enyo, who obviously didn't know all the issues.

"I will, I promise. It's just, there's a lot going on right now."

"Okay, I will not bother you again with it. Tonight, we shall celebrate, not lament."

Emma moved over to Enyo and squeezed him dearly. A small tear formed in her eye. "Thank you, Enyo. I've missed you so much."

"Emma, you are always welcome here," he replied. Sensing she needed more at that moment, he added, "And if you ever need to talk, I have a good ear for that, too."

"I know. Thank you."

Suddenly, Emma felt something pull her leg. It was Gia tugging on her. "Emmy, Emmy, do you want to see my room?"

Emma squatted down to her level and replied, "I thought you'd never ask!"

Emma followed Gia indoors while Logan stayed on the balcony talking to Enyo. Gia's bedroom was small but full of a six-year-old's colorful flair, a miniature chandelier and stuffed animals galore. There were multiple shelves holding up playful clocks, ceramic figurines and other items. Emma's eyes immediately gravitated to a shelf of unicorn figurines, all slightly different in shape, size and color. The collection caught her eye because of the now-defaced etching in Snorri Sturluson's tunnel that Gunnar drew for them in the dirt that resembled a unicorn. She wondered, was there a connection?

"Those are beautiful," complimented Emma, picking up one of the figurines. "They look old. Where'd you get them?"

"Papa," replied Gia.

"Your dad gave these to you?"

"Uh-huh. They were in the memory box."

"Memory box?"

"It's a box with bisnonna's old stuff. They were in there."

Gia was referring to her great grandmother, Isabella. Isabella was Emma's grandmother, Immaculata's sister. They went by Izzy and Immy.

"Well, they're amazing," replied Emma.

"Do you want to meet my stuffed animals?"

"There're quite a lot of them."

"They're all my friends."

"Oh, well then, if they are *all* your friends, I definitely have to, don't I?"

"Yes!" responded Gia with a great, big, dimpled smile. She started introducing Emma to her extended furry family, one at a time. It took a while.

ΔΔΔΔΔΔΔΔΔΔΔΔ

When Gia and Emma finally emerged from her room a half hour later, it was time for dinner. Mimi was handing dishes to Logan and Enyo to carry to the outdoor balcony where the table was set up for dinner. Lorenzo was outside folding napkins, positioning silverware around plates and waiting.

Mimi had just finished preparing a full meal: a caprese salad, an antipasto platter, baked bread, and her incomparable homemade eggplant parmesan. Emma remembered Mimi's rich and messy eggplant parmesan from her visit many summers ago and loved it. To this day, Mimi's eggplant parmesan was the best she'd ever had.

"I can't believe you remembered!" Emma said to Mimi.

Mimi chuckled. "How could I not? Your mother sent many emails asking for the recipe after you stayed here that summer."

"She never could get it quite right," replied Emma.

"Yes, and she sent many more emails about that, too!"

"It smells amazing," stated Logan.

"As it always does," said Enyo, kissing Mimi. They all headed outdoors.

The six of them sat down for dinner on the balcony overlooking the Florentine skyline, while the sun was setting. The ambiance got even more charming when Enyo flicked on the twinkle-lights that lined the balcony, garden plants and apartment walls.

For the next forty-five minutes, they talked about anything and everything except for why Emma and Logan were really there. Enyo and Mimi spent a lot of time catching up with Emma, getting to know Logan, and talking proudly about Lorenzo and Gia. Logan and Emma tried hard to allow their worries to fade away in the dinner conversation, to allow the world to seem normal again, but in the end, they couldn't.

Out of the blue in the middle of the conversation, Emma said, "Enyo, I have a totally random question."

"Random questions are always the most fun," he replied, intrigued.

"Do you know if anyone from our family was from Iceland?"

"From Iceland?" he asked, confused.

"I know it sounds crazy…"

"As in, do we have relatives in Iceland?"

"Yes, or Norway maybe..."

Enyo shook his head. "I don't think so. I have never heard such a thing. Why do you ask?"

Mimi found the conversation humorous. "Hmm... Enyo, have you been lying to me all these years? That might explain some of those stubborn Rossi family genes," she said, touching and playing with Gia's long dirty-blond hair, a color that all the Rossis had.

"Do you mean we're Vikings?!" asked Lorenzo, excited by the prospect of having something new to brag about at school.

"No, we're not Vikings," replied Enyo, finding Lorenzo's question funny.

"Why not? Why can't we be Vikings?" asked Lorenzo.

The table laughed. Enyo responded, "It is not the kind of thing we get to choose." Lorenzo appeared disappointed, while Enyo was curious. "Is this for that genealogy project you called me about awhile back?"

"Uh-huh," replied Emma.

"Well, as far as I know, we are purebred Italians, through and through."

"Are all your relatives from Florence?" Logan asked.

"No, not all. Immediate family from Florence, but I know we have ancestors from Venice, and elsewhere throughout Italy, too. Maybe you can look through Nonna Izzy's box. There is much in there about the family's past for your genealogy project."

Emma's ears perked up when he mentioned the box. "Is that the 'memory box' where Gia said you found her unicorn figurines?"

"Ah, yes. Those unicorns are astounding, aren't they? Passed down from many generations. Fortunate the condition I found them in. Quite remarkable. I considered donating them to the University art museum—"

"No!" barked Gia.

Enyo smiled and kept explaining, "Yes, I know sweetheart. Gia loves them too much. I decided they will stay here for now."

"Can we look through the box after dinner?" asked Emma.

"Most certainly. After dinner, I will be happy to retrieve it."

When dinner was over, Logan, Emma and the kids helped clear and wash the dishes while Enyo went to find the memory box. He returned carrying a large cardboard box and put it on the couch.

"Alright Em, it's all yours. After you look through it, perhaps we can enjoy some espresso on our balcony. It is special bean from the café downstairs, roasted and ground today. Very fresh. It is a sweet bean, like drinking dessert."

Emma, who loved all things coffee and espresso, enthusiastically responded, "Yes, please!" Looking over at Logan, she added, "I love Italy."

After everything was cleaned and put away, Enyo and Mimi went to put the kids to bed. They forewarned it would take a while because they had to get the children to clean their rooms, wash up, brush their teeth, and read them bed-time stories. The timing was perfect because it gave Emma and Logan a chance to go through the memory box.

As they browsed through it, they quickly realized that it was a treasure trove of Rossi family history. There were old photos of Emma's relatives in there, including some of Aunt Izzy and Uncle Francesco, Grandma Immy and Grandpa Matteo. There were photographs of Izzy and Immy as young girls living in a small apartment in Florence with their parents and Emma's great grandparents, Giovani and Angelica. They came across a classic wedding photo of Giovani and Angelica taken in front of a church. The year 1928 was handwritten on the back of the photo. They kept going, finding various other odds and ends in the box, a diary that Aunt Izzy kept, some of Uncle Francesco's business notes, and even an old apartment lease.

"Wow, look at that!" said Emma. "It's my great grandparents' lease for Via di Mezzo, 34, Apt. 4, Firenze FL, dated 1928, the year they got married. That must have been their first apartment before Grandma Immy and Aunt Izzy were born. It even has my great-grandfather, Giovani Romano's signature on it."

Giovani Romano

Logan checked out the old lease and commented, "Crazy, they paid 27,500 lire a month for that apartment."

Emma laughed. "Yeah, but remember, that's Italian lire. Back then, that was probably, like, $17 U.S. dollars a month."

"That makes more sense," acknowledged Logan, laughing at himself.

They continued to thumb through a pile of old black and white wedding photographs of Immy's and Izzy's own weddings at spectacular Florentine chapels.

"Look how stunning they all were," remarked Emma.

"Is that your grandmother?" asked Logan, staring at a wedding picture of a couple standing on the steps of a cathedral.

Emma looked into the eyes of the bride. "Yeah, that's Grandma Immaculata. She really was beautiful."

"I know, and I'm not trying to be corny, but it's incredible how much you look like her."

Emma had never really noticed it before, but their similarity in that particular photograph, more than others she had seen in the past, was unmistakable. "God, I miss her. When I was little, she was always the one who encouraged me to be anything I wanted to be no matter what anyone said. She always wanted to make sure I chose my own path."

"Grandma Immaculata was a wise woman."

"Yeah, she was. She always used to say, 'live your dreams, don't dream 'em.' It didn't matter what was happening, good or bad, Grandma Immy just always knew the right thing to say." Emma kept rummaging through the box.

"Hey, look at this," said Emma, lifting up an old handwritten letter from the pile. The writing was in cursive Italian and slightly degraded, but legible. "Logan, this is hilarious!"

"What does it say?"

"It's a letter to my great-grandfather Giovani, the one who married my great grandmother Angelica, from my great-great-grandfather, Alessandro." She translated for him:

"Dear Giovani:

Please stop writing my daughter.

Sincerely,

Alessandro Rossi"

A handwritten envelope was clipped to the letter. It was addressed to Giovani Romano, Via Cairoli, 18, Firenze FI, and the sender's return address read: Alessandro Rossi, The Rossi Family Home, Calle Scaleta, 5850, Venezia VE.

Emma laughed out-loud. "No wonder Aunt Izzy kept it!"

"I wonder how your great-grandfather ever obtained your great-great-grandfather's blessing to marry his daughter," said Logan.

"I don't know, but that must've been a great story," replied Emma.

She began putting the letter away when Logan noticed something. "Hey, wait a second. Why didn't your great grandmother change her last name."

"Huh?"

"Your great-grandfather's full name was Giovani *Romano*. Your great grandmother's full name was Angelica *Rossi*. Why didn't she change her last name to Romano after they got married?"

Emma explained, "In Italy, women don't change their last names after marriage like they do in the United States. In fact, in Italy, there's actually no way to change your last name."

Somewhat surprised, Logan replied, "I didn't know that! But then, why did Grandma Immaculata and Aunt Isabella also keep the last name, Rossi? Do children take the surname of the father or mother in Italy?"

"Traditionally, in Italy, children take the father's last name, but that's optional; they can choose either."

"Interesting. Growing up in the U.S., I kind of just assumed it was the same everywhere," said Logan. "Why'd they take their mother's name, not their father's?"

"I don't know, family tradition maybe."

"What about your mom? If it was a family tradition, why didn't she keep her maiden name Rossi?"

"Well, she kind of did. She changed her middle name to Rossi when my mom and dad got married, so she's now 'Mary *Rossi* James.' Actually, a lot of women in the United States do that to carry on their family names."

"Huh," replied Logan. He glanced at the letter's envelope again and had another question. "Have you heard of *the Rossi Family Home* in Venice written on the envelope?"

"No."

"What do you think about taking a day trip tomorrow to Venice to check it out?"

Emma loved the idea. "Yeah, okay! We just have to let Evans know what we're doing and coordinate."

Just then, Enyo walked back into the living room.

"Are the kids asleep?" asked Emma.

"Gia is, she never puts up a fight, but it always takes a few extra stories to get Lorenzo down. Mimi's in there now, reading to him. It shouldn't be much longer. Ready for that espresso?"

"Definitely!" blurted Emma, continuing, "but I have a quick question: how long is the train to Venice from here?"

"Eh, about two hours, maybe a little longer. Are you thinking of going?"

"Yeah, we're thinking about taking a day trip there tomorrow. Logan's never been."

"I think that is an excellent idea. I work tomorrow anyway, so that will be perfect. Promise though that we can spend some time together while you're here."

"Are you kidding? I'm not missing out on Mimi's cooking while we're here," assured Emma. "I promise we'll be back for dinner tomorrow night. We're just going for the day."

Enyo was happy to hear that. "Here, let me grab my computer and I will show you the train schedule. What time do you want to leave?"

Emma and Logan exchanged a look. They each knew what the other was thinking: *early morning*. They were both anxious to get to the Rossi Family Home in Venice.

Chapter 8 – Operation 17 Tauri

Captain Velasquez sat with his recon team in a room far below Area 51 wondering how much longer the briefing for Operation '17 Tauri,' named after Electra's official star designation, was going to last. After all, he, along with Commander Davis, were veterans from the last mission when they went through the Vaniryan portal to rescue Emma and the others from the battle in the Hidden City. Thus, he already knew how the portal worked, what to expect and who their enemy was. He just wanted to get back out into the stars, and specifically, to Supay's home planet orbiting Electra in the Pleiades. The four newest members of the team, however, including Lieutenants Williams, Wesley, Hamilton and Bates, had a lot of catching up to do and disbelief to suspend.

Pegasus West's director, Dr. Ehringer, the frazzled, white coat scientist with graying brown hair, thick glasses and a perpetually stressed-out face, and former JPL engineer-turned-Pegasus-operations-specialist, Ian Marcus, were going over the last remaining details for the mission, with others having already covered the reconnaissance objectives and combat contingencies earlier in the day. They paused when Colonel Rodgers, another Pegasus West veteran, stopped in to check on their progress.

"How's it going in here?" Rodgers asked, looking around.

"We're almost done, sir," assured Marcus.

"You said that two hours ago," griped Bates.

Marcus guiltily replied, "I know. Just a few more instruments to go, I promise. These last ones are important, so your team will carry multiple sets just in case—"

"Only some of us make it back, we get it Marcus. Can you cut to the chase?" asked Velasquez, who was in command of the recon team.

"Umm, right," replied Marcus, his voice cracking. "As I was saying, it's important you try to get readings for all the instruments we're sending you with because they'll give us a lot of info about the alien lifeforms, their environment, atmosphere, chemical and mineral elements at their disposal, metallic properties, energy signatures, you name it."

"What's that rod looking thing?" asked Davis, pointing at a metallic rod with a ball at the end.

Marcus responded, "That's the APXS. It'll clip onto the suits you'll be wearing that are currently being prepped over in Equipment."

"I hate acronyms… English please," uttered Davis.

"Sorry, it's the Alpha Particle X-Ray Spectrometer. It uses particle rays to measure the composition and chemical elements in the alien soil, rocks, and metals."

"What about this metallic box here?" asked Hamilton, picking up a square-shaped device.

"That little guy is the BCU, umm, sorry, I meant the Bio Chem Unit for performing chemical tests on any organic matter you find." Marcus studied his smart pad to see where he was on his checklist and then kept going. "Okay, next we've got the Radiation Detector for radiation levels and the Environmental Analysis Device for atmospheric readings… I think those two are pretty obvious. And last but not least, the Gravitometer here. Each works off the press of a button and will be affixed to your suits."

"Yeah, along with the cameras, infrared sensors and audio surveillance devices too," grumbled Davis. "I thought this was a recon mission. You're treating us like Mars-rovers on some science expedition. Can't you guys play NASA another time? It's a ton to carry."

"It's just really important that we learn all we can about our enemy," replied Marcus.

"I don't think anyone doubts that Marcus, but you're asking us to carry a *lot* of equipment. How do you expect us to maneuver effectively in enemy territory carrying all this?" questioned Velasquez. "And remember, it's not just your science gear or the recon surveillance equipment, it's our weapons, too. I'd like to see you carry more than your smart pad into the field."

"Velasquez, lay off Marcus, okay? He's just doing his job," instructed Col. Rodgers.

Brushing off Velasquez's not-so-subtle insult, Marcus explained, "We were, umm, thinking you could find a safe place to stash some of the equipment, you know, only carry what you need."

"And how does that help us if we're under attack the moment we get there? Not everything plays out the way your computer sims predict," countered Velasquez.

Marcus snapped back. "Hey, listen, I know you think all I do is sit in front of a computer and play Call of Duty all day—"

"Don't take it personally, Marcus. I'm just saying it's different in the field than in your labs or—"

"And *I'm* just saying I've got your backs, okay? Your mission might be out there in the stars, but *my* mission is to make sure you guys get the job done and come back safely!"

Velasquez was slightly taken aback by Marcus' feistiness, and impressed. "Alright then... cool. You're right. I was an ass just now. I'm sorry about that." Velasquez walked over to Marcus and fist-bumped him. "You're alright, kid. Maybe I'm more anxious than I thought."

"Thanks," replied Marcus with a grin, adding, "and I think we all are."

"Velasquez, the drop spot is well outside the lion's den based on observations of the planet's surface obtained using the Vaniryan Pyramid," said Col. Rodgers. "We've vetted the insertion point and you should be safe when you get there."

"I guess we'll see," uttered Velasquez, not nearly as confident as Col. Rodgers.

"Do we have to bring all this stuff back with us?" asked Williams.

"No, that's the good thing," replied Marcus, "All your devices, from the science gear to the cameras to the surveillance sensors, are designed to transmit their readings to the data-storage units embedded in your suits. And you're all synched up so that what one of you gets, you all get. So, you guys don't have to bring back *anything* if you don't want to. You can ditch whatever you need to, if necessary, just get what you can."

"That's pretty bad-ass, actually," conceded Williams.

Marcus continued. "Yeah, it is. You can literally leave everything behind if you have to escape, run, hide or just kick some ass—"

"Hell yeah!" chirped the collective SEALS.

Somewhat concerned by the team's reaction to Marcus' last point, Col. Rodgers piped in, "Gentleman, I remind you, the mission is recon only, not engagement. Do not 'kick some ass' unless you're forced to, is that understood?"

"Yes, sir," the team responded.

Williams had another question. "This is awesome and all, but won't these aliens just use their fancy sensors to detect us the second we land on their planet? I mean, on Star Trek, they can detect a single lifeform on the planet's surface from outer space..."

Dr. Ehringer weighed in. "Well, that may be more science fiction than reality, but the good news is that those suits you'll be wearing have some safeguards. They're designed to seal in all of your heat and bio-electric signatures to insulate against infrared and bio-signature-based detection, but in the end, we have no way of knowing what surveillance technology the aliens use."

"That's what the artillery is for my friends!" proclaimed Velasquez.

"Damn straight!" uttered Wesley.

"Only if engaged!" repeated Col. Rodgers.

"You said earlier today that the atmospheric conditions on Supay's planet orbiting Electra are unknown. How long will our oxygen tanks last?" asked Davis.

"Like last time, we're going to try and get a read of the atmosphere with the *p*RAMZA rover first, but beyond that, we're sending you in with a lot of tank refills, which you guys can store, hide or ditch when you get there depending on the circumstances," answered Dr. Ehringer.

"But assuming no refills, your suits have integrated re-oxygenizers built-in to work with the tanks so that should give you up to 24-hours per tank," added Marcus proudly.

"And the plan is for that *p*RAMZA thing to trigger a return portal for us?" Velasquez inquired.

"Yes, but if it doesn't work, like we discussed this morning, we'll be opening up portals for you at the predetermined time intervals," replied Dr. Ehringer.

"Any other questions?" asked Col. Rodgers.

"Yeah, what if my suit rips?" inquired Davis.

"Depends how bad the tear is, but your bags have air-tight, military-grade-adhesive patches to seal up most suit breaches. If you get one too big to patch, I suggest you get back to a portal real quick," said Dr. Ehringer.

"No one said this mission wasn't going to be dangerous, boys," added Col. Rodgers. "Dr. Ehringer, Marcus, anything else?" asked Rodgers.

"No, I think that covers it," replied Dr. Ehringer.

"That's it for me, too," said Marcus.

"Good," said Col. Rodgers. "I will go notify General Nemond that Operation 17 Tauri is on schedule. Marcus, get these men over to Equipment so they can suit up."

ΔΔΔΔΔΔΔΔΔΔΔΔ

Captain Velasquez's team, wearing tough but malleable camouflage-colored space suits and carrying beige aerodynamic helmets, pushed through the door into the giant hollowed-out Vaniryan pyramid under Area 51. Col. Rodgers, Dr. Ehringer, Ian Marcus, and Area 51's commanding officer, General Nemond, were already waiting inside, along with a room full of cameras, monitors, military personnel and doctors. Velasquez and his men approached the five-foot-tall white metallic sphere in the pyramid's center where General Nemond and the others stood. They loaded up with bags of equipment, science gear and weapons, and saluted their ranking officers.

"Captain Velasquez, is your team ready?" asked General Nemond.

"Yes, General, sir."

"Your team's carrying quite a load," commented General Nemond.

Velasquez, glancing at Col. Rodgers, replied, "Yes, sir, we sure are."

"Any final questions about your mission before you boys warp to the other side of the galaxy?" asked Nemond.

Marcus corrected him. "Well, not quite to the *other* side of the galaxy. The Pleiades where Electra is located, is only 400 light years away, while the Milky Way Galaxy is between 150,000 to 200,000 light years across. So, Electra's actually incredibly close, umm, at least from a galactic point of view..." Marcus trailed off when he realized General Nemond was eyeing him impatiently.

"Anything else Marcus?" asked Col. Rodgers, annoyed.

"Umm, no sir."

"Great, we'll practically be next door!" exclaimed Velasquez, throwing some support Marcus' way. Velasquez put his hand on Marcus' shoulder and said, "Just be sure to keep the doors open for us, okay?"

Marcus nodded. "Good luck, Captain Velasquez."

Velasquez turned to face General Nemond. "General, we're ready."

General Nemond gave Col. Rodgers a nod, after which Rodgers announced, "Alright everyone, boot up and bring P-East and the SIT-Room online."

All display monitors and data screens sitting on stands along the pyramid's southern wall turned on. Lieutenant Colonel Ainsley Lain's and Major Bryce Jameson's faces appeared on Pegasus East's screen from their typical post back in the Pentagon, while General Covington, NSA Director Orson, Miles Garrison and several other high-ranking officials appeared on screen from the White House's Situation Room.

"Good afternoon everyone," said Mr. Garrison. "The president sends his regards but he is not going to be joining us. He's got an urgent situation in Kazakhstan that he's dealing with. Captain Velasquez, he wants to wish your entire team good luck."

"And Captain Velasquez, this is Sue Orson… Good luck to you and your men from me, as well," added the NSA Director, staring straight into the screen at Velasquez, the SEAL she had handpicked for the recon mission. She was counting on him to get the job done.

Velasquez looked right back at her in the monitor to acknowledge her, and responded, "Thank you, Director Orson. I won't let you down. General Covington, General Nemond, my team is ready."

"Is Operation 17 Tauri a go?" asked General Covington.

"Yes, general, we are a go," said Nemond through the screen to General Covington.

"Please proceed," said Covington.

Marcus did the honors. He stepped up to the metallic sphere to touch-activate it like Emma had shown them all how to do years ago. After touching it, the sphere lit up with its usual blue energy outlining the continents and land masses of Earth. Marcus next touched in order all the geographic locations around the globe required to activate the sphere: the Château de Falaise in France; Storfjorden fjord in Norway; Stonehenge, UK; Giza, Egypt; Tiwanaku, Bolivia; the Copán Temple, Honduras; Area 51; and lastly, Falaise, again. He kept his index finger fixed on the sphere after touching Falaise the second time and watched as the walls and floor of the pyramid disappeared and a galaxy full of stars holographically appeared around them. Predictably, they lost contact with the outside world.

"Alright Marcus, take us to the insertion point," ordered Col. Rodgers.

Marcus, who had been training for days for this moment, immediately searched the pyramid's stars for the Pleiades star cluster spotted at the right hoof of the bull-shaped constellation Taurus:

"There, I see it!" exclaimed Marcus after finding the Pleiades, which looked like a smaller version of the Big Dipper in the night sky.

He next pointed at Electra, which was located in the bottom row in the middle:

A blue line extended from his finger to the star and off they zipped through the holographic stars until coming to a stop in Electra's solar system. Orbiting the star were two planets: a half-blue, half-green one, dubbed Electra-1, and further out, a red planet covered by large sections of white, called Electra-2. Electra-1 was the one they wanted. That was Supay's planet according to Logan and Dr. Arenot who, along with Bryan Callister and Allysa Anders, had discovered it when going through the portal at Machu Picchu.

"Take us in," said General Nemond to Marcus.

While keeping his index finger on the sphere, Marcus pointed his other finger at Electra-1 and they warped into its orbit. As they had learned to do while working with the holographic technology in the Vaniryan pyramid, Marcus reached his hand toward the planet and, without pointing at it, rotated their position by turning his hand. While Marcus rotated the planet, they saw no civilizations or lights, although in some areas, they saw what resembled destruction or devastation of huge swaths of land and cities that once were there. That was until they rotated to the far side of the planet where there was, just above Electra-1's equator, a section of landmass covered by lights, vibrant structures and buildings, and a massive white dome, all visible from orbit. Because it was the only evidence of advanced life on the planet, Pegasus scientists presumed Supay was there.

Marcus pointed to a darker green section of land just outside the furthest band of lights. Mission analysts had selected that spot because it was far enough away from the lights but close enough for reconnaissance.

A wide portal to the surface opened revealing a forest growing over buildings that had toppled or collapsed, and grass, foliage, vines and moss covering up large broken structures, bridges and tunnels. The forest overgrowth had long since smothered all evidence of a once thriving civilization. There was a bunker approximately 100' in front of the portal consisting of trees, bush and building debris meshed together to form a cave-like place for hiding.

"Team, send in the *p*RAMZA rover," said Dr. Ehringer.

The *p*RAMZA rolled into the portal, instantaneously appearing on the alien soil after traversing the threshold. Slowly, it turned around to face them, and its forward-facing digital screen relayed a message in big, bold, blue letters:

"GREETINGS.

"TEMPERATURE: 90.14° F (32.3°C).

ATMOSPHERE CONSISTS OF: NITROGEN (80.2%), OXYGEN (16.9%), CARBON DIOXIDE (0.7%), WATER (0.4%); HYDROGEN (0.3%); UNKNOWN (<0.7%); POLONIUM (<.08%).

GRAVITY IS 9.941 m/s².

AWAITING FURTHER INSTRUCTIONS."

"Dr. Adams, is Electra-1's atmosphere safe for them?" asked General Nemond, directing his question to environmental specialist, Dr. Haileigh Adams, who was there to analyze the readings.

"Yes, sir," responded Dr. Adams. "The presence of polonium concerns me a little, although it doesn't pose much risk of exposure through their suits. They're well-protected, but I wouldn't want them taking their helmets off or breathing that in. So long as they're suited up, the mission is still a go."

"Alright then. Captain Velasquez, please proceed."

"Yes sir. Team, let's move out."

Captain Velasquez's team put their helmets on and he led the march forward. One by one, his team entered the portal and emerged on Supay's home world. They found themselves in an alien forest, surrounded by the remnants of a civilization that had been overrun by time, the forest, an enemy, or all three. Once they all stepped foot on the alien soil and confirmed the coast was clear, the portal disappeared behind them.

"I don't believe it!" uttered Williams, astounded.

"You didn't think it would work, did you?" queried Velasquez.

"No. I guess I didn't know what to expect, but look at this place…"

"It's freaking wild!" exclaimed Hamilton.

"As wild as it gets," replied Velasquez. "Alright storm troopers, let's get everything secured inside that bunker up ahead so we can get this recon mission started." They all started walking and the *p*RAMZA unit rolled after them, following Velasquez's voice commands.

"You good with 17 Tauri's recon-only directives?" Davis asked Velasquez as they carried their bags, equipment, and weapons to the bunker.

"If you're asking me whether I'll take a shot if I have one, what do you think?" replied Velasquez.

"You guys heard what Col. Rodgers said before about not engaging, right?" asked Wesley, who was walking behind, but he could still hear what they were saying because their helmets were synched up.

"Yeah, I heard what Mister Rogers said," responded Velasquez, "and we're 400 light years away from Earth. They can't help us out here anymore. It's just us, and if we can stop this war before Supay destroys our world, then you can sure as hell count on me trying to blow his head off."

"Are you sure?" probed Wesley. "It's a direct order from—"

"Hey, I ain't saying we go rogue," interrupted Velasquez, continuing, "We're gonna complete this recon mission like we've been ordered to do."

"Good, because we're looking at a court martial when we get back if we don't," stated Wesley.

"That's assuming we return…," said Hamilton forebodingly. He had his doubts.

"Wes, I know what our mission is and we'll follow orders. I'm just saying that if we see Supay, which I highly doubt, but if we do, we can't just do nothing," clarified Velasquez.

Bates wasn't so sure. "Ehringer said they've been working on all kinds of things to figure out how to stop him."

Velasquez disagreed. "Guys, I've spent months in Iceland with the 'experts' tasked with saving our planet. They're awesome, trying their best, but they're getting *nowhere*. They've got no clue what to do next or what they're looking for. They're reading textbooks, and hanging out in libraries and museums. And from what I've heard, back at Pegasus West, weapons development isn't faring much better. We don't have 30 years for the academics and scientists to figure everything out. Supay destroyed the Vaniryan star and planet from orbit! And what are they going to do, throw textbooks at him? Because right now, that's all they got."

"Maybe we just need to give them more time," suggested Wesley.

Velasquez shook his head. "Yeah, well, I'm not waiting for them to solve the next clue or make incremental advances in technology. Screw that. We've all got family counting on us. Hamilton, you've got twins on the way. Bates, you're getting married next year. I've got a little girl at home. I think you get my drift. Are you guys really going to leave it to chance?"

No one responded.

"I didn't think so. If we've got a shot to end this war before it starts, we end it. And if someone wants to court martial me when we get home, so be it. At least we'll have a home to go back to." They reached the bunker. "Alright guys, let's hide the equipment and get organized so we can move out. The clock is ticking."

Chapter 9 – Friendship

Isa grunted as she dragged her hoe through the soil, trying to create a 20-foot-long row in which to plant cabbage seeds. She and her friend Arni, one of Snorri's younger farmhands, had ten more rows to go after this one, and already, she was getting warm under the mid-morning spring sun. She stopped when Snorri arrived to check on her progress while Arni kept hoeing.

"Very good, little one, you are getting the hang of it," said Snorri, examining her efforts, although he did have a suggestion. "You must dig your row a little deeper, like Arni's."

Isa looked over at the handiwork of Snorri's 16-year-old farm apprentice. Arni smirked back at Isa, a friendly yet competitive smirk. Isa looked at Snorri and said, "Isa apologizes."

"*I* apologize," corrected Snorri, having been working with Isa since last season on her common speech and bad habit of referring to herself in the third person.

"*I* apologize," said Isa, trying her best to learn the language so she didn't have to read others' minds to speak.

"There, that's better," said Snorri, proud of her. "But you have nothing to apologize for. Do you try your hardest?"

Isa nodded.

"Good. That is all the gods can ever ask of you."

Snorri got onto his hands and knees beside her and began removing soil from her row with his bare hands. He explained while digging, "The cabbage seedlings like to be buried slightly deeper, and then, we will cover them back up with more soil." When he reached the depth he was going for, he said, "Alright, now lay your seeds down."

Isa reached into the small bucket she was carrying, cupped a handful of seedlings and sprinkled them onto the soil.

"Be sure to space them evenly apart," Snorri instructed her.

Listening carefully, Isa tried to evenly distribute her seeds throughout the section dug by Sturluson. "Like this?" she asked, looking for affirmation.

"Yes! Very good. You have been kissed by Gefjun," he said, referring to the Norse goddess of agriculture. Snorri put his dirty hand on her head and ruffled her hair. A smile beamed across her face. "Now, continue digging your rows for delicious cabbages and ask Arni if you have more questions. I will return later after I solve the mystery of another cage-break by our crafty geese. They are smarter than my men, it seems."

Just then, Isa noticed a tall brown-haired man, wearing a black cloak with large broad shoulder pads, tall boots, gray pants and a dark shirt, walking toward them.

"Who is that man?" asked Isa.

Snorri looked up, and once he saw who it was, his demeanor changed from jovial to serious. He stood and replied, "Little one, continue with your work. When I return later, will you help me collect eggs from the coop? Hallveig wants to make something special for you and Anna today." Anna was Snorri's nickname for Annika.

"Yes!" responded Isa enthusiastically.

Snorri urgently hurried to intercept the man, who appeared to be in his late 40's, before he got closer. The two men came together more than 100 feet away from Isa and Arni.

"Lawspeaker, it is curious how you intend to plant all your fields and grow crops with your help getting younger and smaller each year," said the man, gesturing toward the diminutive Isa working on her cabbage rows.

"Since when do you care about my crops, Gissur?" asked Snorri, suspicious of the comment.

Gissur Þorvaldsson, a fellow parliamentary member of the Althing, replied, "I care about the well-being of all of my parliamentary brothers, and even more so of my friends."

Snorri disagreed. "Your loyalty at parliament has waned, along with our friendship. I seek to put an end to the clan feuds and bring peace to our country, and yet, you oppose me."

"I do not oppose you, Lawspeaker. The clans feud, the chieftains scheme, they do not listen… not to your resolutions, not to the wisdom behind your words, not to the words of their own people. They only seek to tear us apart. It is that which I oppose, not you."

"I work to unify Iceland to bring peace, but those efforts take time. They cannot be rushed."

"Your words are not action, whether spoken out loud at the Althing, or scribed on one of your fancy parchments. They are just words. The chieftains do not care. Your control of the Althing is the only thing that is waning."

"And you've come here to warn me, have you?" questioned Snorri.

"I have come here to help you, as a friend."

"And what would my friend have me do?"

"You must pay a visit to King Hákon. He can help you if you pledge fealty to him. He can increase your numbers by ten-fold."

"To what end? To increase the size of my army so I can start a bloody war?"

"If necessary, yes, but the king does not want war, Lawspeaker. He wants unification of Iceland under Norway and that will lead to the peace you crave."

"The young king is impatient. He does not understand the risk of imprudence because he has never been to war, nor seen it with his own eyes. The chieftains will not unite under him because they do not believe in him. The king himself is the reason why the clans do not unify."

"Then you should return to Norway and tell him yourself. He may still listen to your counsel."

Snorri, although irritated, chuckled. "Gissur, you know it is the king who riles up the chieftains and pits the clans against one another. The king seeks to sow chaos among the chieftains, encouraging the clans to weaken each other so he can come in with his army and unify Iceland under Norwegian rule."

"But isn't that exactly what you promised the king you would help him do, support a union with Norway to achieve peace, a peace you fail to attain with words alone? Sometimes, Snorri, it takes swords."

Snorri did not agree. "Words do not spill blood the way swords do."

"Lawspeaker, your pursuit of peace through words is noble, and it is an effort the king supported when he helped you regain your status as Lawspeaker of the Althing for a second time. King Hákon is why you are where you are, do not forget it."

"Now, it sounds like you are speaking for the king. Are you here doing his bidding?"

Snorri had discerned the motivation behind Gissur's visit, and so, Gissur confessed, "I have recently traveled to Norway and spoken with the king, yes... and he desires to help you, but he questions your loyalty."

"The king asked me to introduce a resolution supporting a peaceful union with Norway, and I have done that. It fails because it is not yet the will of the people."

"It fails because resolutions are for poets, historians and lawyers like you who believe in words. The chieftains aren't cut from the same cloth as you, Snorri. It is time for action yet you fail to act. You have the power but refuse to wield it."

Snorri shook his head. "Wield what? More swords, axes and spears? Unleash my army to cut throats, pillage and burn down peaceful villages? How much harm must I inflict to achieve the king's dream of unification?"

Gissur raised his fist and stated, "No more than necessary if you strike hard with swift force, bringing your enemies to their knees!"

"The Althing was formed 300 years ago so representatives could govern our country through orderly rule of law and conversation. I will not wage war against my own people to appease Norway's king."

Gissur was frustrated. "You do not need to wage a full-scale war. You need only unleash the power that hides here. The moment the chieftains see that you control the destructive power of witchcraft, they will bow down to you and you will accomplish all that you once promised King Hákon you would."

Snorri immediately tensed up at the mention of witchcraft and his eyebrows raised.

Gissur continued, "Use your witches in the name of the king and he will reward you!" Gissur took a step toward Isa, and Snorri stepped in front of him to block his path. "Is that girl one of them?" asked Gissur.

"One of who? She is the daughter of a friend who stays with us. I have put her to work in the fields to earn her keep. They are staying through the season."

Gissur did not believe him. "Is that so? I need not tell you how far the winds of Njǫrd can carry news of the land, even to the shores of Norway."

"I think it is best that you leave, now," insisted Snorri.

"Sending me away from your property will not stop the clans from coming. How long did you think you could hide the witches here before the chieftains came calling?"

"I do not know what you speak of—"

"Rubbish, Snorri, I am no fool! Do you really expect me to believe for one instant that the most powerful chieftain in all the land and Lawspeaker of the Althing is the only man in Iceland who has not heard the rumors carried by the winds of Njǫrd? Kurgandur now has King Hákon's ear, and he has convinced the king that you hide the witches from him because you intend to challenge his rule. You would be wise to go to Bergen to mollify the king. He can still be an ally, Snorri, but you should leave at once, before it is too late. And bring your two 'houseguests' with you. The king would like to meet them. The three of you are called to travel to Norway by formal invitation of the king."

"It sounds like Kurgandur is not the only one who has the king's ear. Tell King Hákon I will continue the work I am doing here, as I pledged to bring peace and cooperation between our two countries through the parliamentary process of the Althing. I do not have witches to deliver to him nor will I deliver myself. I have too much to do here."

"I will tell him what you say, but you are unwise to refuse King Hákon's invitation," warned Gissur.

"And you are unwise to revel in the merits of bloodshed and war. Abandoning the parliamentary process we both swore an oath to uphold is not the way to peace."

"Again, those were just words, Lawspeaker," replied Gissur, side-stepping Snorri to walk toward Isa.

Snorri whistled to get his guards' attention while also hurrying to keep up with Gissur, who was rushing toward Isa. Snorri's men started running toward Gissur. Snorri caught up to Gissur just as he reached her in the cabbage field. She was on her knees gently laying cabbage seeds down, while Arni had already moved next to her to protect her.

"Hello," said Isa, guardedly.

Gissur studied Isa's work on the soil and said, "You are a talented farmer. Your grooves are of perfect depth for cabbage seeds, but your rows must be straighter." Isa did not respond. Gissur glared at the girl who he believed to be a powerful witch, struggling to comprehend why Snorri was wasting her formidable talents ditch-digging in manure-infused soil for cabbage seed planting.

"You will leave now," said Snorri, whose men had just arrived. They put their hands on their weapons in case Gissur's response was anything other than an unqualified *yes*.

"Of course, Lawspeaker," said Gissur, turning around to walk away from Isa and leave the property. He bumped into Snorri's shoulder on his way out and uttered, while looking back at Isa, "What a waste…" Gissur departed, with Snorri's men escorting him all the way off the property.

While Gissur was on his way out, Isa asked, "Was that man a friend of yours?"

"He pretends to be."

"What did he want?"

You, thought Snorri, agitated and forgetting, momentarily, that Isa could hear his rattled thoughts. After settling himself, he said, "Why don't we return to the house early for lunch. You can finish the cabbages tomorrow."

Chapter 10 – The AÁBs

With the oil lamps and fire pit still burning brightly, Isa sat at the dining hall's communal table writing the Icelandic alphabet on a blank parchment. Having just finished dinner, Snorri looked on with interest while Hallveig and Annika conversed.

Isa dipped her new quill pen, which she had personally plucked from her favorite greylag goose, in a tiny bottle filled with thick black ink. She had even named her greylag goose GreyFeather after its grey and white plumage. Because GreyFeather had become Isa's *de facto* pet, Snorri had promised her no one would eat him unless he escaped and flew off to someone else's kitchen. Snorri actually suspected GreyFeather was behind all the recent escape attempts by the geese as he seemed just a bit smarter than the rest.

After Isa finished writing her final three letters, Þ-Æ-Ó, she looked up at Snorri. Snorri pulled lightly at his beard and asked, "Are you certain?"

Isa could tell from his intonation that she had missed something, so she studied her lettering further until spotting her error. "Ö, not Ó," she muttered. "I always get that one wrong."

"Hey, you did it!" blurted Annika, excited by Isa's proper reference to herself in the first person.

Isa's breakthrough also drew praise from Snorri, who shouted, "Very good, little one! Now, write your lowercase letters." Isa used her quill to write out the last three letters of the alphabet in lowercase. When done, Snorri praised her. "You are an excellent scribe." Isa smiled at the compliment.

"Why do you have her write when she can just listen to the thoughts of others?" questioned Hallveig, who herself had never learned to read or write.

Snorri replied in Latin, "Vir sapiens fortis est, et vir doctus robustus et validus."

"What does that mean?" asked Annika in her rudimentary Icelandic that she had picked up over the last year. At Annika's own request, Isa had stopped translating for her. Annika was trying hard to learn the language and believed that, to become conversant, she needed as little help as possible. She had actually gotten quite good at it. Isa only translated now when Annika asked.

Snorri responded, "It is from the Catholic Vulgate... it means, 'A wise man is strong, a man of knowledge increaseth strength.' Even those gifted by the gods must find their way on Earth. If Isa is to live beyond the years any of us have left, she will need more than the power Aurvandil has bestowed upon her. She will need to read and write, too, for that is the key to the knowledge she will require to survive in this world when we have all departed."

Isa didn't like the sound of that. On Vanirya, she had never witnessed others growing older and dying of old age. "I am afraid to watch you all die as the years pass for you but not I."

"It is not cause for sadness, child," Snorri reassured her. "You must rejoice in our aging and passing. The golden hall of Valhalla awaits us in Asgard, hanging highest among the branches of the Yggdrasil. There, we shall spend eternity dwelling with our friends and loved ones, celebrating with an endless supply of exceptionally fine food and drink."

Hallveig, looking at Snorri's robust belly, commented, "With you, Snorri, it is always about food and drink."

Isa liked Snorri's depiction of their future, although still, she was not entirely comforted. "But I am afraid to be alone."

Hallveig got up from the other side of the table, moved to sit beside Isa and hugged the young girl who had become like a daughter to her. "From Asgard's branches, we shall look joyously down upon you in Midgard, watching you with love for all the days of your life until you can join us in the Great Hall. You will never truly be alone."

"You know this to be true?" asked Isa.

"It is what men believe," offered Snorri.

"But I am not a man," rebutted Isa, challenging Snorri's premise. After all, she was Vaniryan.

He had a better answer. "You shall return to the realm of Vanaheimr, the home of the Vanir on a high branch beside Asgard's on the Yggdrasil. There, you shall meet your parents again, and be able to journey freely through the Yggdrasil's branches to visit and rejoice with us in the Great Hall. Your people travel in unlimited ways, unlike men who can only walk upon the soil of Midgard and the heavenly grounds of Asgard. Your coming to our world has proven the Vanir need not walk."

The idea that Isa might one day be able to see her parents again, who were murdered by Supay's Hunt when she was just a small girl barely able to remember them, pleased Isa.

"Isa, it is time for rest," said Hallveig. The evening had grown long, and like children everywhere, in all places in time, she was expected to go to bed early. She kissed Isa on the forehead and told her, "Go wash and ready yourself for bed, and we shall be right there."

Isa stood up and asked Snorri, "Another story tonight?"

Snorri was happy to indulge her. "Of course, little one."

Isa liked Snorri's stories. They were full of the very adventure that had initially spurred her to leave the trees of Jaannos in search of something more than the constricted home life she left behind. Perhaps she had gotten more than she bargained for on her journey, but still, she loved the wonder of adventure and believed that, someday, hers would lead her back to Vanirya.

Isa left the dining hall, heading off to her quarters to change and wash. On the way there, like always, she stepped outside to say goodnight to GreyFeather. When she was gone, Snorri had a worried look on his face. Hallveig picked up on it immediately.

"What is it, Snorri?" asked Hallveig.

Snorri waited to be sure Isa was gone and responded, "Gissur came to visit me today."

"What did that pig want?" scoffed Hallveig, not a fan of Gissur after his frequent attempts to undermine Snorri at the Althing.

"He said he wanted to help me," replied Snorri.

Hallveig laughed, although she wasn't amused. "Help *you*? How? He has no allies on the Althing, and his entire army can fit inside your swine enclosure, which is where he belongs. I do not trust him."

"Nor do I, but it seems he has the ear of the king."

"What could Gissur possibly have to offer King Hákon that the king does not already have?"

"Isa."

"What?!" exclaimed Annika.

"Anna, I am sorry, but your secret has escaped my protection in Reykholt. Your presence here is known to the king, Gissur and others."

Hallveig was incredulous. "Snorri, you have a traitor among your men! Only one of them could have divulged that information."

"And when I find out who, I will personally send him to Helheim," Snorri assured her.

"How do you know the king wants Isa?" questioned Annika.

"Gissur extended an invitation for you and Isa to travel with me to the king's royal estate in Bergen," replied Snorri, referring to King Hákon's European-style stone palace among the fjords in Norway. "The king wants to use Isa's power to expand his empire."

"Isa is not a weapon, she is just a girl!" stated Hallveig. "She will not kill the king's enemies just because he insists upon it."

"The king does not tolerate disloyalty. He kills those who refuse his requests," Snorri reminded her.

"Snorri, they cannot go!" insisted Hallveig.

"I know, which is why I declined the king's invitation and told Gissur there are no witches here."

"Did he believe you?" followed up Hallveig.

"No. He fixed his eyes on Isa. He already knew precisely who and what she was."

"What does this mean for us?" asked Annika.

"It means it is not safe for you here anymore. The king's men will come for you... soon Kurgandur's men will, too. All the clans will come. I am truly sorry. My men are strong and skilled, but I cannot withstand the Norwegian army and the clans that will come after them. Reykholt will be overrun. The plot is already afoot."

"So what should we do?" asked Annika.

"You must leave Reykholt," replied Snorri.

"When?"

"Tonight."

Hallveig was struck by the immediacy. "Must they leave so suddenly?"

"Yes! I fear the king will act quickly. They must leave long before his men get here and his spy learns more. The greater a head start, the better chance they have."

Annika looked flustered. Snorri could see it on her face.

"Anna, we have prepared for this day, always knowing it was a possibility. I have finished penning the *Final Journey of the Vanir* poem and completed the additions to my *Prose Edda*. If my works do survive until your future like you say they will, the messages will reach your friends, but now, it is time for you to run again."

"But to where?" asked Annika.

"For sure, you must leave Iceland, as the winds of Njǫrd have spread your secret too far and wide. You are no longer safe here."

"Into the waters?" questioned Hallveig, knowing that to leave Iceland, the ocean was their only choice, and a concerning one at that. "Hákon commands a formidable naval fleet. He controls the North Sea, the Norwegian Sea, the Denmark Strait to Greenland, and the waters southeast of here that lead to the English king's channel."

Snorri responded, "That is why they must go south."

"What is south?" asked Annika.

"The secret sea on the other side of the Iberian Peninsula. You must sneak into the secret waters and navigate to the papal lands. Neither King Hákon nor the clans will dare follow you there."

"But we are no Vikings. How are we supposed to do that? I've never sailed the ocean in my life," said Annika.

"That is why Hallveig will go with you," responded Snorri.

"Me?" uttered a stunned Hallveig.

"Yes, you come from a family of skilled navigators. You have sailed the oceans with your father, and ridden the waves with me… you know how to work the sea."

"But—" Hallveig started to respond, but Snorri interrupted her.

"And Anna, you say you are a skilled astronomer in your future, familiar with the stars of the heavens. You need only follow the stars at night and the sun during the day to find your way. Do you know the Iberian Peninsula of which I speak?"

"Yes, it is the southwest tip of Europe where modern day Portugal faces the Atlantic Ocean."

"Good. From there, you must enter the secret sea beneath it to find the pope's lands," said Snorri.

"You are referring to the Mediterranean."

"There must be someone else who can do this," pleaded Hallveig, distraught at the idea of leaving Snorri.

"I don't trust anyone else," Snorri replied. "Do you?"

Hallveig shook her head. "But they will question where I am."

"I will tell them that you have died of natural causes, dig a grave for you in the churchyard, and bury your free spirit below a mound of dirt. They will never suspect."

Hallveig was mortified by his sacrilegious plan. She made a cross on her chest and asked, "Snorri, do you truly mean to do this?" Hallveig's eyes looked ready to burst in tears despite that she was a hardened Viking woman who rarely allowed her emotions to show.

Snorri lifted his hand to move Hallveig's hair out of her watering eyes. "Hallveig, my dear, this is the only way I know you will be safe. Hákon's men, Kurgandur's men, the clans, they are all coming. They will kill you if you are here. My love, I wish you to live your full life and not die because of my failings at the Althing."

"So you expect to die?" asked Annika.

Snorri most certainly did, but he responded more optimistically, "Perhaps my tongue will talk me out of an unfortunate fate. There is always hope, but my enemies appear greater than my friends now that the disease of disloyalty has infected my men. I will do my best, but this is how the three of you survive, and I will give my life, if necessary, to make sure that happens."

Annika had a better idea. "You should come with us."

"Yes, Snorri, please!" urged Hallveig.

"I wish I could, but my face is known throughout this land and my disappearance will arouse suspicion the moment I do not greet my men in the morning as I have done every day for the last 20 years. The spy will know something is wrong immediately, before we ever reach the coast. Accompanying you will nullify all that I hope to achieve."

"But Snorri…," muttered Hallveig, her emotions now overtaking her.

Snorri tried to console her. "I may yet reach a satisfactory accord with the king and regain influence over the chieftains. And if I do, I will come find you in the sea city."

"Sea city?" replied Annika.

"Yes, it has been described to me as a city in the sea, filled with canals."

Annika knew the city he was referring to. "You mean, Venice. It is a city of canals on the northeast coast of Italy, at the top of the Adriatic Sea."

"Good. There, you must find a merchant by the name of Vincente Defuseh. I met him in Bergen a few years ago during my time in Norway when the merchants from the Papal States came to sell their wares to the Crown. This man owes me a favor. He will protect you."

"What kind of favor?" asked Annika, curious what Snorri had done for the man to earn such a favor.

"I saved him from the executioner's block to which he was sentenced for philandering among the king's court. Defuseh owes me his life."

"Oh my," replied Annika. "Why did you help him?"

"It is as I said earlier, 'a man of knowledge increaseth strength.' I did it for knowledge. He possessed a very rare map of the eastern world beyond the known lands, brought back from a merchant's travels there, that I wanted to study. Fortunately, the map also detailed the route he sailed from Venice to reach the king's land in Norway. You can take his map with you to help navigate back to Venice."

Annika was confused. "And the king just let you—"

"No, of course not. For some coin to his majesty, to be sure, and a promise to favorably memorialize King Hákon's legacy in my *Eddas*. Defuseh was lucky my coins and quill curried favor back then. He will keep you safe until I arrive."

"If you arrive," replied Annika.

"Snorri, Hákon's reach extends far beyond Norway and Iceland," worried Hallveig, unconvinced they would be safe even in Italy. "You have told me many times that he schemes with the European kings too, especially the Norman kings."

"Aye," acknowledged Snorri. He considered it for a moment, then proposed some additional subterfuge. "You should change your names, also."

"My name in the time I come from is Annika Nikola Kuznetsov," shared Annika, continuing, "I can go by my middle name Nikola, then Anna. I can spell it the Italian way, Nicola Anna. That sounds like a good Italian name."

Snorri approved. "And Isa?"

Annika thought about it and came up with another suggestion. "Isa, Isabel... Isabella... how about Isabella? It is also a common Italian name."

Snorri nodded and lastly asked his wife, "And Hallveig?"

"How is my mother's name, Tora?" asked Hallveig. "It ends in the sound of 'a' much like Nicola, Anna and Isabella."

"I think that will pass as Italian," concurred Annika.

Snorri replied, "Good, it is settled then. You tell Vincente that Hákon threatens your lives. He will know what to do. He will take you in. I will find you when I can."

"Snorri, are you sure about this?" Annika asked again.

"Yes. It must be done. I have a boat at Strandakirkja to the south. Hallveig knows the one."

"Aye," affirmed Hallveig who had sailed it with Snorri before.

Snorri continued, "It is a fine boat, small enough not to be easily seen on open water, with a mast two can manipulate, and sturdy enough to carry the three of you to the secret sea."

"Is it safe for us to sail the ocean in such a small boat?" wondered Annika, worried about the rough waters of the North Atlantic.

"Safer than staying here," replied Snorri, offering little reassurance.

"Do we leave now?" Annika asked.

"No. You will leave in the middle of the night when all others are asleep. No one can see you leave."

"I will go tell Isa," said Annika.

"No," replied Snorri. "I wish to tell our sweet unicorn one more story, and then, let her rest peacefully into the night. She will need her rest."

Hallveig embraced Snorri. The thought of her unexpected separation from her husband of 20 years was tearing her apart inside. It was all so sudden and her pale, shell-shocked face showed pain even as she tried to hide it.

"I know," said Snorri, putting his hand on her cheek to remove a tear. "If it is Odin's will, we shall reunite in Venice. Otherwise, I shall be waiting for you in Asgard, forever proud of how you saved Isa's and Anna's lives."

"And I you," cried Hallveig.

They shared an extended embrace full of love, admiration, and respect for one another and for what each was about to do. Snorri broke off the hug first before Hallveig was ready to let go, although he still held her hand.

"It is time for me to go tell little one her story. When I return, we can finalize plans and say our goodbyes properly." Snorri kissed Hallveig's hand and gazed at the love of his life one more time before turning to go visit Isa's room.

Isa was sitting upright on her thatched bed waiting for Snorri to arrive. She smiled when he walked in.

"Hello, child, are you ready for a story?"

"Yes!" said Isa, eagerly anticipating what Snorri had in store for her that evening.

Snorri sat down in a chair beside the bed. "Tonight, I shall tell you the story of how the god of stars, Aurvandil, learned to fly through the heavens to place his stars in the night sky."

"Even the star I come from?"

"Yes, *all* the stars, including yours! But the story is not just about how Aurvandil learned to fly. He faced a dangerous adversary along the way who sought to undo his work - Loki, the god of evil and mischief - who tried to steal all the stars that Aurvandil left behind."

"Did Aurvandil win?" asked Isa impatiently.

"Do the stars still glint in the night sky?"

Isa looked outside her open wood window at the starry night sky and, with a smile, replied, "Yes! How did he win?"

"You must listen to the story first, little one."

Her impatience rebuffed, Isa huffed but smiled.

"It is a good one, I promise," pledged Snorri. Isa settled in as Snorri began to speak.

Chapter 11 – Norðrljós

Snorri sat on the stone bench in front of his home, staring up at the heavens and the undulating, appearing and disappearing lights of norðrljós, otherwise known as the Northern Lights or Aurora Borealis. No matter how many times he saw the spectacle, it never ceased to amaze him. He gazed upon one of the more vibrant displays in recent memory, with ribbons of green, blue, and violet lights dancing through the night sky like someone was playing chords on a piano. Snorri wished he wasn't alone to see the awesome sight. Normally, he would have shared the wonder with Hallveig.

It had been six weeks since Hallveig, Isa and Annika left in darkness and, to his relief, the winds of Njǫrd had not carried any rumors back to his ears suggesting they had been spotted or captured. Indeed, his men at the port in Strandakirkja had recently reported that his short-travel boat had been stolen. They had no idea who took it. They had apologized profusely for their negligence, and Snorri had forgiven them. After all, it meant his plan was working.

Hallveig's staged burial ceremony drew very few questions and attracted even fewer mourners because her death was sudden and her funeral took place even before most had a chance to learn of her unexpected passing. Of course, that was intentional by Snorri. In the weeks that followed her burial, many came to pay their respects in person, while others sent messages of condolences, reminding Snorri that he still had friends in Iceland. Or perhaps, more accurately, reminding Snorri that Hallveig had captured the hearts of all who had met her, including most permanently, his. Although she was not dead, her loss struck him just as hard. He was heartbroken by the sacrifice he chose to make when he sent her away.

Snorri was enjoying the stars and dancing lights when he heard footsteps coming his way. Three people were approaching by way of the central path through his property. Once the threesome got closer, Snorri could see who it was. It was Gissur escorted by two of Snorri's men, Arni and Símon. Snorri had expected that the next time he saw Gissur, his former friend would be accompanied by a full army coming to kill him. To his surprise, Gissur had come alone just like he did several weeks earlier.

"Lawspeaker, Representative Þorvaldsson is here to see you," said Arni.

"Thank you, Arni," replied Snorri. Arni and Símon backed up to allow Gissur to speak to Snorri privately.

"Snorri, I was very sorry to hear about Hallveig."

"Is that why you are here, to pay your respects, or are you just checking in to see how my crops are growing?"

"I am here as a friend—"

"Enough, Gissur! My friends visited weeks ago, or sent notes in their stead. What does that make you?"

"I shall assume your cross remarks are born of anguish at the loss of your wife. I was detained in Norway, unable to return to Reykholt sooner."

"Now that you have expressed your condolences, is your business finished here?" asked Snorri.

"No… you know why I am here."

"Let me guess… to help transition Iceland into a peaceful union with Norway, or to burn your home country down?"

"You have failed to accomplish peace, Snorri. You had your chance but the country is already burning down with the clan feuds you failed to stop."

"And you can?"

"No, but the king can, with his army and the help of those who hide here. I have come for your witches."

"I have told you before, there are no witches—"

Gissur snapped his fingers. Arni and Símon drew their swords, stepped closer to Snorri and pointed their blades at his chest. Seeing their betrayal cut Snorri deeply but also confirmed that he had done the right thing by sending Hallveig, Isa, and Annika away.

"I see you have spread your disease to others," commented Snorri to Gissur.

Gissur continued, "I want you to think very carefully before you respond again, Lawspeaker. King Hákon has bought your men, and those who imprudently valued honor over money have been killed. Do not make this any harder than it has to be. Now bring me the witches and command them to come peacefully, or we shall do this the hard way."

"It is sad what you have become Gissur. You should be ashamed."

"I have become a very wealthy man and Earl of Iceland, Snorri. Money, power, those are the things that make a man, and get things done, a lesson you have never learned. Words accomplish nothing. Believing in your words for far too long is the only thing I am ashamed of."

Disappointed, Snorri glared at Arni and Símon, whom he had known since they were boys, and said, "This is who you two choose to follow, a traitor?" Neither Arni nor Símon responded. Instead, they conspicuously avoided making eye contact with Snorri, who added, "Gissur leads you both to Helheim, when your fathers rest in Asgard. You disgrace your fathers, and if you ever wish to see them again, you will stop—"

Arni spat at Snorri, angry at him for invoking his father, and perhaps because Snorri was right. "My father died a poor man, serving you to no end. I will not die like him, with nothing to show for it. But you will."

Gissur laughed. "Do you see the respect your words have earned you?" Just then, Snorri noticed that there were more men amassing and surrounding his home. He couldn't tell how many, but there were dozens of them spread around his property. Most appeared to be Gissur's own men, not Snorri's. Many were holding torches. "You see Snorri, you have nowhere to run, and words will not save you. I shall not ask again. Go get the women."

Snorri, defeated, agreed. "I will go get them."

"A wise decision," replied Gissur. "Símon, go with him. And Snorri, if you do not return swiftly with Símon *and* your two houseguests, we will burn your house to the ground with you and your witches in it. My understanding is that they were not fond of flames the last time they encountered them."

Snorri turned around to head into the house and Símon followed him inside. Snorri walked down the hallway toward steps leading up to the second level of his home. As Snorri began climbing the stairs with Símon on his heels, Snorri asked him, "Do you mean to go through with this, Símon?"

Halfheartedly, Símon replied, "I do not have a choice, Lawspeaker."

"You always have a choice, Símon. Your father Jorri was a brave man and I remember you fondly as a sweet boy who grew up playing in my fields."

"I do not want to die, Lawspeaker."

"Símon, Asgard, where your father awaits you, only admits the honorable. Do not do this. If you help me, a far sweeter place with loved ones awaits you in Valhalla than Helheim where Gissur is leading you."

Símon thought about it. With great regret in his eyes, Símon said, "I am sorry for what I have done. Please forgive me, Lawspeaker. You may throw me down the stairs, and when I hit the ground, take my sword and strike me. Please make it a clean blow. If you stage it well, perhaps death will not follow for me."

Snorri placed his hand on Símon's shoulder and replied, "May Odin protect you all the days of your life."

"And you, Lawspeaker."

"Ready?"

Símon nodded, and Snorri forcefully shoved him backwards down the stairs. Símon landed hard on his back and cracked his head as he bounced to the bottom. He was bleeding from the back of his head, and suffered a broken wrist. Although barely conscious, he survived the fall. With a slight smile, Símon whispered, "May we meet again in Asgard."

Snorri grabbed Símon's sword and slashed the young man's right shoulder. He didn't use all his strength because he didn't want to sever Símon's arm. Snorri dropped the bloodied sword and hurried down the steps to a door beside the stairs. It led to an underground passage that continued underneath the house, through the hill behind his property, and all the way to an outer exit at his geothermal spa several hundred feet away.

He ran through the tunnel hoping to escape Gissur's ambush. However, before he reached the other end, he saw the exit door open and torches rush in. It appeared Snorri's secret escape was not so secret. Snorri turned around to head back to the house, but Gissur, Arni and others were already rushing down the tunnel from that direction too, having heard Snorri's struggle with Símon. Snorri was trapped.

When the two sides converged, Gissur spoke first. "Did you really think you could outsmart me, Snorri? Where are the witches?"

"There are no—"

"Your lies do not matter! The men search the house now."

Gissur's men kept Snorri at bay with swords while others searched the house. It wasn't long before one of Gissur's men shouted down into the tunnel, "There is no one here. The woman and girl are gone!"

"Snorri, where have your witches gone?" demanded Gissur.

"I will enjoy my journey to the heavenly gates of Asgard before I ever answer you."

"As you wish. By order of King Hákon, for treasonous disloyalty, an offense punishable by death, you shall be executed. Arni, strike him down!" ordered Gissur.

"Arni, you do not have to strike me. Make the coward do it himself and I will forgive you!"

Gissur screamed at the young man again, "Arni, strike now!"

"Do not strike!" countered Snorri.

Arni stepped toward Snorri with his sword at the ready. He pushed the point of his sword up into Snorri's neck and looked intently into Snorri's eyes. "Where are Isa and Anna?" he yelled before telepathically adding, *If you tell me, I will spare you.*

At first, Snorri was confused, but then he realized Arni was speaking to him in his mind just like Isa used to do.

Where are Isa and Anna?!?! boomed Arni's voice again inside Snorri's head, this time more angrily. Arni got into Snorri's face, nose to nose, eye to eye, with the point of his blade now piercing Snorri's skin.

"I will not tell you," uttered Snorri to the alien who served a master far more dangerous than King Hákon. "Supay will never find them."

Arni sneered. *That is where you are wrong, poet. Supay's power reigns over all worlds.*

"The people will defeat him," Snorri pushed back.

Fool. Supay cannot be defeated. Did Isa not tell you that? I ask you one last time, where are Isa and Anna?

"You are the only fool here if you think I will share that with you."

Undeterred, Arni started forcibly searching through Snorri's mind. Snorri could feel Arni scouring his thoughts, and he tried to resist. Unfortunately, before he could stop it, Snorri inadvertently revealed the direction Isa, Annika and Hallveig had gone: *south.*

Where south? demanded Arni.

Having already said, or rather, thought too much, Snorri tried harder to resist Arni's prying. Snorri, knowing his life was nearly over, turned his final remaining thoughts to Valhalla. In his last moments, he wasn't going to betray Hallveig, Isa or Annika again.

Gissur screamed at Arni, "Boy, strike now or I shall question your loyalty!"

With a mocking grin, Snorri proffered the final words of his poetic life, "You are too late, you have failed your master. Perhaps I will not be the only one to die today."

Perhaps… but you will be the first. Arni stepped back and shoved his sword into Snorri's gut followed by his chest. Snorri fell backward into the low wall of fieldstones, and slumped down, with his back leaning against the stones. Snorri was bleeding profusely from his chest and back. He next slumped down onto his side.

That's when he saw the doors to the golden hall of Valhalla open up, calling for him to enter. Inside, he saw loved ones, places to recline, food, drink, and angelic Valkyries carrying the honorable fallen to other heavenly places deeper in the hall. It was as Snorri had always believed it would be: the perfect place for him to wait for Hallveig. He smiled. A Valkyrie had come to take his hand and escort him in. It was his time to go.

Chapter 12 – Canals of the Past

Logan, Emma, Captain Evans, and Lt. Peters, who came along solely for security reasons, arrived on a train at Santa Lucia Railway Station in the 1,200-year-old canal-city of Venice, Italy. Once the train stopped, they got up from their seats and disembarked, ready to visit the Rossi Family Home. They made their way out of Santa Lucia, passing indoor shops, restaurants and tourists on the way to their next destination: the Grand Canal. The Grand Canal was Venice's most significant water-traffic corridor, winding through the heart of Venice in a reverse-S-shaped pattern from one side to the other, dividing the city in half.

They boarded a pre-arranged water-taxi to carry them to the address Emma's great-great-grandfather had written on his letter to Emma's great-grandfather: Calle Scaleta, 5850. Their water-taxi captain, Filippo, told them that the place where they were going was in the Cannaregio district. In tour guide fashion, he advised them that the Cannaregio was popular among tourists because of its narrow cobblestone walkways lined with shopping opportunities, merchants, and casual canal-side restaurants and bars.

As their water-taxi cruised down the Grand Canal, four and five-story buildings with foundations submerged below water, lined the banks of the waterway. The buildings, most of which dated back centuries, included Venetian palaces, hotels, opulent villas, museums, and churches. After 10 minutes, their taxi veered off to the left into a section of buildings via one of Venice's smaller canals, the *rio San Giovanni Crisostomo*. Set low on the water, their water-taxi motored on the narrower canal, edging by tourist gondolas and underneath walking bridges until reaching a second intersecting canal. They turned right and came to a stop at a platform.

"Here you are," said Captain Filippo, gently sidling their boat up to the stone platform so they could step off. To ensure that they could do so safely, Captain Filippo got up to tie the rocking water-taxi to the platform. After pulling his knot tight, he said, "Now, it is ready for you."

"Thank you," said Captain Evans, standing to exit the boat. She stepped up onto the platform followed by the others. After unloading his passengers, Captain Filippo said "Addio," disconnected his water-taxi and motored away.

They found themselves standing before three arches leading to a passageway under an old, distressed-brick building into a courtyard of more structures. Above the arches was a sign that read "Corte Del Milion." Emma was the only one who could read Italian, so she translated it for them: "Courtyard of the millionaire."

"What does that refer to?" wondered Logan.

"The courtyard of someone rich, I guess," replied Emma.

Unlike the center and right arches which were plain, the arch on the left was a many-centuries-old Venetian-Byzantine-style archway with intricate designs carved into it, including designs of flowers, lions, serpents, jackrabbits, and other imagery.

"Pretty," commented Emma, marveling at the stone archway's exquisite detail.

Off to the right of the arches was the backside of another multi-floor building, with the address 'Calle Scaleta, 5850' identified on a sign.

"That's it, my family's old digs!" blurted Emma, excitedly walking over to check it out.

"I thought we were looking for a house," said Lt. Peters, who had been given very little information about the mission.

"Yeah, we are, but you have to remember, it's different here. In Venice, houses are built more like multi-family dwellings and multi-floor apartment buildings and structures than stand-alone, single-family residences," replied Emma.

There were three glass doors at the back of Calle Scaleta, 5850 but they couldn't enter them because iron bars covered the doors. Inside, they could see a hallway with a door, and a staircase leading up. Overhead on the outer wall of the building between the second-floor windows, was a large square off-white marble plaque with words engraved into it that read:

QUI FURONO LE CASE DI MARCO POLO, CHE
VIAGGIO LE PIU LONTANE REGIONI DELLE ASIA E
LE DESCRISSE. PER DECRETO DEL COMUNE
MDCCCLXXXI

Again, Emma translated the plaque for the rest of them:

HERE WAS THE HOUSE OF MARCO POLO, WHO
TRAVELED THE FARTHEST REGIONS OF ASIA AND
DESCRIBED THEM. BY DECREE OF THE
MUNICIPALITY
1881

"Does that refer to *the* Marco Polo?" Logan wondered, surprised.

"I'm not sure," replied Emma, curious.

"Remind me again who Marco Polo was?" asked Evans, her memory foggy.

Emma explained, "He was an Italian merchant and traveler who was famous for journeying across Asia in the Middle Ages along the Silk Road, and for establishing trade relations between Europe and the Far East."

"So, the place where your family used to live was Marco Polo's old home?" queried Evans.

"I guess… I don't know," responded Emma.

With the back entrance covered by iron bars, Logan said, "Let's see if we can go through the front."

The group walked back to the three initial arches which led into an inner courtyard, and while they were walking underneath them, Emma noticed something on the leftmost arch. "Hey, look at the carving on the far side of that arch, three up from the bottom! Is that a unicorn?"

Logan stepped closer to the arch. "Yeah, it kind of looks like one, or maybe, a lion with a horn coming out of its head."

"You guys and your unicorns," griped Captain Evans.

"There's an identical one on the right side of the arch, too, three up from the bottom," pointed out Logan.

"Guys, it has to be a coincidence," uttered Captain Evans.

"You're probably right," said Emma, although between Gunnar's drawing, Gia's unicorn collection, and now these two, she wasn't so sure.

"Let's keep going... we can always come back," proposed Logan.

They continued under the arches and into the courtyard. Once inside, old buildings surrounded them and there was a corridor at the courtyard's opposite end leading out to other parts of Venice. To the right was the frontside of Calle Scaleta, 5850 and it had a large, red rectangular banner on it that read: "Teatro Malibran."

"The Malibran Theater," said Emma, wondering if that was what had become of the Rossi Family Home. There were doors leading in.

"Peters, hang tight out here and guard the entrance," ordered Captain Evans.

"Yes, ma'am," replied Lt. Peters.

Evans added, "But try not to make it look like you're guarding the entrance. We'll be right back."

Peters chuckled. "Will do, Captain."

Logan, Emma and Captain Evans entered the theater. They discovered a lavishly decorated lobby fashioned in the ancient-Roman style, decorated with ornate columns, statues, paintings, and gold trim everywhere. Further inside were steps leading down into the theater itself. They walked over and peeked.

The theater was taller, and sunk down lower, than they expected. There were five stories of spectator boxes on the walls to the left and right, two levels of seats above and below, and a stage set down at the bottom of it all. Several actors were rehearsing on stage. They took several more steps into the theater.

"This place is beautiful," commented Emma at the unexpected sight of the stunning theater hidden inside Calle Scaleta, 5850.

A theater company performer who saw them poking around, walked up the stairs from the stage and approached them. When he got close, he said in Italian, "Mi scusi, ma oggi il teatro è chiuso."

Emma translated. "He says the theater's closed today."

Hearing Emma and realizing the visitors spoke English, the theater performer added, "Mi dispiace, you speak, eh, English. The theater is open for rehearsals, but not for performance. Today is for study."

"Do you mind if we look around?" asked Emma.

The actor responded, "Yes, is okay. The lobby is always open for visitors as is the gift shop. The theater-portion of Teatro Malibran, however, is open for rehearsal only, not for touring. I hope you understand."

"I'm sorry, one more question," replied Emma. "What's at the back of the theater building? We saw stairs leading up."

"At back of the building on canal-side are apartments the theater uses for storage and office space."

"How long has this theater been here?" followed up Emma.

"Centuries. Over on the lobby walls you might enjoy reading about the history of Teatro Malibran. I hope you enjoy. Mi scusi, but I must return to rehearsal."

"Grazie mille," said Emma.

The actor retreated down the steps to the stage to rejoin his fellow actors and they turned around to head back to the lobby. They stopped at a wall beside the gift shop, decorated with old theater paraphernalia, such as Venetian opera masks and performance programs from the 18th and 19th centuries, according to the descriptive plaques below each item. And there were several displays detailing the history of Teatro Malibran in various languages including English:

THE HISTORY OF TEATRO MALIBRAN

The Teatro Malibran, known over its lifetime by a variety of names, beginning with the Teatro San Giovanni Crisostomo upon its inauguration in 1678, was built upon the place where the well-known wealthy Venetian merchant and traveler Marco Polo's residence once stood.

The famous traveler Marco Polo was born in Venice into a wealthy merchant family in 1254, to parents Nicole Anna Defuseh and Niccolò Polo. Raised by an aunt after his mother died of an illness while he was young, Polo lived in the Cannaregio courtyard from his birth until his death in 1323, except during his famous travels between 1271 and 1295, when Polo journeyed through Asia at the height of the Mongol Empire and joined the court of the powerful Mongol ruler, Kublai Khan, grandson of Genghis Khan. After Polo's death, the wealthy merchant's family and relatives continued to live in the Cannaregio compound for centuries until a fire destroyed most of the residence in 1598.

In 1675, prominent Venetian patrician family, the Grimanis, acquired the property and its belongings from its then-owner, which included several artifacts of exceptional quality and value from Polo's renowned travels to Asia that had survived the fire. The Grimani family donated the artifacts to the Doge's Palace, where they remain on display today in the Doge's Hidden Treasures Reserve Collection.

The Grimani family then had Teatro San Giovanni Crisostomo built where Polo's residence once stood, and had portions of Polo's old residence which survived the fire, including numerous rooms, incorporated into the back of the theatre for actors, singers and theater company employees to live and stay while performing. The theater reopened and became the most luxurious and extravagant stage in Venice, known for its elaborate productions, operas and high-quality singers. It enjoyed a long run of success until the late 18th century when a downturn hit and the Grimani family abandoned the theater.

In 1834, Giovanni Gallo acquired the theater, refurbished and renamed it the Teatro Emeronitto. When the famous soprano Maria Malibran came to sing in 1835, she was appalled at the theater's condition and refused her performance fee, telling Gallo to 'use it for the theater' instead. At that point, he renamed the opera house the Teatro Malibran in the singer's honor and it has stayed that name ever since.

"Quite the story," said Captain Evans.

"Now we know what happened to the house that used to be here, it burned down and was replaced by the theater," added Logan.

"Well, most of it, anyway, except for the rooms at the back that survived the old fire," said Emma. "I wonder if we can have a look at them."

"Why not?" replied Logan, suggesting they go on a self-guided tour of the theater building. They spotted a hallway leading from the lobby to the left behind the spectator boxes and followed it. The hallway wrapped around the rear of Teatro Malibran to a door. They opened it and went in. They stood on the first floor of the building before a staircase, looking out of the same bar-covered glass doors they saw from the outside when they first arrived. They climbed the stairs to investigate the rooms on the upper floors.

They discovered offices and storage rooms on the other floors. Being careful to avoid the janitor who was walking around cleaning, they snuck into the doors to investigate. The various rooms were packed with theater items, costumes, paperwork, boxes, trunks, desks, file cabinets and equipment, among other things. The rooms were small, but years ago, they could have served as residences for theater employees, and even the Rossi family. The interior walls and ceiling all looked recently repainted, so if there was something left behind on the walls to see, it wasn't visible any longer. The wood flooring also looked new.

"Unfortunately, not much to see here," said Logan, who had hoped to find more, but the property's refurbishment had put a dent in that plan.

Emma wasn't ready to give up yet. "Guys, I know we talked about this before, but do you think there's any possible connection between the unicorn in Snorri Sturluson's tunnel and what we saw on the arch leading into the courtyard?"

"That's really a stretch, James," Captain Evans replied.

"I know, but—"

"A *big* stretch," Captain Evans emphasized further. "Unicorns are a universally common mythological symbol."

"Even in the Middle Ages?" challenged Emma.

"Okay, so what are you suggesting, then? That Isa and Annika met Snorri Sturluson in Iceland, carved that unicorn in his tunnel and then, somehow, traveled thousands of miles by sea to Venice where they met Marco Polo and carved more unicorns on the arch, if that's even what they were?"

"Well, I don't know exactly…"

"The time frame does add up," interjected Logan in support of her theory. "Sturluson lived in the 13th century, just like Marco Polo who was born in 1254."

Emma had a rhetorical question for Captain Evans. "I know it sounds crazy, but don't you find it just a *little* odd that we've been seeing unicorns everywhere, from Iceland to my cousin's figurine collection in Florence, and now here on the arch leading into the courtyard where my family used to live?"

"I suppose," conceded Evans. "Okay, assuming for sake of argument that you're right, are you saying *Corte Del Milion* wasn't just Marco Polo's residence, but Isa's too?"

"There's no way to know for sure, but yeah, since my family ended up living here at some point, I think we have to assume it's possible," replied Emma.

"Do you think Isa was living here when your great-great-grandfather did?" asked Logan.

Emma responded, "Maybe, or maybe just until the fire burned the Polo residence down in 1598."

Logan had another thought. "What if Isa was the *owner* of the property when the Grimani family acquired it along with Polo's artifacts in 1675?"

"Hey, wait a second," started Emma, "why don't we go check out the Polo artifacts that the Grimanis donated to the Doge's Palace after buying the property? Maybe we'll find out who they bought the property from."

Captain Evans liked her suggestion. "James, that's not a bad idea. Where is the Doge's Palace?"

Logan looked it up on his phone. "It's next to St. Mark's Basilica in St. Mark's Square, only a few minutes from here."

"Can we just walk in or do we need reservations?" asked Emma.

Logan went to the Doge's Palace website. "It looks like we need tickets. It also says the Doge's Palace can be crowded with long queues, so they recommend booking e-tickets ahead of time. I guess we'll find out when we get there."

"What about the Doge's Hidden Treasures Reserve Collection… same thing?" asked Captain Evans.

Logan dug a little deeper. "Good thing you asked. It says here that viewing the *Reserve* Collection requires special arrangements."

"That shouldn't be a problem," said Emma. "We just need to call General Covington or Mr. Garrison. I'm sure they can arrange it. And if they can't, maybe my cousin Enyo can help."

Captain Evans was ready to get a move on. "Alright then. One of you make the call, and then, let's head over there."

Chapter 13 - The Doge's Palace

After making a phone call to General Covington, who subsequently coordinated a private showing of Polo's artifacts at the Doge's Palace, Logan, Emma, Evans and Peters made their way to St. Mark's Square. Rather than wait for another water-taxi, they decided to walk given that St. Mark's was only a 10-minute stroll through Venice's narrow interwoven cobblestone corridors and canals.

With the benefit of a map on their phones, they started their journey south on Calle Scaleta, crossed over the canal-bridge at *rio de San Lio*, made a right onto Corte Spechiera, a short left at Calle del Forner and quick right on Calle del Pistor. From there, they crossed over additional canals and navigated a dozen more intersecting "streets" that were really nothing more than narrow paths between buildings until reaching St. Mark's Square.

"Look at all those pigeons!" exclaimed Logan. Venice's most popular tourist attraction, St. Mark's Square, was full of them.

"It's just like in pictures!" remarked Emma as flocks of birds flew to different parts of the plaza where people were feeding them. One flew off course and buzzed Logan's head, causing Logan to duck and flail.

The square was several football fields long and wide, surrounded on three sides by stately public buildings and on the fourth, by St. Mark's Basilica and its mix of domes, pointed arches, columns, sculptures and mosaics. Next to the basilica rose the 23-story tall brick bell tower, St. Mark's Campanile, which astronomer Galileo once climbed in 1609 to demonstrate his very first telescope to the ruling Doge of Venice and the Venetian Senate.

St. Mark's Square had served as the epicenter of civic and religious life in Venice for over a thousand years. Today, it was a busy tourist spot, not just because of its stately buildings or the basilica or even the Doge's Palace to the basilica's right, but because the ground floors of the surrounding buildings hosted dozens of shops and elegant cafés, one after another, with outdoor seating. Tourists packed the tables to enjoy café food, espressos, bellinis and other cocktails while sitting outside people-watching on the iconic square. Unfortunately for Logan and Emma, they wouldn't have time to do any of that since they had come to visit the Doge's Palace. The Doges essentially functioned as the kings of Venice, and their huge Venetian-gothic palace turned museum was right in front of them.

"Is that it?" asked Captain Evans, staring at a palace façade with a lower section consisting of ground floor colonnades, columns and pointed arches beneath an open-air second floor with more pointed arches. Above the second floor was a remarkably light-looking upper story made of pink Verona marble, and more pointed arch windows.

"Yeah, that's it," Emma responded.

"It's huge, how do we get in?" wondered Lt. Peters, scanning for the entrance.

They searched the outside of the palace until they found the public entrance, a 15th century Gothic door with lavish sculptures and marble decorations. Per Covington, they were supposed to meet a Doge curator by the name of Chiara. When they walked up to the entrance, Chiara was already waiting for them.

"Buongiorno, I am Chiara," said the woman in her late-20's wearing a navy pant-suit. She carried a computer tablet and a key ring with keycards dangling from it. She looked frazzled, as if she had been interrupted in the middle of her workday to accommodate the American visitors.

"Hi, thank you so much for meeting us on short notice like this," replied Emma.

"It is my job, of course," said Chiara, moderately deflecting Emma's gratitude and implying that she did what her supervisors told her to do. "Please, follow me."

As before, Captain Evans had Lt. Peters wait outside, while Chiara, using her pass, whizzed Emma, Logan and Evans past the gate and lengthy line of tourists waiting their turn. While they were walking into the entrance, Chiara asked Emma, "Have you been to the Doge's Palace before?"

"No."

"Oh, well, there is so much to see. You could spend days just touring the palace!" said Chiara confidently.

"I'm sure that's true."

"How long are you in Venice?"

"Just today."

"One day? That is hardly any time at all! We must hurry!"

Chiara ushered them through the palace's opulent halls of paintings and gilded ceilings to the Doge's private rooms. Chiara guided them down a secluded corridor to a heavy door with a sign above it that read, "Collezione della Riserva dei Tesori Nascosti del Doge," standing for "The Doge's Hidden Treasures Reserve Collection." Chiara used her key card to unlock the secure door. Through it they walked, and back in time they went...

They stood in a long rectangular room with arched windows offering a clear view of the domes of the neighboring basilica. The ceiling was flat and covered from side to side with paintings, heavily gilded and carved with wooden trim, just like the walls. Various exhibits filled the space, ready for viewing. There were ancient suits of armor in the far-left corner; gems and jewelry on a stand in the middle; weapons from the Middle Ages; Far East statues; and many other ancient artifacts to see. But what they had come for was kept in an open display case near the back, namely, artifacts attributed to Marco Polo.

"Right this way," said Chiara, leading them to the collection. When they reached it, she added, "Please let me know if you have any questions."

The exhibit consisted of multiple glass shelves of historical relics: a white and red Chinese porcelain jar from the court of Kublai Khan; a bronze compass believed used by Marco Polo; an ivory tusk; a collection of green, yellow and white jade jewelry; an old cartographic map charting the world beyond the known lands, believed created by Marco Polo's father, Niccolò Polo; and a chao, an ancient form of paper currency used by the Mongols in the Yuan Dynasty. All of the artifacts were astonishingly well-preserved.

They carefully studied the porcelain jar, the jade collection and other items looking for clues, unicorn imagery, or Emma and Logan's favorite pastime, numbers that looked like coordinates. They found none.

"Incredible… all of this stuff really belonged to Marco Polo?" asked Emma.

"At one time, yes," answered Chiara.

"How do they know for sure?" questioned Logan.

"Well, eh, of course, when items donated in the late 17th century, Marco Polo had been dead for centuries, so it is true, no one can verify. But according to the records that accompanied the donation, the items were the property of Milione and many scholars have validated the claim."

"Who was Milione?" questioned Emma.

Chiara replied, "Milione was the nickname for Marco Polo, who was also called 'Messer Marco Milione,' meaning 'Mr. Marco Millions'. He got the name when he returned to Venice after staying in the court of Kublai Khan, whose wealth Polo described to be in the 'millions.' And the riches Polo brought back with him from Asia cemented that nickname for him."

"Do the donation records still exist?" asked Emma.

Chiara responded, "Yes, in fact, they are in the display case just over to the right." She pointed at a glass case a few feet away. Logan, Emma and Captain Evans walked over to have a closer look. Inside was a light-brown parchment encased in a gold frame and laminated under glass, with faded but legible lettering on it that said, according to the English translation beside it:

"The Honor of Donation

To the 106th Doge of Venice, Alvise Contarini, House of Contarini

Here is the true history of Venice which I possess, the artifacts of Milione, salvaged from the flames of *Corte Del Milion,* which I acquired from Sir William Richard Stanley, 9th Earl of Derby, along with his property; artifacts of Milione's travels across land to Asia and back, which connected Venice to the world. Possessed first by Sir Stanley's grandmother, Elizabeth (de Vere) Stanley, before passing to her son James Stanley, 7th Earl of Derby, before passing to his son, Sir William Richard Stanley, and then, to me, it is time for Milione's belongings to return home for good.

140

Donated this day, 16 September 1675

My pledge to the Doge hereby committed.

Vincenzo Grimani"

The year of the donation caught Logan's eye. "1675 was the year the Grimani family acquired the Polo property," he remarked.

"From William Richard Stanley, though. I guess Isa wasn't the prior owner of the property, after all," lamented Emma.

"It says Stanley's grandmother, Elizabeth Stanley, came into possession of Polo's artifacts first. I wonder how," said Logan.

Chiara was confused. She didn't quite understand what they were talking about. Fortunately for her, her phone rang. "I am sorry, but I must answer this. Please enjoy the exhibit and I will be back shortly." Chiara walked off to the other side of the room for some privacy.

Emma said to Logan, "Can you look Elizabeth (de Vere) Stanley up on your phone?"

Logan pulled out his cell and googled the search terms, 'Elizabeth de Vere Stanley.' "Good call... I found a page about her on www.royalpedia.com." Logan read it aloud:

Elizabeth de Vere Stanley

Born: 2 July 1575 in Hertfordshire, England

Father: Edward de Vere

Mother: Lady Anne Cecil

Occupation: Maid of Honor for Queen Elizabeth I

Died: 10 March 1627

Spouse: William Stanley, 6th Earl of Derby (married, 1595)

Children:
– Robert (1596 – 1632)
– Anne (1600 – 1657)
– Susan (1602 – 1605)
– James, 7th Earl of Derby (1607 –1651)
– Isabel (1598 – unknown)

"She had a daughter named Isabel!" exclaimed Emma. "Isabel could be a variation of Isa!"

Logan continued:

"Background: Elizabeth de Vere was born 1575 as the elder daughter of Edward de Vere and Lady Anne Cecil, Queen Elizabeth I's Maid of Honor. Like her mother, she spent most of her life in the personal service of Queen Elizabeth I as the queen's next Maid of Honor, acting as both a personal aid and secret confidante. The queen, who never married, treated her like a daughter, and they were believed to be very close.

Queen Elizabeth I (1533-1603), her reign made famous by her defeat of the Spanish Armada in 1588, was the daughter of Anne Boleyn, the Queen of England from 1533-1536 until her husband, and Queen Elizabeth I's father, King Henry VIII, beheaded her. Elizabeth de Vere was named after Queen Elizabeth I by her mother Lady Anne Cecil, much to the queen's liking. Lady Elizabeth de Vere married Sir William Stanley, 6th Earl of Derby, in the summer of 1595.

It has been said that Queen Elizabeth I, as a wedding gift to her dear friend Elizabeth, commissioned William Shakespeare to write a play for them, *A Midsummer Night's Dream*, and that Elizabeth de Vere and William Stanley's wedding was the occasion of the play's first performance."

"You've got to be kidding me... *William Shakespeare!*" uttered Emma, finding the convergence of names in Elizabeth (de Vere) Stanley's background about kings, queens and playwrights they'd all heard of, interesting. Logan kept reading...

"The midsummer night's dream did not last long, however. While William and Elizabeth had numerous children together, their relationship was tumultuous with rumors of affairs by Sir Stanley. While Sir Stanley was away on one of his many multi-year traveling adventures around the world, it was rumored that Lady Elizabeth had an affair of her own with an Italian merchant named Antonio Rossi, and a child Isabel out of wedlock in 1598."

"Oh my god, Isabel's father was an Italian merchant named Antonio *Rossi!*" uttered Emma, her family name finally making an appearance in their mystery. "That has to be her!"

Captain Evans nearly did a double-take. "You're not seriously suggesting that this Isabel was Isa, are you? Because if we're talking about the same Isa we met on Vanirya, how is it possible that she was *born* in 1598?"

"Maybe Isabel's birth was staged or maybe the Isa we're looking for changed her appearance to play the part," theorized Logan.

"Are you saying she turned herself into an infant?" asked Captain Evans.

"Vaniryans *can* change shape, so I'm just saying anything's possible," replied Logan.

"I'm not sure if it's the same Isa or not, but this all means something," insisted Emma. "Somehow, Elizabeth Stanley ended up with Polo's artifacts, passed them down to her son James Stanley, who passed them down to his son, William Richard Stanley, who returned them to Venice when he sold Polo's property where my family used to live, back to the Grimanis."

"And I'm guessing Antonio *Rossi* is the one who gave the artifacts to Lady Elizabeth," said Logan. "Especially considering 1598, the year Isabel was born, was the same year Polo's residence burned down!"

"I know!" agreed Emma. "Maybe you were right and Isabel's birth was staged or Isa changed shape."

"There's only one way to find out, we need to know more about Isabel," replied Logan.

"What does the rest of the royalpedia article say?" asked Emma. Logan went on to read the rest of it:

> "When many might have shunned Elizabeth and her illegitimate child, Queen Elizabeth I embraced them and took the child into her court for care, because they knew Sir Stanley would never accept Isabel upon his return from his travels. Queen Elizabeth I's tolerance of Lady Elizabeth's transgression surprised no one. After all, the queen cared for her very much and was extremely popular for her tolerance. Indeed, she was credited with being the first English monarch who understood that a monarch ruled by popular consent and truth, not force and cruelty, an opinion she likely formed when her father, King Henry VIII, beheaded her mother. She was similarly tolerant of all religions, believing that faith was personal and that she did not wish to "make windows into men's hearts and secret thoughts," according to Sir Francis Bacon (Lord High Chancellor of England from 1617-1621).

Owing to all of the secrets they held and knew, the Cecils and Stanleys remained very close to – some have said guarded by - the monarchs for centuries."

"It doesn't say much more other than that she was the illegitimate daughter of Elizabeth Stanley and that Queen Elizabeth I took her in," said Logan, noticing that Isabel's name was hyperlinked in the webpage. He clicked on it and it led to another page about Isabel with some additional information which he again read aloud:

"Lady Elizabeth Stanley's illegitimate daughter Isabel spent her life in the personal service of the monarchy, even after Queen Elizabeth I passed away and her mother, Elizabeth Stanley, relocated with her husband, Sir William Stanley, 6th Earl of Derby, to the Isle of Mann. As the Earls of Derby were the hereditary heads of state of the Isle of Mann, Sir Stanley took up the title of Lord of Mann in 1609 following an Act of Parliament, and they relocated to the Isle. Little is known about Isabel's life after her mother moved away, although it is believed Isabel never saw her mother again and she remained unmarried. Her date of death and place of burial remains unknown."

"That doesn't help much, either," said Emma. "Are there any other websites talking about her or Antonio Rossi?"

Logan did some more googling but nothing came up other than the original royalpedia page they had already gone over.

"Maybe we can visit where Isabel used to live with the Queen's court," said Emma.

Logan looked that up on his phone, too. "Umm, that's going to be difficult." He was looking at a webpage called *Queen Elizabeth I – Royal Palaces of the Royal Family*. "It says here that the queen owned and used more than a dozen palaces all over England beginning with Greenwich Palace, where she was born in 1533, and ending with Richmond Palace, where she died in 1603. Here's a partial list…" He showed Emma and Captain Evans:

Greenwich Palace

Hatfield Palace

Enfield Palaces

Hampton Court

Whitehall Palace

Windsor Castle

Oatlands Palace

Tower Of London

Eltham Palace

St James's Palace

Nonsuch Palace

Richmond Palace

Emma was exasperated. "Which palace did they live in? That's a lot of palaces to cover."

"And don't forget, Isabel presumably only lived with Queen Elizabeth I from 1598 until 1603 when the queen died," said Captain Evans. "After that, who knows where she ended up. That royalpedia page says she spent her life in the personal service of the monarchy, but it doesn't say with who or where. And even if we could narrow down the locations, we're talking about royal palaces. It's not like the British are going to just let us walk in and poke around."

"Why not?" countered Logan. "It's just another phone call to Covington."

"I'm not so sure it'll be that easy," rebutted Captain Evans. "If the monarchy entrusted their Maids of Honor with guarding their secrets, I think it's safe to assume the royal family might not want those secrets exposed, not even today."

"Wow!" blurted Emma, having spotted something else.

"What?" replied Logan.

"Look at the coat of arms above Queen Elizabeth I's name, where it says the Royal Coat of Arms for the United Kingdom!" exclaimed Emma, pointing to a shield center page hovering over the queen's name.

The shield was quartered, depicting in the first and fourth quarters over a red backdrop, the three guardant lions of England; in the second, over a yellow backdrop, another lion and the flowery arms of Scotland; and in the third, over a blue backdrop, a yellow harp for Ireland. The crest or top of the shield had another lion wearing a crown, himself standing on another crown. Supporting the shield on the left was a crowned English lion, and on the right, a white *unicorn*. The lion and the unicorn both stood on greenery.

"There's a unicorn!" stated Emma, excited.

"I don't believe it," uttered Logan. "That has to be a coincidence. We're talking about the freaking Royal Coat of Arms of the United Kingdom." Logan quickly googled it and confirmed that the image they were staring at was, indeed, the *official* and *current* Royal Coat of Arms for the United Kingdom.

Captain Evans, rarely one to be shocked, this time, was. "I have to admit, that's pretty wild, but the monarchy has been around a long time, which means that coat of arms probably has been, too, since long before Antonio Rossi came along and Isabel was born."

Logan was curious, so he looked it up, and Evans was right. The English monarchy had been around since at least the 9th century, when Alfred the Great became the King of Wessex. He also found a page describing how the official royal coat of arms represented the union of England, Scotland and Ireland under the United Kingdom and a blending of elements of those countries' various shields over time, including the unicorn. Still though, just when he thought his search had confirmed Evans' instincts, he saw another astonishingly coincidental fact…

"You guys aren't going to believe this… the monarchy's been around since the 9th century, but the United Kingdom adopted the current Royal Coat of Arms with the *unicorn* on the date of the Union of the Crowns, March 24, *1603*, which was the date of Queen Elizabeth I's death. It says she approved the new coat of arms in her final weeks before she died in private succession meetings with her cousin and soon-to-be-successor, King James I. It's almost like Queen Elizabeth I preserved a clue about Isa in the Royal Coat of Arms as her final gesture before her death."

"Guys, it seems like Queen Elizabeth I left us a Royal Coat of Arms-sized breadcrumb for Isa that has survived since 1603," said Emma.

Just then, Chiara returned from her phone call. "I am sorry, but I'm scheduled to give another private guided tour in a few minutes at another part of the museum. My regrets, but I cannot leave you in here. Before we leave, do you have any more questions?"

"No, no more questions, and thank you for this," said Emma. "Everything we've seen has been amazing."

"I am happy to hear that. Let me show you out." Chiara escorted them out of the Reserve Collection hall and back down to the first floor of the palace. She took them to the exit and said goodbye, heading off to her next appointment.

Once outside, they met up with Lt. Peters and wandered around St. Mark's Square until they found an empty table in front of a café where they could sit and chat. Captain Evans had Lt. Peters stand off to the side of the outdoor café to keep watch and secure the perimeter.

Emma jumped right into it once they got settled in. "That website about Isabel said that little is known about her life after her mother moved away except that she remained unmarried and in lifelong service to the monarchy. I bet there is someone who knows more about her."

"Who?" asked Logan, curious.

"The Queen."

"*The* Queen, as in, the *current* queen of the United Kingdom, Queen Elizabeth II?" Logan replied, ironically referring to Queen Elizabeth I's namesake.

"Exactly."

"Are you serious, James?" questioned Captain Evans.

"Completely serious. We're talking about secrets kept close by the English monarchy for centuries, and about a little girl named Isabel, whose father was Antonio Rossi and who Queen Elizabeth I took in and raised among the royal family. Perhaps Queen Elizabeth II knows what happened to her, or maybe the answer is sitting in a little royal book of secrets like the one U.S. presidents pass on to each other."

"You know that little book of secrets isn't a real thing, right?" replied Captain Evans.

Emma smirked and continued, "I'm sure it's a thing. Can you think of any other way to track Isa down?"

"No," replied Evans.

"Exactly!" uttered Emma, continuing, "The needle on the compass is pointing straight to the British royal family. I think that has to be our next move."

"Emma's right, we should talk to the queen," agreed Logan.

"Okay, but how do we do that?" inquired Captain Evans.

"We call Covington," answered Emma.

"Arranging a tour of the Doge's Palace is one thing, but this… this is on a whole 'nother level," Captain Evans responded.

"Yeah, I know," said Emma. "The president himself is probably going to need to make a phone call if we have any hope of arranging an in-person meeting at Buckingham Palace with Queen Elizabeth II."

"Who knows, maybe the queen likes to do video conferences," suggested Logan.

"Yeah, right," scoffed Emma, preferring a trip to Buckingham Palace over a video call, anyway.

"Hey James, do you have a pen in that bag of yours?" asked Captain Evans.

"Yeah, why?"

"I just want to jot down a few notes before we call Covington so we don't forget anything."

"Sure no problem." Emma reached into her bag and pulled out a blue ballpoint pen. She handed it over.

"Thanks. So here is what I am thinking we tell Covington..." Captain Evans started writing on a napkin in oversized lettering, large enough for Logan and Emma to see:

DON'T REACT

DON'T LOOK AROUND

WE R BEING WATCHED

"Those are good points," said Emma, trying to keep her cool. "But don't you think General Covington is going to want to know *where* to look?"

"Yeah, you're probably right. How about we tell him this?" Captain Evans jotted down a few more notes:

4 TBLS OVER

2 UR RIGHT

PETERS IS MISSING

Emma, suddenly nervous, feigned calm. "Hmm, those are excellent ideas. Any other thoughts?"

"I'm not sure, but what do you think of this?" Captain Evans flipped the napkin over because she needed more space and scribbled: *THEY R LISTENING 2 US WTH A DEVICE.*

"Hey, do you think this place allows orders to *go*?" asked Logan.

"Yeah, I think so," responded Captain Evans.

"When do you think I should put in a to-go order?" followed up Logan.

"How about *now*," replied Evans.

With Evans' cue, they got up and started walking away toward one of St. Mark's Square's many exits. Wherever Lt. Peters was, Captain Evans hoped he was watching and following. Sure enough, three men sitting four tables over from them got up to pursue. With the volume of tourists flooding the square that afternoon, Emma, Logan and Captain Evans found themselves weaving in and out of the crowd, while the three men picked up their pace and began pushing tourists out of the way.

"Guys, run!" shouted Captain Evans.

They took off with the men chasing them, and still, Peters was nowhere to be found. Something had obviously happened to him, but they didn't have time to worry about that at the moment. They raced through the crowd, bouncing off people.

"There, straight ahead!" hollered Evans, who had spotted an escape route. She guided them toward a walking bridge over a canal. There was a passenger-less water-taxi on the move in the canal heading under the bridge. Evans led them up the steps of the bridge and just as soon as the boat crossed under, yelled, "Jump!"

They scaled the bridge's railing and leapt for the water-taxi when it passed underneath. It continued on its way after they crash-landed onto the boat's deck. The men chasing them reached the bridge a second too late. Still, one of them climbed the railing and dove for the boat, trying to catch them. He smacked into the back of the hull and fell into the canal. The other two men slammed their hands on the railing and began looking for a boat of their own.

Meanwhile, their water-taxi captain appeared stunned. Looking over his shoulder, he shouted, "Who are you?!"

"Please just keep going!" yelled Evans.

"Get out of my boat!" he demanded, easing up on the motor to slow the boat down.

"Please, those people are chasing us! We'll pay you $500 to get us out of here!" responded Evans.

"No, get—"

"$5,000! We'll pay you $5,000! Please just go!" urged Evans, upping her ante.

"For $5,000, Luca will get you out of here!" agreed the captain. Luca sped up.

Back at the bridge, Logan and Emma watched the two men commandeer a boat of their own by throwing its captain overboard. Worse, that boat looked bigger and faster than the one they were in.

"Hurry!" shouted Emma. "They're coming."

"Does this thing go any faster?" questioned Evans.

"Eh, yes, I try," replied Luca, kicking his engine into its highest gear, but it still wasn't enough. The other boat was already catching up.

"They're gaining!" yelled Logan. They heard gunfire! All of them ducked to avoid the bullets.

"Dio mio!" exclaimed Luca.

"They're shooting at us!" screamed Emma.

Evans pulled out her own gun and returned fire. She hit the other boat's windshield, causing it to swerve. One of the men leaned around the windshield to fire back at Captain Evans.

"Merda!" shouted Luca after a bullet struck his instrument panel, just missing him. He was seriously regretting what he had gotten himself into. Luca pulled a sharp right down a narrow waterway between two 500-year-old Venetian buildings.

The other boat followed, although it had difficulty navigating the turn because of its size. More bullets whizzed by overhead as the other boat closed in, striking surrounding buildings and potted plants on windowsills. Residents who had popped their heads out their windows to see what was happening, ducked back inside. Captain Evans again returned fire but the enemy boat kept charging until it rammed into the back of their water-taxi! The impact pushed their boat toward the foundational brick wall of the building on the left side of the canal. Luca threw the steering wheel to the right in an effort to lessen the impact and steer the boat away, but impact was inevitable…

"Hold on!" he shouted just before the left side of their boat struck the building. Fortunately, the impact caused only minimal port-side hull damage, and after a crunching bounce off the building, Luca sped away from it.

Undeterred, the enemy rammed into their stern again. This time, their boat lurched forward on impact, knocking Logan and Emma off their feet while Evans, who had managed to maintain her footing, fired at the other driver to force him to back off. Luca pulled another sharp left at the next canal-intersection. The enemy boat, whose new 'captain' did not have Luca's skill navigating the sharp turns of Venice's waterways, temporarily fell behind. Luca tried to put as much distance as he could between them at that moment, but the advantage was short-lived because the other boat's engine was too powerful. It predictably closed the gap quickly.

Luca turned right to avoid another rear-end collision and aimed for a smaller canal corridor up ahead. He pushed his engine to its breaking point while gunfire continued to strike their hull and they continued to duck. Captain Evans kept firing back while Luca zig-zagged to keep the enemy off their tail until they could reach the smaller corridor. When they finally did, their boat barely squeezed through the two venerable brick buildings just as Luca knew it would, while the other boat, which was much wider, didn't fit…

It crashed into the bricks on both sides of its hull, with only the boat's middle squeezing through the buildings. The men pursuing them were ejected over the bow while the boat's port and starboard sides broke apart. Logan, Emma and Captain Evans gleefully watched as the hull fell into the water, and the boat exploded.

"Grazie dio!" hooted Luca, speeding away.

"You did it!" exclaimed Logan.

"Oh, thank god!" said Emma. Turning to Luca, she added, "Thank you! Thank you!" Then, she surveyed the damage to Luca's boat. "I am so sorry about your boat! We work for some people who will fix it right up, or buy you a new one, I promise!" assured Emma.

Luca seemed relieved to have escaped and, with an oddly thankful grin, replied, "Eh, it is all right. It is company boat."

Emma laughed. Thankful, she replied, "Well, I'm sure they'll still take care of everything!"

Luca was pleased with himself. "It is not every day that we have high speed chase through the canals of Venice, but Luca did alright!"

"More than alright! You were amazing!" declared Logan.

"Can you take us to the airport?" asked Captain Evans.

"Eh, sí."

"How far is it?" followed up Evans.

"Twenty minutes over the Venetian Lagoon to airport."

"Do you think your boat can make it?"

"Oh, yes, they did not hurt her too badly."

"Perfect," replied Captain Evans. "Twenty minutes should be more than enough time for Covington to make arrangements to get us the hell out of here." Glancing over at Luca, Evans added, "No offense."

"No offense taken," responded Luca nonchalantly.

Emma let Luca know, "Covington is our boss. He'll make sure you and your employer get paid for your trouble."

"Grazie. So, eh, who was chasing you?"

"Good question, that's what we have to figure out," replied Emma.

"Whoever they were, I have a feeling they've been on our tail since Iceland," stated Captain Evans.

"They're probably the same people who defaced the rock in Sturluson's tunnel, too," said Logan.

Captain Evans nodded in agreement. "Yep. Let's call Covington."

"And then, Em, you have to call Enyo," said Logan. "We can't go back to Florence after what just happened."

"Definitely not," chimed in Captain Evans.

"Yeah, I know. Enyo's going to be so disappointed," replied Emma, feeling bad about their sudden change in plans.

"We'll go back soon, I promise," assured Logan.

"I hope so," replied Emma. In all the commotion, Emma had almost forgotten about Lt. Peters. Suddenly worried about him, Emma asked, "What do you think happened to Peters?"

"I don't know. Covington's gonna have to get some agents over to St. Mark's Square ASAP to look for him," replied Captain Evans, although privately, she was worried that he was already at the bottom of a canal somewhere.

Chapter 14 – Il Mercato Di Rialto

On a rainy 13th century morning in Venice, Venetians descended upon the bustling outdoor market along the Grand Canal just north of the Rialto bridge. The large, covered, canal-side marketplace had stalls of fish, seafood, fowl, fruits and vegetables, and customers were busy buying up all they could before the day's supply ran out. The smell of warm fish and fowl laid out on slabs or in buckets, permeated the air.

Just off to the side of the main market in an adjacent stone courtyard was another tarp-covered area of merchants selling exotic goods imported from distant shores, including spices, wine, furs, fine cloth, glass, jewelry and more. The merchant-market was more lively than the food market, with Venetians bartering and negotiating their way through every purchase.

Rain dripped through the holes and gaps in the merchants' trading stall tarps. In the middle of the drenched marketplace was a booth, better-covered from the rain than most, where a young peddler was urgently trying to convince the booth's older more experienced-looking merchant, Vincente Defuseh, to buy his goods.

"Defuseh, I assure you, it is spice from Asia, very valuable to you for resale," urged the peddler.

Unsure, Vincente stuck his nose in the box and replied, "Severino, it smells like galingale." Defuseh dipped his fingers into the box for a pinch of the spice. He brought his pinched fingers to his tongue and after sampling it, said, "It tastes of galingale and sugar."

"No, it is an exotic spice I bring back from Karakorum, ground of cinnamon and clove… very rare," insisted Severino.

Vincente did not believe him. "You try to sell me common spice."

"I would not do such a thing," scoffed Severino.

Vincente turned to another merchant in an adjoining booth and said, "Niccolò, this peddler claims to offer spices he brought back from Karakorum."

"Is that so?" replied Niccolò Polo, one of the younger merchants in Venice, although he already had a reputation as a shrewd trader and cunning explorer. More importantly, he had actually been to Karakorum, the capital of the Mongol Empire in Mongolia's Övörkhangai Province, which was why Vincente had called over to him.

Niccolò walked over to Vincente's booth. In his youthful days, Niccolò had apprenticed under Vincente before going out on his own. Now, he regularly collaborated with his mentor on trade opportunities. Niccolò eyed Severino, trying to read his eyes and body language. "You have been to Karakorum, you say?" asked Niccolò.

"Yes," answered Severino, nervously looking away.

"Then you must have stayed in the court of Ögedei Khan, the Great Khan of the Mongol Empire," responded Niccolò, referring to the third son of Genghis Khan, who succeeded his deceased father as the second Great Khan of the Mongol Empire.

"Of course," replied Severino, although by his blank expression, it looked like he had no idea who Niccolò was talking about.

"And what did you offer to the Great Khan to pass through the four gates of Karakorum?" questioned Niccolò.

"I offered, eh, a spice for trade cultivated from the dark-leaved evergreen myristica."

Now, both Niccolò and Vincente suspected Severino was lying, since nutmeg, the ground spice made from the myristica fragrans tree, was typically imported *from* Asia, not *to* Asia.

"Staying in the emperor's opulent palace in Karakorum must have been a welcome improvement over the rank smell of fish here on the canal," remarked Niccolò, humoring Severino.

"Indeed, it was the honor of this Venetian's lifetime to stay in the Great Khan's court," bragged Severino.

"You must also have met the emperor's powerful sons, Ghengis and Kublai... what were they like?" asked Niccolò, testing him further given that he was referring to Ögedei Khan's father, Ghengis, and nephew, Kublai, and not Ögedei's sons, at all.

Severino smirked, thinking he was getting away with his ruse. "Yes, the emperor's sons were his mirror image, a testament to the enduring strength of the Great Khan's lineage." Vincente gave Niccolò one final glance while Severino kept talking, "Now Defuseh, back to the box, I sell it to you for—"

Niccolò grabbed Severino and threw him face down onto Vincente's table. He then thrust a knife up against Severino's neck. "Peddler, we offer you a different deal. Your life for your box."

Suddenly shaking uncontrollably, Severino squeaked out, "It is a mistake. I do not—"

Niccolò pressed his knife a little deeper into Severino's skin. "You are unwise to challenge your fate here," snapped Niccolò, ready to punish the deceitful peddler.

"You misunderstand my intentions," cried Severino, still hoping to talk his way out of the situation.

"What is there to misunderstand?! You are attempting to trick Defuseh," retorted Niccolò, tightening his grip. Other merchants in the area were taking notice of what was happening in Vincente's booth. Cheats were not welcome in the merchant-market, to put it mildly.

In a last second change of heart, Vincente, more merciful than Niccolò, uttered, "Severino, you're not worth the worthless box of common spice you peddle here." Vincente snapped his fingers and over walked two burly men who served as guards for the wealthier merchants. Vincente advised them, "This man wishes to leave il Mercato di Rialto."

The guards hoisted Severino right out of Niccolò's hands and high off the ground, while the peddler pleaded, "No! No!" They next walked Severino's flailing and protesting body to the bank of the Grand Canal and threw him in. Severino splashed and screamed while the water's current carried him off.

Chuckling, Niccolò asked Vincente, "What do you want done with the peddler's box of common spice?"

"I'm sure we can sell it for a few coins to help fund your next trip up the Silk Road. Perhaps you can obtain some of that cinnamon and clove spice that Severino was boasting about."

Vincente laughed while Niccolò joined him. It was just another day at the merchant-market, that was, until three women dripping from the rain approached Vincente's booth. Without saying a word, one of them laid down on Vincente's table a map and unrolled it for him to see. Defuseh recognized the map immediately, as did Niccolò, who had had a hand in creating it.

Vincente and Niccolò looked with great curiosity at the faces of the women standing before them. They saw a child, a woman who could have been the girl's mother, and a more mature woman who appeared approximately the same age as Vincente.

"Vincente Defuseh?" asked Annika. Other merchants in the rainy marketplace had pointed them in Defuseh's direction but she wanted to make sure they had the right merchant.

In Italian, Defuseh responded, "Sí." Pointing to the map, he asked his own question: "Come hai ottenuto questa mappa?" [*How did you get this map?*]

It was fairly obvious to Annika what he was asking about because he was pointing at the map, plus, she understood a few words of Spanish and Italian. She responded, "Snorri Sturluson."

"Snorri Sturluson gave this to you?" asked Vincente, intrigued but skeptical.

With Isa translating and feeding her words, Annika responded, "Yes, Snorri sent us from Iceland. King Hákon threatens our lives and Snorri said you would help us."

Vincente, still curious, delved a little deeper. "And how do you know the Icelandic Lawspeaker?"

This time Hallveig responded in Italian with Isa's assistance, "We are, eh, friends of the Lawspeaker. I am Tora, and," pointing to Annika and Isa, "this is my sister, Nicola Anna and her daughter Isabella."

"Hmm... Icelandic names that sound Italian, I am sure quite unusual in your part of the world... It seems you have planned for today," replied Vincente, picking up on the fact that they were traveling under aliases.

"Snorri says you owe him a favor for saving you from the block," said Annika.

"Indeed," conceded Vincente with the cock of his head, and a reminiscing chuckle.

"Defuseh, you never told me about your brush with the block," commented Niccolò.

"The incident was nothing more than the squabble of an envious monarch, wealthy and powerful but without a purpose."

"Is that all it was?" pried Niccolò, suspecting there was more to the story.

"It is time for you to repay the favor, Snorri says," said Annika, very direct and to the point.

Her confident, insistent tone impressed Niccolò, who liked Annika's take-charge demeanor. He suddenly felt compelled to introduce himself. "Signorina Nicola Anna, my name is Niccolò Polo. It is a pleasure to make your acquaintance." Isa translated for her.

"Hello," replied Annika, momentarily caught off guard by Niccolò's charm. Niccolò next introduced himself to Hallveig and Isa.

"Ah Niccolò, il mercante ammaliatore," mocked Vincente, referring to Niccolò as "the merchant charmer." Annika wasn't the first woman Vincente had watched Niccolò introduce himself to. "Niccolò, perhaps you should not visit Bergen, either," remarked Vincente, convinced Niccolò would find himself in the same trouble in Norway that he did. Turning his attention back to Annika, Vincente announced, "I will help you," much to Annika's, Isa's and Hallveig's relief. After all, they had traveled a long way from Iceland to Venice, and while they trusted Snorri's expectations as to how everything would play out, it wasn't until Isa translated Vincente's words that they truly felt like they had made it to safety.

"Thank you. Hákon will kill us if he finds us," said Annika.

"Then we will have to make sure he does not find you. Having been on the king's block before, I understand why you have traveled so far from home to get here. Where is Snorri?"

164

"Snorri will join us if he can, once he resolves his dispute with the king," replied Annika, although she did not say it with much confidence.

Vincente had his doubts, too. Nonetheless, he graciously responded, "Then, my home shall be your home for as long as you need until he arrives."

"Thank you again," said Annika.

"There is no need to thank me, especially after what he did for me. I will take you back to my courtyard over the canal when the market closes."

Niccolò had a different idea as he glanced at Annika, with whom he was already smitten. "Vincente, it is, eh, slow today as the rain discourages interest in my booth. I am happy to escort your guests to your home now so that they might get settled for when you return." Looking at Annika, he added, "It is near the San Giovanni Crisostomo church in Cannaregio, just over the Rialto. It is a very beautiful courtyard, with many buildings and rooms, and a garden for you to enjoy."

"Why am I not surprised that you are offering to take them to my home?" asked Vincente, amused.

"I am, of course, happy to do so," responded Niccolò while gazing at Annika. Niccolò, who did not have much on his table for sale that morning, moved over to his booth, swiftly swept his wares into a sack and announced, "And someday Defuseh, I plan to buy that beautiful courtyard of yours."

Now, Vincente was really amused. He knew Niccolò was just trying to impress Nicola Anna, but Vincente was more than willing to entertain Niccolò's ambitious notion. "Niccolò, may you achieve enough success to one day buy my home from me, so that I might be able to retire a wealthy man and to a simpler purpose."

"That is the plan. One day, I shall have millions," replied Niccolò.

Again chuckling, Vincente replied, "Ah! Aspiring to such greatness and wealth is an admirable trait, Polo. You have learned much from me."

"Shall we?" Niccolò asked Annika, Isa and Hallveig, gesturing for them to follow. He started leading them out of the marketplace back toward the Rialto bridge. As they departed the market, Niccolò politely offered to take Annika's hand as he guided them to Defuseh's courtyard home in Cannaregio.

Vincente smiled and shook his head. He got back to work as Niccolò led his new houseguests away, although Vincente, like Niccolò, expected to finish early that day. He was very interested in learning more about his guests' predicament and what they, and Snorri, had done to draw the king's ire. Somehow, he suspected their story was going to be an interesting one.

Chapter 15 – Electra-1

"It looks like we found the lost city of Atlantis at the bottom of a swamp after someone drained it," remarked Captain Velasquez. He led his team through a maze of toppled structures and broken buildings covered by green foliage, blue moss, yellow vines and other unusual plant life.

It was day three of Operation 17 Tauri. They had spent the first few days examining the terrain near home base to get acclimated, collect basic data, and survey the surrounding areas. Today, they were finally on their way to the dome they had spotted from Electra-1's orbit when they first arrived. They could see it off in the distance through the fractured buildings, although the dome could be seen from nearly everywhere given its massive size.

"What happened here?" wondered Davis, surrounded by broken structures and buildings, some in piles, others lying on their sides, but all badly damaged, charred, riddled with blast marks, or missing entire sections completely.

"Looks like they were attacked," said Williams.

"It's been that way everywhere we've gone. Whoever lived here got wiped out by somebody or something," responded Wesley.

"Yeah, by Supay," presumed Bates.

"Or something else," implied Velasquez.

"Are you suggesting that Supay didn't do this, and that there might actually be something *besides* Supay on E-1 that destroyed this city?" questioned Hamilton.

Velasquez put it in perspective. "There's probably a thousand things on this planet that can kill us, Hamilton. I wouldn't spend too much time worrying about it."

"Hey, over here, more remains," said Wesley, finding bones and skeletal fragments amid a field between structures. Hamilton walked over to join Wesley.

"Vaniryans?" wondered Hamilton.

"How would I know? I missed the class in basic training when they taught Vaniryan anatomy," retorted Wesley.

"Since this isn't Vanirya, I doubt it," replied Velasquez.

Looking around, Wesley suddenly realized that they weren't standing beside just one set of remains, but rather, in an entire field of them. "Look at them all."

"What is this place, a cemetery?" asked Hamilton, bending over to pick a fragment up.

Wesley shook his head. "These remains are shielding their faces. I'd say this looks more like an execution field. I want to get a few bone samples for the BCU," said Wesley.

"Okay, and while he's doing that, let's use the particle spectrometer on the blast marks on that building over there," requested Bates, pointing at a nearby structure with holes in its thick metallic walls. "What kind of weapon can penetrate metal ten feet thick?"

"Something with serious firepower," remarked Davis.

"No kidding. We've got to get as much data as we can so they can try and duplicate the energy source used to cause that kind of damage when we get home," said Bates.

"Alright, but then let's keep going. We've gotta reach the dome today. That's our primary objective," Velasquez reminded them.

"How much longer until we reach that thing, anyway?" wondered Hamilton.

"It's close," Velasquez replied.

"When something's as big as that, it always looks close," countered Williams.

After they finished collecting samples, they resumed their trek through the post-apocalyptic cityscape. Travel was slow going because, despite no obvious evidence of intelligent life beyond bird-like animals and small critters scurrying on the ground, they couldn't be sure. They had to treat it like any other covert-mission in enemy territory. That meant moving station to station, clearing movement between structures or obstacles one at a time, with a forward scout clearing each segment and waving everyone through while a rear soldier provided cover for those on the move. They weren't taking any chances.

They heard rumbling overhead.

"Ships!" shouted Hamilton.

"Hide!" ordered Velasquez. They ducked into a tall, circular skyscraper with moss and vines wrapping around it all the way to the top. It was one of the few buildings in the city that remained standing. Peeking back out, they could see at least ten dark, triangular-shaped ships flying overhead.

"Those are the same ships we saw in the battle in the Hidden City," said Velasquez.

"That means we're going the right way," stated Davis.

Hamilton filmed the encounter, including how the ships effortlessly rotated and turned in the green sky as if the basic laws of gravity and physics didn't apply to them. The ships eventually disappeared from view.

"They're heading toward the dome," said Velasquez. "Let's keep moving."

Davis had an idea. "Hold on. This is the tallest building we've encountered so far. Why don't we try and get a view from the top to see what's ahead?"

"Good thinking, Davis," agreed Velasquez, looking around and continuing, "Does anyone see a way up?"

The team searched the bottom floor for staircases or something similar, but didn't find anything. There was a round clear tube in the center of the ground floor and a circular platform inside it approximately 10' wide.

"What do you think that is?" asked Wesley.

"Some kind of elevator shaft or something?" guessed Williams.

"Yeah, looks like one, but where's the elevator or lift?" asked Davis.

"Maybe it's stuck in the tube higher up," Hamilton theorized.

"Is there a ladder in the tube we can climb up?" wondered Davis, walking out onto the round platform to check it out.

"Do you see anything?" asked Velasquez.

"I don't—" Davis stopped mid-sentence. The entire platform lit up in a bright light that filled the round platform from the ground up, engulfing Davis. When the cylinder of light dissipated, Davis was gone.

170

"Davis!" screamed Williams.

"What happened to him?" shouted Wesley.

Hamilton and Wesley immediately took out their various devices to take readings, but then, they heard something through their comm units.

"Guys, this is Davis… do you copy?"

"Damn, you scared the crap out of us!" uttered Williams, relieved.

"Good to hear your voice, Davis!" exclaimed Velasquez. "Where are you?"

"The thing sucked me up and dropped me on the top floor. I don't know what happened, but I'm literally standing at the top of this freakin' skyscraper looking at the whole city. I can see the dome from up here, and you guys aren't going to believe what else."

"What?" asked Velasquez.

"You have to come up here to see it."

"I'm not getting in that thing," uttered Wesley.

"Me, neither," announced Williams, reminding everyone that, "Someone's gotta stay down here and keep watch anyway."

Velasquez replied, "Bates, Hamilton, what about you guys? You okay going up there with Davis to check things out? The rest of us will stay down here and hold the fort."

"Yeah, I'm good," said Bates. "Davis, you sure this thing is safe?"

"I'm standing up here, ain't I?" replied Davis through the comm.

"Captain, I'll go," said Hamilton.

Hamilton and Bates walked onto the platform, and within seconds, it lit up just like before, encompassing the two men and taking them up.

"Davis, do you have them?" asked Velasquez.

"Yes, sir, they're standing right in front of me."

"Alright, we're gonna keep things under control down here. Report back when you're ready. Velasquez out."

"Yes, sir," replied Davis.

Velasquez, Wesley and Williams walked around the bottom floor which was covered in plant life that had moved indoors during an extensive period of abandonment. It wasn't long before Hamilton reported back…

"You guys are missing one hell of a view!" announced Hamilton.

"What are you guys seeing?" asked Wesley.

Davis tried to describe it. "Hamilton's filming it, but we can see the rest of the city from up here… it goes on for miles. The whole city is covered by overgrowth."

"And the dome?" asked Velasquez.

"Yes, sir, we can see the white dome. The thing's huge, it's gotta be at least ten miles long, and it's quite a bit further away from here than we thought. It's sitting right in the middle of a crazy-looking city with tall metallic buildings, all built in bizarre shapes, curves or angles. They must've used some pretty freaky engineering 'cause we got no clue how they did it from up here, but Bates has already picked out the venue for his wedding reception next year... and there are platforms floating in between the buildings with more buildings on them."

"Tell Bates his girl ain't gonna stick around another year with that personality of his. He'd better seal the deal real quick," mocked Wesley.

"Alright boys, let's plan the bachelor party later... anything else?" asked Velasquez.

"There are a lot more ships buzzing around that dome," answered Davis.

"Can you guys zoom in with the surveillance camera?" asked Velasquez.

"Yes, sir, doing that now," affirmed Davis.

Bates reported back, "Captain, there are at least fifty of those triangle-shaped ships hovering around that dome and a couple big ones, too... they're huge, like floating aircraft carriers!"

"What are they doing?" followed up Velasquez.

"They appear to be circling in a holding pattern and... you gotta be kidding..."

"What? What are you seeing, Bates?" Velasquez asked.

"Hundreds more of those ships are amassed way out there, like they're stationed at an air force base or space-force base or—"

"Something else is happening, sir!" announced Davis. "The dome is opening up."

"Opening up? In what way?" asked Velasquez.

Davis explained, "It's like one of those retractable roof stadiums. The roof is rolling back and all the ships that were hovering above it are flying into the dome." There was a short pause, and then Davis continued, "It looks like all the ships are inside it now, and by the size of that dome, probably a few hundred more could fit in there, no problem."

"What are they doing, can you tell?" Velasquez asked.

Davis reported back, "The top of the dome is closing and... the whole dome just turned black, and if our surveillance cameras aren't messing with us, from here, it looks like the inside of the dome just turned into a galaxy of stars... Wait, there's movement inside the dome and... the whole thing just flashed and turned white again. Whatever happened, it's over."

"Captain, the guys back home aren't going to like this, but if I had to guess, I'd say that dome is another one of those Vaniryan portals like the pyramid below Area 51," speculated Bates, adding, "But instead of a small 20' wide portal allowing a few of us to walk through, that thing can transport an entire fleet, all at once."

"That's a *huge* problem," uttered Velasquez. "As if Supay's ability to destroy a planet from orbit wasn't bad enough, he can send his entire arsenal anywhere he wants on Earth in the blink of an eye."

"Wait, something else's happening...," blurted Hamilton.

"What?"

"Something's coming out of the side of the dome!" Hamilton responded.

Velasquez wanted more. "C'mon guys, talk to me!"

"Captain, we've been made! Ships are flying this way and they're pointing some kind of weapon straight at us!" hollered Bates.

Velasquez yelled back, "Guys, get out of there! Get to the elevator tube and let's—"

A loud high-pitched boom interrupted Velasquez. It was the dome's weapon – a laser cannon - firing. The entire building shook on impact when the laser struck it. Velasquez could tell it was a solid hit by the ferocity of the vibrations.

"Williams, Wesley, let's go!" shouted Velasquez, bolting out of the bottom floor of the building. They ran for their lives as the building started to collapse. The laser cannon had destroyed the upper portion of the building, with the explosion and falling debris causing it to crumble in on itself.

By the time Velasquez, Williams and Wesley got out of the bottom floor, the entire building was crashing downward. Velasquez and Williams got far enough away, but a metal beam struck Wesley as he was trying to escape, knocking him to the ground. A split second later, the rest of the building came down on top of him. The force of the structure plunging into the ground created a whole lot of dust and a small shock wave that threw Velasquez and Williams forward.

When they got to their feet, Williams turned back toward the fallen building to search for the others, but Velasquez grabbed his arm to stop him.

"Williams, they're gone. There's nothing we can do. We've gotta get out of here before those ships arrive, or no one's ever going to learn what we discovered."

"Yeah, okay," replied Williams, devastated, but he knew Velasquez was right.

Velasquez, his helmet and suit covered in dust and debris, looked at the digital display on his wrist for the *p*RAMZA homing beacon at home base. After cleaning it off so he could read it, he quickly re-oriented himself and said, "C'mon, Williams, follow me!"

They took off at full speed, no longer moving station to station or cautiously. There was no time for that. Any moment, enemy ships were going to reach the area looking for survivors, and neither Velasquez nor Williams had any intention of being around when they got there. They frantically raced back to home base, hoping to get off Electra-1 as soon as possible. Operation 17 Tauri was over.

Chapter 16 – Buckingham

Emma and Logan sat anxiously on a sofa in Queen Elizabeth II's private Audience Room at Buckingham Palace, the London residence and administrative headquarters of the monarch of the United Kingdom. Dr. Arenot and Professor Quimbey, who had flown in from Iceland for the audience with the queen, sat across from them in two chairs on the other side of a circular table draped with a tasseled tablecloth. The table, chairs and sofa were centered before a grand fireplace, with a large mirror in an ornate gilt frame hanging over the mantle on a pale blue wall. The ceiling was slightly arched and designed using a pattern of symmetrically arranged gilded triangles.

While Emma, Logan and the professors chatted, General Covington walked around the room looking at the artwork. Captain Evans and the other security officials who accompanied them on the trip had been asked to wait in the entrance hall to Buckingham Palace because the queen had only approved the five of them for a personal audience.

The queen's personal assistant, Miss Charlotte, kept them company while they waited for Queen Elizabeth II's arrival. "Her Majesty won't be much longer," said Miss Charlotte, looking at her watch.

Nervously making small talk, Emma asked, "How big is Buckingham Palace?"

Miss Charlotte, an expert on the five-floor square-shaped royal palace with an inner courtyard, was happy to answer her question. "The palace measures 108 meters long across the front, 120 meters deep and 24 meters high. Many Americans are interested to learn that Buckingham Palace is nearly 15 times larger than the White House."

"Wow, how many rooms does it have?" wondered Emma.

"775," answered Miss Charlotte.

"That's a lot of rooms!" blurted Logan. "How many does the queen use?"

Miss Charlotte replied, "Her Majesty is very modest. She only uses a handful."

"So what are the rest used for?" followed up Logan.

"Staff bedrooms, one of which is mine, offices, bathrooms, guest bedrooms, state rooms, dining halls, meeting halls, you name it."

"How long has the monarchy lived in Buckingham Palace?" asked Emma.

"The building at the core of today's palace was originally constructed as a townhouse for the Duke of Buckingham in 1703. King George III acquired the private residence as a summer home for Queen Charlotte in 1761 and it became known as The Queen's House. During the 19th century, the monarchy added three wings around the center courtyard to resemble the building that exists today. Buckingham Palace finally became the official London residence of the British monarch on the accession of Queen Victoria in 1837."

"What do we do when we meet Her Majesty, do we bow?" asked Logan.

Miss Charlotte responded, "There are no obligatory codes of behavior when meeting the queen, but many people wish to observe the traditional forms. For men this is a neck bow from the head only, while women do a small curtsy. Other people have preferred simply to shake her hand in the usual way, but that is assuming she asks."

"Is there anything else special we should do or not do?" inquired Logan, continuing, "I'm sorry, I know I'm probably asking a lot of protocol questions but I've never met a king or queen before."

Miss Charlotte shook her head. "Not to worry. We get these questions all the time. Her Majesty won't bite your hand off, but there are some general guidelines we recommend you follow. Avoid touching the queen unless she reaches out to shake your hand or invites it. Try to remain standing at all times, sitting only when beckoned by Her Majesty to do so. Don't speak unexpectedly to the queen unless she is conversing with you, and please do not interrupt Her Majesty because the queen does not look favorably upon it."

"Of course," replied Emma.

Miss Charlotte, with one finger on an earpiece and listening intently, announced, "Her Majesty, Queen Elizabeth II, is on her way… please stand and join me in the center of the room."

All of them rose to their feet and moved to the center of the Audience Room. Through a private door in the wall opposite the one they had entered came Queen Elizabeth II. She was in her mid-90's, still moving spryly and presenting an aura of elegance befitting a monarch representing a lineage of kings and queens dating back over a millennia. The queen approached them. Taking Miss Charlotte's lead, they all bowed or curtsied in the formal way.

Her Majesty surveyed the group and offered a very polite generalized hello. She then reached out to shake hands, one at a time. Having been prepared for the private audience by her aides, the queen addressed each of them by name. When Queen Elizabeth II got to Emma to greet her, her gaze lingered. She seemed to study Emma's face for a split second longer. Emma smiled back. Finally, when the queen got to Professor Quimbey, to the professor's surprise, Queen Elizabeth II spoke to her.

"Professor Quimbey, you know, I met your grandmother once when we were both young girls, on a visit to the Ayrshire with my father. He took me along on an excursion to meet your great-grandfather, Lord Alfred Quimbey. I don't remember what it was all about, but I remember your grandmother. She was very sweet, introduced me to the horses in her stables."

Professor Quimbey seemed surprised. "Your Majesty, it is an honor to know that you remember that. I had heard that story from Grammy a long time ago."

"It was only a short visit to the shores of the Firth of Clyde. My father allowed your Gran to steal me away for a few minutes. We rode a couple of her ponies. I loved the horses growing up. I still do. I'd ride more often if everyone around here wasn't so afraid of me falling and breaking a hip."

"I'm sure you wouldn't do that," stated Professor Quimbey.

With an appreciative smile, the queen replied, "I was quite the equestrian rider in my youth, or so I fancy."

"From everything I have read about Your Majesty, you still are."

"Well, as we say, if the tabloids are saying something kind about us, it might be true."

"I'm sure it is, Your Majesty."

"You are very sweet, dear, just like your Grandmother. Please remind me again what her name was?"

"Grammy Sophie."

With yet another great big royal smile, Queen Elizabeth replied, "Yes, that was it... Sophie. One of the few girls I ever met with the courage to ask to steal me away. That was a fun morning. Please let her know I remember her fondly."

"Unfortunately, Your Majesty, Grammy passed away a few years ago."

"Oh dear, I am sorry to hear that. She was very kind." Queen Elizabeth turned to General Covington. "General Covington, your president had many fine things to say about you."

"Thank you, Your Majesty. President Barrett is very much looking forward to hosting you at the State Dinner in Washington next month." General Covington handed Queen Elizabeth II a formal invitation to the State Dinner as well as a special gift: a set of strawberry jams, the queen's favorite, from Jamestown, the first permanent English settlement in America. Courtesy of a well-informed U.S. State Department, it was the perfect gift for the queen who absolutely loved jam pennies—small sandwiches filled with jam and cut into circles the size of an old English penny. "Your Majesty, I offer you this set of jams to celebrate Jamestown's heritage of English-style strawberry farming, from a local Virginia farm tucked away within the mountains of Stellenbosch."

"Thank you," said Queen Elizabeth, taking hold of the jam set. Miss Charlotte immediately approached to take the gift off the queen's hands.

"It seems like only a few years ago that I celebrated the 400-year anniversary of the Jamestown settlement with your former President George Bush when we visited the States in 2007. I don't know how much you know about the Jamestown settlement, but it was sponsored by King James I shortly after Queen Elizabeth I passed away in 1603. The colony was founded by the Virginia Company of London whose charter King James I approved in 1606 to support England's national goals of expansion and economic interest in finding a northwest passage to the Orient."

Her Majesty was quite knowledgeable of her kingdom's history. Indeed, Queen Elizabeth II believed it her royal duty to know, and know well, the history of her kingdom and subjects. The general, like all of them, was impressed by the queen's knowledge. The queen continued. "It is ironic that you come here today to ask me about a child who lived with the very same King James I, a child who, quite possibly, could have been in the room during King James I's audience with the Virginia Company of London when he approved the proposed expedition to the Americas."

Before anyone could ask about the child the queen was referring to, Queen Elizabeth II continued, "It is a pleasure to have an audience full of such fine people this morning. Please accept my apology, but if I may, I would like to speak to Ms. James for a few minutes, alone."

"Me?" asked Emma, shocked. She glanced over at Logan, and then Professor Quimbey, both of whom looked equally stunned.

"Yes, you, dear," replied the queen. "And when we return, I would be delighted if you would all join me for some tea pennies to sample that exquisite-looking jam of yours." Addressing Miss Charlotte, the queen said, "Dear, can you please arrange that?" The queen started walking back to her private door.

Miss Charlotte, more than a little surprised herself, responded, "Of course, Your Majesty."

Emma, who had been holding Logan's hand, let go and followed the queen. She hurried to catch up and open the queen's door for her. The two disappeared into Queen Elizabeth II's private apartments.

Miss Charlotte looked back at the rest of the group, and with genuine surprise, said, "I have never seen Her Majesty do that in all my years working at the palace."

ΔΔΔΔΔΔΔΔΔΔΔ

Emma walked beside the queen, being careful not to step ahead of her, trying to match the queen's gait while they proceeded down the Queen's Corridor. Her heart was racing as they slowly walked down a hallway decorated with lavish drapes covering floor-to-ceiling windows, oriental vases and paintings on the walls, making their way to the Queen's Sitting Room.

"I saw Mr. West holding your hand, dear. Very sweet," said the queen.

"Yes, Your Majesty, Logan is very sweet."

"He seems like a fine young man. He fancies you."

"I know."

"And you him?" asked the queen.

"Yes, Your Majesty."

"Could he be the one for your hand in marriage?" pried Queen Elizabeth II.

"Someday. It's complicated right now."

"Oh, I'm not sure that it is, dear."

"Then why does it always feel like it is?"

The queen thought about it. "Because young people make everything complicated. I'm not suggesting it's your fault, or that I was above doing so myself when I was your age, but young people are always worrying about tomorrow, convinced they have all the time in the world that they forget about today. Take it from me, a queen approaching her centennial, it goes by in a flash. It seems like just yesterday I was crowned at Westminster Abbey at 25, following my father's passing. Quite honestly, it doesn't feel like 70 years ago. My point is, dear, tomorrow is not guaranteed, not for this queen, not for anyone."

"I'm just afraid of him getting hurt."

"If he loves you, he stands to suffer far more if you don't let him in than if you do."

"I'm sorry Your Majesty, but that isn't quite what I mean."

"You know, the child you have come here to ask me about left everyone she loved behind so they wouldn't get hurt, or so the story goes. It must have been hard for her to do that. After death, heartbreak is truly the hardest living tragedy to recover from. It would be unfortunate if you followed her fate. Perhaps it is in your blood."

Emma found Queen Elizabeth II's remark curious. Did she know something about Isabel and her possible relation to Emma?

"We are here," stated the queen, leading Emma into her private Sitting Room, another regal space overflowing with royal décor, paintings, sofas, tables, flowers, tapestries, vases, and crown molding.

The queen escorted Emma to a sitting area consisting of matching light powder blue sofas angled to allow their occupants to easily converse with one another, and a tea table between them. An elegant tea set was prepared and waiting on the table. She motioned for Emma to sit on the adjoining sofa, which Emma did, her knees knocking.

"It smells delicious," said Emma nervously.

"Earl Grey," replied the queen.

"I like Earl Grey tea," Emma responded.

The queen appeared pleased. "It is my favorite, with a splash of milk and no sugar. Would you care for some?"

Emma was not about to say no to tea with the Queen of the United Kingdom! "Yes, please!" she blurted, perhaps a bit too excited. Her nervous energy was running amuck.

"Wonderful, although no need to be anxious, dear. You are safe in here."

"Yes, Your Majesty," said Emma, doing her best to appear poised and proper.

"How do you take your tea, dear?"

"A splash of milk and no sugar is perfect for me too, Your Majesty," replied Emma. The queen grinned back at her.

As the queen made herself and Emma a cup of tea, she said, "Did you know that Earl Grey tea was named after Charles Grey, 2nd Earl Grey, British Prime Minister in the 1830s? He abolished slavery during his time in office, you know. It is a pity he is most remembered for the tea, which he didn't even discover or invent. It was imported. He merely preferred it, no different than you or me."

"I did not know that," responded Emma, still finding it hard to fathom where she was and what she was doing.

"The Grey family is splendid. Still a delight," remarked the queen, handing Emma her cup.

"Thank you," said Emma.

After they spent a moment sipping their tea, the queen said, "Around the room are many fine paintings of the royal family over the years, some recent, many dating back centuries. Truly remarkable portraits. You might enjoy them."

Something in the way the queen said it gave Emma the impression that Queen Elizabeth II wasn't making a comment, but rather, a suggestion. Emma put her teacup down and rose from the sofa. She stepped away and looked back. The queen continued to sip her tea without batting an eye or turning her head, as if it was exactly what the queen expected Emma to do.

Emma approached the closest wall, the north wall, which had a slew of paintings on it arranged at different heights. There were portraits of kings and queens, at times alone, other times together or with family or their courts. The portraits portrayed royals sitting on thrones, dining, enjoying the outdoors or rejoicing in banquet halls. Emma wasn't familiar with the faces depicted, but she did not doubt that they accurately resembled their subjects given the portraits' incredible artistic detail.

When Emma was finished looking at the portraits on the north wall, she turned to the paintings on the east wall, still unsure what she was looking for. She only knew that she was doing precisely what the queen wanted her to do because Queen Elizabeth II continued to just sit there, quietly enjoying her Earl Gray tea, a peaceful smile on her face.

Emma kept perusing the paintings until she came to one that struck her, a scene depicting a royal family along with children of varying ages posing for what looked like a family photo. Two over from the king was a young blonde girl, wearing a full-length, maroon, medieval gown and her hair braided back, that stopped Emma in her tracks: the girl's face was unmistakably similar to Emma's, so much so that, for a moment, Emma thought she was staring at a younger version of herself. Emma glanced below the frame to see if there was a description of the painting, but there wasn't.

When Emma looked back at Queen Elizabeth II to ask about the portrait, the queen was already on her way over, for as soon as Emma had stopped at the portrait, the queen already knew what her next question was going to be. She knew it from the first moment she laid eyes on Emma.

"Your Majesty, this portrait here, this girl in the maroon gown, is that Isabel?" asked Emma.

The queen grinned. Only someone who knew who or what they were looking for would have stopped at the portrait Emma was asking about out of all the portraits in the Sitting Room, which purposely had no plaques or descriptions to assist a viewer in discerning what they were looking at. Emma had chosen correctly. "The portrait is of King James I, his queen, Anne of Denmark, their children, Henry, Prince of Wales, Charles I, Elizabeth of Bohemia and others in King James I's court, including—"

"Isabel, daughter of Elizabeth Stanley and Antonio Rossi," interrupted Emma, mortified at herself for interrupting the queen. "I am so sorry, Your Majesty."

Queen Elizabeth II wasn't offended. At that moment, the queen knew very well the source of Emma's unchecked enthusiasm. "Yes, dear, it is. The portrait was painted shortly after Queen Elizabeth I succumbed to illness. She loved that child, and decreed that the royal family would care for and protect her. And King James I honored the queen's request on her death bed, as did many to follow."

"Your Majesty, I know this is a strange question, but was Isabel born as an infant to Elizabeth Stanley?"

"It is a strange question, dear, but you already know the answer, I suspect. We did what we could to protect the girl from those who would harm her after they burned down her home and chased her from Italy. We staged what we could, but the girl, as you know, did most of her own staging."

The queen reached for the right-hand side of the painting's floral, gilded frame and pulled it toward her. The frame swung out to reveal a large safe behind it with a keypad. Emma looked away while the queen pressed buttons, although the queen didn't seem remotely concerned with Emma's peering eyes. When she was done, the safe opened to reveal yet another inner safe that looked hundreds of years older, made of thick iron. On the front of the safe was a medieval combination lock with five columns on rotating wheels. It resembled a combination lock on a high school locker, only this one used calligraphic letters instead of numbers.

"If you know her name, her secret is yours," said the queen, pointing to the safe, and specifically, to the medieval cryptological combination lock.

It was one final test. Emma studied the cryptological lock and its five column-combination. With butterflies in her stomach, she examined the letters to assess the combination options. "If you know her name, her secret is yours," she whispered to herself. "Rossi is five letters," she mumbled. She turned the five combination wheels until landing on R-O-S-S-I. Nothing happened. She then tried the next logical answer, the reverse spelling, I-S-S-O-R, adjusting the column wheels accordingly. On the last column, when she turned to the letter "R," she heard a *click!* The medieval safe popped open, releasing a waft of trapped air.

"That's what I thought," remarked Queen Elizabeth II, "but I had to be sure." The queen reached into the surprisingly deep, dark safe and pulled out two items: a heart-shaped pendant necklace and a letter. The queen first handed Emma the necklace.

"I am told she loved jewelry, animals, flowers, and the stars. She had the Royal Jeweler fashion this necklace, it is said, and when she left, she chose to leave it behind for those who would search for her someday... I suppose, you, dear."

Emma's eyes welled up. It was as if she had found Isa, or a piece of her, even if the little girl was not standing in front of her. The necklace mirrored the one Isa had once admired hanging around Emma's own neck on Vanirya. Isa had liked it so much, in fact, that Emma had left it behind with Tassa to give to Isa the day Emma and the others departed Jaannos to continue on their journey to the Hidden City. Only, Isa never received that necklace because of her decision to join them on that journey which, of course, resulted in Isa ending up on Earth before she could ever return home. Apparently, Isa remembered the necklace well enough to have it re-made. Emma clutched the necklace, and tears openly flowed down her cheeks.

"Have you seen this necklace before?" asked the queen, taken aback by Emma's strong connection to a necklace that had been locked away for centuries, one that Emma could not possibly have seen before.

Emma chuckled through her tears and replied, "Yes, Your Majesty... I mean, one just like it, anyway."

The queen's own eyes welled up. "Dear, it is not often that I am humbled."

Emma wiped her tears away with her sleeve. "I'm sorry I'm crying, Your Majesty. It's just..."

"Oh dear, happiness requires no apology." The queen gave Emma a second, and then, handed her the note that accompanied the necklace. "Here, I suppose Isabel left this letter for you, as well."

"Her real name was Issor, but she liked Isa most," said Emma, smiling through her tears. Emma unfolded the old piece of paper and read it. It took her a moment longer to understand the note because of the Old English alphabet which, in the 18th century, did not have the letters 'J' or 'U.' Instead, it used the dual-purpose letters 'I' for 'J' and 'V' for 'U.' The note said:

"I sovght the adventvre of a lifetime when I left my home, and that is exactly what I fovnd. I have seen so many wonders of this world, bvt with my lifetime have I also witnessed so many lifetimes pass, so many loved ones lost. If immortality lives in the poems of the greats, so too does my pain, the price I did not anticipate immortality asking me to pay, made worse by the evil that continves to hvnt me. Somehow, it smells my scent again. I mvst leave all that I love behind once more. To the end of the world I will sail this time, far away from what I know. I hope that will be far enovgh, for Arcadia is as far as the admiral can take me. There, I will wait for yov, hiding among the fire and ice, bvt beware: the Hvnt tracks yovr scent too. - I"

"Oh, thank goodness!" exclaimed Emma after finally finding evidence that Isa's life had continued on Earth after they lost her in the portal on Vanirya. However, just as soon as the words left her mouth did her heart also sink at how Isa described her suffering from the curse of her Vaniryan lifespan, virtually immortal by human standards. And worse was the foreboding reference to the Hunt. It was a frightening reminder of why they were all there and how the battle that started with Supay on Vanirya had never ended. Instead, it had come to Earth.

Emma, wiping away more tears, read a portion of the note again: *To the end of the world I will sail, far away from what I know. I hope that will be far enough, for Arcadia is as far as the admiral can take me.* She thought about it. The words in the last sentence, *Arcadia* and *admiral*, conjured up something Emma had learned sophomore year about one of the world's top uncracked ciphertexts: *The Shugborough Inscription.*

The Shugborough Inscription was a cipher well-known to any cryptology major because, much like the Voynich Manuscript, it had never been solved. It consisted of a 10-letter sequence carved into an 18th-century monument called the Shepherd's Monument, right below a mirror image relief of Nicolas Poussin's painting, the *Shepherds of Arcadia*, which depicted four shepherds standing over a tomb in a mythical utopian forest with rolling hills called *Arcadia*. But that was not all. The Shepherd's Monument was located on the grounds of Shugborough Hall in Staffordshire, England, a property once owned by none other than First Lord of the Admiralty, *Admiral* of the Fleet and Royal Navy, *Admiral* George Anson, 1st Baron Anson!

The inscription carved into the Shepherd's Monument below Poussin's *Shepherds of Arcadia* relief, was broken into two lines, an upper and a lower one. On the upper line was a sequence of eight letters - O U O S V A V V- and on the second lower line a sequence of two letters, D and M. The D and M bookended the upper line of eight letters from beneath, with the D placed below and to the left of the eight-letter line, and the M placed below and to the right:

D   OUOSVAVV   M

The inscription had never been satisfactorily explained or solved. Over the centuries, it had generated many theories, with some suggesting that the letters represented the initials for a phrase, others hypothesizing that they were coordinates to long-lost treasure or even to the Holy Grail. And of course, many believed the letters were coordinates to Poussin's mythological Arcadia or the location of the tomb depicted in his painting:

But Emma now wondered, did the inscription indicate something different altogether? Had *Admiral* Anson sailed Isa to the end of the world, to *Arcadia*, and did the inscription on the monument located on his property provide coordinates to her location? Isa's comment that she was "surrounded by fire and ice" certainly didn't sound like the mythological utopian place that Poussin painted, but there was only one way to find out if the inscription led to Isa's Arcadia...

Emma suddenly felt compelled to leave Buckingham Palace for Shugborough Hall to get a closer look at the inscription on the Shepherd's Monument on Admiral Anson's property, which Emma now suspected indicated where the admiral had taken Isa. "Your Majesty, how far from London is Staffordshire?" asked Emma.

The queen knew exactly what Emma was thinking. "Admiral Anson's property is just a few hours northwest of here, dear," replied the queen.

"Your Majesty, do you know where the Shugborough Inscription points to? Where Arcadia is?"

"No, dear. It is a secret kept even from us. For Isabel's protection, no doubt."

"Your Majesty, I can't believe I am saying this, and I sincerely apologize, but I think we have to go."

The queen did not look surprised. "I understand. We swore an oath to protect the special little girl, and now, that oath is yours. Godspeed, dear."

"Your Majesty, is there anything more you can tell me about Isabel?"

"Unfortunately, no, very little of her secret is known."

"I don't know how to thank you, Your Majesty."

"When the time is right, dear, please come back and we will enjoy another cup of tea and jam pennies properly. And maybe, you can tell me more about Isabe—... *Isa*. I should very much like to hear more about her."

Emma smiled politely and replied, "Yes, Your Majesty, I will."

Chapter 17 – Cryptological

The road to Shugborough Hall took them northwest through the English countryside on the way to Staffordshire. Given what had transpired in Venice, they rode in a CIA-arranged shuttle, followed by several other cars full of CIA agents for extra security. The drive was nearly three hours long, which was perfect because it gave the team time to work.

General Covington spent much of the drive marshalling resources back home to locate, vet and transmit potential solutions for the Shugborough Inscription, with new ones coming in every fifteen minutes or so. Unfortunately, there were a lot of them. It wasn't that no one had come up with theories for solving the ciphertext before, but rather, that there was no way to verify the solution. After all, Admiral Anson had been dead for over 250 years. Further casting doubt on any of the possible solutions was the fact that no one had found buried treasure, the Holy Grail, mysterious tombs, religious artifacts or anything else of interest wherever their solutions had led them. But if the team wanted to find Isa before Supay did, cracking the cipher on the Shepherd's Monument was exactly what they needed to do.

During the drive, they studied photographs of the Shepherd's Monument and proposed solutions sent to the encrypted tablets they were using in the shuttle. Covington, who had been on his cellphone with Mr. Garrison, hung up to report back on his conversation. "Miles says they're sending a few more over."

"How did his call with the Shugborough Hall Foundation people go?" asked Logan.

Covington shook his head. "Not well. The Foundation's Director Graves told him that they get five or six people a week at Shugborough who believe they've solved the cipher and just as many unsolicited emails, so they're a bit wary of cryptologists and treasure hunters at this point. He told Miles that two centuries of unsuccessful solutions and wasteful treasure hunting quests had left the National Trust and the Shugborough Hall Foundation profoundly skeptical of such efforts and that they've moved on to things more worthy of their time, such as caring for the estate on behalf of the people of the United Kingdom."

"Well, of course they're skeptical! Everyone's been looking for lost treasure, religious artifacts or a sacred tomb when they should have been looking for Isa!" replied Emma.

"Totally," concurred Logan.

Professor Quimbey, looking out the windows at the CIA escort surrounding their shuttle, said, "General, aren't you guys worried about someone tapping our communications and reading our devices after everything that's happened?"

"Professor, these phones and tablets are military grade encrypted with the latest technology. There's no way anyone is listening to our phones or reading our communications," assured General Covington.

"Are you sure?" Quimbey pushed back.

Logan chimed in, "*Someone* knew we were going back to that tunnel in Reykholt to look at the carving on the stone and *someone* knew we were going to be in Venice."

The general replied, "Listen, I know you guys are worried. We don't know where the leak is yet and we'll find it, but until then, we're surrounded by security and the NSA tells me they're confident our phones and tablets aren't the problem."

"That's not very reassuring," remarked Professor Quimbey.

"No, it isn't, and I'm sorry I don't have better assurances, but let's focus on what we need to do today, okay?" responded the general.

"Yeah, okay," said Logan, ready to get back to work. "Hey Em, can you pull up the picture of the Shepherd's Monument again on your tablet?"

"Sure." Emma, using her tablet, pulled up an image of the centuries-old Shepherd's Monument in Shugborough Hall's exterior gardens. The outer form of the monument was a stone portico with two Doric columns on the sides holding up a heavy, rectangular stone set lengthwise on its side. The upper portion of the monument had carvings of laurel wreaths and stone heads while a row of radiating round petals decorated the top.

Inside the portico was a rusticated arch which framed a marble-engraved copy of Nicolas Poussin's painting, *The Shepherds of Arcadia,* showing four shepherds, including one woman and three men, holding staffs and mourning over a stone tomb. Two of them were on their knees pointing to lettering on the tomb that read 'ET IN ARCADIA EGO,' while the other two looked on.

And right below the marble engraved copy of Poussin's painting was a marble plaque with the *Shugborough Inscription* engraved into it. The inscription was broken up into two lines: O U O S V A V V on the upper line, and D and M on the lower line bookending the above eight letters:

D OUOSVAVV M

198

"Thanks," responded Logan. Emma handed him the tablet displaying the Shepherd's Monument. He reverse-pinched the image on the screen to enlarge the view of the marble-engraved ciphertext:

"There are so many possible solutions. How will we know which is correct?" wondered Logan.

"You just need to think cryptologically," declared Emma.

"Cryptologically?" Logan replied.

"Yeah."

"Is cryptologically even a real word?" inquired Logan.

"Yes, as a matter of fact, it's my word, so therefore, *yes*, it *is*," retorted Emma.

"What do the letters on the tomb say that the shepherds are pointing to?" asked Professor Quimbey.

Emma, who was very familiar with the painting and the inscription below it from cryptology class, replied, " 'ET IN ARCADIA EGO,' meaning, 'I am also in Arcadia.' "

"Hmm, that could refer to Isa being in Arcadia, I suppose," remarked Logan.

"But it says, 'I am *also* in Arcadia,' suggesting that someone else was *also* with her," said Professor Quimbey.

"Like Supay," Captain Evans darkly suggested.

"Let's hope not," replied Dr. Arenot.

"General, which of the Shugborough Inscription solutions do the Pegasus lads back home think are the most plausible?" asked Professor Quimbey.

General Covington sorted the solutions the Pegasus think-tank had sent over, ranked by plausibility, and reported, "The top results are all Latin initialism theories."

"What's an initialism theory?" asked Logan.

Aspiring cryptologist Emma quickly answered, "It's when the letters refer to the *initial* letter in each word of a sentence or phrase, like L W stands for Logan West, based on the initial letters of your first and last name."

"Right," said General Covington, "at least, that's what it says here on my screen. The top proposed solution says the eight-letter sequence is actually a dedication by Admiral Anson to his deceased wife, and that Anson used Poussin's *Shepherds of Arcadia* to symbolize his wife's burial in the tomb over which the shepherds are mourning. The solution suggests the letters are an initialism for the Latin epitaph, 'Optimae Uxoris Optimae Sororis Viduus Amantissimus Vovit Virtutibus,' which means 'Best of wives, best of sisters, a most devoted widower dedicates (this) to your virtues.' "

"An epitaph? That's a long way from coordinates leading to Arcadia," bemoaned Logan.

"Unfortunately, that's not the only one," said General Covington. "Another solution interprets the letters as standing for the Latin phrase from *Ecclesiastes* 12:8, 'Orator Ut Omnia Sunt Vanitas Ait Vanitas Vanitatum,' meaning, 'Vanity of vanities, saith the preacher; all is vanity.' And recently, a former NSA linguist concluded the letters are an initialism for the Latin phrase, 'Oro Ut Omnes Sequantur Viam Ad Veram Vitam,' which translated, says, 'I pray that all may follow the way to true life,' in reference to the Biblical verse John 14:6."

"I don't like *any* of them," said Emma. "Plus, all those solutions are only eight words, which account for the middle eight letters in the inscription, but completely ignore the D and M that bookend it on both sides. You can't just ignore those letters. It has to be something else!" insisted Emma.

"Emma's right. General, did the Pegasus team find *any* non-Latin-initialism theories in there?" wondered Logan.

General Covington replied, "No, but there are some theorizing the inscription is a code leading to buried treasure or a captured Spanish galleon that Admiral Anson hid somewhere in the ocean, or a powerful secret of some kind."

"What is the 'powerful secret' theory based on?" asked Logan.

General Covington, reading from his tablet, responded, "It's based on a letter sent to representatives of King Louis XIV of France in the 17th century."

"Written by who?" asked Dr. Arenot.

"By Frenchman Abbé Louis Fouquet to his brother, Nicolas Fouquet, Superintendent of Finances to King Louis XIV, describing a meeting he had just had with *Nicolas Poussin* in Rome, Italy. Here's a type-written copy of a portion of the letter's text from French archives."

A Rome, le 17 apvril 1656.

J'ay rendu á M. *Poussin* aujourd'hui. Lui et moi avons discuté de certaines choses, que je pourrai facilement vous expliquer en détail – choses qui vous donneront, par M. Poussin, des avantages que même les rois auraient beaucoup de mal à tirer de lui, et que, selon lui, il est possible que personne d'autre ne puisse jamais redécouvrir dans les siècles à venir. Et, qui plus est, ce sont des choses si difficiles à découvrir que rien maintenant sur cette terre ne peut prouver une meilleure fortune ni être leur égal.

"It's in French," griped Logan. "Did they translate it for us?"

General Covington replied, "Yes, here is the translation of the section of Fouquet's letter they wanted us to look at." He showed it to them. It read:

"In Rome, Italy, April 17, 1656

I met with Monsieur *Poussin* today. He and I discussed certain things, which I shall with ease be able to explain to you in detail – things that will give you, through Monsieur *Poussin*, advantages which even kings would have great pains to draw from him, and which, according to him, it is possible that nobody else will ever be able to rediscover in the centuries to come. And, what is more, these are things so difficult to discover that nothing now on this earth can prove of better fortune nor be their equal."

"Fouquet's letter suggests that Poussin, who was also French, told him about something so powerful that nothing on Earth could prove of better fortune nor equal," repeated Logan, intrigued.

"Maybe, something not of this world, *like Isa*," Emma hypothesized. "Seems like they may have been on to her scent in Italy."

"By 'they,' you mean Fouquet and Poussin?" asked Logan.

"And the French king, Louis XIV. Seems like he was also interested in Poussin's secret," intimated Emma.

"Who was this Abbé Louis Fouquet who supposedly met with Poussin in Rome?" asked Dr. Arenot.

Logan looked him up on the tablet. "Abbé Louis Fouquet was the younger brother of Nicolas Fouquet, France's Superintendent of Finances and bishop-count of Agde and chaplain to King Louis XIV. Abbé Louis supposedly conducted secret missions of state for the Crown, including numerous visits to Italy and around Europe."

"That explains why he was in Rome," observed Dr. Arenot.

Logan continued, "And for his service to the king, he ascended to distinguished orders, including the Order of Saint-Michel and the Order of the Holy Spirit, which conferred upon him the benefits of nobility without being of royal blood."

Emma was impressed. "Sounds like he moved his way up in ranks by carrying out secret missions for the king, and acquiring and delivering information like that message from Poussin," commented Emma.

Logan spotted something else. "Huh. Interesting. It also says here that he was involved in an underground order called the Christ's Templars, a secretive off-shoot of the dismantled Knights Templars who were supposedly banned from France by King Phillip IV after the Crusades."

"If by banned, you mean arrested, tortured, executed or exiled, then you are correct," expounded Dr. Arenot, who knew a bit about the history of the Knights Templars. "The Knights Templars had a strong presence in France during the middle ages. They were a devout Christian military order who carried out important missions for the Church, like protecting Christianity and pilgrims journeying to the Holy Land. But after the Crusades ended, they fell out of favor and usefulness, and at the beginning of the 14th century, King Philip IV resolved to bring down the Knights Templars and even pressured Pope Clement V to dissolve their order. Tens of thousands of Knights Templars who weren't arrested or executed dispersed throughout Europe and even up into Russia, with many of them absorbed into other orders or underground organizations such as the Knights Hospitallers, the Order of Christ, and apparently, this Order of Christ's Templars that Logan just mentioned."

"What was this secret Order of Christ's Templars all about?" asked Emma.

Logan read further. "They were a shunned underground order of Knights Templars who believed in recapturing the divine power from Christ's disloyal subjects who abandoned Christ after the Crusades, and using it to start a new crusade to take over the world. Their symbol was a right leaning version of the normal red Knights Templar cross, encased in a red circle. Here, look at it…"

"They sound like a fun bunch," said Captain Evans. "I can see why Fouquet was interested in meeting with Poussin to discuss a secret that nothing on this earth could prove of better fortune nor equal. Not sure who was more interested in Poussin's information about this powerful secret, Fouquet and his power-hungry cabal or King Louis XIV."

"Maybe both," replied Logan. "Apparently, Abbé Louis Fouquet was exiled from the king's palace in Versailles after it was discovered that he was part of the Christ's Templars. He was exiled to a French commune in the south of France called Villefranche-de-Rouergue, which—"

"He wasn't arrested or expelled from France altogether?" questioned Dr. Arenot, surprised.

Logan replied, "Exactly! Many found it odd that he wasn't arrested or expelled from France given the country's law at the time. Coupled with the contents of the letter about Poussin he sent to King Louis XIV, many believed that the king may have secretly been part of that underground Christ's Templar order and that he might even have been the order's Grand Master."

Emma jumped back in. "I can see why researchers believe Poussin's *Shepherds of Arcadia* and the Shepherd's Monument hold the key to some kind of powerful secret with no equal on Earth. King Louis XIV and the Order of Christ's Templars were chasing after it, and the English monarchy was protecting it. And when they got close, the monarchy had Admiral Anson hide it elsewhere."

"By 'it,' you mean, Isa," stated Logan.

Emma nodded. "Yes. They were all after her, Supay, the French king, the Order of Christ's Templars, *everyone*; that's why Admiral Anson sailed her to the end of the world, Arcadia, as far away as he could, to hide her from it all."

"We just have to figure out where Arcadia is and what the inscription is trying to tell us," said Logan.

Emma responded, "You know, the Knights Templars, the Freemasons and Freemason-offshoots like the Great Enlightened Society of Oculists and the Odd Fellows, *all* used secret codes assigning number values to letters. It could be something like that."

"Was Admiral Anson a member of any of those societies?" Dr. Arenot asked Emma.

"Yes, Anson's family was a well-known Freemason family. The list of Freemasons is like a who's who in history: Winston Churchill, Wolfgang Amadeus Mozart, George Washington, Benjamin Franklin and more. Even Sir Francis Bacon and William Shakespeare belonged to a secret society that used cipher codes, called the Rosicrucians."

"Okay, so what kind of code are you talking about?" asked Dr. Arenot.

"Well, for example, the English alphabet has 26 letters. So, imagine the letter A equals the number 1, B equals 2, C equals 3 and so forth, until you get to Z which equals 26. They used all kinds of different cipher codes like that, some equating letters to numbers and counting up, others counting backwards or stopping halfway through the alphabet and reversing direction, or adding a plus one, or subtracting one, etc. There are dozens of codes out there that were once used by the various secret societies, and that's assuming Anson used a *known* code on his monument. Who knows if he did or not."

"So, you're suggesting the letters in the Shugborough Inscription represent a series of numbers, then?" asked Professor Quimbey.

Emma conjectured, "It's possible. The inscription says O U O S V A V V, right?" Everyone nodded, so she kept going. "So, for example, using the English alphabet of 26 letters, O would equal 15, followed by the letter U which equals, um…" Emma counted on her fingers before resuming, "21, followed by the 15th letter again, S which is the 19th, V is… 22… A is 1, then we have two V's, so that's 22 and 22 again. So 15, 21, 15, 19, 22, 1, 22, 22. Then maybe we turn them into coordinates."

"I see what you're doing," said Logan. "We just have to figure out where to put the decimal point like we used to do."

"Or not. I don't know if it works the same way as it did before. And also, we still have to figure out where absolute zero is and which side is latitude and longitude, but yeah, that's kind of how it works. I remember learning in cryptography class that some suggested that the letters D and M, which bookend the Shugborough Inscription's eight-letter sequence, indicate longitude and latitude because, using Masonic code principles, you add one number value to each letter in a letter code, so D becomes E and M becomes N… E for East, N for North. That's just one theory, of course. Maybe the numbers are coordinates for a map, or maybe we simply add the numbers up… so 15 plus 21 plus 15 plus 19, equals, um, 70 East, by

22 plus 1 plus 22 plus 22, which equals 67. So 70 East by 67 North starting from some absolute zero point."

Logan quickly computed Emma's 70 E by 67 N on his phone. "Those coordinates of yours plot out virtually right over a town in Russia called Yar-Sale, in western Siberia."

"Now that's beginning to sound more like the end of the world to me, a place where a person can hide among the fire and ice, or at least, ice," commented Captain Evans.

Logan shook his head. "Yeah, but I did that calculation using the modern day absolute zero which, as Emma and I learned senior year, wasn't established until the International Meridian Conference in 1884."

"When was the Shepherd's Monument built?" asked Captain Evans.

Logan looked it up. "It says here that the Shepherd's Monument was built sometime between 1748 and 1763, commissioned by Admiral George Anson's brother, Thomas Anson, paid for by Admiral Anson himself, and fashioned by the Flemish sculptor Peter Scheemakers."

"Okay, so the modern day absolute zero doesn't work and those Yar-Sale coordinates aren't correct," said Captain Evans.

"Right," said Logan.

Emma piped up. "Guys, I was just giving you an example before. I don't know where absolute zero was in the 18th century when the Shepherd's Monument was built, and back then, the Old English alphabet didn't even have 26 letters. I was just shooting from the hip coming up with those 70 East by 67 North coordinates to make a point, but that's the kind of cryptological thinking we're going to need to figure this out."

"Then, I suggest you all keep trying to crack this," said General Covington. "We've got 1½ more hours before we get to Staffordshire. And Ms. James, for the record, I'd take your 'shooting from the hip' over someone else's hard research any day."

Chapter 18 – Shugborough Hall

They pulled up to Shugborough Hall, the stately ancestral home of Admiral Anson in Staffordshire, England, just as the church bells were ringing at 3 pm. The land around the sprawling estate, which Anson's family first acquired in 1624, was largely flat and impeccably landscaped. Trees, gardens, trails, creeks, a farm, walking paths, and water features could be found all around the property, in addition to a number of unique follies and structures including the Red Iron Bridge, The Chinese House, The Doric Temple, The Tower of the Winds, the Arch of Hadrian, and what they had come to see, The Shepherd's Monument. The estate property was a vast parkland filled with exhibits to see and things to do and, as a result, there were a lot of visitors touring the grounds.

Their shuttle and security entourage drove up a private road to the property's main building, a well-preserved three-story mansion with a porticoed entrance fronted by ten Ionic pillars that welcomed guests into a neo-classical structure encased in slate and sanded to resemble stone. They had to park in a lot far away from the building, with the area around the mansion reserved for foot traffic only.

As they got out of the shuttle to head over to the mansion, they saw costumed staff walking about the property, adding 18th century period charm to the experience of visiting Shugborough Hall. The National Trust, which assumed ownership of the estate in 1960, and the Shugborough Hall Foundation charged with preserving it, had taken great care to transport visitors of the sprawling estate back in time with period costumes and décor.

"This place is adorable," commented Emma.

"It looks like a walking history lesson," remarked Captain Evans.

"I hope so," Dr. Arenot replied.

"I think it's sweet," said Emma.

General Covington spoke to some of the CIA agents and told them to spread out and keep their distance, but to stay close enough to act on a moment's notice.

They continued to the main building, through the pillars and up the steps. There was a sign indicating that the Mansion Tea Room was to the left, and the Guest Information Center and Gift Shop, their destination, was straight ahead. In the Gift Shop, they were supposed to meet a staff member to escort them to the Shepherd's Monument.

Once they reached the Gift Shop, it was chock-full of Shugborough Hall-related paraphernalia like a gift shop at the end of an amusement park ride, crammed with merchandise. There were estate guidebooks, history books, photobooks, calendars, tea sets, coffee mugs, sweaters, sweatshirts, miniature monuments, trinkets and knick-knacks on every shelf in every corner of the gift shop. While they waited for their guide to arrive, Emma and Logan perused the merchandise. They didn't have to wait long.

"I apologize," said an older man wearing a gray suit, dressed out of character from the rest of the staff donning costumes. He surveyed their faces. "My name is Gerold Graves, Foundation Director here at the estate, and I am sorry for being late. I am here to show you to the Monument."

Emma, suddenly realizing that they were talking to the same Shugborough Hall Foundation Director who, several hours ago, had shot Mr. Garrison's Shugborough Inscription inquiries down, replied, "I thought you were profoundly skeptical of us cryptologists and treasure hunters wasting your time."

"I was until I received a call from the Lord Chamberlain's Office requesting that I personally oversee your visit. My dismissal of Mr. Garrison's inquiries earlier today was rude and uninformed."

"Thank you," said Emma, glad to hear that the queen's staff at Buckingham Palace had set him straight.

"Shall we shove off and have a look?" asked Mr. Graves. He turned around without waiting for an answer and led them out the gift shop and down the front steps of the mansion. He announced, "We shall follow the path of our Monuments Stroll. It's one of the many walking tours on our map. I know you are all here to see the Shepherd's Monument, but on the way there we will pass more gardens and The Doric Temple, as well as our famous arching Red Iron Footbridge, which spans the River Sow and leads to The Chinese House."

"He sounds like a tour guide without the costume," whispered Logan to Emma.

Unfortunately, Mr. Graves overheard him. "Long ago, I once was, dear boy, when I first began my employ here at the estate... when the period costumes were just a few years closer to the 18th century than they are now. Much closer than I'd like to admit."

Somewhat embarrassed, Logan apologized. "Mr. Graves, I'm sorry for—"

"Nonsense. I am quite certain I had that coming after how short I was with Mr. Garrison earlier today. I, too, once had a sense of humor, closer to when I was wearing the period costumes, of course."

They passed a decorative fountain tossing waterspouts to and fro, and soon after, the Greek-style Doric Temple set amongst a backdrop of trees in a grass lawn. The temple, which was not full-sized but rather, a smaller copy of one, had six Doric columns fronting the structure, capturing the ancient Greek architectural form. The Doric Temple, like The Chinese House, The Tower of the Winds, the Arch of Hadrian and The Lanthorn, all reflected memorable places around the world that Admiral Anson had once been. The renowned world-traveler had brought his favorite memories from abroad home, permanently memorializing smaller versions of them in the structures built around his property.

Once they passed the Doric Temple, they followed the walking path through more trees and gardens until they reached another wooded area that housed the Shepherd's Monument.

"Look at the size of that thing!" uttered Logan as they walked up to it. The Shepherd's Monument stood approximately 25' tall and 15' wide. The large and ornate work of stone and its three-dimensional marble relief of Poussin's *Shepherds of Arcadia*, was far bigger in real life than it appeared in pictures.

Knowing that they had come to make a go at solving the inscription, Mr. Graves remarked, "You know, some of the United Kingdom's greatest minds, like Charles Darwin and Charles Dickens, have tried to crack the code, and many others not named Charles. And maybe they have, but unfortunately, the answer to this mystery died with Admiral Anson in the 18th century. Did you know several places in your United States are named after him, including Anson County, North Carolina and Anson, Maine?"

"I didn't know that," responded Dr. Arenot, while everyone else shook their heads likewise.

As they approached the Shepherd's Monument, Mr. Graves spoke to several costumed staff members to have them usher their tour groups onward toward the Red Iron Footbridge over the River Sow. He advised his staff to let their groups know that they could come back to the Shepherd's Monument later if they wished. Within minutes, Logan, Emma and the professors had Anson's mystery to themselves, and a handful of CIA agents surrounded the area for protection and surveillance.

Logan, Emma and the professors studied the oversized portico and engraved relief of the *Shepherds of Arcadia*. They walked around the back of the monument, looking for little clues, etchings, or other markings, but experts had been doing that for centuries and found nothing.

"Any ideas, Mr. Graves, which of the wasteful Shugborough Inscription theories your Foundation deemed the most credible over the years?" asked Dr. Arenot.

"The Foundation ceased its decryption program years ago, but during its time, the Latin-initialism theories tended to be the best ones. Who are we to say which is correct?"

"What about all the treasure map theories?" asked Logan.

"Those tended to be the wildest of the bunch, inspired by Hollywood-driven plots and conspiracy theories ranging from a treasure map leading to buried Spanish galleon treasure, Captain Kidd's lost gold or Blackbeard's treasure hoard, to claims that Admiral Anson knew where the Holy Grail was or that he had discovered the lost city of Atlantis on one of his ocean voyages, you name it."

"*Any* theories that stood out?" prodded Emma.

"As I said before, our preferred solutions consisted of the Latin-initialism theories. All the rest, I am sure your team has seen before. Many make mathematical sense and point to an island or location because someone reverse engineered a formula designed to achieve that precise result, but who is right can only be confirmed once someone finds something at the end of the proverbial rainbow. And to date, so far as we know, no one has. Suffice it to say, none of the proposed solutions have inspired the Foundation to affix its stamp of approval on them." While Mr. Graves' attitude had certainly improved since he spoke to Mr. Garrison earlier in the day, his answers were no more helpful.

Wanting to get a closer look, Dr. Arenot approached the foot of the Shugborough Inscription plaque and lowered himself onto one knee to analyze the letter sequence as if he was back in Honduras studying hieroglyphics on the steps of the Copán Temple. Professor Quimbey knelt beside him to gaze at the inscription:

D   OUOSVAVV   M

General Covington stood back with Mr. Graves and Captain Evans while Emma and Logan moved closer to talk to the professors.

"I was really hoping when we got here that seeing it in person would help," said Emma

Logan replied, "It's helped a *little*. I can actually see the relief better now."

"Oh really... how?"

"Well, I can see what the kneeling shepherd is pointing at," replied Logan.

Professor Quimbey was confused. "We already know that. He's pointing at the word—"

"Arcadia, yeah, I know. When we saw the images online, maybe the resolution wasn't good enough, but now that we're here in person, it's pretty obvious he's pointing at the letter 'R' in the word Arcadia. Maybe the 'R' stands for something, like, another initialism thing."

"Like Rosicrucian?" speculated Emma.

"I don't know. You're the cryptologist, but maybe—"

"Or Rome!" blurted Emma, interrupting Logan. "That letter Abbé Louis Fouquet sent to King Louis XIV through his brother Nicolas Fouquet, described a meeting he had just had with Poussin in *Rome*, discussing a secret that 'nothing now on this earth can prove of better fortune nor equal!' I'm sorry, I totally interrupted you... what were you going to say?"

"Forget it. Nothing nearly as good as what you came up with," replied Logan.

"Come on, what?"

"Trust me, Rosicrucian or Rome makes a lot more sense than what I was thinking of."

"Logan!?"

"Okay, fine…" Slightly hesitant, Logan responded, "I was thinking the 'R' might signify something a little less fancy than Rosicrucian or Rome, like, 'right,' or 'reverse.' "

"Logan, you're brilliant!" declared Emma excitedly, much to Logan's surprise.

"I am?"

"You are!" Emma quickly pulled up on her phone an image of Poussin's original *Shepherds of Arcadia* painting to show them all:

She explained. "I had totally forgotten about this. The *Shepherds of Arcadia* engraved on the Shepherd's Monument is a mirror image copy of the painting by Poussin, meaning the one on the Shepherd's Monument is the *reverse* of it!"

Logan, Professor Quimbey and Dr. Arenot looked at the Shepherd's Monument's relief, and Emma was right. While the painting and the relief had obvious differences, the biggest one was that the relief of the *Shepherds of Arcadia* was a reverse version of the painting, with all the shepherds standing on the exact opposite side from the original painting. Indeed, the kneeling shepherd pointing at the letter 'R' was down on his right knee in the monument's relief instead of his left, and he was pointing to the letter 'R' with his left hand instead of his right like in the original painting:

"You're right, it's the reverse," said Professor Quimbey.

Emma explained, "So I was thinking, maybe we need to do the same thing with the inscription and 'reverse' it, so instead of the letters reading O U O S V A V V on the upper line, and D and M on the lower line, we flip them so they read, V V A V S O U O on the upper line, and M and D on the lower line."

"That still doesn't spell anything in English," said Logan.

"Well, it wouldn't if it's one of those codes Emma was talking about in the shuttle on the way here where the letters translate to numbers, or if it's another Latin-initialism thing," said Dr. Arenot.

"We can try a code and see what happens… I mean, that's kind of our thing, right?" replied Emma, addressing Logan.

"Yeah, it kinda is. So which code are you thinking?"

"Well, like I said in the shuttle, Admiral Anson was from a known influential Masonic family and the Freemasons used a code that converted letters into numbers based on where they appeared in the alphabet."

"Is that the one where A is 1, B is 2, Z is 26, etc.?"

"Yeah, but remember, in the 18th century, the Old English alphabet only had 24 letters, with no U or J. They used V for U and I for J. They began to phase those dual-purpose letters out when J and U were added in the late 18th century."

"It's a good thing you decided to major in cryptology," said Logan, thankful for her expertise. "How far do you think we'd have gotten if you'd done what your dad wanted and gone into pre-law?"

"Not far," Emma responded.

Logan chuckled and continued, "So, what do we do now, just assign each letter a number?"

"Exactly," replied Emma. "We have O U O S V A V V, which equals, with no J or U in the alphabet..." She started counting on her fingers for a moment, and then continued, "14, 20, 14, 18, 20, 1, 20, 20. And if we reverse it, it becomes 20, 20, 1, 20, 18, 14, 20, 14. I need to write these down before I forget." Emma quickly entered the numbers in a note on her phone.

Logan jumped in, "The D and M get reversed too, becoming M and D, and you said on the way here that Freemasons added one to each number, so M moves up 1 to N and D moves up 1 to E, right? So, North and East?"

"Yep. But remember, we also need to add one number to the *other* numbers, too." Emma looked at her phone again and continued, "So... 20, 20, 1, 20, 18, 14, 20, 14 become 21, 21, 2, 21, 19, 15, 21, 15."

"Okay, now what?" asked Logan.

"Well, a lot of the cartography theories split the inscription in half, using the first four letters for North, and the second four letters for East. So that would leave us with 21, 21, 2, 21 North by 19, 15, 21, 15 East."

Now, it was Logan's turn to take out his phone and work through the numbers on his notes app. "Okay, after combining them, they read 2121221 by 19152115. Now, we just have to figure out where to put the decimal point. The only way for 2121221 by 19152115 to end up with the same number of digits after the decimal point so that we know we're comparing apples to apples is for it to be .2121221 by 1.9152115, leaving 7 numbers after the decimal; or 2.121221 by 19.152115, leaving 6 digits after the decimal."

"What about 21.21221 x 191.52115, leaving 5 digits after the decimal?" asked Emma.

"That doesn't work because Admiral Anson, Britain's foremost naval navigator in the 18th century, would have definitely used the standardized latitudinal and longitudinal navigation system that existed at that time in history. And because, when plotting latitudes and longitudes, the most you can have for latitude is plus or minus 90 degrees, and the most you can have for longitude is plus or minus 180 degrees, in the 18th century, 191.52115 wasn't a viable longitude."

"Are you sure?" asked Professor Quimbey.

"Yeah. I remember reading about implementation of the more standardized coordinate plotting systems in modern times when Emma and I were researching the Copán numbers three years ago."

Emma was ready to try his first two suggestions. "Alright then, let's plot them out."

"Let me just quickly look up absolute zero in the 18th century," said Logan.

"Can't you just treat the Shepherd's Monument as absolute zero like you guys did with all the Copán coordinates, when you always treated the current location as absolute zero?" asked Professor Quimbey.

"We only did that before because the Vaniryans left behind coordinates at a time in history when there wasn't a standardized absolute zero, whereas that wasn't the case for Admiral Anson." Logan quickly looked it up on his phone and confirmed that Admiral Anson did have an agreed-upon absolute zero point to work with. "It says here that in the 18th century, the British Navy used an absolute zero point based on the British Royal Observatory in Greenwich Park, England. The observatory was commissioned in 1675 by King Charles II, and was established as the official point in 1714 by Queen Anne. We should use the Royal Observatory Greenwich point because that's what Admiral Anson would have done."

"He's right," said Dr. Arenot. Everyone else nodded.

"Okay. First, I'll try .2121221 by 1.9152115, then 2.121221 by 19.152115, using the Royal Observatory as absolute zero." Logan searched the location of the Royal Observatory Greenwich, and then, using the map app on his phone, inputted the coordinates, calculating their location using the Royal Observatory as absolute zero. When he was done, he read the results out loud: "Okay, so the first set of coordinates plots out over the North Sea, 50 miles off the coast of Great Britain. There's nothing there but water, and the second set puts us in the middle of farmland in Butowo, Poland. Neither of those places really sound like the 'end of the world' or places of 'fire and ice' to me."

Dr. Arenot had another idea. "Maybe we didn't reverse the coordinates correctly."

"I'm not sure what you mean," replied Logan.

Dr. Arenot tried to explain. "The original inscription says O U O S V A V V, which, in the Old English alphabet, equals, 14, 20, 14, 18, 20, 1, 20, 20, right?"

222

"Uh-huh," agreed Logan and Emma.

"Okay, and we reversed it so it became 20, 20, 1, 20, 18, 14, 20, 14, right?"

"Yeah," said Logan.

Dr. Arenot shook his head. "But that's not the mirror image reversal, is it?"

Emma and Logan looked at each other. He was right. Emma replied, "So, you're saying that the coordinates, instead of becoming 20, 20, 1, 20, 18, 14, 20, 14, that the mirror image reversal of those numbers should have been 02, 02, 1, 02, 81, 41, 02, 41?"

"Yes!" responded Dr. Arenot.

"And if we get rid of the unnecessary zeros, it becomes 2, 2, 1, 2, 81, 41, 2, 41," said Emma.

"Correct," said Dr. Arenot. "And using your Freemason code trick of adding one number, it becomes 3, 3, 2, 3, 82, 42, 3, 42. And if we separate it for North and East, it becomes 3, 3, 2, 3 by 82, 42, 3, 42."

"Those hardly look like coordinates anymore," commented Logan. "If it really is 3, 3, 2, 3 by 82, 42, 3, 42, the number of digits is way off. I don't see how that can work. To have the same number of digits after the decimal point so that we are comparing apples to apples, the best we can do is .3323 by 824.2342, and that's not a plottable coordinate around the globe."

"You know," said Emma, "what about the other trick I mentioned on the way here, the one used by the Rosicrucians who summated the number values? That's actually how they wrote their names. Sir Francis Bacon, who was known to be the Imperator of the Rosicrucians in the 17th century, used the cipher system to write his own name. He summated his name in numbers and came up with 100. That was his name among the Rosicrucians: 100."

"So, instead of coordinates, we're supposed to add the 3, 3, 2, 3 together and the 82, 42, 3, 42 together, to come up with an aggregate total for each?" asked Logan.

Emma replied, "I mean, if we're going all the way with this theory, then yes. 3 plus 3 plus 2 plus 3 equals 11, and 82 plus 42 plus 3 plus 52 equals 169. So that would be 11 North by 169 East."

"Interesting," remarked Professor Quimbey.

"Logan, do you want to try the coordinates again, using those numbers?" asked Dr. Arenot.

"Sure. Okay, so using the summation approach, we have to go 11 north of the Royal Observatory and 169 east of it." After doing the calculations, he reported back, "A little better. That puts us further east in the Penzhinsky District of Kamchatka Krai, more than a hundred miles inland, in the middle of some mountains in northeast of Russia."

"Hmm, it's definitely better, but I'm still not sure how Admiral Anson could have sailed there since it's in the middle of the mountains," said Dr. Arenot.

"Well, if Poussin's *Shepherds of Arcadia* holds the secret, maybe there's another clue in there," alluded Professor Quimbey.

"What do you mean?" asked Emma.

"I liked Logan's theory earlier that the kneeling shepherd is purposely pointing at the letter 'R,' but perhaps the letter isn't trying to tell us to reverse the numbers. I was thinking this before, but the relief itself is already a mirror image reversal of Poussin's original *Shepherds of Arcadia* painting and, by its very reversal, already suggests what to do with the numbers, which is to flip them as we've done. The 'R' standing for 'reverse' is redundant of what the *Shepherds* relief already tells us to do, no?" She paused waiting for a response, then posed another question. "Why have two clues both telling us to do the same thing? It's repetitive."

"I suppose," agreed Emma. "So what are you thinking?"

"That the shepherd isn't pointing at the letter 'R' to tell us to reverse the numbers, but rather, to do something else."

"Rosicrucian? Rome?" threw out Emma, recycling her ideas from earlier.

Professor Quimbey shook her head. "No, I was thinking Logan's *other* guess from before might be the right one."

"You mean the word 'right'?" asked Logan, who had theorized before that the letter 'R' stood for either 'reverse' or 'right.'

"Yes," confirmed Professor Quimbey. "I think it's possible that the 'R' is telling us we need to go right to come up with the final coordinates."

"Go right, but how far?" asked Emma.

The professor responded, "I'm hopping completely off the rails here, but look up at the monument." They all looked up, and the professor continued. "There's a Roman numeral embedded in the middle of the *Shepherds of Arcadia* relief, do you see it? The shepherds' staffs appear to form the Roman-numeral VI."

"You're totally right!" exclaimed Logan, noticing it for the first time.

"So, you think the shepherd is pointing at the letter 'R' to tell us to go 'right' by 6?" asked Emma.

"It's an off the rails theory, but as good as any."

"It's worth a shot," said Logan, ready to try it. "Alright, let me run the coordinates again doing what I did before, using the Royal Observatory as absolute zero, and adding six more degrees to the right, *i.e., to the east* this time." Logan calculated 11 degrees north of the Royal Observatory and *175* degrees east of it by adding 6 to the previous longitude summation of 169, and said, "Guys, that plots out over a village called Khatyrka on the east coast of Russia in northeast Siberia." He showed them on the map:

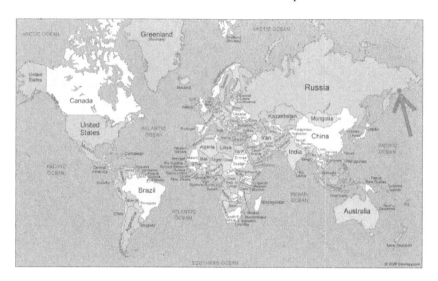

"I've never heard of Khatyrka before, but that definitely looks closer to the end of the world to me... cold and icy, too," remarked Emma.

Logan clicked on it for more information. "It says Khatyrka is a fishing village in the Anadyrsky District of Chukotka Autonomous Okrug, Russia, located on the shore of the Bering Sea, just below the Arctic Circle. The Chukotka region is the easternmost federal subject in Russia with a population of 50,526."

"Definitely reachable by Admiral Anson's boat," opined Dr. Arenot.

"Wow, you guys aren't going to believe this!" blurted Logan.

Emma smacked his shoulder. "What? Spill it!"

Logan read what he was looking at aloud: " 'Khatyrka is one of the oldest settlements in the Anadyrsky District, founded around 1756. The geography of the Anadyrsky District was formed by long lava flows which disrupted the valley of the Monni River. Later, a volcanic cone formed, experiencing explosive activity and eventually extruding a long lava flow. The volcano was considered to have been active during the 14th through 18th centuries.' *And...* 'Khatyrka sits at the northern edge of the Kamchatka Peninsula, which is designated as a UNESCO World Heritage site because it is home to 178 volcanoes, one of the most active volcanic areas in the world.' UNESCO says that 'Despite its cold and often frozen terrain, it might just be one of the hottest places on Earth, geologically speaking!' "

Emma started working things out in her head. A coastal village founded in 1756 at the northeastern tip of Eurasia, where the near-arctic terrain consisted of ice and snow, surrounded by volcanoes on the Pacific Ocean's volcanic Ring of Fire. Emma recited Isa's note in her mind: *'To the end of the world I will sail this time, far away from what I know. I hope that will be far enough, for Arcadia is as far as the admiral can take me. There, I will wait for you, hiding among the fire and ice.'* Khatyrka, located on the other side of Russia at the top of the world near the Arctic Circle, certainly seemed about as far away as Admiral Anson could have taken her.

"When was the Shepherd's Monument built again?" asked Dr. Arenot.

Logan, who had looked it up earlier in the shuttle, replied, "Sometime between 1748 and 1763."

Emma smiled. "1756, the year Khatyrka was founded, is smack in the middle of that date range!" Emma cupped her hand around Isa's heart-shaped pendant necklace that the queen had given her at Buckingham, which now hung around her own neck, and squeezed it. She felt like they were on the verge of finally finding Isa. "Guys, this is it! She's in Khatyrka. I'm sure of it!"

"Someone else has to have come up with this inscription solution before, right?" asked Logan.

"Maybe," replied Emma, "but how many of them traveled to Siberia looking for Isa rather than buried treasure?"

"Probably none," replied Logan.

"Exactly!" exclaimed Emma. "Let's talk to Covington to see if he can get us to Khatyrka."

"After what happened in the Chersky Mountains on your last mission, and with Prime Minister Menputyn supposedly not cooperating with the United States anymore, it's not going to be easy getting us into Russia," said Dr. Arenot. "They do not want Menputyn to get a hold of Isa. They're worried about what he might do and what his intentions are."

"Not to mention Menputyn took us hostage and threatened to kill us the last time we dealt with him," Logan reminded everyone, referring to his and Dr. Arenot's run-in with Viktor Menputyn's men on their way to Machu Picchu.

"Yeah, I know, but we don't have a choice... we have to go," replied Emma.

"I guess that's true," conceded Dr. Arenot.

They all turned around and got General Covington's attention.

ΔΔΔΔΔΔΔΔΔΔΔΔ

Emma, Logan and the professors stood impatiently in the Shugborough Hall parking lot outside the shuttle while General Covington, who was inside, spoke privately with the president, General Nemond and NSA Director Orson about a mission into Russia. Captain Evans stayed near while several CIA agents guarded the shuttle. It seemed like forever until the general's door popped open and he told them all to get back in the shuttle, which they did.

"So, what'd they say?" asked Emma.

Very calmly, the general replied, "They're going to let you go."

"Awesome! So what's the plan?" asked Logan.

"Khatyrka is a fishing and hunting village that exports fish and game product and imports its necessities through a low-yield, minimum security harbor on the Bering Sea. The CIA's going to sneak you in through an import export barge that serves Khatyrka's harbor. It'll be a joint CIA-NSA operation."

"Sounds like a covert spy op," said Professor Quimbey.

"It is, and it's dangerous, which is why we're only letting Emma and Logan go."

"What?" blurted Dr. Arenot.

"I'm sorry Jonas, Jill, but any more than that, along with all the agents who'll have to accompany them, compromises the mission."

"I'm not going anywhere without Captain Evans," insisted Emma, who had grown to trust Evans above anyone else.

The feeling was mutual. "I'm going with her," stated Captain Evans, leaving no debate about it.

"That can be arranged," replied General Covington.

"Why can't we just use a portal to get into Khatyrka?" wondered Logan, ready to use the Vaniryan technology to their advantage.

"Because Pegasus West and the only working *p*RAMZA are all tied up on Operation 17 Tauri, and we're pretty sure the Russians can track the use of zeutyron signals now. They'll know if we use z-particles to portal into their country. It's a last resort option only, especially after what went wrong in Chersky. Emma, Logan, I don't have to tell you, but the mission is risky. There are a lot of unknowns. We plan to deploy the U.S.S. Ronald Reagan, which is currently stationed at Yokosuka Naval Base in Japan, north into the Bering Sea to Attu Naval Station, but that's as close as we can get without encroaching Russian waters. We can't afford to start another international incident, with things already tense enough with the Russians."

"Where's Attu Naval Station?" inquired Logan.

"Attu Island, it's the westernmost point of Alaska, part of the Aleutian Island chain extending from the Alaskan Peninsula. We can park the U.S.S. Reagan just north of there. The island is mostly just a historical landmark now. We closed Attu Naval Station over a decade ago, but it still gets strategic use from time to time, and if we deploy the Reagan north of there, we can get within a few hundred miles of Khatyrka. But make no mistake about it, those fighter jets of ours and other assets will still be several hundred miles away. If you guys find more than you're bargaining for in Khatyrka, you're on your own for at least 15 minutes until we can extract you."

"What do you expect us to find there other than Isa?" wondered Emma. "Russian resistance? If Menputyn doesn't know we're there, it shouldn't be a problem."

"We don't know," replied the general. "And with the leak issue—"

"Are you worried Supay could be waiting for us there?" Emma asked.

"Yes, that too, but truthfully, no one knows what will happen if you find her, Ms. James. There are a lot of theories about what could happen and a concern that finding Isa might trigger the next set of events in Supay's timeline, let's just put it that way."

"Like what?" asked Logan.

"I don't want to speculate, okay?" requested the general, who wasn't prepared to go into all the doomsday scenarios that the Pegasus team had come up with that finding Isa might trigger. "Like I said, the mission is dangerous. Are you two sure you still want to go?"

"When do we leave?" replied Logan.

Chapter 19 – 1598

Isa sat outdoors on a stone bench working on her manuscript in the middle of Corte Del Milion. People milled about while children laughed, played and ran around. Long ago, she was one of those children, but over time, she had grown up, or at least, simulated doing so to fit in among the Venetians. She pushed her elegant silver hair out of her middle-aged face, which was one of many she had worn over the last 350 years, as she changed her appearance whenever it was necessary to start over. For the last 50 years, however, her appearance had once again resembled Emma's, albeit an older version of her, since there was no one currently living in Venice who was alive the last time Isa borrowed Emma's smile.

Isa had lived in Vincente Defuseh's, and then Niccolò and Marco Polo's old courtyard estate since arriving in Venice with Annika and Hallveig. Where once she felt trapped in her Vaniryan tree home, desperate to see the world, Isa felt no such frustration in Corte Del Milion. While she missed Tassa and her extended family in Jaannos, after running from danger nearly her entire life, Isa finally felt like she had found a home. And she was happy.

"Mother," said a young man in his thirties. He approached her, sat down and kissed her forehead. "Why do you still work on your manuscript? I thought it was finished."

"I was just updating it."

"What did you add this time?"

"A few new pages. One on botanicals. See..." Isa turned the manuscript to show Antonio her latest page displaying colorful hand-drawn illustrations of plants, roots, and other imagery along with text written in Isa's beautiful Vaniryan lettering:

(Credit: Voynich Manuscript, Beinecke Rare Book & Manuscript Library, Yale University)

Antonio read it and remarked, "Your Vaniryan handwriting has always been better than your Italian."

"Yes, Tassa taught me well. And you would do well to practice yours, too, before you forget it."

Antonio chuckled. "And what about this page here? I have not seen this one before, either," he said, pointing to a loose page showing a tree with extensive lush branches, overly long tree roots and a large opening near its base.

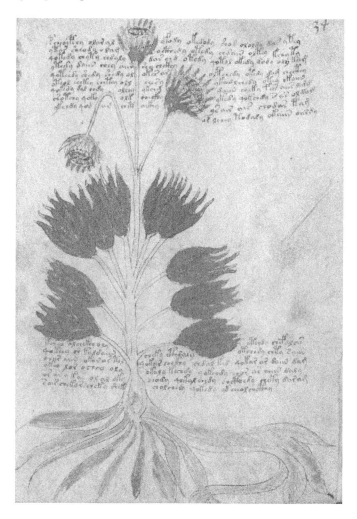

(Credit: Voynich Manuscript, Beinecke Rare Book & Manuscript Library, Yale University)

"That is a Tree Gate. Although the trees take many forms, this one was always my favorite," replied Isa.

"Are those the trees on Vanirya that you said carried people to different places?"

"Yes, the doorways to the forest. I have studied the trees on Earth and am convinced they also have the energy to do this, just like on Vanirya. They all live and breathe the same energy. We all do. I have described here how I think it can work but I do not yet know how to teach the trees of this world the way."

"If there's anyone who can figure it out, I am sure it is you, mother. And what about this last page... it looks like four people sitting inside a circle surrounded by rings of words. I don't remember this one. Is it also new?"

(Credit: Voynich Manuscript, Beinecke Rare Book & Manuscript Library, Yale University)

"Yes. My illustration is poor, but it shows my first human family here on Earth—Snorri, Hallveig, Annika and myself—soaking together under the stars in Snorri's outdoor bath in Reykholt, discussing the legends of the heavens. I wrote the names of his favorite myths in the outer rings. He really loved that circular bath, almost as much as he loved his *Eddas*, maybe more. I miss him. I hope the golden halls of Valhalla are feeding him well, and rewarding Hallveig with much-deserved rest."

"What became of Hallveig after you came to Venice?" inquired Antonio.

Isa thought back three centuries. "After news of Snorri's murder reached us, she was devastated at first, consumed by thoughts of revenge, but she was strong, stronger than any woman I've ever met. So, she resolved to take care of me with Annika. After a few years, Vincente asked Hallveig's hand in marriage and she obliged. That's how we all became part of the Defuseh family. And we were a family, at least, until the charming Niccolò Polo wooed Annika away from us. He was smitten with her from the moment he laid eyes on her at the Rialto market, just like you were with Mariella."

"That, I was," reminisced Antonio with a warm grin.

"Annika resisted Niccolò's charm for a while, but eventually, his cunning spirit and love won her over. They married next door in the San Giovanni Crisostomo church, and at her request, Vincente gave her hand away in marriage. Niccolò and Annika actually had their wedding celebration right here in this very courtyard. The festivities were quite lavish, guests came from all the districts, and Cannaregio's canals were packed with boats hull to hull, so much so that one could not leave the wedding celebration early even if they wanted to. Annika always used to say that was human history's first traffic jam. I never really understood what she meant by that, but she always remembered her wedding fondly that way."

"She died young, right, like Mariella?"

"Yes. A tragedy the cruel diseases of this world. When Niccolò was away on a long journey east, Annika took ill and passed away while their son, Marco, was young, leaving Hallveig and I to raise him, much like you've had to do with—"

"Nonna Isabella!" screamed a tiny voice running up from behind her grandmother. The 8-year-old girl squeezed Isa tightly.

"Anna, you get prettier and stronger by the day!" proclaimed Isa while Anna bear-hugged her.

"Did you finish your chores?" Antonio asked.

Somewhat evasively, Anna responded, "Ah, yes…"

Antonio could tell she wasn't being completely truthful. "Anna…"

In the face of modest pressure, Anna confessed. "Almost, papa. Please, can I go play with my friends in the canal? I promise to finish them when I get back."

"Not before—"

"Oh Antonio, let her play with her friends. Since Mariella died, she has handled more than her fair share of the load, more than most children her age. You push her too hard."

Although annoyed at his mother for undermining his parenting right in front of Anna, he loved his mother too much to hold it against her, and in this instance, he knew she was right. "I just want her to be ready for what awaits her."

"It is her time to be young. Her mother's death has forced her to grow up too fast. I missed my childhood for the same reason. I don't want that for her."

Antonio looked at Anna, considering her request. Anna, feeling the momentum shifting in her favor, asked, "So can I go?" Her eyes were wide with hope.

Momentarily lost in her gaze, Antonio eventually responded, "You remind me so much of your grandfather. Yes, you can go!"

"Thank you!" shouted Anna excitedly, throwing herself into her father's arms before bolting toward the canals.

As she was running off, Isa commented, "And I was going to say she looks more like her mother every day."

"I miss them both so much," said Antonio, referring to his late wife, Mariella, and Isa's late husband, Angelo.

"Me too," replied Isa. "Every day."

"Lady Isabella, there are some people here to see you," shouted Stefano, one of the courtyard's Keepers, interrupting their conversation as he approached. The Keepers doubled as caretakers and guardians of the courtyard estate, along with other estates in the Cannaregio and surrounding Venetian districts.

"Who?" wondered Isa.

"About a half dozen knights, my lady."

"Knights?"

"They appear to be."

"A half dozen?" asked Isa, surprised.

"Yes, my lady."

"Is it the Knights Hospitallers again? Tell them we have no sick or wounded today."

Stefano shook his head. "No, my lady, I do not think so."

"How do you know they are knights, Stefano?" questioned Antonio.

"I do not know for certain, but they arrived carrying flags with a coat of arms on them and they are wearing armor."

"What does their coat look like?" asked Isa.

"A right-leaning cross in a red circle. I do not know it. They have called for you."

"Mother, what do they want?"

"I don't know."

"I will go out to meet them," offered Antonio.

"No, I will go," insisted Isa. "Manners are always to be true and first."

"Then I will go with you," Antonio said.

Isa grinned appreciatively at her son's over-protectiveness. "Of course. But you have no reason to worry—"

"Lady Isabella!" yelled a voice. Isa spun around and saw several armor-clad men letting themselves into the courtyard.

Isa stood up and walked toward them with Antonio and Stefano. Isa and Antonio saw the right-leaning cross in a red circle insignia that Stefano had mentioned and did not recognize it, either:

Isa was irritated by the intrusion. "It is rude to enter another's home without invitation."

"Are we intruding? I had not noticed," said the man nearest them.

"Who are you?" demanded Isa.

"I am Lord Phillipe Nemond, and it is I who has come to extend an invitation to *you*, Lady Isabella."

"Is that so? Of what invitation do you speak?"

"An invitation to come with us." The other men closed in behind Lord Nemond.

"Go with you, where?" questioned Isa, not prepared to accept but curious. At this point, others living and working in the Milione courtyard were gaining interest in the conversation and gathering around. This included the property's Keepers, friends, family, and Anna, who had come back to see who her father and grandmother were talking to. After all, it was not often knights visited the Corte Del Milion and she, like everyone else, was curious.

"France," responded Lord Nemond.

Isa laughed out loud, stunned. She had expected him to say a place nearby, maybe central or southern Italy, but not somewhere so far away.

"France?!" exclaimed Antonio. "Are you mad?"

Lord Nemond eyed Antonio with annoyance, putting his hand on the hilt of his sword.

Antonio, be careful, he brings danger here, said Isa to Antonio telepathically.

"Where in France?" inquired Isa, playing along.

"I am not prepared to tell you yet."

"You ask me to go with you, but you keep secrets," criticized Isa.

"Some secrets are better off not shared aloud, don't you agree, Lady Isabella?" responded Nemond.

Lord Nemond's response threw her. Did he know her secret? For three centuries she had been safe in Polo's courtyard, having escaped the never-ending pursuit of the Hunt on Vanirya and the power mongering claws of King Hákon IV of Norway, but for the first time since arriving in Venice, she wondered whether the time to run again had arrived. With a family here in Venice, it was not so easy to do anymore. Isa always worried that having a family would make her and them vulnerable, and suddenly, her worst fear was coming true. Isa responded, "Why would I want to go to France with you when my home is here and I have no business in France?"

"That is where the Grand Master lives, and he would like to speak with you."

"The Grand Master of what?" questioned Antonio.

"The Order of Christ's Templars."

"I thought all the Templar orders were dismantled, disbanded, or arrested," countered Antonio.

With a sinister sneer, Lord Nemond replied, "Only the dishonorable ones."

"Whatever your intentions, honorable or not, my mother is not going anywhere with you without a just reason," stated Antonio.

"Lady Isabella surely already knows," responded Nemond.

Isa suspected what he was implying. Worried, she replied, "Lord Nemond, I suggest that you have your Grand Master come visit me. I have no reason to leave my home, especially for a journey as far as you propose. I am sorry, but you have come a long way for nothing."

"There is always something."

Isa could perceive from Lord Nemond's thoughts that he did not intend to leave without her. Still, she tried to stall. "Not today, but I would be happy to receive a formal invitation from your Master so I can make proper arrangements."

"The Grand Master does not stand on ceremony. His invitation is not to be refused. I only wish to save you from the inevitability of heartbreak," cautioned Lord Nemond. "We do not wish anyone to get hurt."

Antonio stepped in front of his mother. "Was that a threat?"

"No, young man. I offered my words sincerely, and for everyone's sake, I hope your mother will reconsider."

"You need not concern yourself with our well-being," uttered Stefano. His fellow Keepers stepped up beside him with swords in hand, outnumbering the Christ's Templars eight to three.

"I think you should leave," insisted Isa.

"As you wish, Lady Isabella. We will return." Lord Nemond and his cohorts turned around and departed.

"Mother, what was that all about?" asked Antonio above the worried whispers of others. Anna ran up to her father and clutched his leg, frightened.

"Antonio, assemble all the Keepers from Cannaregio and any of the surrounding districts that you can. Hurry!" urged Isa.

"Mother, they have gone for now. Need we act so hastily until we know what they wanted?"

Isa shook her head. "Antonio, we do not have time to waste. Their withdrawal was temporary. They want me. My presence here endangers you all."

Stefano replied, "Lady Isabella, rest assured, my men will protect you."

"No, the time has come," replied Isa.

"The time for what has come?" asked Stefano, confused. "Why do they want you, Lady Isabella?"

"Stefano, I am afraid it is an old family quarrel, and the Christ's Templars have come to resurrect it, it would seem. You are all in danger as long as I remain here. I am sorry."

Stefano had heard enough. "Lady Isabella, Antonio and I will immediately gather all the Keepers and—" *THUD*. Stefano stopped mid-sentence. He collapsed to his knees, blood flowed out of his mouth, and he fell forward, face down. There was a large crossbow bolt sticking out of his back.

A high pitch scream cried out from the crowd as two dozen Christ's Templars, far more than the initial half dozen originally estimated, stormed into the courtyard carrying torches, crossbows and swords. Corte del Milion was under siege. The intruders began firing off crossbow bolts and attacking with swords. The Keepers quickly rallied around Isa, Antonio and Anna to protect them.

Everyone started to scatter, trying to take cover from the attack, but the Christ's Templars began setting buildings on fire by lighting oil flasks and throwing them inside. Their plan was to force those hiding indoors to run out and to prevent Isa and anyone else from running in. And sure enough, as the fire grew, those hiding inside were forced outside due to the smoke and flames.

"Antonio, take Anna away from here!" screamed Isa, leaning down to pick up Stefano's sword. Antonio grabbed Anna's hand and ran for an exit. Meanwhile, Isa swung at the intruders trying to grab her. The Keepers valiantly fought to protect her, but the Christ's Templars' skills with a blade and use of crossbows were overwhelming them. One after another, the Keepers fell, while buildings continued to burn and innocent people continued to die.

Isa could not simply fire her blue Vaniryan energy at the Christ's Templars. Her family and friends were everywhere, some fighting the enemy, some fleeing on foot, but all intermixed with the intruders. It was perfect chaos, as if the enemy had purposely attacked from all sides to prevent Isa from having a single target to focus on. A discharge of her potent energy had just as much chance of hitting friend as foe, not to mention the fact that she had not used her Vaniryan powers publicly in over three centuries. Every time she did, trouble always followed. Not doing so had helped to keep her and her family safe for hundreds of years, but if ever there was a time to use them again…

Isa heard a familiar scream. It was Anna. Isa looked over and saw Antonio crumpled on the ground with a crossbow bolt in his chest and Anna crying on top of him. Seconds later, a Christ's Templar hoisted Anna off her father's dying body, yanking her up by the hair. It was Lord Nemond. He pulled Anna into his chest and put a sword to her throat.

"No!" screamed Isa. "Stop!" She threw down her weapon and put her hands up.

Lord Nemond shouted to his men to cease the slaughter and put everyone face down on the ground for execution in case Isa retracted her cooperation. In short order, everyone Isa knew and loved was lying on their stomachs while the surrounding buildings remained ablaze.

"I only wished to save you from heartbreak, Lady Isabella. I did not wish to hurt anyone," said Nemond.

Isa was too enraged to allow tears to flow for her dying son just yet. "You lie! You came here to harm."

"If you mean I did not expect you to go quietly, you are correct. And if you come with us now, no one else needs to suffer, you have my word."

"The word of a murderer."

"But my word, nonetheless. The choice is yours." Lord Nemond stuck the point of his blade deeper into Anna's neck, hurting the girl.

Isa nodded that she was ready to cooperate. She slowly approached Antonio's body which was lying in a pool of his own blood. She got onto her knees to speak to him. "I am so sorry, Antonio, this is all my fault." Now, tears openly flowed down her cheeks.

"Mother, do not blame yourself... is Anna safe?" asked Antonio weakly while the color drained from his face.

Isa looked up at Anna who was still in Lord Nemond's grasp and replied, "Yes, she is safe now."

"Good... mother... I am sorry I could not protect you," whispered Antonio in a voice so faint that only Isa could hear him.

Isa stroked his face. "You have always protected me. I love you."

Antonio used what little strength he had left to whisper, "Mother, please protect Anna... I love—" Antonio stopped talking. He was dead.

Isa cried over her son's dead body and Lord Nemond released Anna to join her, shoving her forward. He motioned for numerous Christ's Templars to fix their crossbows on the little girl in case Isa chose to recant her coerced cooperation. Anna fell on top of her father, devastated and weeping.

Isa stood up and glared into Lord Nemond's eyes. Despite his outward persona of intimidation, Isa saw fear in them. She knew he was afraid of her. Isa ended the stalemate first. "You call yourselves an order of Christ but the Knights Templars would never—"

"The Knights Templars were weak! That is why they were wiped out!" shouted Lord Nemond.

"And you think you are strong because you can kill innocent people? The Knights Templars would never have harmed the innocent the way you have."

Lord Nemond retorted, "If only you could ask those who did not accept Christianity during the Crusades how the crusaders of Christ treated them."

"You are no crusaders of Christ, nor are you knights or Christians."

"May I remind you, Lady Isabella, that neither are you. Do you want to tell all the people lying face down on the ground awaiting execution, who you really are and what it is you secretly do in the caves in the mountains?" Isa did not speak. "I did not think so. You will go with us now, or the girl and everyone else in this courtyard dies."

Isa looked around at her friends and family lying flat on their stomachs with swords at their backs, praying for the standoff to end, fearful for their lives. So many more were already sprawled out on the ground, dead. She looked at Anna who was on top of her father, sobbing. She wasn't about to fail her. She was going to protect her just as Antonio asked, and to do that, she had only one choice…

"I will go with you to meet your Master," Isa informed Lord Nemond, wanting to end the bloodshed. She knew that if she remained at Corte Del Milion, everyone would be in danger, including Anna.

Lord Nemond seemed pleased. "A wise decision. It would have been a shame for more to suffer because of your selfish indulgence."

"Nonna, no!" screamed Anna, running up to her grandmother.

"It is going to be alright, Anna. You are safe now," replied Isa, trying to console her.

"Please don't go!"

"Anna, it is the only way to protect you."

"But I am afraid to be alone."

Anna's words crushed Isa, who long ago had uttered precisely those same words to Snorri and Hallveig. Their response back then comforted her, and so, Isa offered Anna a similar one. "Anna, wherever I am in this world, I will always be with you, watching over you. You will never truly be alone until, hopefully, we can be reunited again." Isa hugged Anna snugly and telepathically conveyed a message to her that no one else could hear: *Until then, you must go to the Grimanis. They will take care of you.* Isa was referring to the Grimanis, a prominent Venetian family that had grown close to the Polo and Defuseh families over the years.

Okay Nonna, replied Anna.

There was one more thing Isa needed Anna to do, something Isa had been contemplating for a long time. *Anna, I need something else of you... do not use the last name Defuseh anymore. It is not safe. Do you understand me?*

Yes Nonna, but what should I use?

From now on, you shall go by Anna Rossi, responded Isa while the two continued to embrace.

Rossi?

Yes, Rossi, the reverse of my given Vaniryan name. This is very important. This name is how I will find you again, if I can. Can you do this for me?

Yes, Nonna. I love you.

I love you, too, sweet Anna. You are stronger than you know…

Nemond motioned with his hand for his men to pry Anna away from Isa. They started pulling Anna off but she refused to let go.

"No! No! No!" cried Anna.

Nemond's men eventually used extra force to pry Anna away from Isa, and afterwards, they threw Anna to the ground.

"You did not need to do that. She is just a little girl," Isa said to Lord Nemond.

Lord Nemond, indifferent to Isa's concerns, replied, "Even little girls can be dangerous, don't you think?"

Nemond motioned to his men and they pulled Isa's arms behind her back and bound her wrists together. They next placed a hood over her head and tied it tightly around her neck, cutting into her skin.

"Let's go!" ordered Lord Nemond, and the Order of Christ's Templars started marching off.

"Nonna!" screamed Anna as they left the courtyard.

It was the last time Isa ever heard her granddaughter's voice again.

Chapter 20 – Revenge

More than a week of travel on horseback had passed since the Order of Christ's Templars attacked Isa's home in Venice, and just as long since she saw daylight. She couldn't see where they were going because Lord Nemond's men were under orders not to remove her hood, although they had cut a small slit into it so she could breathe. Other than that, she was trapped with her thoughts in darkness, reliving the horror from the siege over and over again. The pain had yet to subside. Much like the heartache she had suffered long ago from losing her parents to Supay, Isa doubted it ever would.

Isa had seen as much cruelty on Earth as she ever did on Vanirya, and just as much death. It seemed that wherever she went, no matter how many worlds or homes she fled to, suffering and pain followed her. She couldn't escape it. Perhaps it was just part of being Vaniryan and human, and after living in borrowed human skin for 350 years, she considered herself equal parts both. She could not distinguish her humanity from her Vaniryan identity anymore. She hoped in some ways that made her a better version of both, not that that helped her now.

Her body, secured by rope to her horse's neck with her hands still tied behind her back, ached due to the constant pounding and bouncing from her horse's gait. At one point, Lord Nemond's men had referred to the horse carrying her as Belle. Isa could hardly blame Belle for her body aches. Belle seemed like a sweet mare and Isa spoke to her often to let her know that she didn't hold her captors' crimes against her.

During the journey to France, Isa listened to the Christ's Templars' whispers and thoughts about the woman they were carrying back to their Grand Master. Some were afraid of her, but most didn't believe she was some all-powerful being. After all, they wondered, if she was, why didn't she stop the attack in Venice and help her people? Wouldn't she have done so if she possessed the divine power that the Grand Master had promised? Lady Isabella certainly didn't appear powerful, and the ease by which they captured her had them doubting she was capable of helping the Order of Christ's Templars take over the world.

While Isa listened to the thoughts of the fanatics who followed a delusional Grand Master, she wondered why power spoke so strongly to the ill-minded rather than those who would use it for good. Thinking about Supay, King Hákon of Norway, and even the Grand Master who she was off to meet, she realized that this problem was not uniquely Vaniryan or human, it was a problem born of evil that infected all species and worlds.

Lord Nemond and his men stopped to rest in the early evening. Two of his men took Isa off Belle, put her on the ground and secured her to a tree for the night.

"Are you hungry?" asked a voice. It was Lord Nemond.

"No," responded Isa. "Extending me kindness now cannot erase what you did."

"Neither can starving yourself."

"I will make that choice for myself."

Nemond chuckled at her stubbornness. "I will have my men bring you some food in case you change your mind."

"Where are we?" asked Isa.

"We are in the south of France, a beautiful countryside, nothing around but rolling hills. I grew up in a countryside like this. It is a shame you cannot see it. Perhaps you would think differently of France."

"Remove my hood and we can gaze upon its beauty together."

"If I trusted you, perhaps I would."

"What do you expect me to do?"

"I do not know what you are capable of, Lady Isabella, only what the stories say, but that is not for me to decide."

Isa laughed at Lord Nemond. "What kind of man does not make decisions for himself?"

"The Grand Master knows much. I have learned to trust his wisdom."

"You sound like a faithful pet, not a man," Isa replied, ridiculing him.

"You will see it differently tomorrow when you meet him."

"I doubt that. So, tell me, how did you find me?" Isa asked Lord Nemond.

"You forget that Normandy in northern France and the Norman Kings descended from Norse Vikings and the region has remained close to Norway ever since," Lord Nemond responded.

"And let me guess, the Nemond family clan descends from the Norman Kings?"

"No, but the House of Nemond, like the Grand Master, has strong roots in northern France. Did you really think your secret would remain buried in Reykholt forever?"

Suddenly, it was clear to Isa that she had never really escaped King Hákon IV. His obsession with her power and finding her had outlived even him, spilling into France and the Order of Christ's Templars.

Someone approached. "Lord Nemond, I bring the lady's food."

"Thank you, Garen. I will take it." Not long after, Nemond said, "I have food for you. Please, open your mouth, you are not helping anyone by refusing food."

"Was it your Master's orders to make sure that I am well fed so that my powers are plump and powerful?" mocked Isa.

Lord Nemond sneered and lifted Isa's hood to her nose so he could put bread into her mouth. Isa bit his finger and spit out the bread.

"Ah!" shouted Nemond. He pulled his hand away in pain, angry. "Suit yourself, Lady Isabella. You will learn to cooperate when we get there, I assure you."

"And I assure you that you are wrong," replied Isa.

"Then, you will learn what torture feels like, starting with tonight." Nemond looked around and ordered his men, "Put her back on the horse. She can spend all night sitting upright on horseback. Perhaps that will teach her some respect."

Lord Nemond got up and walked away, and his men did as asked, hoisting Isa back up onto Belle. Once Nemond's men secured her, Isa realized time was running out. What awaited her in France, including torture, frightened her. If she was going to escape without others seeing her use her powers, which would only lead to more rumors and another cycle of people hunting her down, this was her chance.

Lord Nemond had said that they had made camp in the French countryside, with no one around except for the Christ's Templars who planned to use her Vaniryan abilities to kill more people. She had planned to kill the Grand Master when they got to their destination, but she could no longer wait. It was too risky. She had to escape now, and to do that, she had to do what she abhorred: kill her captors.

She was not a killer. She was a peaceful Vaniryan girl hiding in human skin, wanting nothing more than to make a life for herself. The idea that her power enabled her to kill another living being horrified her, which was, in part, why she believed she hesitated during the siege at Corte Del Milion. She was afraid of what she could do and what it might turn her into. She did not want to kill, not for the Christ's Templars, not for anyone, but Nemond and his men had murdered Antonio and others in Venice; and so, they deserved what she was about to do...

"I am sorry, girl. Please forgive me," Isa said to Belle, and Belle neighed back. "That's right, girl. These men will not win. Evil never wins. Soon, you will be free to roam in the heavens."

Isa closed her eyes and in an instantaneous display of raw power which she had only practiced in mountain caves, she released a blast of blue energy from her hands that radiated outward hundreds of feet in every direction. Her energy struck all who were lying, sitting and standing in the camp. There was no escaping it. Lord Nemond, his men, and regrettably, their horses too, including Belle, all fell to the ground, dead. Because Isa was tied to Belle, when the mare collapsed, she landed partially on top of Isa, crushing Isa's right leg and ribs.

In excruciating pain, Isa next used her blue energy to burn off the ties around her body and wrists, and then, she removed her hood. While still pinned under Belle, she saw one of Lord Nemond's men who was outside the blast radius, running away scared for his life. There wasn't much Isa could do about it trapped under Belle. She worked to dislodge herself, wincing in pain as she did so.

After getting out from under Belle, she looked around at all the dead bodies and horses. The fact that she could cause so much death so quickly terrified her, and it was why she never wanted to use her power, but Lord Nemond had left her no choice. At least she knew these men would never hurt anyone else again. There was only one thing left to do...

Isa closed her eyes one more time and allowed her Vaniryan energy to consume her in light and reconstitute her energy into something new. When done, Isa had taken on new form: her son, Antonio, with all her body parts remade and healed anew. The Grand Master's men, including the escapee who had evaded her blast, would be looking for Lady Isabella. Isa had made sure they would never find her again.

Isa looked down at her clothes which had torn apart in the transformation, too small and tight for an adult male. Isa removed her clothes, and borrowed clothing and boots from one of Lord Nemond's dead men. Once dressed, she walked over to Belle and kissed her goodbye.

"Thank you, sweet girl, for giving me your life. Now, you are free. May you roam joyously in the heavenly grounds of Asgard."

Isa stood up tall and proud as her son, Antonio *Rossi*, and began jogging southwest toward Spain. She had to get out of France as fast as she could. She could not return to Venice. It was too dangerous.

Over the last week, Isa had learned the heavy price of her own existence and resolved herself to never put Anna in danger again. She only hoped that having Anna change her surname to Rossi and move in with the Grimanis would keep her safe, because Lord Nemond was right: her self-indulgent desire to live a normal life had put others in harm's way, especially those she loved the most. She couldn't let that happen again. She couldn't be selfish anymore. As heartbreaking as it was to leave those that she loved behind, she had to do so.

Tears welled up in her eyes at the thought of never seeing Anna again. It was probably how Snorri felt when he made the choice to send Hallveig to Italy three centuries earlier, knowing he would likely never see her again. As much as it hurt, he knew it was the right thing to do, and now, it was Isa's turn to do the same. It was time for her to take her human journey on a new path, and she knew where she had to go.

Several years earlier, during Venice's famous yearly Carnevale celebration, which attracted visitors from all corners of Europe, Isa had met a kind woman from an aristocratic English family named Elizabeth Stanley. Elizabeth was in Carnevale with her travel-hungry husband who liked to attend Carnevale because it gave him a chance to philander while wearing the famous Venetian Carnevale masks. Carnevale's masks allowed people to engage in otherwise forbidden activities such as mocking the government, making fun of the aristocracy, mixing it up with high society, or in Sir Stanley's case, mixing it up with other aristocratic women. Sir Stanley always fancied himself smart but Elizabeth was never fooled. Unfortunately, it was not something she could control.

One evening while Sir Stanley was off philandering, Isa and Elizabeth struck up a friendship and Isa invited her to visit Corte Del Milion. To Isa's surprise, the following afternoon, Elizabeth accepted her invitation and came to Isa's home bearing gifts. In return, Isa gifted Elizabeth several unique artifacts of her own from Niccolò and Marco Polo's impressive collection, which she had maintained over the years.

In their time together, Elizabeth Stanley had described Queen Elizabeth I as the most caring, tolerant, trustworthy and powerful monarch the world had ever known – and even bragged about the queen's crushing defeat of the Spanish Armada a few years earlier. Elizabeth told Isa that if she ever wanted to visit or needed a place to stay, that she could call upon Elizabeth in England, and that the queen's court would receive her kindly.

Isa had never expected to take Elizabeth up on her offer, but after all that had happened, Isa realized that she needed help. She couldn't do this alone. She needed the help of a friend, one who could bear the responsibility of her greatest secret. And, more importantly, she needed the protection of the most powerful monarch and army the world had ever known. Isa needed to go to England…

Chapter 21 – Portal Protocol

Dr. Ehringer sat at his desk in Pegasus West's underground hangar beneath the Nevada desert several miles away from Area 51. It was there from his raised platform where he oversaw the teams responsible for testing and operation of the United States' classified zeutyron particle technology, portal implementation, *p*RAMZA rovers, and the Stationary Zeutyron Accelerator (called 'Station' for short) that communicated with the *p*RAMZA rovers.

At the moment, he, along with his trusted civilian sidekick, Ian Marcus, were working late like they had for days, monitoring for signals from Electra-1. The Pegasus team estimated Operation 17 Tauri would last up to a week, and as they got closer to day five, neither intended to sleep until Captain Velasquez's team came home. In fact, nearly the entire Pegasus crew was awake and working, even at the late hour. That included Lt. Col. Lain and Major Jameson at Pegasus East, who were operating the U.S.'s top-secret high-orbit telescope, the "PAPA," scanning for z-particle signals from Electra-1.

Dr. Ehringer eyed a box of two-day old donuts sitting in the middle of the table, wondering if he should have his eighth donut of the week. After some initial hesitation, he grabbed a chocolate donut and took a bite. It wasn't fresh, but he didn't care.

"You know, if you're hungry, we can order something," Marcus reminded him, surprised his boss went for the two-day old donuts, which were only still there because no one had bothered to throw them out.

Dr. Ehringer replied, "Sometimes, a person just needs chocolate, even if it's a two-day old donut."

"I know," responded Marcus. "It's pretty intense around here right now."

"Intense is a polite way of putting it. I've got Col. Rodgers breathing down my neck and General Nemond and General Covington asking me for updates every half hour, it seems. The military brass has me a little on edge."

"I think they've got us all on edge. What do they think's going to happen every thirty minutes?"

"I don't know."

"You know the whole team's got your back, right? You can count on us, Dr. Ehringer."

"I know, Marcus, but it's not my back I'm worried about. It's the team 400 light years away that I'm thinking of."

"We've done everything we can to help them, Dr. Ehringer. We just have to hope it's enough."

"I hope so. I'm not sure I can live with myself if they do their job, but we still can't get them home."

"Those military guys all signed up for this. They knew the mission and still wanted to go."

"I'm not sure they signed up for *this*, but Captain Velasquez's team is brave as hell, if you ask me. To go to another world hundreds of light years away like that, into the enemy's stronghold, with no guarantees of getting out... I'm not sure I could do it."

"I'm sure you'd be the first one—"

"Don't say it, Marcus. Talking brave and being brave are two totally different things. Those men are heroes. I'm no hero. Do you think I had any idea when I majored in astrophysics at Berkeley that I was signing up to save the world someday? Me, the kid who liked math and science but was afraid of his own shadow growing up? Go figure."

Finding Dr. Ehringer's story amusing, Marcus inquired, "And if you had known then what you know now?"

"18-year-old-me probably would have changed his major."

Marcus chuckled. "And 50-year-old-you?"

Dr. Ehringer thought about it. "You know, I'm a lot braver than I used to be, inspired, really, by what the people involved with the Pegasus project have done, not just Captain Velasquez's team, but *everyone*. What about you, Marcus, is this what you signed up for—"

The monitors all started beeping and a two-foot-thick transparent aluminum panel began rising out of the floor all the way up into the ceiling in front of a smaller adjacent hangar until it completely sealed the adjacent hangar off. Something had activated Station's portal protocol.

"Dr. Ehringer, Station's receiving a signal!" exclaimed Marcus.

"Team Two, can you confirm the signal?" asked Dr. Ehringer, wanting to make sure something wasn't malfunctioning.

"Yes, Dr. Ehringer, a z-particle signal has activated Station's portal protocol," responded a member of Team Two.

"Team One, notify Col. Rodgers and General Nemond at once. Someone get me Pegasus East online..." Within seconds, Pegasus East was on the phone. "Lt. Col. Lain, Station is receiving a zeutyron signal. Can you confirm?"

After a couple second hold, Lt. Col. Lain responded, "Confirmed, the PAPA is tracking a z-particle signal to your location."

Before anyone could ask another question or say another word, a large portal materialized in the adjacent hangar sealed off by the transparent aluminum panel. They were staring at a rectangular-shaped portal, 20 feet wide and 10 feet tall, with a clear view of a forest-like environment and structures covered by foliage. They also saw the *p*RAMZA unit which had activated the Stationary Zeutyron Accelerator. And then, they heard laser fire, saw a ground explosion and heard screaming...

Captain Velasquez was running toward the portal at full speed, avoiding laser blasts on the way there. He dove through the portal's threshold and immediately yelled, "Close it! Close it!" They could hear him through the microphone installed in the sealed-off adjacent hangar, which was transmitting into the main hangar. Almost stunned by what was happening, no one reacted at first. Velasquez shouted again, "Close the portal!"

In the background, they saw a triangular-shaped fighter ship flying straight for the portal, on a collision course to fly right into the Pegasus West hangar!

"Team Three, deactivate the zeutyron field! Hurry! Hurry!" yelled Dr. Ehringer, with the ship flying at break-neck speed and about to penetrate the portal's threshold.

Seemingly milliseconds before the fighter ship reached them, and just as Pegasus West personnel started screaming, the portal disappeared. Those who had closed their eyes in fear kept screaming for a few seconds more.

"Portal deactivated!" announced Team Three, followed by a huge sigh of relief. They had done it, although just barely. Captain Velasquez was sprawled out on the floor inside the smaller adjacent hangar.

"Medical team to the hangar, STAT!" shouted Dr. Ehringer into the intercom. "Lower the panel!"

Captain Velasquez was laid out, his helmet cracked open, and his face bloody. He was struggling to breathe, sucking for air, rolling around on the ground. Dr. Ehringer, who had raced down the platform steps, got to Velasquez first, followed by Marcus.

"Captain, are you alright?" asked Dr. Ehringer, wanting to help him.

A few seconds later, a medical team came rushing into the hangar and up to Captain Velasquez's flailing body. Velasquez was trying desperately to get his helmet off. After taking a few breaths, he screamed, "Get it off!" He was panicking, struggling and suffering, all at the same time.

The medical team worked with Dr. Ehringer and Marcus to remove the helmet and help get Velasquez out of his suit. They couldn't simply cut him out of it because the material was specially designed to be puncture resistant. Several members of the medical team had to hold Velasquez down to calm him while they got the suit off him. Once they succeeded, he began to relax.

The medical team put an oxygen mask on his face to help him breathe, which he tolerated well. The doctors started taking Velasquez's vitals and other readings.

Although the doctors were still working on him, Dr. Ehringer felt compelled to ask, "Where are the others?"

Velasquez shook his head and responded, "They didn't make it."

"They didn't make it to the portal?"

Velasquez whispered, "No… they're all dead."

Dr. Ehringer's and Marcus' faces went flush, shocked by his response. Before Dr. Ehringer could respond again, the medical personnel interrupted the conversation. "Dr. Ehringer, I'm sorry, but we need to get him to the Medical Unit… his oxygen levels are saturated with polonium. We've got to get him treated ASAP."

"Of course," said Dr. Ehringer, backing up.

"Will he be okay?" asked Marcus.

"Yes," assured the medical team.

They lifted Captain Velasquez onto a stretcher to take him away. As they began wheeling him off, Velasquez looked back at Dr. Ehringer and Marcus and uttered, "Call Nemond, Covington. They're coming…"

"Who's coming?" asked Dr. Ehringer.

As he was being rushed away, Velasquez despondently replied, "…and there's nothing humanity is gonna be able to do to stop it."

Chapter 22 – The Drunken Unicorn

Thirty-six hours. That's how long Emma, Logan and Captain Evans had been traveling to get to Khatyrka, starting with the drive from Shugborough Hall to Lakenheath AFB in Suffolk, England. From there, they flew aboard a military transport to Yokosuka Naval Base in Japan, followed by another one to Attu Naval Station in the Aleutian Islands, and then a helicopter ride to the U.S.S. Ronald Reagan, which was already sailing into the Bering Sea. And finally, they sailed north on the Ronald Reagan until meeting up with the NSC Reliant, a cargo vessel operated by Bering Exports, a Canadian shipping firm conveniently owned by a U.S.-based parent company, Global Freight Logistix, Ltd.

Bering Exports' fleet of cargo ships made regular trips to Khatyrka and other locations in the Bering Sea. Through cooperation coordinated by the NSA—and some financial incentives granted by the U.S. government to Global Freight Logistix—Bering Exports agreed to include Emma, Logan, Captain Evans and several other military operatives into the NSC Reliant's crew manifest. The NSA took care of all their paperwork and passports.

Since departing Shugborough, Logan and Emma had not spent much time alone together because they had been traveling non-stop with Captain Evans and participating in meetings for the mission. But after changing into Bering Exports-issued uniforms to resemble crew members, and while they were still about an hour outside of Khatyrka Harbor, they had a few extra minutes to kill on the NSC Reliant's upper deck.

"I wonder when we'll finally be able to see Russia," said Logan, leaning over the starboard railing and peering into the deep blue ocean.

Emma looked ahead to see if she could catch a glimpse of Russia's coastline and responded, "She's out there, that's for sure."

"Russia or Isa?"

"Both," Emma replied, clutching the heart-shaped pendant hanging around her neck.

"What if she's not?"

"Then we just keep looking."

"To be honest, after what happened to Captain Velasquez's team on Electra-1, I'm not sure how much longer they're going to give us."

"Yeah, I know," responded Emma, staring into the open water.

"What if we never find her or the Leyandermál? How do we stop Supay then?"

"I don't know," responded Emma.

"I'm worried that if we don't find her soon, based on Velasquez's intel, the military's going to do something stupid like send an assault team loaded with explosives to Electra-1 to blow up that dome, or worse, send in nukes," said Logan.

"Well, that would be about the dumbest thing they could do. They have no idea if that would work, or what they're dealing with. That would probably just trigger the beginning of the end. Fortunately, Barrett's smarter than that."

"But is he that desperate?" asked Logan. "Captain Evans told me that Covington and Nemond interviewed Velasquez to ask him about the battle in the Hidden City, about how much earlier in time his team would have needed to arrive to change the outcome or rescue you guys even before you reached Qelios' compound, among other things they could have done differently, all the way back to the Chersky mission."

"I thought Barrett was adamantly against playing god and changing the past?" asked Emma.

"Yeah, well, that was then, before Velasquez returned with news of what he saw. Who knows what they'll do now."

Emma had a concerned expression on her face. Logan picked up on it immediately.

"What's wrong?"

"I'm fine," replied Emma, fighting back tears.

"Em, I can—"

"It's nothing."

"Em, I can tell something's wrong."

With a tear now running down her cheek, Emma capitulated. "Logan, I'm really scared I'm not supposed to be here."

"If you don't want to go on this mission, you don't have to. It's not too late for Covington to—"

"That's not what I mean."

Slightly confused, Logan replied, "Okay, then what are you saying?"

"That none of this is supposed to be happening, and that I shouldn't even be alive."

"What? Em, of course you're supposed to be alive!"

"Are you sure? If I don't get trapped on Vanirya with Jill, Carrie and Annika after the Chersky accident, we don't meet Isa in Jaannos… and if we don't meet Isa, she doesn't go with us to the Hidden City… and if she doesn't go with us to the Hidden City, she doesn't escape with Annika through the portal in Qelios' compound and end up in Iceland 800 years ago… and if she doesn't do that, my family doesn't exist and I'm never born."

"That's assuming you are actually related to her," interjected Logan.

"And when we find her, that's when I'll know if I'm, like, the offspring of a mistaken alternate timeline that was never supposed to happen."

Logan had never thought about it that way before but he refused to accept it. "Emma, you know that's not true. You're—"

Emma cut him off, because she had been thinking about the reality of her own existence for months. "Logan, if I'm related to her, that means there's a timeline where I don't exist, and somehow, something changed it. *I* changed it! I don't even know how it's possible that I could have caused the very chain of events that led to my own existence. All I know is that I'm nothing more than the product of some messed up alternate timeline that will vanish as soon as someone fixes the timeline or if the president does any of those things you just mentioned."

"Emma, that's crazy."

"Logan, you and I both know I'm right. If I'm related to her, I'm not supposed to be here."

"Or maybe Einstein was right!" countered Logan.

"What do you mean, 'or maybe Einstein was right'?" asked Emma, wiping her eyes.

Logan explained, "Einstein always said time is relative and flexible and that the dividing line between the past, present, and future is an illusion. It was something he called 'non-linear time theory' in which every moment in time, and every alternative on any given timeline, are all occurring simultaneously. It means, the past, present and future don't necessarily follow a straight linear timeline, but rather, are a quantum of alternatives all happening at the same time."

"Logan, c'mon... how is it possible that something that happens in the future can change the past? It doesn't make any sense."

"Well, a lot of stuff Einstein said in 1905 didn't make sense back then, but turns out he was right about most of it. It doesn't make any sense to us now because humans still don't understand how time works, not really. We can't fathom time unfolding any other way than linearly. My point is, if Mr. Jackson hadn't given us the Copán project, none of us would be here right now. We are *all* a byproduct of alternate timelines that converge and intersect, and this is *your* timeline. You are here because you are supposed to be."

With his words making her feel somewhat better, Emma replied, "And you still love me even though my entire existence might be an illusion, a mistake that gets erased tomorrow?"

"Is that what's been bothering you lately?"

"It's on the list. I know it's stupid. Score one for insecurity, I guess."

"Em, you are nobody's mistake, and there's nothing messed up about this timeline or you, okay? You're here now, and that's all that matters."

Logan's rather insistent and reassuring words brought Emma out of her funk. She leaned forward, hugged him and replied, "No one ever believes me when I say you are the smartest person I have ever met."

Logan thought about it. "Wait... who doesn't believe you?"

"There you guys are, I've been looking all over for you," interrupted Captain Evans, sneaking up behind them.

"Why, what's up?" asked Logan.

"We need to head below deck. The NSC Reliant's second in command, Chief Mate Burrows, has some info to share with us about Khatyrka." Suddenly, Captain Evans picked up on the fact that she had interrupted an intense conversation. "Everything okay with you two?"

"Yeah, everything's fine," replied Emma, wiping her eyes.

Captain Evans didn't believe her. "So, you guys are good, then? Because now really isn't the best time for—"

"Carrie, we're good, seriously," said Logan.

"Good, 'cause I don't do counseling or breakups on missions."

"Would you stop it!" snapped Emma, now completely ready to get back to work.

"Okay, follow me." Captain Evans led them below deck to where Chief Mate Burrows was waiting with the other mission operatives: Agents Stephenson, Nuñez and Taylor. When they walked in and closed the door, Chief Mate Burrows launched right into it because time was short.

"Alright, since none of you have been to Khatyrka before, they wanted me to tell you a bit more about the place, because I have," said Burrows.

"Great, so what's there?" asked Captain Evans.

"The short answer is, not much."

Unamused, Captain Evans prodded, "And the long answer?"

"You are dealing with an old Russian coastal village that stopped evolving decades ago. Everything's rundown. The main occupation in Khatyrka is livestock. Its economy is supported entirely by its fishing and hunting operations, with the most successful one being a reindeer herding, hunting and processing enterprise."

"Reindeer?" uttered Emma, horrified.

"Yes, ma'am. You ain't gonna find Rudolph, Dasher, Prancer or Comet vacationing anywhere near Khatyrka."

"Does anyone vacation in Khatyrka?" asked Stephenson.

"Nope, especially not in the winter months when the average high is sub-zero. Plus, there ain't much to do in the village, which is nothing more than a one-road town with a couple off-shoots to residential neighborhoods and small businesses. In addition to the industrial structures, you'll find a boarding school, kindergarten, hospital, recreation center, library, post office, a bakery, and my favorite stop, a bar. Not exactly a vacation hotspot."

"Sounds like there's not much there," remarked Logan.

Burrows continued. "The village folk keep to themselves, friendly enough, but in the winter months when it's freezing like today, they don't go out much, and prefer to disappear after hours. Khatyrka is the opposite of lively, except of course, when the cargo ships come into the harbor and their crews disembark for a little vodka and pelmeni."

"Is there a centralized area where people meet up or go?" wondered Emma, trying to figure out where to begin their search for Isa.

Burrows chuckled. "There ain't no town square, if that's what you're asking. The only place I've ever seen more than a handful of people gathered at once is the bar, and that's usually because I brought 'em there."

"Where would you start if you were looking to find someone?" asked Captain Evans.

"Well, I suppose if I wanted to find someone, I'd start at the bar. They know everybody in town, even the kids. But be prepared to drink because the owner doesn't let foreigners lounge on her benches or ask questions without paying the price."

"Paying the price of what?" replied Emma.

"Of vodka. The owner of The Drunken Unicorn is a shrewd businesswoman."

Emma did a double-take. "Did you say 'The Drunken *Unicorn*'?" Logan, Captain Evans and Emma all shared an optimistic glance.

"Yep, or as they call it in Russian, 'P'yanyy Yedinorog.' "

"That's where we have to go," stated Emma.

"Alright, then, I suggest your team does whatever it needs to do to get ready, because we'll be pulling into the harbor in about an hour. From there, it sounds like you cats are going drinking," said Chief Mate Burrows.

ΔΔΔΔΔΔΔΔΔΔΔΔ

When the NSC Reliant pulled into the harbor midday, the crew started prepping the cargo for offloading while the Khatyrka Harbor Authority came on board to check the crew manifest, passports and cargo deliverables. It was an impressively efficient operation of manpower, cranes, forklifts and clipboards. Once the boat reached port, many of the higher-ranking crewmembers whose jobs did not involve offloading cargo containers, deboarded to go into town. Today, that group included Logan, Emma, Captain Evans, Stephenson, Nuñez and Taylor, along with Chief Mate Burrows, who was more than happy to escort them to The Drunken Unicorn.

They proceeded down the main street, passing the various storefronts and buildings Burrows had told them about earlier. Like Burrows had described, the buildings looked old, rusty or in need of renovation. Khatyrka had the look of a dying fishing village that was barely holding on.

When they got to The Drunken Unicorn, they saw a dilapidated building that was connected to the bakery next-door. It did not qualify as cute, although it had a large overhead sign of a unicorn rearing up on its hind legs with its horn sticking through an oversized beer mug.

"Classy," commented Emma.

"Looks like my kind of place," remarked Captain Evans.

Burrows laughed. "Wait 'til you see the inside."

The group of seven entered the bar. It was full of wooden benches and tables. There were booths along the walls, and the walls were decorated with neon signs, vodka bottles, and reindeer antlers. The bar-top itself was made of reclaimed wood and finished to capture the wood's natural coloring, with unicorns carved into its forward-facing wood base. There were bar stools in front of the bar-top, and behind the bar, shelves of bottles, beer taps and a grumpy-looking older male bartender.

They sat at a table in the center of the bar, while a few patrons came in and sat in a booth in the corner right after them. If there were others working at the bar beside the bartender, they were hiding in the backroom or office.

"I wouldn't recommend the beer, it's usually flat. Who knows how often they get shipments in. I know we don't bring it," advised Burrows.

The bartender knew they were English-speaking when they walked in because he was familiar with Bering Exports' crewmembers who often came in during stops. He approached and asked Burrows in his more than serviceable English, "Your usual?"

"Yep, a round of shots for everyone."

"What are we drinking?" asked Captain Evans, keeping an eye on the two men in the corner who were minding their own business, just in case.

"Stolichnaya vodka," he replied.

"Actually, I do not want any, but thank you," said Emma. Everyone looked at her, shocked she said no, but Emma knew what she was doing. "Really, I'm good, but thank you."

"It is always the woman who does not drink," griped the chauvinistic bartender.

Annoyed by the bartender's sexist comment, Captain Evans replied, "On second thought, I'll have two shots. Now please, be a good boy and go get the Stoli." The bartender eyed Captain Evans, grunted, and walked off to go take the corner booth's order before fetching their liquor.

"What are you guys doing? Are you trying to cause trouble?" asked Logan.

"Yeah, actually," answered Emma. "And if we cause enough of it, I assume The Drunken Unicorn's proprietor will be coming out to introduce herself any minute."

"You could have just asked to see her, you know," Logan responded.

"And miss out on the fun?" countered Captain Evans. "Besides, by the looks of this place, they're not turning any business away, so you've got nothing to worry about."

"I like a woman who starts her day with two shots of vodka," said Stephenson, grinning at Evans.

"That's because it's the only way she'll talk to you," mocked Evans, drawing a good laugh from Nuñez and Taylor at Stephenson's expense.

Not long after, the bartender returned carrying a tray full of shots, and a large bottle of alcohol, which he placed on the table. "Here is vodka."

"You have high hopes for us, Oleg," replied Burrows, who obviously knew the bartender's name.

"Natalya says you drink whole bottle."

"Oh, does she?" questioned Burrows, although he knew Natalya's M.O. He had predicted it on the ship.

"Business light this month. She says drink up. You buy bottle."

Emma piped in, "Tell Natalya we want to thank her."

"Natalya busy now."

"Tell Natalya if she comes out, we will buy a second bottle," replied Emma.

Intrigued, Oleg challenged Emma, "You drink shot, then I get Natalya."

It was a bit of a standoff, but Emma decided to go along with it. After all, she'd done plenty of shots at Georgetown. She picked up a shot glass and downed it, scrunching her face because it burned on the way down. Everyone else at the table followed suit. When all the empty shot glasses hit the table, Oleg, pleased, said, "Now I get Natalya."

He walked back behind the bar and disappeared through a door. Soon after, Natalya emerged. She was a tall, middle-aged, burly Russian woman, whose face appeared severely weathered by Khatyrka's freezing conditions over time. Natalya approached their table.

She spoke first. "Oleg says the Bering's crewmembers are giving him trouble today." Eyeing Burrows, she added, "I thought you had that crew of yours under control, eh?"

Slightly embarrassed, Burrows responded while looking over at Emma and Evans, "Not the new ones."

When Natalya glimpsed Emma and Captain Evans' direction, her eyes widened. Emma removed Isa's heart shaped pendant necklace from beneath her shirt to allow it to dangle outward.

"That is a very pretty necklace," remarked Natalya, whose eyes fixated on it.

"It belonged to someone very special," replied Emma.

"Are you Americans?" asked Natalya.

"Yes," Emma replied, while Captain Evans and Logan watched the interaction between the two of them.

Natalya said, "You know, some of my favorite Vodka actually comes from a place one would least expect... Iceland. It is called Reyka Vodka, made by a distillery there that uses water from a 4,000-year-old lava field. The taste is smooth and warm with a touch of vanilla. Have you had?"

"No, but I have been to Iceland recently. I will try it the next time I am there." Emma stood up and approached Natalya to introduce herself. "My name is Emma." Natalya smiled, and Emma sensed Natalya knew who she was, so Emma added, "For a girl who was looking to see what life was like outside of the trees, you sure have seen your fair share."

Natalya smiled, and then, unexpectedly, and to Oleg's astonishment, hugged Emma. It was a firm, full embrace, the kind that looked like Natalya had just been reunited with a long-lost friend or relative. Both of them had tears of joy in their eyes.

Oleg asked Natalya in Russian, "Vy dvoye znayete drug druga?" ["*Do you two know each other?*"]

"Da," replied Natalya. After finishing her extensive squeeze, Natalya said to Emma, "I have a bottle of Reyka in my office, if you are interested in seeing it."

"Yes, very."

"Follow me."

The two of them started walking behind the bar heading to Natalya's office. Logan began to rise, intent on following, but Captain Evans put her hand on his leg to indicate that he should stay put. "Give them a moment to talk," she whispered. Natalya and Emma disappeared into the office and closed the door behind them.

"Well, Evans, looks like your little search party is already over," said Burrows.

"Something like that," replied Captain Evans.

"Do you still want that second shot of vodka, Captain?" asked Stevenson.

"Sure, pour another one for all of us."

About a minute or two later, a bright light flashed from behind Natalya's office door, with light leaking out of the door jamb's seams and the open space at the bottom of the door. Captain Evans and Logan knew, or suspected, what had caused it: Natalya changing shape.

Oleg, however, did not. "What in the world are they doing in there?" he asked.

After a few more minutes, another light surge emanated from behind the door, but this time, it was followed by a loud banging noise, the sound of furniture crashing, and shouting. Captain Evans and her team leapt into action.

"Logan, stay here!" yelled Captain Evans, racing toward the office with the others. They heard more shouting and then saw another light flare. They crashed through the door only to find smashed up furniture, a broken desk, and papers scattered about the floor, but nothing else. Natalya, who Evans now assumed was Isa, and Emma, were gone.

"Where'd they go?" asked Stephenson.

There was a window in the office, but it was way too high off the ground and too small to easily fit through in such a short time, plus, it wasn't open or broken. There was a door in the wall which Captain Evans promptly opened, but it was a supply closet with no exit.

"Oleg, is there another way out of this room?" asked Captain Evans.

"No. Only way out is through side door near bar and front door. No other door in office. Where are they?"

"We don't know," said Captain Evans, hurrying out of the office, looking for the two customers who had been sitting in the corner, but they were gone, too—and worse, so was Logan!

"Damn!" yelled Evans, running outside with Stephenson, Nuñez and Taylor to look for them, but they were nowhere in sight. "Does anyone see them?" No one did. Evans called out to Logan, shouting his name, but she received no response. "Alright, Taylor, Nuñez, you guys spread out and start looking for them, and if you don't have any luck, return to the ship in fifteen minutes," ordered Captain Evans. "Stephenson, you're with me."

Captain Evans ran back into the bar with Stephenson. "Oleg, did you see what happened to our friend?"

"No, I was looking at Natalya's office, and then, I followed you in there."

"Did you know the two customers who were sitting in the corner?"

Oleg looked back at the booth where the patrons had been sitting. "No, I had not seen them before."

Captain Evans was sick to her stomach and fuming. "Damn it! Damn it!" she cursed, angry at herself for letting Emma go into Natalya's office alone. Logan's instincts were correct, but Captain Evans had stopped him. She had let her guard down, overly swayed by the emotional moment between Emma and Natalya, and had made a horrible mistake. She had failed to protect them and compounded that mistake by leaving Logan alone.

"This is all my fault!" she uttered to Stephenson. "Let's go, we've got to make some phone calls ASAP! Emma and Logan were wearing trackers. Hopefully, the NSA's still got them."

Of course, Captain Evans knew that if Emma and Logan were no longer on Earth, their trackers would be useless.

Chapter 23 – The Red Room

Dr. Arenot anxiously sat beside Professor Quimbey on a sofa in the Red Room, one of four state reception rooms on the 1st Floor of the White House's Presidential Residence, waiting for General Covington to arrive. As its name implied, the room's walls were painted red. The sofa on which the professors sat, along with all the other furniture in the room, were upholstered in red silk and constructed using finely carved and finished woods dating back to the early 19th century.

"How much longer do we have to wait?" complained Dr. Arenot, who was devastated by the outcome of the Khatyrka mission and impatiently awaiting an update on Logan and Emma.

"I'm sure they're just taking their time to gather as much information as possible," replied Professor Quimbey.

"I wish I could have been there to help them."

"And what would you have done, Jonas, that Captain Evans and her team didn't? I'm sure they did everything they could."

"I know, it's just… I just want to help somehow! All this sitting around is driving me crazy."

"You can't fix everything, Jonas. I know you want to, but this time, we might not be able to."

"There's always a way."

"How?"

In walked General Covington carrying a tablet device.

"We can talk about it later," said Dr. Arenot.

Once the doors closed behind him, General Covington said, "Jonas, Jill, I'm sorry for keeping you waiting. The president will be here shortly, once the others arrive. I know how close you both are to Logan and Emma. How are you holding up?"

"Honestly, we're worried sick for them," replied Dr. Arenot. Professor Quimbey put her arm around him. Logan was like a son to him, and Emma like a daughter to her. They had grown very close to the teens turned college students, colleagues and friends over the last 3½ years, especially after everything they had been through together.

"That's understandable. I've grown fond of them, too," replied the general as sympathetically as possible.

"Any sign of them?" asked Professor Quimbey.

"No. Their trackers went offline when they disappeared inside The Drunken Unicorn. Nothing since."

"Are they still on Earth?" inquired Dr. Arenot.

"We have no way of knowing. There were multiple z-particle signals at the source and their trackers stopped transmitting instantly. We have no idea where they are and we've received no reports out of Russia suggesting Menputyn has them, either. We are doing everything we can on the counterintelligence side to shake some intel loose."

"Are they sure it was Isa in Khatyrka?" asked Professor Quimbey.

The general nodded. "Captain Evans is, yes."

"How does she know for certain?" wondered Quimbey.

"She doesn't, but she said she's willing to bet her life on it based on the woman's conversation with Emma, the expressions on her face, her reaction to a few of Emma's comments, and her intuition."

"Carrie's intuition has always been good enough for me," Professor Quimbey remarked. "Could Supay have been behind what happened?"

"Possibly. I don't want to speculate. It could have been Supay *or* the Russians. Evans said two men followed them into The Drunken Unicorn and disappeared with Logan."

"They could have been Supay's Hunt in disguise," countered Dr. Arenot, who had watched Supay change shape to mirror Logan's appearance when he and Logan ended up at Supay's stronghold after going through the portal at Machu Picchu.

"Right, or Russian operatives," theorized the general.

"If it was the Russians, how did they know exactly where Logan and Emma were going to be?" blurted Professor Quimbey angrily. "If that's the case, you guys have a leak the size of your Grand Canyon in this so-called top-secret operation of yours! I'm surprised cable news hasn't started reporting on the Pegasus Project's dailies by now."

General Covington knew she was right. "We are trying to get to the bottom of it, I promise."

"Are you? Because Logan, Emma and Isa are gone because of it, and I don't see what you guys are doing to fix it!" snapped Professor Quimbey.

General Covington was trying hard to remain calm and not take anything personally because he knew they were upset. "Rest assured, we are looking at everything and we've put all military units and bases on high alert."

"None of that's going to do any good if Supay blows Earth up from orbit," commented Dr. Arenot, continuing, "Thank god he doesn't have the Leyandermál yet."

"We are not certain of that," said the general.

"What?" uttered Professor Quimbey.

Dr. Arenot was equally surprised. "What are you talking about?"

"Emma," Covington responded.

Professor Quimbey didn't understand. "What do you mean, *Emma?*"

"There is some concern among the highest levels that Emma could *be* the Leyandermál."

"That doesn't make any sense," said Dr. Arenot, confused.

"Among the highest levels? Who?" questioned Professor Quimbey.

"The president, myself, NSA Director Orson and a geneticist."

"No one else?" followed up Dr. Arenot, surprised.

"Correct."

"Who is the geneticist?" asked Quimbey.

"I can't say."

"Okay, fine, but why a geneticist? You still believe Emma's human, right?" replied Professor Quimbey.

"Yes, more or less."

"What does that mean?" asked Dr. Arenot.

"Emma's suspicion that she is related to Isa is correct. She is definitely part Vaniryan."

"How do you know?" asked Dr. Arenot.

"Because we found multiple strands of long white hair on Emma's clothing after Captain Velasquez's team rescued you all from the Hidden City, and ran a DNA comparison. We assumed the hair strands were Isa's based on your description of her, and the comparison matched."

"The comparison matched what?" inquired Dr. Arenot.

"Emma's DNA," answered the general. "It's not just Emma. Other members of her family whose DNA we were able to covertly collect, seem to share the same fused human-Vaniryan DNA."

"Does that mean Emma and her family share some of the same qualities or abilities that Isa displayed on Vanirya?" asked Professor Quimbey.

"We asked the geneticist that same question and her response was that there are probably some latent qualities in the Rossi's DNA that have not manifested themselves or perhaps never will given the infusion of human DNA over the centuries, or maybe the Rossis don't know how to access it. We obviously have no idea."

"Why use an outside geneticist who is unaffiliated with Pegasus?" wondered Dr. Arenot.

"Well, she's not entirely an outsider. She's a classified geneticist who works with us on other projects. We used her because she's discrete, one of a kind and only reports to the president and me. The fewer people who know that aliens have been walking on Earth since the middle ages, living in Italy and the United States under the surname Rossi, and *paying taxes*, the better. The panic, the conspiracy theories, and the retribution against everyone in the world named Rossi will spiral out of control. We can't let this get out."

Dr. Arenot replied, "Okay, to some extent, based on Emma's observation that her last name Rossi was the reverse of Issor, and based on everything we've learned recently, this doesn't entirely surprise us, but what makes you think Emma is the Leyandermál?"

General Covington explained, "It is just supposition so please bear that in mind when I tell you this, but it starts with the Copán map the kids discovered 3½ years ago."

"The map of coordinates left behind by the Norwegian Albo?" asked Dr. Arenot.

"Yes."

"How?" inquired Dr. Arenot.

"Let me show you…" The general pulled up on his tablet a map of the Copán coordinates from Logan and Emma's initial adventure that started it all, showing in red dots the locations of the Château de Falaise in France; Storfjorden, Norway; Stonehenge, UK; Giza, Egypt; Tiwanaku, Bolivia; Copán, Honduras; and Area 51, Nevada.

He then used his finger to draw on the tablet's Copán map, drawing a red line from Area 51 in southern Nevada, down through the Copán region of Honduras until reaching the Gate of the Sun in Bolivia. It formed a straight line:

"Immaculata," he said, referring to the letter "I" that he had just drawn from Area 51 down to Tiwanaku. "Remember, Emma's first name is Immaculata." Next, he put his finger on the Storfjorden cave plot point in Norway, drew a line downward to the Great Pyramid of Giza in Egypt, then looped to the left and back up through the Château de Falaise and ended at Stonehenge. It formed a letter J:

"The Copán map's coordinates form the initials for Immaculata James—I J—which is why we think there might be more to Emma than just a genetic relationship to Isa. Plus, her name's on the Vaniryan sphere beneath Area 51. Someone foretold her coming a long time ago, and the Leyandermál could be why."

The professors were shocked. They had studied the Copán map for years and had never noticed that before. Still, Dr. Arenot wondered, "Beings with the ability to travel through time foretelling our future in order to tell us something they wanted us to know, does not alone mean she is *the* Leyandermál."

"There's more," alluded the general. "I'm going to get this wrong because I am not a scientist, but DNA is made up of molecules called nucleotides," the general began to say.

Dr. Arenot jumped in, "Right, and the nucleotides attach together to form a structure called a double helix, which looks like a spiral ladder, with phosphate and sugar molecules constituting the ladder's sides, and nucleotide base pairs consisting of adenine, thymine, guanine and cytosine, serving as the ladder's rungs. Remember, you're talking to two scientists here."

"Yes, I realize that," replied the general, "and feel free to correct me, but as I understand it, human DNA is made up of around 3 billion base pairs coiled tightly to form structures called chromosomes, with 23 pairs of chromosomes stuffed inside every human cell's nucleus."

"Sounds like you know quite a bit already," said Professor Quimbey.

"That's because I've asked a lot of questions, Professor. Anyway, according to the geneticist, the Rossi's cells contain the normal 23 chromosomes that all human cells have, plus additional genetic material within each."

"What kind of additional genetic material?" inquired Dr. Arenot.

"The geneticist says that hidden within each of their chromosomes are 7 sub-chromosomes or micro-chromosomes which she believes come from Isa and are Vaniryan because Isa had them, too."

"*Sub*-chromosomes?" Professor Quimbey asked the general.

"Yes, and they would never show up on any standard genetic DNA test which only searches for ordinary human DNA markers. What's more, Emma's DNA not only includes the 7 sub-chromosomes that her family has, but 6 more sub-chromosomes unique to her. Not even Isa has them. The geneticist says her additional 6 sub-chromosomes contain triple the base pairs that normal human chromosomes have – so, 9 billion instead of 3 billion - and they vary from cell to cell at a rate of .0008%, resulting in an estimated 13.3 million variations."

"That's not possible," uttered Dr. Arenot. "DNA's supposed to be identical in every cell in the body."

"Well, not in Emma's case."

"But how's that possible?" asked Professor Quimbey.

The general replied, "The geneticist compared Emma's DNA from before she went through the Vaniryan portal in the Storfjorden cave in Norway during your original adventure years ago, to her DNA today. Before going through, Emma's DNA was the same as the rest of her family, but afterwards, her sub-chromosome count increased from 7 to 13. Something happened when she went through that portal. They did something to her or changed her DNA."

Professor Quimbey responded, "I remember Emma describing to us what happened on that first encounter. She said the Vaniryans told her how it was time for mankind to travel the stars and how the planet was in danger, and at one point, the Vaniryans entered her mind and flooded it with information. She said they shared information directly into her head like they were uploading data into a computer, and that she became so overwhelmed that she blacked out."

Picking up on what Professor Quimbey was implying, Dr. Arenot said, "We've always assumed that the Leyandermál was a book, a writing or object of some kind, but what if it's not? What if they hid the Leyandermál in Emma herself, concealing the information directly in her DNA?"

"That's our theory," replied General Covington. "We don't know if the information hidden in her DNA can be read, or if it's a code or if it's information at all, or whether it will manifest itself in some way that Emma has access to or can use it. All we know is that each of those extra 6 sub-chromosomes of hers have 9 billion base pairs of unique genetic code multiplied by 13.3 million distinctive combinations. If we think of each base pair like a character or letter in a book, there's enough written there to fill 400 billion average length books or the Library of Congress 10,000 times over. That's a *lot* of information."

"Enough to contain all the secrets of the universe?" posed Professor Quimbey. Dr. Arenot and General Covington shot a look at her, considering the implications.

They heard a knock on the door. A secret service officer poked his head in and said, "Loretta Richards is here. Should I let her in, sir?"

General Covington replied, "Yes, please."

Logan's mom had arrived, and seconds later, she walked in, appearing frightened and stressed. When she saw the professors, she rushed up to them. The professors, who had had dinner with Loretta on numerous occasions when she visited Logan at Georgetown, stood up and hugged her. She had tears in her eyes.

"Loretta, I am so sorry," said Professor Quimbey, consoling her.

"Jill, I'm really worried about them," Loretta replied.

"I know."

"Logan and Emma are stronger than everyone we know. If anyone's going to be okay, it's those two," offered Dr. Arenot, feeling the urge to say something positive.

Loretta pulled away. "How did they get wrapped up in a mess like this with Russian terrorists?" she asked, referencing the only detail about the incident she knew. She had known for a while that Logan and Emma were interning at the Pentagon, although she never quite understood what they did because Logan had said it was classified. She always assumed it was some kind of think-tank internship.

"Loretta, this is General Warren Thomas Covington," said Dr. Arenot, introducing her. "He can answer your questions."

She shook the general's hand, wiped her face and tried to straighten her hair which she had been running her hands through for hours. "I'm sorry, I'm such a mess."

"You have nothing to apologize for, Ms. Richards," replied the general.

"Please tell me they're going to be okay... Logan and Emma are my whole life. I don't know what I'd do without—"

"General Covington, the Jameses are here," announced the secret service officer poking his head through the door.

"Please, let them in," said General Covington.

In walked Emma's parents, Robert and Mary James. They walked right up to the general without acknowledging the others in the room. They knew Loretta, but had never met the professors before.

"Mr. and Mrs. James, thank you for coming. My name is Warren Covington."

"General Warren Thomas Covington, of course we know who you are. An honor to meet you, General," said Mr. James. He turned to Loretta and could only coldly muster, "Loretta."

Emma's mom was far warmer. She hurried up to Loretta and hugged her. "Hi Loretta, how are you doing?" she asked. The two of them had always gotten along.

"Hi Mary. Not great. You?" Loretta replied.

"I just don't understand what's happened and what this is all about," Mary responded.

"I'll tell you what it's all about!" stated Mr. James. "Ever since Emma started dating Logan, it's been nothing but—"

"Hey, don't you blame this on Logan!" snapped Loretta.

Mr. James didn't back down. "Your kid has been a bad influence on Emma ever since high school, always convincing her to do things she would never have done had he not gotten into her head. She dropped out of law—"

"That was always your dream, not hers! Maybe you should listen to your daughter once in a while," retorted Loretta.

"Yeah, well now she's practically dropped out of college because of him and who knows what other trouble he's gotten her into!"

"That boy of hers happens to be a fine young man and one of the most extraordinary in the country," interjected President Barrett, walking in through the Red Room's doors unannounced in the middle of their heated conversation. Emma's father immediately stopped talking. The president approached Loretta, shook her hand and said, "May I call you Loretta?"

"Yes, of course, Mr. President," replied Loretta, stunned that President Barrett even asked.

"Please, Andrew will be fine, and thank you for coming. I know this is hard but I promise you we are doing everything we can to help your son."

"Thank you, Mr. President… I'm sorry, I mean, Andrew."

The president smiled politely, stepped back and turned to face Emma's parents. "Mr. and Mrs. James, thank you for getting here so quickly. I promise we are doing everything possible to get Emma back. Your daughter is a brilliant and brave woman and you should be very proud of her. I think you should know that their decision to drop out of college this semester was my idea, not Logan's. I'm sure you understand that a lot of what goes on around here is classified, so they probably never told you the real reason behind their decision. I'm sorry it had to be that way. Unfortunately, apologies come with the job."

Somewhat humiliated, Mr. James responded, "I'm sorry, I did not know that. I, um… Loretta, I owe you a huge apology."

"Mr. James, I have a daughter of my own—Ella, I know you all know that because her face is splashed throughout the media far more than she'd like—but let me tell you, when you watch those little princesses grow up, there is nothing you wouldn't do for them. When they hit those teenage years, oh boy, hold on, because that's when the boys start coming around trying to take that little girl away from you. And when that starts happening, you're sure none of 'em will ever be good enough for her."

Everyone in the Red Room chuckled respectfully while the president meandered through his story, but Mr. James only slightly grinned because he knew the story was meant for him. President Barrett continued…

"I must have chased dozens of boys away from my daughter over the years, always thinking I knew what was best for her, and I'm sure I was right a few times, but not always. I was probably an ass more than I'd like to admit. Anyway, they grow up and one day, you remember: you raised a special little girl, you taught her to take care of herself and to make good decisions. And now, as a grandfather with kids running around the White House during the holidays, when I watch them wreck the halls, I know that's exactly what she did.

"Mr. James, Logan loves your daughter very much, and I know this not just because he's told me so multiple times but because I can see it when he looks at her. And getting to know Emma as I've had the chance to do over the last few years, no one pushes her around, not even me. I'm confident she wouldn't have let Logan into her life the way she has if she didn't want him to be there and if it wasn't the right decision for her. Trust me when I say, he's a keeper. They both are."

The president paused to let his words soak in while he walked over to an ornately carved 19th century wood coffee table surrounded by sofas. He continued… "So, now, why don't we all sit down and talk about what's happened to Logan and Emma, what we know, and what we're doing to try and help them. Can we do that?"

"Of course, Mr. President," replied Mr. James, followed by the others.

They all sat down on the sofas surrounding the coffee table and President Barrett started explaining everything, to the extent that he could. In total, he and General Covington spent about thirty minutes discussing the situation, giving a classified briefing on what had happened, and more importantly, what they were trying to do to rescue Logan and Emma. They spent most of their time discussing the latter since that part was actually true. The president hated that he couldn't be more forthright with Emma and Logan's parents, but he simply couldn't compromise national security, and thus, he made no mention of aliens, Vaniryans or supervillains.

When it was over, everyone left the White House, feeling confident that the president was doing everything possible to rescue Logan and Emma from whoever had captured them. All except for Dr. Arenot and Professor Quimbey. They knew better. They knew the situation was more dire than the president had let on, and they were determined to do something about it.

After leaving the White House, Professor Quimbey immediately turned to Dr. Arenot and said, "Jonas, you said earlier that there's *always* a way. Okay, how?"

Dr. Arenot replied, "It's time to pay a visit to **Dewey's Comic Books & Hobby Shop**."

Chapter 24 – Heroes

Dr. Arenot and Professor Quimbey pulled up to Dewey's Comic Books & Hobby Shop in downtown Philadelphia early Friday evening and parked the car. Just like the last time Dr. Arenot visited, the place was packed with customers, not only inside Dewey's, but next door, too. Dewey's had taken over the adjoining space. Apparently, Bryan Callister had expanded his empire.

"What's going on here?" wondered Professor Quimbey.

"Looks like Bryan is holding another one of his gaming tournaments," replied Dr. Arenot.

"Do you really think he can help us?"

"I don't know, but every time Logan gets in a jam, this is where he comes, and somehow, it always works out."

"That doesn't sound very scientific," commented Quimbey.

"No it doesn't. Are you ready to go in?"

"Into a frenzied gaming mob? Can't wait..."

They crossed the street and pushed through the door into a crowd of gamers cheering on a match taking place in the arena. Bryan had blown out the wall between Dewey's and the space next door to create a supersized Dewey's.

The old part of the store still had all of Dewey's classics: action figures, comic books, model trains, dollhouses, board games, figurines, remote-controlled cars, planes, computer games, gaming equipment, and other hobby items. In the new space, Bryan had built an e-arena surrounded by two rows of seating along the walls with table space equipped with hook-ups for each gamer's laptop. At the back was a huge projection screen that took up nearly the entire wall. It displayed all of the gamers' screens through wireless connections. There was a gaming pit in the middle with two combatants wearing virtual reality headsets going head-to-head in a VR boxing match. The action was being projected up onto the screen so others could watch.

Bryan's loyal assistant store manager, Zack, approached them to collect the entrance fee. "$5 bucks a head," he said, holding out his hand.

"Just to walk in?" questioned Professor Quimbey.

"It's the price of walking into our noble gaming domain, my lady," responded Zack. "Plus, it helps pay for all the pizza and drinks we ordered."

Dr. Arenot reached into his pocket and grabbed two $5's. "No problem. Here you—"

"Professors?! You gotta be kidding me!" yelled Bryan, who had just spotted them from across the room. He rushed over to save them from Zack. "No way! Your money's no good here! Zack, these two are cool."

"You sure?" asked Zack.

"Yeah. Go hit up those 13-year-olds in the corner who just snuck in the side entrance." Bryan pointed to a couple teens trying to set up their laptops.

Zack replied, "Yes, master." He bowed and took off to intercept the intruders.

Bryan closed his eyes, embarrassed. "I hate it when he does that!"

"I don't blame you," remarked Professor Quimbey, finding Zack a bit *too* loyal.

"Look at this place, Bryan! You've completely revamped everything. It looks great!" complimented Dr. Arenot.

"Thanks, it does look pretty awesome! We finished the upgrades a few weeks ago. The store's totally blown up. I have an e-sports league event every night now. Wednesday night's a virtual reality bowling league for old-timers like you, Doc. You should come by."

"Thanks, but I don't own a VR headset," replied Dr. Arenot.

"No problem, I've got 'em available for rent. Bringing in an older crowd with that league. Turns out the older customers spend more money in my store than the kids do, always buying new toys for themselves and their children, nieces and nephews. I used to spend all my time trying to get the younger crowd in here. Boy was I wrong. The VR bowling league is a 'virtual' goldmine."

"Jonas, finally a sport you can play where you won't throw out your back," mocked Professor Quimbey.

"Don't count on it," Dr. Arenot responded.

"If you really need to slow things down, we've got virtual bingo Sunday nights. This Sunday's virtual bingo on Mars. Should I count you in?"

"Let me guess... the grandparents spend a fortune buying stuff in your store for their grandkids?" asked Dr. Arenot.

"Bingo!"

"Speaking of spending a fortune, where'd you come up with the cash for all this?" inquired Dr. Arenot.

"I took out a small business loan to help take this place to the next level. And it's working, too, because we've already been approached by the downtown city center to open up another location there."

"Wow, you are—"

A loud roar interrupted Dr. Arenot as gamers cheered on the VR boxing match taking place mid-gaming-arena.

"GodzillaRocks is killing it!" blurted Bryan, pointing to one of the contestants throwing upper cuts and body blows at the air.

"GodzillaRocks?" replied Professor Quimbey.

"Yep! It's the finals of tonight's boxing tournament. GodzillaRocks hasn't lost in a month, a total natural in the VR boxing ring."

They watched the wall display showing a split-screen of the two VR fighters going toe to toe, throwing upper cuts, jabs, hooks and body blows. The contestants' names were identified at the top of their respective sides. GodzillaRocks on the left was getting the best of SuperMario13 on the right, landing punches and avoiding counterpunches with good glove work. A massive uppercut by GodzillaRocks leveled SuperMario13, sending GodzillaRocks' virtual opponent to the canvas. The VR fight referee jumped in to start the countdown, joined by the rowdy crowd of gamers: Ten... nine... eight... seven... six... five... four... three... two... one... out! SuperMario13 failed to stand up and the virtual referee called the match! The crowd erupted! GodzillaRocks had won again!

"Like I said, a total natural. Seriously, I don't know how she does it!" said Bryan, wowed.

GodzillaRocks removed her headset. It was Allysa Anders, their freshman friend from Georgetown who, months earlier, had gotten involuntarily roped into their whirlwind adventure to Peru, Sweden, Area 51, Electra-1 and Vanirya. Allysa came bounding over, totally proud of herself...

"Did you see that?!" she uttered, practically jumping into Bryan's arms and kissing him. Clearly, they were more than friends.

"You crushed it like always!" declared Bryan.

Just then, Allysa realized Bryan was talking to Dr. Arenot and Professor Quimbey. Surprised, she said, "Professors… what are you doing here? I thought you were in Iceland."

"We just got back," Dr. Arenot responded.

"Where are Logan and Emma?" Allysa followed up.

Dr. Arenot replied, "In trouble."

"Uh-oh," said Bryan.

"We need your help," said Dr. Arenot

"Zack!" shouted Bryan to get his assistant manager's attention. "We're doing the battle dungeon tournament next. Can you load it up and get everyone started?"

Zack appeared confused. "Don't you want in? You own the battle dungeons."

"Nope. I'm going to sit this one out. We're going to talk to the profs in the office."

"Sure thing, mast—"

"Don't say it! I swear to god if you call me master one more time, I'm going to delete all your avatars!"

Zack wasn't discouraged. "Yes, my lord." He took off to coordinate the next tournament.

Irritated, Bryan shook his head. "Alright, let's go." He led the way to the back.

Once inside Bryan's office, Dr. Arenot noticed some changes, including much-needed organization, a few plants, better lighting, file cabinets, and a couple pictures.

"Nice. It looks like a real office in here," complimented Dr. Arenot.

"All Allysa," replied Bryan.

Allysa added, "They might hold battle dungeon tournaments at Dewey's but that doesn't mean the place has to look like a dungeon. It needed some sprucing up."

"So, what's up with Logan and Emma?" asked Bryan.

"They found Isa," Dr. Arenot answered.

"That's great. Where?"

"Khatyrka," replied Dr. Arenot.

"Where's that?" asked Allysa.

"Far northeast Russia," answered Professor Quimbey.

"So, she's alive? That's amazing!" responded Bryan. "That's good news, isn't it?"

Dr. Arenot responded, "Yes, but right after they found her, someone abducted them all."

"Holy hostage! Who?" inquired Bryan.

"Was it that Russian guy who hijacked our plane at Martin State Airport?" guessed Allysa, still upset about Menputyn taking them hostage on the flight down to Peru.

"We don't know," replied Dr. Arenot.

"Then, who?" wondered Allysa.

"It might have been Supay," answered Dr. Arenot.

"That's bad," murmured Bryan.

"Yeah, well, it gets worse," said Dr. Arenot.

"How can it get worse?" Bryan questioned.

"Whoever has them might also have the Leyandermál," replied Dr. Arenot.

"You mean, the thing that's supposed to contain all the secrets to the universe about creation, destruction, life, death, power, the stars, dimensions, other universes... *everything*?" asked Allysa.

"That's the one," stated Dr. Arenot.

"How'd they find it?" asked Bryan.

"They found Emma," responded Dr. Arenot.

Bryan was confused. "I don't understand... what does Emma have to do with—"

"Emma *is* the Leyandermál," Professor Quimbey announced.

"What? Sweet, coffee obsessed Emma? How's that possible?" responded Allysa.

"We don't have time to explain it all, but apparently the Vaniryans hid the Leyandermál's information directly in Emma's DNA, or at least, that's what the government thinks," said Dr. Arenot.

"You forgot about the map," chimed in Professor Quimbey.

"What map?" asked Bryan.

Dr. Arenot replied, "The map of Copán coordinates Emma and Logan chased down three years ago."

"We know the one," said Bryan.

Dr. Arenot continued, "Well, it turns out Emma's initials were embedded in that map the whole time. Here, let me show you." Dr. Arenot searched the internet for a global map on his phone and asked, "Hey, can I print this?"

"Yeah, send it to my wireless printer. You should see one pop up in your Bluetooth options called, um, AllysaRocks," said Bryan.

"AllysaRocks?" asked Dr. Arenot.

"Yeah," said Bryan, blushing, while Allysa smiled.

"You two are too cute," commented Professor Quimbey.

Dr. Arenot sent the image to the printer and Bryan grabbed it. "Here you go."

Dr. Arenot laid the printout on Bryan's desk, grabbed a red pen and drew small circles to signify the location of all the Copán landmarks. When done, he swapped out his red pen for a blue one.

"Okay, Emma's actual first name is Immaculata. Watch me draw a line from Area 51 in Nevada down to the Gate of the Sun in Bolivia, and then, a second line from the Storfjorden cave in Norway down to the Great Pyramid, looping to the left and back up through the Château de Falaise and ending at Stonehenge. The Copán map's coordinates form the initials for Immaculata James—I J."

"Dude, that's insane!" blurted Bryan.

"I know. Between her DNA and this map, you can see why they think Emma is the Leyandermál. Covington said there's enough extra genetic coding in her DNA to fill 400 billion books."

"Does Emma know?" Bryan asked Dr. Arenot.

"That she's the Leyandermál? We don't think so, or she's never said anything."

"So, what does it mean?" Allysa inquired.

"It means that if Menputyn has them, once he figures out that Emma is the Leyandermál, he might try to use her to take over the world. And if Supay has her, he'll have what he needs to take over the *universe*, or destroy it, starting with Earth," responded Dr. Arenot.

"Where are they?" asked Allysa.

"No one knows. They might not even be on Earth," said Professor Quimbey.

"Oh, this is really really really bad," Bryan replied.

"But what can we do?" wondered Allysa.

"Help us find them," said Dr. Arenot.

"How?" questioned Bryan. "The government has access to the most advanced technology and surveillance equipment in the world. If they can't find them, what chance do we have?"

Dr. Arenot didn't disagree, but he replied, "All I know is that if any of us were missing, Logan would be here trying to find us. Emma and Jill got lost halfway around the galaxy on Vanirya, 800-years in the past, and Logan didn't give up. He found a way. There's always a way."

"You're right, it's hero time!" declared Bryan, ready to tackle the challenge. "Okay, so what would Logan do if backed into a corner, up against supervillains?"

Allysa replied, "There's only one thing you can do: you have to fight supervillains with superheroes. You have to find the Va, the original guardians of the Leyandermál, if they still exist. Maybe they can help rescue Emma and Logan and show her how to use the Leyandermál to defeat Supay and Menputyn."

Professor Quimbey responded, "You know, when I was in Jaannos with Emma and Carrie, they showed us the Scroll of the Va which was supposed to depict where the Va went. The answer is in there."

"Do you remember what it looks like?" asked Bryan.

"Yes. When we got back from the Hidden City, General Covington had us all sit with a sketch artist to recreate the Scroll from our collective memories. We worked on it for days until we got it right. I've got the image burned in my mind at this point. Here, hand me a piece of paper." Bryan removed a sheet from his printer and handed it to her. She grabbed a black sharpie and started drawing the Scroll of the Va from memory. When done, she announced, "There! It's not perfect but it's pretty close." She showed them:

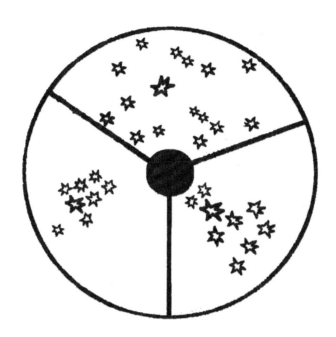

They stared at a black and white image of a large outer circle with a smaller black circle in the middle. Three lines extended outward from the inner circle to the outer ring, dividing the whole up into three equal pie-chart sections with stars in each.

"The bottom-right quadrant with nine stars represents our solar system, with the largest star, the third one in, representing Earth," said Professor Quimbey.

"So that quadrant's out," remarked Dr. Arenot.

Professor Quimbey nodded. "And the bottom-left section represents the Pleiades constellation with Electra being the largest star in that group. And we know from your visit there and Captain

Velasquez's report, that Supay's there, not the Vaniryans. So, that one's out, too."

"Okay, so, it has to be the top section of stars then, right?" said Bryan.

"Right," replied Professor Quimbey, pointing at it.

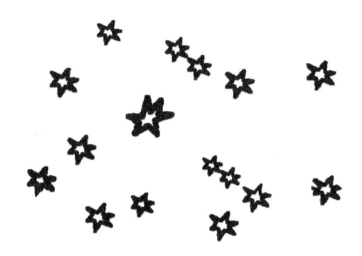

"If that big star in the middle is meant to indicate where the Va went, how do we figure out where that is?" asked Allysa.

"Logan and Emma would look for constellations," replied Bryan.

"That's exactly what they would do!" agreed Dr. Arenot. "Let's pull up constellations on our phones and see what might—"

"Wait," interrupted Professor Quimbey. "That's not going to work. The Va didn't render those star drawings from the perspective of the stars as seen on Earth. There's no point in looking at constellations when our stars don't match theirs."

"So what do we do then?" wondered Allysa.

"What about comparing the Scroll's stars to the Copán map?" suggested Bryan.

"Why?" queried Dr. Arenot.

Bryan replied, "It just seems like there's a lot of information hidden in that Copán map. It told humanity how to find Vanirya. It predicted Emma's coming with her initials. Maybe there's still more to it, some correlation between the Copán map and the stars in the upper section of the Scroll of the Va."

"Jonas, can you print another copy of the global map off your phone and re-draw the Copán landmarks so we can lay the two side by side?" requested Quimbey.

"Sure." Dr. Arenot sent the map to the printer. Bryan grabbed it, handed it to him and he re-drew the Copán landmarks. He then laid it beside the Scroll of the Va stars:

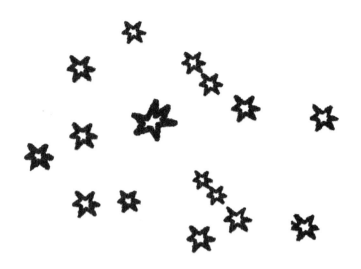

"Huh," said Bryan.

"Do you see something?" asked Dr. Arenot.

Bryan nodded. "There's a line across the middle of both."

"Where?" asked Allysa.

"Here, I'll draw it out." Bryan grabbed the blue pen that Dr. Arenot had been using earlier to draw a line on the Scroll of the Va page from left to right across four stars in the middle. On the Copán map, he drew a similar line from Area 51 to the Château de Falaise in France, and then slightly beyond it. "I drew the line farther out on the Copán map because I have an idea, but what do you guys think?"

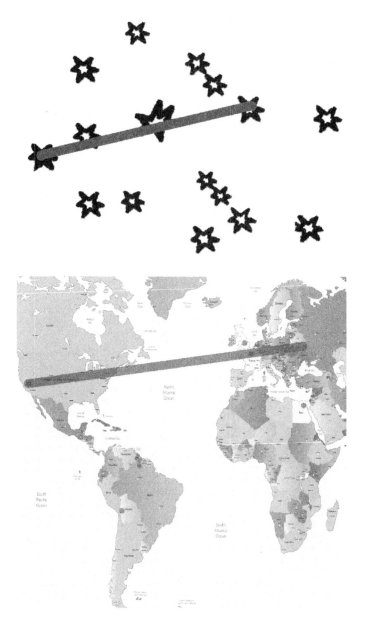

Dr. Arenot was intrigued. "Okay… what else are you thinking?"

Bryan continued to explain. "I also see two lines, angled downward and slightly to the right, that look like back-slashes. Here, look…" Bryan drew two lines through the Scroll of the Va's stars down and to the right, connecting stars instead of dots. On the Copán map, he drew lines from Area 51 down to the Copán Temple in Honduras and from the Château de Falaise down to the Great Pyramid in Egypt:

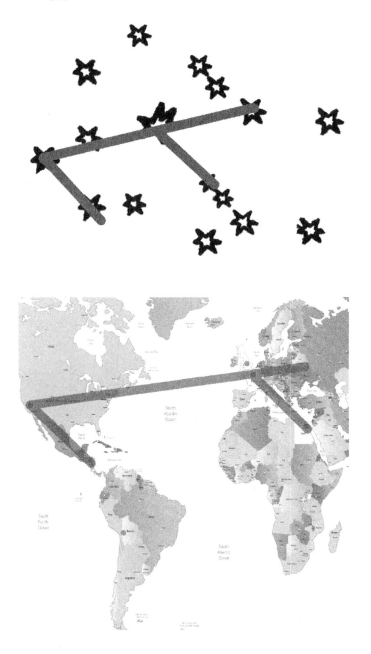

"There, don't you guys see the similarity?" asked Bryan. He continued to mark up the images, drawing a triangular-shaped head at the right side of both lines and another line passing through the tops of the triangles like a horn…

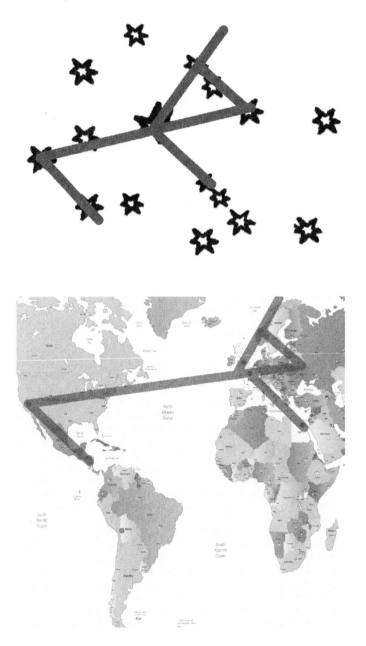

"Whoa!" uttered Allysa. "Those coordinates and stars, when connected, look like—"

"Unicorns!" interjected Dr. Arenot, well aware that they had been chasing down unicorns since Reykholt.

"Wait a second," said Professor Quimbey. "Jonas, pull up the picture you took of Gunnar's drawing from Sturluson's tunnel, the one he drew in the dirt." Dr. Arenot found the image on his phone and showed everyone what Gunnar had drawn:

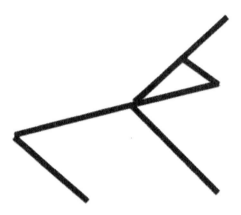

"Would you look at that," uttered Dr. Arenot. "There's a strong resemblance between all these drawings. Not identical, but they all look like stick unicorns with legs slanted forward, backs slightly angled up to the right, a triangle for a head and a horn sticking out of it."

"Maybe the Vaniryans never intended the Copán coordinates to mirror Emma's initials at all, but instead, to look like a unicorn," suggested Bryan.

"Perhaps, perhaps not. I guess we see what we want to see in the stars," replied Dr. Arenot, continuing, "or perhaps the stars are

314

telling us exactly what we should see, and that Immaculata James has been the unicorn we've been looking for this whole time."

"If the stars tell us what we should see, then, isn't there a constellation that looks like a unicorn?" asked Allysa.

Bryan googled it on his phone. "Yep, Monoceros!" he answered. "Oh, you guys are gonna love this..." He printed the Monoceros constellation and laid the printout beside the other drawings:

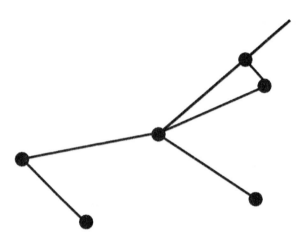

"It looks like another stick unicorn!" yelped Allysa.

"... with the same forward-slanted legs, a back angled slightly up and to the right, and an odd-shaped triangle for a head with a horn sticking out of it," observed Professor Quimbey.

"Just like the other ones," commented Allysa.

"You know," said Professor Quimbey, "in the Scroll of the Va, the enlarged star in each section represents where you are supposed to go, and the enlarged star in the upper section of stars I drew equates to the front shoulder of the unicorn. See..."

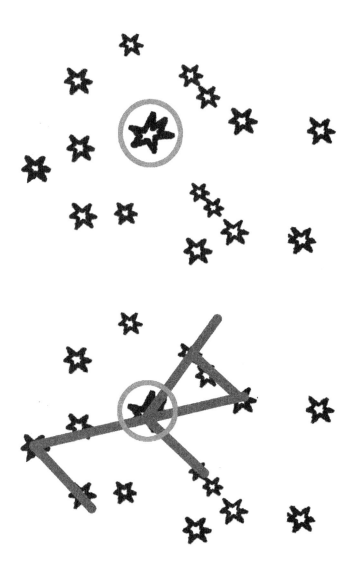

She continued, "So, if that's the case, which star in the Monoceros constellation is the front shoulder of the unicorn?" queried Professor Quimbey.

Bryan searched Google and replied, "*Delta Monocerotis!* It's a white main sequence star about 375 light years away from our Sun."

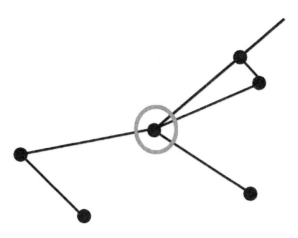

"That could be where we are supposed to go... maybe Delta Monocerotis is where the Va escaped to," suggested Professor Quimbey.

Dr. Arenot was curious. "Which landmark on the Copán map equals the front shoulder of the unicorn?"

They looked at the map and saw that it was the Château de Falaise in northern France:

"What are you thinking, Jonas?" asked Professor Quimbey.

"That we should pay another visit to the Château de Falaise," replied Dr. Arenot.

"But we've been there before, 3 years ago, and found nothing," said Professor Quimbey.

"Yeah, I know, but after seeing all this, maybe we missed something. Bryan, can you pull up a picture of the Château de Falaise?"

"Sure thing, Doc." Bryan pulled up a picture of the castle on his screen.

"That's the castle?" asked Allysa.

"Yep, that's it, the Château de Falaise in the Normandy region of Falaise, France," replied Bryan.

"Can you find an overhead map of the castle's floor plan?" asked Dr. Arenot.

"I think so." Bryan searched for one but couldn't find any.

Allysa had a suggestion. "What about a Falaise historical society or tourist website, something like that? Maybe you can find one there."

Bryan searched and found a website dedicated to the Château de Falaise at https://www.chateau-guillaume-leconquerant.fr/, which, roughly translated, meant "The Castle of William the Conqueror," referring to the Château's occupant in the 11th century.

"There, go to the 'Virtual Visit' link on the home page," blurted Allysa excitedly.

Bryan clicked the link and perused the options but saw nothing resembling a floor plan. There was a *Camarades* link (for Fellows) on the site. Bryan clicked the link and it asked for a username and password. "Well, we've been here before," uttered Bryan, remembering back to a similar hurdle he, Logan and Dr. Arenot previously faced when trying to gain access to the *Final Journey of the Vanir* records locked away on Uppsala Library's restricted members-only page.

"So, are we stuck?" asked Professor Quimbey.

Bryan laughed and replied, "No way! A low-security tourist website like this won't take more than a jiff for my 'CodeCracker' software to break."

"Is that the website penetration software you used last time?" asked Dr. Arenot.

"Yep, the same one. Here goes nothing." Bryan ran the software and they watched while the program worked its magic on the *Camarades* page. Bryan's screen flashed with hyper-fast activity, with the program force-feeding millions of usernames and passwords per second into the *Camarades* page as part of its brute-force attack methodology. It didn't take long.

"And...we're in!" announced Bryan.

The *Camarades* page had additional materials not publicly available, including a 'Castle of Honor' link listing top donations from Fellows; a 'Board of Trustees Minutes & Agenda' page; an 'Original Documents' link; and a 'Renovations Update' link.

"Click on the Renovations page," suggested Professor Quimbey. "Maybe it has plans, architectural drawings or schematics, who knows."

"Alright," said Bryan, clicking the Renovations link.

"There! Phase I Renovation Schematics!" screamed Allysa enthusiastically, looking at the link right above Phase II Renovation Schematics and Phase III Renovation Schematics.

Bryan clicked on Phase I Renovation Schematics, and up popped a page with an Original Building Plan and Proposed Renovations for the East and West Corridors.

"Well, I'll be damned, there's an Original Building Plan," said Dr. Arenot, kissing his wife on the cheek. "You never cease to prove how much smarter than me you are."

"Don't you forget it," chirped Professor Quimbey.

Bryan clicked on the Original Building Plan, and up came a castle schematic. He printed and set it on the table...

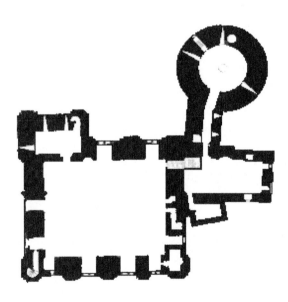

"Hey, I might be imagining things here," said Allysa, "but that castle's floor plan kind of resembles a unicorn, too." She grabbed a red Sharpie and traced over the floor plan. It required some imagination, but the resemblance wasn't that far off either...

Allysa continued. "And if you angle it slightly in a counter-clockwise direction, it sort of looks like the same unicorn shape we've been looking at..." She rotated the picture 15 degrees counter-clockwise.

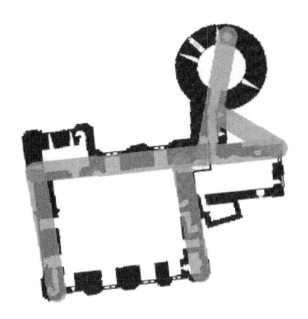

"No way!" blurted Bryan, looking at a castle floor plan design that looked like all the other unicorns they had been looking at. Five stick-figure unicorns each bearing an uncanny resemblance…

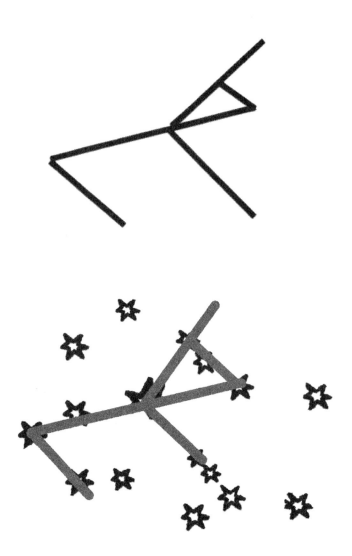

The Final Coordinate by Marc Jacobs

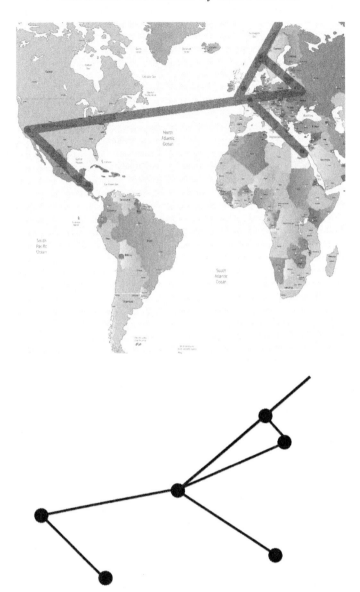

"Jonas, you're right, we've got to call Covington and get to France immediately to have another look at that castle!" exclaimed Professor Quimbey.

"What about going to Delta Monocerotis?" asked Bryan.

Professor Quimbey shook her head. "Jonas is right. We need to go to Falaise first."

"What you really need to do when you get there is check out the walls in that castle located where the front shoulder of the unicorn would theoretically be," remarked Allysa, based upon Professor Quimbey's comment that the largest star in each Scroll of the Va section always signified where one was supposed to go.

"Damn, GodzillaRocks with another knockout blow! She's right!" blurted Bryan. He grabbed the Château de Falaise's Original Building Plan page that Allysa had marked up and circled the section of the castle where the unicorn's theoretical front shoulder would be...

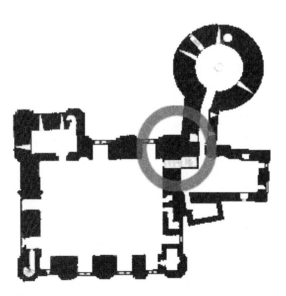

"There's a staircase there, and a few thick walls," continued Bryan.

Dr. Arenot replied, "We'll check those out, and if there's nothing there, then we can go to Delta Monocerotis, that is, if they'll still let us after what happened to Captain Velasquez's team on Electra-1."

"What happened to them?" Bryan asked, remembering Captain Velasquez from their rescue mission to the Hidden City on Vanirya.

"Only Velasquez made it back."

"Oh," replied Bryan.

"Okay. Bryan, Allysa, you have been incredibly helpful, as always," said Dr. Arenot, getting ready to leave.

"Wait, that's it?" asked Bryan, seemingly unsatisfied.

"Yeah, I think so. Jill and I need to head back to DC to get to France ASAP," replied Dr. Arenot.

"Not without us, you're not," stated Allysa, itching for another adventure. "We want to help."

"Logan and Emma are our friends too, and friends always stick together! Plus, you need us," added Bryan.

Dr. Arenot chuckled. "I'm not going to argue with you. Com—"

"Jonas, do you really think that's a good idea?" questioned Professor Quimbey.

"Jill, trust me, we're not going to talk them out of it. Besides, they've already got all the security clearance they need after the rescue mission to Vanirya, and he's right, we can use all the help we can get."

"So, we can come?" replied Bryan.

"Yeah, get your stuff. We gotta move fast though," responded Dr. Arenot.

Bryan jumped up and opened the office door. "Zack!" he hollered. His dutiful assistant manager came running around the corner. "Hey dude, I need you to take care of the store for a few days. Cool?"

"Sure thing. What's up?"

"Allysa and I are getting out of town for the weekend."

"Oooh, a little romantic getaway, huh?" giggled Zack.

"Busted," replied Bryan, not telling Zack what they were really doing. Bryan thought it was probably best not to mention anything about flying to France to save their friends, or the world, for that matter. After all, Zack had other things to worry about, like battle dungeons.

Chapter 25 – The Painful Truth

Logan was tied to a chair in a poorly lit room, his wrists and ankles bound by rope, and his arms secured behind his back. He didn't know where he was. It had been several days since he was captured by a group that he assumed was Russian, based on their accents and the language they were speaking.

Every six hours or so, someone came in to interrogate him, asking questions about the Leyandermál. Each time they did, he told them he didn't know anything and they responded by punching or kicking him. He didn't know how much more of it he could take; all he knew was that his responses weren't going to change.

A number of hours had passed since the last interrogation, and predictably, in came another interrogator. The metal door flung open at full speed, smashing into the steel wall to purposely jar Logan.

"You know, you're never going to get your security deposit back if you keep doing that," said Logan, who hadn't seen the interrogator before.

"Shut up," responded the interrogator as he approached without closing the door.

"You're going to leave it open? If I escape, that's on you."

"Be my guest," replied the interrogator. In came a second man holding a camera and tripod. He closed the door behind them. "There, do you feel better?" the first interrogator asked, while the second flicked on a light and started filming.

"Much."

"You know, they said you have sense of humor. Maybe I see it once I get warmed up," said the interrogator, throwing a harsh right hook into Logan's ribs. Logan coughed out some blood, grimacing from the pain. The blow hurt. There wasn't much he could do to hide that fact.

"There, now you are funny," uttered the interrogator, drawing pleasure from Logan's pain. "Now, where is the Leyandermál?" he demanded.

"How many times do I have to tell you guys: I. Don't. Know." Logan was struggling to breathe. He was pretty sure his captors had broken several of his ribs over the last couple days, and was on the verge of passing out.

"Wrong answer!" shouted the interrogator. He punched Logan again, this time in the face, and followed it up with a shot to Logan's gut, all while Goon #2 continued filming.

Logan coughed hard. Staring into the camera, he muttered, "I hate documentaries."

"Your girlfriend seems to like them. Now, if you don't know where it is, then tell me, *what* is the Leyandermál?"

"I've already told them five times, I don't know!"

"I don't believe you," growled the interrogator. "If you don't know what the Leyandermál is, then why do you search for it?!"

With the few ounces of strength he had left, Logan mustered one more, "I already told you—"

The interrogator kicked Logan in the chest. He fell backward in his chair, cracking the back of his head on the ground...

ΔΔΔΔΔΔΔΔΔΔΔΔ

Emma tried hard to hold back tears as she watched the video of Logan getting beaten up, which was being projected into her and Isa's cell on a split-screen digital display. Russian Prime Minister, Viktor Menputyn's face was visible on the other half of the screen. It was the third time they had shown her a video of them beating Logan, and he was looking worse each time, yet his black and blue eyes conveyed the same message every time he looked into the camera: don't give up, don't give in, and don't worry about me. He even mouthed the words 'I love you' into the camera at one point.

When Menputyn saw Logan mouth the words 'I love you,' he commented, "How sweet."

Emma and Isa had been held captive in a solid metal cell for days. Isa again resembled an 11-year-old-looking version of Emma, after changing back to that form at The Drunken Unicorn, right before Menputyn's men abducted them. She had been in the middle of showing Emma the different appearances she had assumed while living on Earth when Menputyn's men showed up. Now, her arms were tied behind her back using chains and her hands were bound inside thick metal contraptions, one on each hand, designed to contain her Vaniryan powers.

"You are beating him up for nothing! He doesn't know anything!" shouted Emma.

Menputyn replied, "Then your fiancé will die for nothing."

"Fiancé?" uttered Emma, allowing her momentary confusion to slip off her tongue.

Menputyn cackled at having spoiled the surprise. "I did not realize Mr. West hadn't popped the question yet. Perhaps he changed his mind about asking you. Young people these days, so fickle. Sad, too, because the ring he bought you really was beautiful. It would be a shame for it to go to waste. I will be sure to have one of my men retrieve it from his apartment so I can give it to someone more deserving."

"You are not deserving of the air you breathe!" said Emma.

Menputyn was unphased by her insult. "You are not the first to say that. Now, tell me, where is the Leyandermál?"

"We already told you we don't know," stated Emma.

"Then I suggest you try harder because the next time we visit your fiancé, we will cut off his left hand unless you tell me what I want to know."

"You can't do that!" yelled Emma, enraged.

"But I can. He has no use for his ring finger anyway. And if he doesn't bleed out and die, we will cut off another extremity every hour until you cooperate."

Isa interjected, "It is men like you who bring death and chaos into the world who deserve to die."

Menputyn sneered, "Men like me bring order to the world!"

"You aren't going to get away with this!" exclaimed Emma.

"I already have," countered Menputyn.

Emma replied, "President Barrett will find us and when he does—"

Menputyn stopped her mid-sentence. "I don't think so. There are hundreds of mountains in Russia. Your U.S. won't have time to look underneath every one of them, and Mr. West is being kept somewhere totally separate from you two. And as for the rest of your friends, they are all flying to France as we speak, looking for more clues in castles. We will deal with them when they get there. You have fifteen minutes."

Desperately, Emma yelled, "Menputyn, you can't—"

The video feed cut to black. Menputyn was gone.

Emma screamed, furious.

"I am sorry," said Isa, trying to console her.

Emma put her hands in her face and dropped to the ground with her back against the wall. She started to sob slightly behind her fingers, terrified for Logan, terrified for everyone.

After a few seconds, Isa sat down beside her as best she could with her arms tied behind her back and said, "It's going to be okay."

In a tearful voice, Emma replied through her hands, "How?"

"I don't know."

Emma lifted her head out of her hands. "You know, Logan and I were talking about this exact scenario happening not long ago, about me making a decision that might get him killed. It's like we spoke this into existence."

"You know that's not true. Menputyn's the one who spoke this into existence. What did Logan say about it then?"

"In typical brave, selfless Logan fashion, he said 'even good decisions have consequences, and 'there are no guarantees in life.' "

"He was right, and he would want you to remember that now," replied Isa.

Emma didn't feel satisfied with the inevitability of it all. "Well, it's stupid. Any decision that gets him or anyone else killed is a bad one."

"It is what the Leyandermál does, it kills people."

"But why does it have to do that?" asked Emma, somewhat rhetorically.

"Because absolute power corrupts everything and everyone," surmised Isa.

"Not you. It wouldn't corrupt you."

Isa shook her head. "Don't be so sure. I've done things since I came to this world that I wish I hadn't. When I watched Supay murder my parents, I promised myself that, one day, I would get revenge. And now that you've told me what he did to Vanirya, if I had the Leyandermál in my hands, I'm not so sure I wouldn't use it to kill Supay, his whole world and every living thing on it, or worse," said Isa, who was still reeling from the shock of learning from Emma two days earlier that Supay had destroyed Vanirya.

"I guess none of it's ever going to matter if we don't get out of here."

"We will," Isa assured Emma, still confident that things would work out.

Emma changed her tune. "*When* we get out of here, we need to promise each other to put an end to this somehow, and when we do, we're gonna go back and rescue everyone, starting with your parents and Annika!"

"Annika wouldn't want that," Isa responded.

Surprised, Emma replied, "Why? She wouldn't want to come back to live in her own time with her family?"

"No. Annika found her family with Niccolò. Those two were inseparable, and that boy of theirs, Marco, she loved him more than life itself. So did I. He was like my little brother. One of the last things Annika ever said to me before she died was that she did not want to be rescued anymore, that she did not want things changed. Marco meant everything to her, to all of us. She died happy."

"I suppose I never thought about it that way," said Emma.

"And I know you know this having grown up reading your history books about Marco Polo, but rescuing Annika would change the development of trade relations between the Far East and Western world in the 13th century that shaped the modern world. I even went on a few of those Far East journeys with Marco, among the most amazing adventures of my life. But the ramifications from any changes we make now are too great. I've had more than 800 years to learn Earth's history and consider our role in it, and I know that, like it or not, we are all now inextricably tied into its fabric. Finding a path forward is the only way out of this."

"When did you become so smart?" asked Emma.

"I have had a lot of time to think about things, along with learning over 200 languages since coming to this world," responded Isa, the depth of her eight centuries of wisdom and life experience on Earth obvious behind her 11-year-old-eyes. It was evident to Emma that Isa was no longer the same little girl she lost in the portal on Vanirya despite her appearance.

"Any brilliant ideas now?" asked Emma, closing her eyes, fearing the moment when Menputyn returned.

We give him what he wants, Isa replied telepathically, not wanting to take the chance that Menputyn was listening to their conversation. In fact, she assumed he was.

We give him the Leyandermál? Emma replied.

Yes.

Emma was confused. *But we don't know where it is.*

We have to buy time until your people can rescue us, responded Isa.

Emma knew Isa was right. They had to come up with something to stall until someone could rescue them, and so, that's exactly what Emma did…

As expected, Menputyn's face returned to the video screen at the fifteen-minute mark. "So, have you decided to save Mr. West's hand?"

336

"You have no idea how shortsighted you are," critiqued Emma.

"Nor do you," countered Menputyn.

"Listen to me, you need to let us go. Please! Supay is going to kill us all if we don't work together to stop him. He will destroy Earth. None of this will matter if we don't stop him!" insisted Emma.

"Once I find the Leyandermál, the most powerful weapon in the universe, I will stop him, and then, the whole world will pledge allegiance to Russia."

"So, this is all about politics?!" asked Emma, stunned, but more so, offended.

"Stupid girl. This is not about politics. It is about power, as it has been for a thousand years. Either you tell me the truth, or we will start with Logan's hand. From there, we will cut off one extremity at a time until he dies, then, we will move on to your parents."

Menputyn snapped his fingers and a split-screen visual of Logan popped up on the video display. Logan looked badly beaten. His eyes were fixed on the machete being held by one of Menputyn's men standing over him, while another held down his arm over a table, and a third restrained his body. Logan kept trying to yank his arm free, but he couldn't.

"Logan…," pleaded Emma, frightened for him.

"Shall I, Ms. James?" taunted Menputyn.

"No!" screamed Emma.

"Now!" shouted Menputyn.

"Giza!" hollered Emma, offering up the biggest bluff of her life while tears ran down her cheek.

The split-screen display of Logan disappeared. Emma had no idea if Menputyn's men had gone through with it.

"There, that wasn't so hard, was it?" questioned Menputyn.

"You are a monster!" yelled Emma.

"To some, I am a hero. The Leyandermál is in Giza?" questioned Menputyn, confirming what he had just heard while glaring at Emma.

"Yes, in the Great Pyramid," replied Emma, hoping her poker face held up.

"Hmm. That pyramid was one of the coordinates on your Copán map," said Menputyn, considering what she had said. "If you are lying, we will not just cut off Mr. West's hand, we will cut off his head, do you understand?"

Emma gulped. "It is in the 30-meter-long-void discovered inside the Great Pyramid using cosmic particle rays in 2017."

"There is no access into the Void, Ms. James. I know you know that. Do you think I am stupid? Ever since that landmark showed up on your coordinates map, I have studied it. Scientists have been looking for a way into that Void since its discovery."

"There is a way if you portal in using zeutyrons," responded Emma.

Menputyn hadn't thought of that. "And what will my men find when they get into the Void?" he asked.

Emma laughed at him. "Your men? The most powerful weapon in the universe and you are really going to let someone else find it first? He who finds the Leyandermál will rule over everything. Sounds like we will be dealing with a new Prime Minister soon. I honestly thought you were smarter than that."

Menputyn considered her point. "And what will *I* find inside the pyramid?" he asked, apparently changing his mind.

Isa answered, "We do not know. It is Vaniryan legend that the Leyandermál is the greatest source of power and knowledge in the universe, but we do not know what is inside the Void. It is possible there will be another clue to solve in order to access or use the Leyandermál. We just know that it is hidden inside the stones of Giza."

Menputyn responded to Isa, "Your people were clever to hide the Leyandermál inside 6 million tons of rock in a secret void with no human access. That is about as safe a place on Earth as they could have hidden it. If you are lying or do not cooperate when we get to Giza, we will kill Logan, are we clear?"

"You deserve to rot in hell," responded Emma.

Menputyn smirked. "Yes, well, I have no doubt the zeutyrons can transport me in and out of there, too, but we will start with Giza. And I suggest you two prepare to join me."

Chapter 26 – Full Circle

It had been nearly four years since Logan and Emma ducked into a café in Bologna to decipher the coordinates left behind on the walls of the Archiginnasio. There, the Norwegian Albo had painted a coat of arms depicting a white brick castle with two towers flanking a third larger tower in the middle, set on a dark hill against a red skyline, and a thin banner with Roman numerals partially covering the castle. The coat of arms was a replica of the shield for the Château de Falaise, the commanding Castle of the Dukes of Normandy, including Guillaume le Conquérant or *William the Conqueror*. The Château de Falaise was also positioned on Logan and Emma's Copán coordinates map at a location that corresponded with TYC 129-75-1, the Vaniryan home star, which had since been destroyed.

As a result, because of its importance in the Copán coordinates map, during Emma and Logan's freshman year at Georgetown, after the Pegasus project got underway, one of the first things President Barrett had them do was fly back to Falaise with Dr. Arenot and Professor Quimbey to investigate the castle. They had searched for hidden corridors, underground chambers, inscriptions, or other clues hidden in the ancient structure, and found nothing. This time, the professors, driving in a van up the road to the stone keep sitting atop a rocky outcrop overlooking Falaise, hoped for a different result.

Agent Stephenson drove the van with Captain Velasquez sitting shotgun, the professors in the second row, Bryan and Allysa behind them and Captain Evans alone in the back row. Given all the security leaks they had encountered lately, General Covington and General Nemond insisted they limit the mission's participants to the same trusted few, and keep intel about their Falaise trip to a

340

minimum number of people, but that still didn't stop the professors from worrying. Not Bryan, though. Off on another galactic adventure with Allysa to save the day, he couldn't be any more excited or oblivious to the stress of the moment.

"Look at this place!" he blurted when the van reached the top of the rocky hill just outside the Château's fortified walls. "Le Conquérant's haunt was bad ass!"

"Let's hope it was more than that," said Captain Evans, still reeling from the loss of Emma, Logan, and Isa, and desperately hoping there was more to find at the Château de Falaise than history. What had happened in Khatyrka was as painful for her as when she lost her team on Peak Pobeda during the Chersky Mission. It was yet another failure that sowed doubt in her mind as to what she could have done differently. Covington had given her the opportunity to pass on the Falaise mission to regroup, but like Velasquez, who was fresh off the loss of his own team on Electra-1, she insisted on continuing. They both did. If there was any chance this mission could lead them back to Logan, Emma and Isa, any hope, both Evans and Velasquez wanted that chance at redemption and Covington wasn't going to stand in their way. Plus, their familiarity with the enemy and knowledge of all aspects of the Pegasus project rendered them near-indispensable.

As they came to a stop in the parking lot, Dr. Arenot said, "General Nemond's contact in Normandy arranged for us to get in two hours early before it opens. We're a few minutes ahead of schedule but let's see if they're ready for us."

All at once, they poured out of the van. Dr. Arenot and Professor Quimbey went to the back to retrieve their equipment. Dr. Arenot reached for his trusty cosmic particle detector, 3D laser scanner and bag of tools, while Professor Quimbey grabbed her gravitometer and a few other devices.

They walked through the outer gates to where Pierre, a staff member, was waiting for them. The professors remembered him from their prior visit to the castle. Apparently, he came with the keep.

"Welcome back to Château Guillaume-le-Conquérant, professors," he said to Dr. Arenot and Professor Quimbey. Addressing the rest of them, he continued, "I am Pierre, Head Groundskeeper." Finally, noticing the bags of gear the professors were carrying, Pierre added, "You bring a lot of equipment."

"We definitely do," replied Professor Quimbey. "It is a pleasure to see you again, Pierre."

"And you, as well, Mademoiselle. So what is it that your group looks to study this time? Perhaps I can be of assistance."

Dr. Arenot responded, "We are studying construction techniques."

"Not my, eh, forte, I am afraid. It takes seven of you to study the construction?"

"I teach a popular class at the University... That's what happens when you're the professor who gives easy grades," replied Dr. Arenot.

Pierre chuckled. "What happened to the students from last time?"

Knowing that Pierre was referring to Logan and Emma, Dr. Arenot responded, "They graduated. On to better things than staring at old stones, I hope."

Pierre eyed Bryan and Allysa. They looked young enough to be students but he wasn't so sure about Captain Evans, Captain Velasquez, or Agent Stephenson. "Are you three students, too?"

Before anyone could answer, Dr. Arenot jumped back in, "They're my, umm, grad students."

Pierre seemed to buy it. "Ah, I see. For you new students, if the professors did not already mention, eh, you might find it interesting to know as you look at the imposing keep perched on a spur of rock

342

high above town, that Falaise literally means 'cliff' in French. Our town was named after the keep on the cliff."

"Huh, interesting," replied Allysa.

Pierre, who was ready to take them in, said, "Please, follow me." He turned and walked toward the castle, guiding them over a bridge and through a public entrance into a large room called The Aula. The room had a high ceiling, walls and flooring made up of a mix of old stone and newer building materials, and large ornate Norman Romanesque windows to let light in. "Dr. Arenot, Professor Quimbey, have you taught your students about this great hall?"

"No, please, go ahead," replied Dr. Arenot, who had heard Pierre's spiel before.

Pierre explained, "This room is called The Aula. It was once the center of the castle, the Grand Hall and throne room where the king-duke presided over assemblies, passed judgments, received petitioners and visitors, and resolved disputes. It was, eh, the home of the first Norman King of England, Guillaume le Conquérant... William the Conqueror to you. Did you know that every English monarch who has followed William, including Queen Elizabeth II and her family, is considered a descendant of the Norman-born king? Some genealogists claim that more than 25 percent of the English population is distantly related to him, as are countless people with British ancestry around the globe. This place you stand in literally *is* history."

"I could totally see holding a Dungeons & Dragons tournament in here," remarked Bryan, wowed by the castle's dungeon-like atmosphere.

"How much of this place is original?" asked Dr. Arenot, looking at the hall's newer walls.

Pierre replied, "Much of the castle has undergone refurbishment over the years. The walls and floor in The Aula and Small Keep, in particular, have been substantially reinforced over time to prevent the keep from collapsing."

"Is any portion of the castle still original?" asked Allysa, suddenly worried that they had come a long way to look for clues in a portion of the castle where the structure had been rebuilt.

Pierre nodded. "Eh, yes. The stair corridor, lower rooms and The Talbot Tower remain fully intact as original. Please let me know if you need anything. I will be outside with my staff preparing the grounds for today's visitors."

"Merci," responded Professor Quimbey. Pierre turned and walked out.

"Phew," mumbled Allysa, relieved that the section of the castle where they planned to start their search was still original.

"Okay, let's head over to the corridor leading into the Small Keep where there is a staircase down to the lower rooms," said Dr. Arenot. That was where Allysa had proposed they start based on the location of the theoretical unicorn's front shoulder.

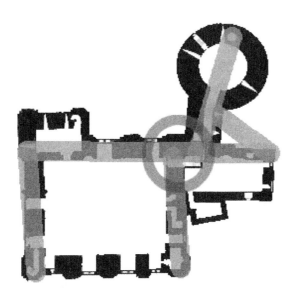

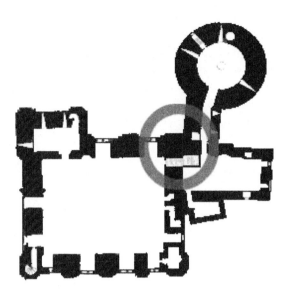

"It's this way," Dr. Arenot informed the others, leading them toward the corridor and stairs on the northwest end of the hall.

They followed Dr. Arenot to the staircase, which was narrow, poorly lit and had a low 6½ foot ceiling. The first flight of stairs descended through walls of stone halfway down to a landing, turned right, and continued down further to the lower rooms. The corridor's walls were made of medium-sized stone blocks fit together with mortar.

"Alright, let's get to it," said Dr. Arenot. Turning to Capitan Evans, Captain Velasquez, and Agent Stephenson, he added, "You three keep watch at the top of the stair corridor."

"You got it," replied Captain Evans.

She, Velasquez, and Stephenson kept watch in The Aula while the professors, Bryan and Allysa headed down the steps, looking for clues using the devices the professors had brought with them. They scanned the walls and steps looking for open spaces behind or under the stone, and searched for markings, for about an hour.

"Stymied again," lamented Professor Quimbey after concluding the results were no different than the first time they visited.

Allysa was disappointed. She had taken personal ownership of her idea to search where the theoretical unicorn's shoulder was supposed to be. "Darn. Are you sure you're using that doodad correctly?" she asked Dr. Arenot.

Dr. Arenot half-heartedly grinned. "This 'doodad' is a cosmic particle detector, and the muons spilling out of it don't lie. They didn't the last time we were here, either. If there was a hidden corridor or room, we would have found it."

"Well, maybe we're not looking for a hidden corridor or room," suggested Allysa.

Dr. Arenot replied, "Then what are we looking for?"

Allysa responded, "Maybe something smaller, something that wouldn't look like a corridor, passageway or room... like a small compartment or maybe even something smaller than that."

"Can we review the data the cosmic particle detector sent to the 3D scanner?" inquired Bryan, who was holding the scanner.

"Yep," answered Dr. Arenot, taking hold of the device from Bryan. He sat on a step next to Bryan's feet to study the data images. Bryan plopped down beside him and Allysa one step up.

Dr. Arenot began reading the scanner's display which had synced with the particle detector to render a complete digital record of what was behind and below the stone walls and steps.

"What about there!?" blurted Allysa over Dr. Arenot's shoulder as he flipped through the images, one frame at a time.

"That, my young archeologist, is a crack in the mortar," the professor replied. He had spent years studying images like this and knew a mortar crack when he saw one.

"Oh," muttered Allysa, momentarily thinking she'd found something. Dr. Arenot kept shuffling between images until Allysa excitedly exclaimed again, "There! How about that one!?"

Dr. Arenot chuckled. "That is a gap between stones. When constructing these castles, they didn't use engineering software, modern techniques, or machinery. The placement of the stones is going to be imperfect. Castles built in this time period typically have spaces behind stones where the fit isn't tight. Keep up those eagle eyes, though," he encouraged Allysa.

"How's it going down there?" asked Captain Evans from above.

"Swimmingly," Professor Quimbey shouted back up.

"Sounds good... let us know if you need anything," Captain Evans replied.

Dr. Arenot kept clicking through the images. After a few more minutes, Allysa once again got excited…

"There!" she yelped, pointing to a section of the staircase on the north side of the lower corridor where there appeared to be a small line inside the wall.

Dr. Arenot theorized, "Maybe it's another gap between stones."

"Are you sure?" asked Bryan. "Because it looks to me like the line is in the middle of a stone block, like someone cut into it."

Dr. Arenot, playing devil's advocate, replied, "Perhaps they were trying to fit two stones together."

Professor Quimbey begged to differ. "If that was the case, the stone would look like it was in two halves. I don't know what it could be, but Bryan is right, that line looks like it's in the middle of the stone."

Dr. Arenot replied, "Why don't we go take a closer look?"

They proceeded to the lower corridor and stopped where the suspicious stone was located. Dr. Arenot went into his tool bag and pulled out some flashlights for better lighting. He distributed them. Everyone pointed their flashlights at the stone.

Professor Quimbey remarked, "It's slight, but if you ask me, the stone is discolored. Hard to notice in the dim lighting down here, but the shade is darker than the rest, and the mortar smooth around it."

Dr. Arenot wasn't convinced. "Discoloration isn't unusual."

"Even if the rocks came from the same place?" asked Bryan.

Dr. Arenot nodded. "Possibly. Even stones from the same quarry can have color variations."

"What about the mortar, Jonas? It looks smooth around the edges, more so than the others," observed Professor Quimbey.

"I agree, it does," conceded Dr. Arenot, "but think about what you're proposing... cracking open the walls inside a historic castle based on a hunch. General Covington told us not to break the stones in here unless we were absolutely sure because he's going to have to explain it to the French. And we all know what he meant... only do it if we discover something obvious that we can't walk away from."

"How about taking a higher resolution image to get a better sense of what this is?" proposed Professor Quimbey.

Dr. Arenot liked her suggestion. "If I tighten the muon beam, it may generate a more precise image of what is directly in front of the particle detector, but with limited 3D width or depth perception."

"Let's do that!" said Allysa enthusiastically.

"Alright." Dr. Arenot changed the settings on the particle detector to narrow the muon beam. He turned it on and slowly scanned the stone. He moved along the face of the stone deliberately, one inch at a time. When done, he announced, "Okay, finished."

"Dr. Arenot, there's a perfect line inside that stone," uttered Bryan.

Dr. Arenot looked at the scanner. "Hmm, I love it when the stones make a fool out of me. You're absolutely right... there is a perfectly-straight line in there, it looks like a groove about eight inches long."

"Jonas, that doesn't look natural to me. How did we miss this the last time we were here?" wondered Professor Quimbey.

Jonas responded, "Well, we were looking for bigger spaces, something far more obvious and not nearly this small. And we had a whole castle to search. Other than that, I don't know, but we did. We definitely missed it."

"Now do you want to break it open?" asked Allysa.

"Bryan, can you grab the chisel?" requested Dr. Arenot, answering Allysa's question with one of his own.

Bryan reached into Dr. Arenot's bag and pulled out the chisel. "Here you go, Doc."

"Thanks." Dr. Arenot put the chisel's tip on the mortar, and with the palm of his hand, smacked the back of it…

Pop! The chisel went straight in and the mortar collapsed around it.

"That was easy," commented Dr. Arenot, surprised. "The mortar around this stone is not compacted, at all." Dr. Arenot, using his chisel, quickly cleared away the mortar from all four sides of the stone. "Okay, guys, give me a hand with this."

They all grabbed hold of the stone and pulled. It was a medium-sized stone, not so big that the four of them couldn't move it with some effort. It shimmied an inch. "Let's keep going," urged Dr. Arenot. "On the count of three again… one… two… three." They pulled the stone block out a little more. "We've almost got it, it's nearly halfway out. One more time." Everyone readied themselves as Dr. Arenot counted again: "One… two… three, pull!" They pulled, and the rock slid forward even more.

"There it is!" exclaimed Allysa. She could see a straight groove on top of the stone, smack in the middle. And true to the scanner, it looked about eight inches long, and was one to two inches deep.

Dr. Arenot, using his flashlight, examined the groove. "Huh," he uttered.

"What do you see?" asked Professor Quimbey.

"There's something in there." Dr. Arenot, using his right index finger and thumb, reached in and pulled out a worn-down, folded up brown parchment. After he unfolded it, it had a familiar albeit faded design on it: a large outer circle with a smaller solid circle in the middle, three lines extending outward from the inner circle to the outer ring dividing the whole up into three equal pie-chart sections, and stars in each section.

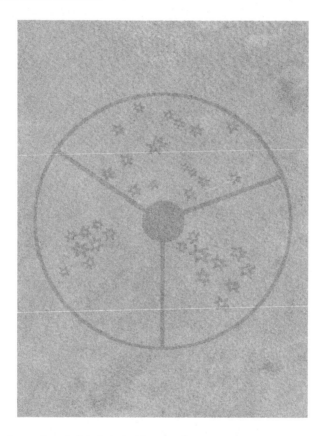

"Is that what I think it is?" asked Dr. Arenot.

"It looks just like the Scroll of the Va we saw in the tree city on Vanirya," replied Professor Quimbey.

"Would they have made two of them?" wondered Allysa.

"Maybe they made an extra copy and left it on Earth in case something happened to the original," suggested Bryan.

"Wait! There's something written on the back," said Dr. Arenot. He flipped it around for all to see. Written on the back of the parchment was a note in worn-out, barely legible ink:

Par dessus tout, que Dieu règne en maître et que
la foi au Christ soit à jamais inviolée. En guise
de gratitude pour le cadeau du Norvégien de b
c faite du soulèvement des croisés templiers,
je m'engage à garder son secret en sécurité a
l'intérieur de ces murs jusqu'à ce que son héritier
se lève et revienne. On ne sait ni comment ni pourquoi,
on sait seulement ce que le Norvégien a fait pour sauver
la Maison de Normandie. Dans le sang et le serment,
je garderai son secret pour l'éternité.
Décrète ce jour, le roi Guillaume 3er

"It's in French. I don't suppose anyone can read this," stated Professor Quimbey.

"I can," Bryan announced.

"Really?" replied Allysa, surprised.

"Uh-huh. Some kids took Spanish in high school. I took French." All eyes remained on him, so he felt the need to explain further. "I thought it would impress the girls."

"Oui," responded Allysa, indeed, impressed.

"I never really thought I'd use it again after high school."

"Well, now's your chance," said Dr. Arenot, handing the parchment to Bryan.

Trying to lower expectations, Bryan added, "I mean, I'm not fluent or anything, but—"

"Just give it a whirl," interrupted Dr. Arenot.

"Okay. I'll try, but it's pretty faded. Here goes nothing." He took hold of the parchment and translated it out loud as best he could… "It says, umm…

> Over this things… is God govern highest… faith in Christ keeps forever in violation. Thankfulness of the Norwegian's present, defeating revolt of Templar crusaders, I promise to hold his private safety in the wall until relatives float and return. We do not understand how or why, we know only merely of ask the Norwegian if save the House of Normandy. In blood and swear or vow… my castle should hide secret his for forever. Commanded today, King William I"

"What in the world does that mean?" asked Allysa.

"I'm sorry guys, my French needs serious work… I butchered the whole thing."

"It's okay," said Allysa, proud of him for trying. "You still did really good."

Dr. Arenot wasn't disappointed. "Actually, I heard the word Norwegian in there. Did I hear you correctly?" he asked.

"Yep."

"Could that be referring to the Norwegian Albo?" speculated Professor Quimbey.

Dr. Arenot thought about it. "It's possible given everything we know."

"Maybe we can try Google Translate or something later," suggested Bryan.

"Wait, that's a brilliant idea!" said Allysa. "Why didn't I think of that?! I have a translation app on my phone!" Allysa pulled out her phone, took hold of the parchment from Bryan, and keyed in all the words. After doing so, she read the translation aloud:

> *"Above all things, may God reign supreme and faith in Christ be kept forever inviolate. In gratitude for the Norwegian's gift of defeat of the uprising of the Templar crusaders, I pledge to keep his secret safe inside these walls until his heir shall rise and return. We do not know how or why, we know only what the Norwegian did to save the House of Normandy. In blood and oath, my keep shall guard the secret of his scroll for eternity. Decreed this day, King William I"*

"Huh. I was close," remarked Bryan.

"Yes, you were," replied Allysa, giving the document back to Dr. Arenot.

"So, what does it mean?" wondered Bryan.

They heard shouting coming from The Aula.

"Something's going on upstairs!" stated Professor Quimbey.

"Darn!" uttered Dr. Arenot. He placed the parchment inside his bag. "We'll have to go over this later. Let's shove the stone back in place."

They all leaned in and pushed the stone back into the wall. The grooves around it remained exposed but there wasn't much they could do about it at the moment.

"Alright, let's head up and see what the commotion is about," said Dr. Arenot. They walked back upstairs. When they got there, Captain Evans, Captain Velasquez and Agent Stevenson were gone, and they heard screaming outside. Then, they heard gunshots! Multiple gunshots!

"Bloody hell, here we go again," muttered Professor Quimbey.

Suddenly, Captain Velasquez, Captain Evans and Pierre came running back into The Aula to escape enemy fire. Pierre scrambled for cover while the captains each took a side of the door. One at a time, they peeked around the edge and returned fire.

"What's going on?!" bellowed Pierre, covering his ears at the sound of gunfire.

"We're being ambushed," replied Captain Velasquez, stating the obvious.

"Someone knew we were coming!" screamed Captain Evans.

"Where's Stephenson?" hollered Dr. Arenot.

"Stephenson's down!" replied Captain Evans.

The assault intensified. Incoming bullets were pulverizing the stonework outside the entrance and flying into The Aula.

"Everyone back up!" ordered Captain Evans. "Pierre, how do we get out of here?"

"That entrance is the only way out of this castle!" exclaimed Pierre.

"Who builds a castle with no other exits!?" griped Captain Evans.

Pierre suggested, "In the lower rooms below the Small Keep, there are slots that were built for the archers to defend the keep. They might be wide enough to squeeze through, with only a short drop down to the hill on the south side of the castle."

Several objects flew into the entrance. Smoke began flooding The Aula, along with more gunfire.

"Crap, smoke bombs!" yelled Captain Evans. They could hear the enemy closing in on the entrance. "Guys, get down those stairs to the lower rooms like Pierre said!" shouted Captain Evans, firing back to provide cover while retreating deeper into The Aula to avoid the smoke.

Pierre led the way down to the lower rooms. Everyone followed, while enemy soldiers raced into The Aula with guns blazing. Captain Velasquez and Captain Evans stopped just below the top of the staircase corridor to assume defensive positions.

"Go, all of you!" barked Captain Evans to the group after they hesitated at the midway landing. "Hurry!"

Evans and Velasquez fired shots into The Aula to keep the enemy at bay. Unfortunately, more enemy soldiers were pouring in and firing semi-automatic weapons.

"I count at least 10 of them!" stated Evans, ducking to avoid enemy fire. Bullets struck the staircase, pushing Evans and Velasquez further down the steps toward the landing. "Velasquez, we're running out of room!" Just as Velasquez turned his head to see how much room they had left, an enemy intruder leaned around the corner at the top of the stairs and took a shot at him.

"Look out!" shouted Captain Evans, leaping in front of Velasquez to protect him while firing back at the same time. She killed the enemy but took the bullet meant for Velasquez in her upper right chest next to her shoulder, just below her collarbone. "Ah!" she cried, falling hard to the ground. She immediately grabbed her upper chest in pain. Fortunately, the bullet had missed her vital organs, but it still substantially incapacitated her. "Goddammit!" she screamed.

Velasquez started firing wildly up the stairs to keep the enemy back.

"Velasquez, c'mon, we can't go out like this. We've gotta do something!"

Velasquez nodded. He had something in mind. He looked at Captain Evans, and unexpectedly, his eyes flared a bright blue color.

Captain Evans was stunned. "What in the world… what are you?" she uttered.

Velasquez did not respond. Instead, the energy inside his body started swirling into a new form. He still had shape, but he looked more made of energy than humanity. Velasquez bolted up the stairs toward the enemy, suddenly unconcerned about the risk of gunfire. Bullets passed right through him in his new state of energy.

Evans, who could not follow Velasquez up the stairs given her injury, heard gunshots. Then, she saw a flash of blue light, an explosion of energy followed by the sound of falling bodies. When it was over, all was silent. Evans weakly crawled up the stairs to see what had happened. She saw a room full of dead bodies and Velasquez standing in the middle, reconstituting himself back into human form. She struggled to her feet despite the gunshot wound. Velasquez started walking back toward her.

"Oh my god, thank you. Are you a Vaniryan? A Remnant?"

"We are the future for humanity," replied Velasquez.

"I don't understand."

Velasquez looked at Evans and replied, "You will soon. Captain Velasquez would have been proud of how you fought today. He too fought courageously up until his death."

"What?!" Evans uttered.

The alien posing as Velasquez lifted his gun and shot Evans in the stomach. She collapsed onto her side on the floor of The Aula with her legs partially dangling down the staircase. She gasped for air as blood filled her lungs and spilled out of her mouth. With what little life she had left in her eyes, she gazed at Velasquez and whispered, "Why?"

Velasquez gazed at her, almost as if, deep down, he admired her. After all, she had saved his life. "Do not be afraid. Soon, all of humanity will die with you."

"But you—"

"No one can know my secret."

Velasquez took aim and shot her again. She slumped onto the floor. He leaned over and grabbed her gun. He began methodically walking around The Aula shooting all the dead bodies in their chests, stomachs, or heads to make it appear as if they had died from gunfire. He alternated weapons between his and Captain Evans' so it looked like they both had defended the keep until the end. Once done, he wiped off her gun and put it back in her hand. He could hear sirens racing up the hill to the keep. He had to hurry. He was just about out of time...

ΔΔΔΔΔΔΔΔΔΔΔΔ

The professors, Bryan, Allysa, and Pierre hid in the lower rooms at the bottom of the stairs, hiding behind a locked wooden door, although they knew a few well-placed gunshots could obliterate the lock. The arrow-slits created for archers that Pierre had suggested might be wide enough to escape through turned out to be too narrow. They were trapped with nowhere to go, forced to listen to the gunfire and screaming from the castle's upper floors.

After a few minutes, everything got silent. They weren't sure what was happening, but they heard sirens approaching, and then, loud pounding on the door.

"Open up!" yelled a voice.

"Don't open it!" shouted Allysa, afraid.

"It's Velasquez! Hurry, open the door!" yelled the alien pretending to be Velasquez.

Dr. Arenot rushed to open the door. Velasquez hurried in. He had blood all over his shirt.

"Oh my god," uttered Allysa, horrified at the sight of all the blood.

"Where is Captain Evans?" Professor Quimbey asked.

"She didn't make it."

Professor Quimbey closed her eyes and lowered her head, saddened by the news. She, Captain Evans, and Emma had grown very close while trapped together on Vanirya and in the months that followed.

"Is everyone okay in here?" asked Velasquez.

"Yes, we're fine," replied Dr. Arenot, "but I hope you weren't looking for a way out. The arrow slits Pierre mentioned, make better toothpicks than doors."

Captain Velasquez, after seeing the thin arrow slits that Dr. Arenot was talking about, lifted his gun and pointed it straight at Pierre's forehead. "You must have known they were too narrow to fit through. You're the Head Groundskeeper. How could you not have known?"

Pierre's knees were shaking uncontrollably. "I... I thought—"

"Were you in on the ambush? Did you send us down here to trap us? Our friends died up there!" yelled Velasquez at Pierre. With his free hand, he grabbed the front of Pierre's shirt and pulled him in close, ready to pull the trigger.

"I swear, I did not," squeaked Pierre meekly and unconvincingly.

"Hey, let's everyone settle down, okay," urged Dr. Arenot. He wasn't sure if Velasquez was right about Pierre, but he wasn't keen on seeing Pierre's brains splattered all over the wall, either.

"Fine," said Velasquez. He clocked Pierre in the side of the head with his gun, knocking him out cold. Everyone looked shocked. Velasquez explained, "I do not trust him. Did you find anything in the stairs?"

Dr. Arenot replied, "Yes, we found this." He pulled out the parchment and gave it to Captain Velasquez to look at.

Velasquez examined both sides of it very carefully. Before he could ask any more questions, they heard police rushing down the steps to the lower rooms. He handed the parchment back to Dr. Arenot. "I suggest everyone put their hands up."

Captain Velasquez laid his weapon on the ground and lifted his hands high in the air. They all followed suit, putting their hands up just before the French police crashed into the room with guns drawn.

"Nobody move!" screamed the officers in French.

Nobody did.

Chapter 27 – The Void

When Emma and Isa walked through the portal into the Void, the stale air smelled as ancient as the 4,500-year-old Great Pyramid of Giza itself. The fact that there was air in there at all told Emma that there might be a small crack or hole somewhere, but they couldn't see anything because it was dark except for the light coming from the portal. Several armed Russian soldiers carrying containers, multiple scientists, and Prime Minister Menputyn, followed them into the Void.

The scientists immediately began testing the air quality inside the Void using oxygen sensors. They reported back to Menputyn in Russian that oxygen was limited and of poor quality, and that they should limit their exposure. The scientists also suggested wearing the supplemental oxygen masks they brought with them, but Menputyn dismissively waved them off.

Meanwhile, the soldiers were busy removing battery-operated floodlights from the containers and placing them on the floor to illuminate the Void. Once they were finished, everyone could see for the first-time what archeologists using cosmic particle rays had discovered four years earlier: a 30-meter long and 10-meter-wide cavity inside the upper middle section of the Great Pyramid with no discernable access points.

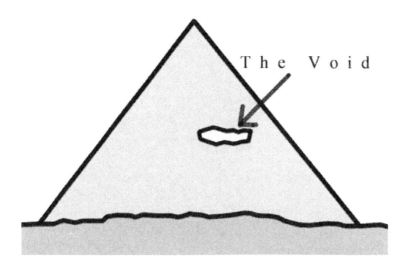

The Void

"Close it!" shouted Menputyn in Russian to his science team who, in turn, signaled to the scientists on the other side of the portal. The gateway vanished, trapping Emma and Isa deep inside 6.5 million tons of limestone with Menputyn and his men. Menputyn glared at Emma's anxious face and asked, "Why the worry, Ms. James? No harm will come to you or anyone else you care about, *if* you both cooperate."

"I don't trust you," Emma replied.

Menputyn sinisterly chuckled. "I remind you that if you are lying to me about the Leyandermál or if I do not walk out of here alive, Moscow has instruction to kill Mr. West, and then, to move on to someone else you care about, and so on and so forth, until you cooperate." Emma appeared angry and frustrated. "Good, it appears we understand each other. Now, let's find the Leyandermál, shall we?" Menputyn gestured for Emma and Isa to lead the way.

They started exploring the Void, which was generally rectangular except that the floor and ceiling undulated up and down and walls in and out in a jagged pattern. There were no rooms or tombs inside the Void, or Egyptian artifacts, treasures, or relics to be seen. There was an altar made of limestone blocks in the middle with nothing on it. Still, the Void was not empty…

Egyptian hieroglyphs covered the walls from end to end, sparing no inch of limestone. It was an astonishing discovery of Egyptian history never before seen by modern man. They surveyed the walls and hieroglyphs while Russian soldiers kept their guns aimed at them. At the same time, the scientists photographed and videoed everything to create a complete record of what they were seeing.

After a while, Menputyn commented to Emma, "Stunning, isn't it? So much history locked away in here for thousands of years."

Emma found his comment surprising. She doubted he cared much about history. "Yeah, incredible," she responded sarcastically.

Menputyn continued, "The story the Egyptians hid in this tomb of dead space must have been about something remarkable."

Emma, fairly certain he was alluding to the Leyandermál, replied, "Uh-huh."

"Where is it?! There is nothing here!" shouted Menputyn furiously, revealing what he was really interested in.

"Do you not see what is right before your eyes?" responded Isa, slowing down at a group of hieroglyphics on the wall in the center of the Void right in front of the altar.

"What are you talking about?" asked Menputyn.

Because her arms and hands were still tied behind her back, Isa motioned to the hieroglyphics on the wall with her head and replied, "There is writing there that is not Egyptian, mixed in with the hieroglyphs. It is faint, but it is there."

"Where?" Menputyn questioned, moving close to her.

"Untie my hands, and I will show you," replied Isa.

Menputyn scoffed and responded, "Try a little harder."

"Fine." Isa used head gestures to direct Menputyn's eyes toward faint sweeping, looping, and flowing letters below a hieroglyph of wavy lines. "There," she said.

Menputyn called his two scientists over to inspect the wall. They came quickly, examined the hieroglyphs and lettering, and confirmed that the wavy lines were the Egyptian symbol for water but the lettering below was not Egyptian. Isa was telling the truth.

Isa added, "And there is writing under several other hieroglyphs, too."

"The lettering reminds me of the Voynich Manuscript," said Emma.

"That is because it is Vaniryan writing," said Isa.

"Fascinating," remarked Menputyn, stepping up and running his fingers over the lettering, and that's when Isa saw it… a silver ring on the ring finger of Menputyn's left hand that had a silver insignia on it which Isa recognized: a right-leaning cross in a circle.

Isa's stomach turned. It was the coat of arms of the Order of Christ's Templars brandished by Lord Phillipe Nemond and his men when they attacked Corte Del Milion. Suddenly, a tidal wave of painful memories of her son dying in her arms at the hands of Nemond's murderous army overwhelmed her. Menputyn, noticing Isa's eyes fixated on his ring, promptly pulled his hand away, stepped back, and asked his scientists to take a closer look at the hieroglyphs with Vaniryan writing below them.

As they were doing that, Emma could see in Isa's face that something was wrong. She put her hand on Isa's shoulder and, knowing Isa could read her thoughts, asked in her mind, *Are you alright?*

His ring bears the insignia of the Order of Christ's Templars who attacked my home in Venice and murdered my son, replied Isa telepathically.

Are you sure? Emma replied. She recognized the name 'Order of Christ's Templars' because she, Logan and the professors had been discussing the Christ's Templars in the shuttle on the way to Shugborough Hall.

Yes! I will never forget the coat of arms waved by Lord Nemond's twisted Templars. I thought they had faded away centuries ago, but I was wrong.

Nemond? wondered Emma, confused, since she had never mentioned General Bernard Nemond to Isa before.

Yes, Lord Phillipe Nemond and his men attacked my home in Corte Del Milion. They burned down our buildings, murdered innocent people and tried to capture me! Menputyn's ring bears the insignia.

Suddenly, it occurred to Emma that General Nemond might be a descendant of Lord Phillipe Nemond, a disciple of the Christ's Templars, and that he might have been the source of the leaks to Russia the whole time.

Menputyn could see Isa angrily staring at him. He could see the fury in her eyes growing, and even saw a flicker of her deadly energy flash in her pupils. He, like all Christ's Templars, knew the stories of the otherworldly power their Order had tried to corral in the middle ages. Knowing her hands were secured behind her back, Menputyn stepped into Isa's face and warned, "Do not tempt yourself, girl, or everyone Emma James has ever cared about will die, do you understand?"

"Leave her alone!" snapped Emma, stepping in between them.

Menputyn's men lifted their guns high and pointed them straight at Emma's forehead. Menputyn chuckled and replied, "Do you really think you can save her by stepping in front of me?"

"It wasn't her I was saving," countered Emma.

Menputyn coughed and wheezed from the limestone dust in the air. "We do not have time for this. Where is the Leyandermál? I will not ask again."

366

Isa walked up to the wall of hieroglyphics and said, "This is what you are looking for."

Menputyn was incensed. "Do you really expect me to believe these hieroglyphs with Vaniryan lettering contain the secrets of the universe, the greatest power ever known to mankind?!"

Emma interjected, "Did you really think the Egyptians built these pyramids on their own?" Emma was bluffing, of course, as she didn't actually believe the Egyptians had extraterrestrial help building their pyramids, but she was desperate to come up with something Menputyn might buy.

"And do you, Ms. James, honestly believe that if the Egyptians possessed the greatest power in the universe, that Egypt would not now be the world's sole superpower today? I am not stupid, Ms. James. These hieroglyphs are nothing more than art on walls glorified by archeologists like your Dr. Arenot merely because they are old."

Emma replied, "These hieroglyphics—"

"Then, tell me, Ms. James, what makes this the Leyandermál? You said it was in Giza to stop me from cutting off Mr. West's hand, and here we are. So, show me, or blood will spill, starting with Mr. West."

Emma couldn't show him. She was out of ideas. Their bluff had reached the end of the line.

"I didn't think so," said Menputyn.

"Prime Minister, we have completed our photo-documentation of all the walls," reported one of the scientists.

"Good," responded Menputyn. Just as he said it, a bright, rectangular portal opened up precisely where it had earlier. "Right on time," remarked Menputyn. Returning his attention back to

Emma, he asked, "Do you still refuse to tell me? So be it. You will soon enough. Let's go!" said Menputyn.

His soldiers and scientists began cleaning up their equipment, and that included the floodlights. In short order, the only light remaining was that emanating from the portal. When the clean-up was complete, Menputyn snapped his fingers and began walking toward the portal with his men. Emma and Isa started to follow but Menputyn's men stopped them.

"You will both stay here," Menputyn said.

"You can't leave us here!" snapped Emma.

"I warned you there would be consequences for lying to me. We will start with Mr. West and when we return, perhaps you will have more to say." Isa quickly tried to read Menputyn's thoughts to see if he knew where Logan was being kept, but he didn't. Presumably, his ignorance was intentional to prevent Isa from gleaning the information from him. Menputyn continued, "And if you do not have more to say, Enyo Rossi's family will be next. That way, all of the Rossis feel some pain." He looked directly at Isa when he said it.

"You can't do that!" screamed Emma.

"Unfortunately, gas leaks in older Florentine apartment buildings happen. It is not within my control. That is, unless you want to tell me something new?"

"It seems the Order of Christ's Templars have not changed," uttered Isa. "All your cabal does is kill innocent people."

Staring Isa down, Menputyn replied, "We are not the only ones who kill the innocent." Isa knew he was referring to the day she had killed Lord Nemond and his men to escape from the Order of Christ's Templars.

"I've only killed those who deserved it," she replied.

368

"Really?" questioned Menputyn. "Has everyone you killed deserved to die, or were some just following orders, with families and children at home waiting for them to return the night you killed them?" Menputyn pulled out a gun and pointed it at the head of the soldier to his right. "Does Andrei deserve to die?" Andrei instantly tensed up and started sweating. The young soldier wasn't sure if Menputyn was bluffing.

"Menputyn, what are you doing?" asked Emma, also worried for the soldier.

"Andrei, do you have a family at home?" asked Menputyn in an eerily calm voice.

"Yes, Prime Minister, a wife and daughter," replied Andrei, swallowing hard and shaking.

Looking at the frightened soldier, then at Menputyn, Isa said disdainfully, "The dishonor of the Christ's Templars knows no bounds."

"You should remember that. Now, do you want to tell me where the Leyandermál is, or shall I kill him?"

"This is insane!" exclaimed Emma. "Menputyn, seriously, think about what you are—"

Menputyn fired, shooting Andrei in the head, killing him. Andrei's lifeless body fell to the floor, stunning Emma and Isa.

"There, yet another innocent person you have killed," said Menputyn. "Now that you both know the lengths I will go to demonstrate my resolve, do not forget it when I return or more will die." Looking at Emma, he added, "I will give Mr. West your love before we kill him." Menputyn turned to leave with his men.

"The Voynich Manuscript!" shouted Isa, offering up another lie, hoping it would work.

Menputyn and the scientists spun around. Menputyn responded suspiciously, "The Voynich Manuscript?"

Isa replied, "Yes. It is written entirely in Vaniryan, just like the lettering on these hieroglyphics."

"How can the Voynich Manuscript be the Leyandermál?" questioned Menputyn, unconvinced.

"The Vaniryan writing on these hieroglyphs describes how the manuscript tells the secrets of the universe, how to create, how to destroy, and how to generate the infinite power source that controls it all. It is what has been hidden from Supay," replied Isa.

Menputyn spoke to his scientists for a moment. Isa could hear them discussing the famous medieval text written in an unknown alphabet that scholars, cryptologists, graphologists, linguists, experts, and amateurs had been trying to decode for centuries. Isa knew it well because she had written it…

Unfortunately, after the Order of Christ's Templars burned down Corte Del Milion, her beloved manuscript was lost in Europe. She was relieved when she heard it had resurfaced, even if it was at an estate sale in Italy in the late 19th century. That was where antique bookseller, Wilfrid *Voynich*, had purchased it. Sadly, she had never had the chance to see her original manuscript again, although she had followed its journey through the ages, and knew that it was now kept safe in Yale University's Beinecke Rare Book & Manuscript Library.

"So, Issor, you say that the book written in a language no one can read is written in your language?" asked Menputyn.

"Yes," Isa replied.

"And you can read it?" asked Menputyn.

"Yes."

One of Menputyn's scientists had a question for her. "The Voynich Manuscript's pages are displayed in books, and its text and images available all over the internet. Are you saying the whole world has access to the Leyandermál?"

"No. You need the original. The lettering below the square arch hieroglyph says that the 'secret hides behind.' It is the way of the Remnants. It means there are words on the pages that can only be seen on the original parchment when zeutyron energy particles are shown from behind. It is like the Scroll of the Va in the tree sanctuary in Jaannos, its words can only be seen when the energy illuminates the pages from behind."

This was actually something Menputyn believed could be true. He was familiar with the Scroll of the Va because Emma, Professor Quimbey and Captain Evans had reported what they saw in Jaannos to General Nemond, General Covington, the president, and the rest of the Pegasus team when they returned from Vanirya. And of course, General Nemond had leaked the information to him.

Menputyn's scientists had another question, one which experts had been asking for centuries. "Then, what do the words in the Voynich Manuscript that can be seen, say?"

Isa replied, "They describe Vaniryan herbology, astronomy, cosmology, balneology, pharmacology, biology, and horticology. It is the words hidden behind the pages that you seek."

"Let's hope so," said Menputyn. With the flick of his hand, he pointed at Isa. "Take her," he ordered and Menputyn's soldiers grabbed her. He continued, "I will play along a little longer, but not much. Do not try anything, Vaniryan. You will come with us to translate the Voynich Manuscript for me and show me how it works, and if this is another one of your tricks, others besides Andrei will die, starting with Mr. West *and* the Rossis. Do you understand me?"

"Yes," Isa replied.

Isa, are you sure about this? Emma asked Isa in her mind.

Isa responded, *We have no choice. If I don't, Menputyn will kill Logan, your family, or you.*

But Isa, when he finds out you are lying—

Menputyn's men started pushing Isa into the portal, and with her arms tied behind her back and hands bound in metal, she was in no position to resist. Before it was too late, Isa tried to communicate with Emma one last time…

Emma, the Vaniryan writing on the hieroglyphs are—

But it was too late. Menputyn's men forcibly pushed Isa through the portal before she could finish her sentence. Emma went after her but another one of Menputyn's soldiers intercepted her.

"But I could die in here!" exclaimed Emma, worried about the lack of oxygen.

"Perhaps that will incentivize the Vaniryan to cooperate with haste. If she is telling the truth, then I will know where to find you. If not, I am afraid you will run out of air right about the same time we kill Mr. West and the rest of the Rossis. For your sake, I hope your Vaniryan friend is not lying." Menputyn and his remaining team walked through the portal.

Emma had no intention of being left behind. She ran toward the portal but it disappeared before she reached it. She ended up running straight into the stone wall behind where it had been.

"No!" she shouted, finding herself trapped in the pitch-black Void with Andrei's dead body. She slumped to the ground and yelled, "Ugh!"

She moved her hand in front of her face but she couldn't even see her own fingers two inches from her nose. As she took a shallow breath of the limestone-dust-filled air, she hadn't the slightest idea what to do next.

Chapter 28 – Awakening

"Now what?" groaned Emma, sitting alone in the dark, her back up against a wall. Surrounded by 2.5 million limestone blocks, she knew screaming was useless, and worse, she'd use up her air. She also knew there was no physical way out of the Void, as archeologists and pyramid experts had studied the muon topography of the Void in the Great Pyramid for years, and found none. Perhaps there was another way out though, considered Emma, a Vaniryan way, like the portal inside the cave in Norway. But even if there was, trapped in darkness, how would she see it? How would she find it? Emma thought about it and came up with an idea, albeit a morbid one…

She began crawling on her hands and knees toward Andrei's dead body, hoping he might have a digital watch, cell phone, flashlight, or something else on him that could provide light. She kept crawling until she felt wet, slippery stone under the palms of her hands. She had crawled into a pool of Andrei's blood. She gagged, but it meant she was close, so she continued to inch forward with blood soaking through her pants at the knees until reaching his dead body.

Emma rolled Andrei's body, which was lying face down, over onto his back so she could feel inside his pockets. She patted down his clothes, searching for anything useful. "Andrei, I'm sorry. You didn't deserve to die, and your wife and daughter didn't deserve to lose you like this. But c'mon, please help me out…"

Almost as if Andrei was listening, she felt an object in his front left pants pocket. She reached inside and found a cigarette lighter! She pulled it out and flicked it on, generating a small flame to illuminate the area around her. She immediately saw Andrei's open, lifeless eyes staring back at her, frozen in shock from what Menputyn had done to him. Startled, she lurched backwards, jumped up and moved away.

Using the cigarette lighter to guide her, Emma walked toward the center of the Void to the wall in front of the altar where they had spotted the hieroglyphics with Vaniryan writing. If there was a Vaniryan way out, she knew that wall was where she had to start. When she got there, she released the button on the cigarette lighter to think for a moment, allowing the Void to become pitch-black again. She had no idea how much fuel the small lighter had left, but conservatively, she had to assume that, if run non-stop, it only had a few minutes of life remaining. Of course, if the lighter was brand new, it might have longer. And then, there was the not so small problem of the flame using up her dangerously-limited oxygen supply. Regardless, to be safe, she had to be efficient.

She sparked the lighter again and the wall of hieroglyphs lit up from the small flame. There were a ton of symbols to look at. Since she couldn't read Vaniryan, her initial plan of attack was to assess *which* hieroglyphs the Vaniryan lettering accompanied to see if there was a pattern.

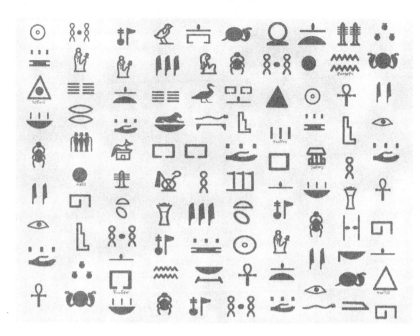

The first Vaniryan letters she spotted were found right below a hieroglyph depicting three vertically-standing, parallel rectangles on the wall's upper right…

She saw more Vaniryan writing higher up the wall and further to the right, underneath the wavy symbol that the Russian scientists indicated earlier was the Egyptian symbol for water…

She kept looking and found Vaniryan letters beneath a triangle symbol lower on the right, near the bottom of the wall...

And then halfway up the wall again, just to the right and slightly below the three vertically-standing, parallel rectangles, she spotted Vaniryan writing below a hieroglyph of some kind of structure...

She continued to scan the wall, bringing the flame with her as she side-stepped left until she found more hieroglyphs with Vaniryan lettering on the left-hand side of the wall. First, midway up, there was Vaniryan writing under a circle symbol…

Then, above that, again on the left-hand side of the wall, there was Vaniryan lettering beneath another triangle hieroglyph, but this time, the triangle had a circle inside it…

And after some more searching, she found Vaniryan lettering beneath a squared arch on the bottom-left of the wall...

That was the last one she could find.

By now, she was familiar with how the Vaniryans did things, hiding patterns in stones waiting to be touched in sequence to activate their portals. Because she had already spent about 10-minutes studying the wall, she let go of the lighter to save fuel and think about what she had just seen. Was there a pattern there? And then, it hit her...

It was just like the cave in the Storfjorden fjord in Norway, but instead of boulders positioned on a cavern floor to form a map of the Norwegian Albo's Copán coordinates, the Egyptian hieroglyphs with Vaniryan lettering were positioned on the wall in a way that replicated the placement of the Norwegian Albo's landmarks around the globe. It was the Copán puzzle, all over again. All the same landmarks were there…

First, there was a squared arch hieroglyph that reminded Emma of the Gate of the Sun in Tiwanaku, etched on the bottom-left of the wall, possibly approximating where Tiwanaku would be located on a global map in western Bolivia, far to the south:

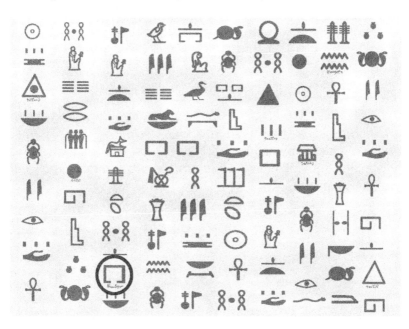

Second, there was a triangle or "pyramid" hieroglyph etched into the wall where the Great Pyramid of Giza in Egypt would hypothetically be located, if the wall was a map, on the wall's bottom right:

Third, there was a circle, perhaps symbolizing the spherical Chamber of the White Eyed Star God in the Copán Temple in Honduras, etched above and slightly to the left of the squared arch of Tiwanaku, positioned where Honduras would hypothetically be, if the wall was a map:

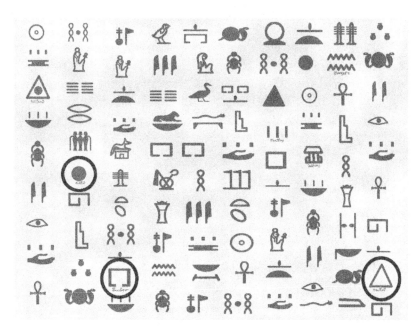

Fourth, there was a hieroglyph of vertically-standing, parallel rectangles, symbolizing the standing stones of Stonehenge, located on the wall where England would theoretically be, north and west of the Egyptian pyramid:

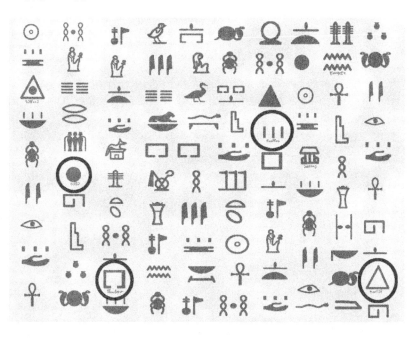

Fifth, and this is what had Emma convinced she was correct, there was a pyramid with a circle in it, just like the hidden Vaniryan pyramid beneath Area 51 that had a Vaniryan sphere inside it! And it was positioned high above the Chamber of the White Eyed Star God's circle hieroglyph, approximating where Nevada might be located in relation to Honduras:

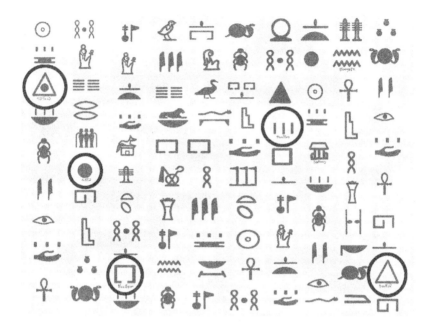

Sixth, there was a hieroglyph that resembled a structure, potentially symbolizing the Château de Falaise, located on the wall where France would be, slightly south and to the east of England's ancient Stonehenge landmark:

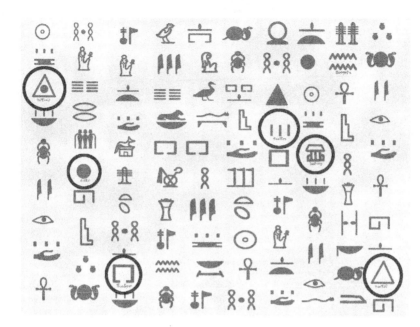

And finally, there was a hieroglyph of wavy lines, the Egyptian symbol for water, carved right where the Storfjorden fjord in Norway would be located, high up near the top of the wall on the right hand-hand side…

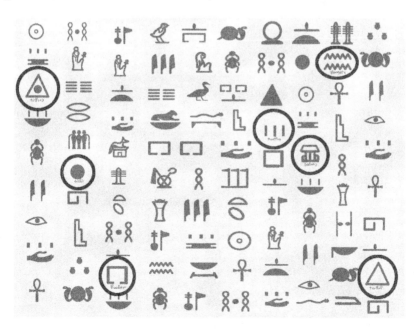

All seven Copán landmarks were represented in the hieroglyphics on the wall! While their placement on the hypothetical map wasn't perfect, the position of each was unmistakably similar to their analogous location on the Copán map. It was another coordinate puzzle left behind by the Vaniryans on a wall of hieroglyphics just waiting to be pressed in order to activate the technology, and Emma knew exactly what to do: press the hieroglyphs in the same order as she did with the boulders in the cave in Norway, and on the Vaniryan sphere below Area 51!

She started with the structure hieroglyph located where the Château de Falaise was; then, she touched the hieroglyph of wavy lines representing Storfjorden next, followed by the vertically-standing, parallel rectangles symbolizing Stonehenge; next, she touched the pyramid hieroglyph representing Giza; then, the squared-arch symbol for Tiwanaku; the sphere representing the

384

Copán Temple, the pyramid symbolizing Area 51, and lastly, the structure hieroglyph representing the Château de Falaise again, in that order. Precisely as Emma hoped, something happened...

The altar started glowing, the walls and floor of the Void disappeared and a holographic pyramid as tall and wide as the Great Pyramid of Giza itself formed around her. It was like the entire pyramid was hollowed out on the inside and she was standing within it. Not only that, but she found herself standing on an oval-shaped platform in a pyramid with no visible bottom, with the altar that was on the floor now at the oval's center.

Although the Great Pyramid of Giza was solid, the holographic pyramid inside it was not. She could see right through it. Billions of stars surrounded the pyramid, which seemed to be floating in the heavens. It all reminded her of the very first time she met the Vaniryans after going through the portal in Norway.

Back then, in the middle of an ambush in a cave adjacent to the Storfjorden fjord, Logan had shoved her through a portal to save her. She emerged on an oval-shaped platform within a pyramid with no visible bottom, floating in the heavens over Vanirya, inside a pyramid with four slanted walls that peaked hundreds of feet above her head.

It was déjà vu. She found herself once again standing inside a huge pyramid on an oval-shaped platform surrounded by holographic walls and stars. Her memory of that day suddenly triggered by what she was seeing, thoughts of how the Vaniryans approached her in that pyramid 3½ years ago, how they started communicating with her in her mind, and *what* they said, all started coming back to her. She wasn't just recalling what they said, but how they inundated her mind with words, images, diagrams, and equations, uploading information into her brain like they were uploading data into a computer. It was all coming back to her with perfect clarity!

She recalled how overwhelmed she felt from the avalanche of information at the time, but this time, she didn't feel overwhelmed. After spending years trying to remember precisely what had happened that day, she was recalling memories that had been locked away for years! All the words, images, diagrams, and equations they showed her were flashing before her eyes as if it was happening all over again, only this time, she was remembering *everything!*

The glowing altar caught Emma's eye, reminding her that if she wanted to escape the Void and save Logan and Isa, it was time to go. She reached out and touched it with her left hand. She could feel the Vaniryan energy moving up her arm and coursing through her body, as though she was part of that energy. And in that moment, it suddenly all made sense to her... the energy that was at the center of the Vaniryan pyramid, of Vanirya and of the Vaniryan's technology, was the same energy that moved through everyone and everything, everywhere. The same electrons, protons, neutrons, atoms, molecules, and particles that made up energy, matter and life on Earth, also created life, energy and matter on Vanirya, too, only the Vaniryans understood it. They understood how to use it, and they understood how the energy that flowed through everyone and everything interacted with space and time. In Emma's mind, she could finally see how it all worked, she could feel it, and she was ready...

It was time to escape the Void. Logan, Isa and Enyo were in trouble. She had to warn everyone about Menputyn's plan, and about General Nemond! As she did with the Vaniryan sphere below Area 51, Emma kept her left hand on the altar, used her right index finger to point outward and—

Everything started flickering around her, reminiscent of a short circuit occurring. The holographic pyramid formed, deformed, surged, reformed, partially disappeared, re-emerged in sections, and then vanished completely. The holographic pyramid was gone, and the altar in the middle had turned back into plain stone.

"No!" screamed Emma. She flipped on the cigarette lighter, only to see that she was still stuck in the Void. "It's fine, just try again, Em," she said to herself, not ready to give up.

She walked up to the wall of hieroglyphs, reignited the lighter so she could see, and touched the symbols in the same order as last time. She let go of the lighter and, for a fleeting moment, heard an energy surge and saw a flicker of energy as the mechanism was trying to re-activate itself. But then, again, everything stopped. It didn't work.

"What's wrong with this thing?!" exclaimed Emma, frustrated. She sparked the cigarette lighter and tried again, pressing the hieroglyphic symbols in order, but this time, even less happened than before. She heard and saw nothing, no noise, no energy surge, only darkness. She tried again and again, like a driver stuck in a broken-down car on the side of the road trying futilely to restart a dead engine. It was useless, and if that wasn't enough, the cigarette lighter ran out of fuel!

"Damn it!" she cursed, throwing the lighter against the wall. She had to get out of there, and soon! If she didn't, Menputyn was going to kill Logan, Isa, Enyo's family and who knew who else, just as soon as he discovered that Isa was lying to him about the Voynich Manuscript.

"Please work!" she yelled tearfully, desperately smacking the stone altar with her hand, hoping it would make a difference. It didn't. "Ouch!" she cried, hurting her hand but doing nothing to the altar. She began coughing and wheezing from all the limestone dust that she was inhaling while screaming and sucking for air.

"This can't be happening!" she uttered. "I have to get out of here!" she screamed, and just then, she could feel it, the energy that was coursing through her body earlier was still there, dancing in her fingertips, waiting to burst out. It always had been, she realized, and she was ready to unleash it…

She pointed at the wall and angrily screamed at the top of her lungs one last time, "Let! Me! Out of here!" Blue energy exploded from her fingertips, striking the limestone blocks in front of her, partially disintegrating them. She had blown a hole in the wall four feet in diameter and several feet deep. More than ever, she knew she was related to Isa. That part of her had finally awakened!

"I can't believe it!" she exclaimed, shocked. It was as if, one minute, she didn't know how to wiggle her ears, and the next, she did. She suddenly felt capable of doing things with the energy inside her that she didn't know she knew how to do.

She sent another blast of blue energy toward the wall, and the hole went even deeper. Of course, she could only see the hole when the blue energy shooting out of her hands lit up the Void. She did it several more times until eventually breaking through to the outside, midway up the pyramid. A thoroughly pleased grin stretched across her face. Menputyn wasn't going to get the best of her today.

Emma crawled out of the hole she had created. Fortunately, it was nighttime and the Giza Pyramid Complex was closed. No one had seen her blast out. She had a long but manageable climb down the step-pyramid, but first, she eagerly took in the cool Cairo air. She was free! She wanted to scream out loud, but the only words she could form while looking at the hole she had put in the pyramid were, "Mr. Jackson is going to be so mad at me."

Chapter 29 – An Act of War

President Barrett sat behind his Oval Office desk in the early evening, listening intently to General Covington. Covington, who was standing in front of the desk while addressing the president, explained, "Lucky for Ms. James that the dead Russian soldier had a grenade and AK-47 on him that she could use to blast her way out, otherwise, she might never have escaped."

"Lucky is right. How's she feeling?" asked the president, leaning back in his chair.

"She has some minor injuries and is pretty shaken up from the whole ordeal, but under the circumstances, that's to be expected, Mr. President. She's a tough kid."

The president concurred. "That's for sure. Have you notified her parents that she's been found safe?"

"Yes, Mr. President. They have expressed their appreciation. Mr. James has asked if you might have a few minutes for him to thank you in person?"

President Barrett emphatically shook his head and replied, "*No.* I don't have time for him. Besides, it isn't me he needs to thank. We didn't do anything. Ms. James saved herself. He should be thanking her."

"Yes, sir. I'll let him know."

"Where is she now?"

"At the U.S. Embassy in Cairo."

"How's she getting back to the States?"

"I've already dispatched some agents to meet her at the Embassy and fly her home, Mr. President."

"Good. What about the others?"

"Arenot, Quimbey, Callister and Anders are on their way back with Captain Velasquez, as we speak," replied General Covington. "The same pilots who flew them to France are flying them home."

"Any word on what they found in Falaise?" asked President Barrett.

"Dr. Arenot said it might be significant, but he was reluctant to discuss it over the phone."

"After all the security failures, can you blame him?"

"No, sir."

"What about Captain Evans? How is she?"

"She got out of surgery a few hours ago and is now fighting for her life in the ICU. Doctors say it's too early to tell if she's going to make it. She lost a lot of blood and there was a lot of internal damage. She's in a medically induced coma for at least a week."

The president looked down, closed his eyes and replied somberly, "Alright. Let's pray she comes through this. She's one of the good ones. She, Velasquez and Stephenson all deserve medals of honor for what they did."

"I am told Velasquez felt so bad, he was refusing to leave Evans' side... that was until he learned Ms. James was still alive and returning to the States. He said coming home to protect the Pegasus team is what Captain Evans would have wanted."

"Good, I'm glad he's on his way back. He's one of the few people we can trust," commented the president.

General Covington added, "He, Evans and Stephenson put up a hell of a fight in Falaise to hold off the ambush. Quimbey, Arenot, Callister and Anders all owe them their lives. Have you had a chance to notify Stephenson's family?"

"Yes, I spoke to his mother an hour ago. Sweet woman, so proud of her son. I hate making those calls, Warren. It's the worst part of my job. Just make sure everyone gets back safely so I don't have to make any more tonight, will you?"

"Yes, Mr. President."

"What about Nemond?"

"He's been placed under arrest, sir."

"Bring him here. I want to talk to him."

"That's not a good idea, Mr. President."

"Dammit, Warren, I don't care if it's a good idea! He compromised national security, right under our own noses! He betrayed us! He's a goddamn traitor!" snapped the president, slamming his fist on the desk.

Trying to calm President Barrett down, Covington replied, "Mr. President, I know you're angry, but—"

"You're darn right, I'm angry!" The president stood up and started pacing. "How could this happen, Warren? What kind of country do we have when we can't even trust our own generals? Nemond swore an oath to protect and defend the constitution and people of this country, and instead, he sold them out to Menputyn! And for what, a membership in the Christ's Templars?! The bastard tipped Menputyn off about the Chersky Mission and Captain Evans' team died because of it. He did the same thing in Reykholt, Venice, Khatyrka, and Falaise. Stephenson's dead, and Evans is barely hanging on. Not to mention all the other security breaches Logan, Emma and the professors have had to deal with, *all* because of Nemond! I swear to god, Warren, if Nemond was here right now, I'd probably kill him."

"And that's why we're not going to bring him here, Mr. President. I'm as outraged by Nemond as you are, sir, but respectfully, you've got other things to deal with right now."

"You know I have the authority to order you to bring Nemond to me, right?"

"Yes, Mr. President, but that's one order I won't follow. You'll get your chance to talk to him, I promise. Just not today."

The president appreciated General Covington's efforts to keep him from doing something he might regret, even if he didn't like it. He turned around to look out one of the floor-to-ceiling windows behind his desk overlooking the South Lawn, which was all lit up at night. With his back to General Covington, he said, "Sun's going to be up in Cairo in a few hours. I imagine once the Egyptians see what happened to their pyramid, they're going to be outraged. I'm expecting all hell to break loose. I don't know what hell breaking loose looks like, but I want the Joint Chiefs to have a Gulf contingency plan ready in an hour."

"Already working on it, sir."

The president turned back around to face Covington. "Is everything arranged with the Beinecke?" he asked.

"Yes, I've coordinated with the Head of Security at Yale and the Director of the Beinecke. They've swapped out the original Voynich Manuscript for a replica which they usually use for bigger audiences. He said it looks virtually identical to the real one."

"And they hid the tracker inside the binder?" asked the president.

"Yes, sir. The tracker's signal is muon based, so it's a little slower but will transmit through stone, rock, etc."

"Good. Let's hope Menputyn makes his move in the next few hours because once the sun comes up in Cairo and word breaks out about what happened at Giza, he'll know Ms. James escaped. Are the troops ready to go?"

"Yes, sir. Yale's given us access to the security camera feed in the subterranean vault where they store the Voynich at night. We expect Menputyn will try to take it by portaling right into that vault. We'll have a strike force outside the vault doors ready to pounce if Menputyn or his men brings either Issor or Logan along to assist in examining the manuscript. However, we think it's more likely they'll try to take the Voynich back to Russia where they can study it more carefully. If they do, the tracker will tell us exactly where they are, and we'll use our own z-particle portal to transport SEALs to the source of the signal."

"I hope this works. It won't take Menputyn's scientists more than a minute to figure out that the manuscript is a fake or for Russia to pick up the tracker's signal. This could be our only shot to bring Isa and Logan back alive."

"You realize, Mr. President, that while it's likely Issor will be with the Prime Minister based on what Ms. James told us, Logan probably won't be. The moment we intervene, even if we rescue Issor, that might lead to them killing Logan."

"That's why I want your men to bring Menputyn back with them through the portal, if they can."

Surprised, Covington replied, "You want to take the Russian Prime Minister hostage?"

"I'm done playing games with Menputyn. If Logan isn't there, then I want Menputyn instead, is that clear?"

General Covington looked shocked. "Yes, Mr. President, but you know taking the Russian Prime Minister hostage could be deemed an act of war?"

"And murdering our soldiers, taking our citizens hostage and conspiring with General Nemond to steal state secrets isn't? We're already at war. Maybe not with Russia, but certainly with Menputyn. Act of war or not, I have no intention of calling Loretta Richards to deliver bad news about her son. I want Menputyn captured alive."

"Yes, sir. I will go relay the order to Col. Rodgers now."

"And Warren, make sure the soldiers are ready."

"Of course, sir. They wouldn't be going in unless they were."

"I'm referring to them being ready for the elephant in the room that we haven't even talked about tonight."

"What is that, sir?"

"Supay."

"You think Supay is coming for the Voynich Manuscript, too?"

"I don't know what I'm thinking. It's just been a little too quiet on the Supay front. He's lying-in wait, I can feel it. And I'm beginning to wonder if there's a connection between Supay and Menputyn."

"Do you think Menputyn could *be* Supay, Mr. President?"

"No, but maybe Menputyn's helping Supay somehow, I really don't know. I'm just starting to get a bad feeling about all this, the closer to the truth we get. And after what Supay's forces did to Captain Velasquez's team on Electra-1, I want to make sure our men are prepared for whatever they might encounter, in case they find something other than Russian forces when they get there."

"Understood, Mr. President. I will discuss this with Col. Rodgers *and* the NSA Director when we're done here. Will there be anything else, sir?"

President Barrett shook his head and motioned to the Oval Office's door, indicating that it was time for General Covington to go call Col. Rodgers and Director Orson.

On his way out, Covington said, "Yale is expected to relocate the Voynich replica to the vault at the top of the hour. Do you want to join us in the Sit Room for the vault's live feed when that happens?"

"Yeah, I'll see you down there."

Chapter 30 – The Beinecke

"**A**ttention!" called out the officer manning the door inside the Situation Room when President Barrett entered with Miles Garrison at his side. Everyone stood, and that included Beinecke Rare Books & Manuscript Library's Executive Director, Michelle Avery, a young, meticulously organized woman who looked nervous to be there, and Yale University's Head of Security, Alex Gibson, an executive-type who looked like he had never worked a day of security in his life.

"At ease everybody, we've got a long evening ahead," said the president, motioning for everyone to sit. The president took his place at the head of the Situation Room's conference table with Mr. Garrison on his left and General Covington on the right.

General Covington introduced the new faces sitting beside him. "Mr. President, I'd like you to meet Beinecke's Executive Director, Michelle Avery, and next to her, Yale's Head of Security, Alex Gibson. They've been instrumental in coordinating the logistics, staging and execution for the Beinecke Operation."

"Good evening to you both. I hope your trip down from Connecticut was an easy one," said the president. "I bet you didn't wake up this morning thinking you were going to spend your Saturday night in the White House Situation Room."

Ms. Avery spoke first. "No, Mr. President, definitely not, but it is, umm, truly an honor to meet you, sir. I've voted for you in the last two elections."

"Thank you. It's always nice to know I'm locked in here with constituents who like me. What about you, Mr. Gibson?"

Mr. Gibson looked flustered. "I, uh…"

"Well, things just got awkward, didn't they?" said the president, having a little fun with Mr. Gibson and drawing some laughs.

"Yes, Mr. President," replied Mr. Gibson, embarrassed.

"That's alright, Mr. Gibson. There are several officers in here who didn't vote for me either, but we've got a country to run, so down in the Sit Room, we're all one big happy family… in-laws and all." Ready to move on, the president turned to NSA Director Sue Orson and asked, "Sue, what's the status?"

Director Orson answered, "The target was relocated to the subterranean vault on its regular nightly schedule a few minutes ago, sir."

President Barrett glanced at Ms. Avery and said, "I also bet you never expected to hear your Voynich Manuscript referred to as 'The Target.' "

"No, sir. This is quite an evening of firsts for me," replied Ms. Avery, who looked concerned about the prospect of military action taking place at her beloved library.

"I promise you, we won't let anything happen to the Beinecke," assured the president.

"I hope so, Mr. President. There is so much history in there," replied Ms. Avery. "If anything should happen to the Tower…"

"The Tower?" asked the president.

Director Orson turned on the oversized monitor in the Sit Room to show the president what Ms. Avery was referring to. The Beinecke's security cameras, which were now patched directly into the Sit Room, provided a live video feed of the Beinecke's main cathedral-like exhibition hall. Dominating the hall, shown from two angles on a split-screen, was a six-story tall, glass-enclosed tower of book stacks, visible through large windows made of translucent 1¼-inch thick glass fortified in a truss of steel, clad in marble and granite. A warm hue of light illuminated the hall and Tower, which itself had interior spotlights to shine additional focus on the stacks and rows of rare books and manuscripts displayed behind the thick glass.

"Stunning," uttered the president. "How many books does that Tower hold?"

"180,000 volumes, Mr. President, most of them older and far more important than any of us," she responded, her eyes nearly tearful with worry. Just in case she offended the president, she added, "Umm, no disrespect intended, sir."

The president shook his head. "None taken. For 8-years, my job is to serve and protect this great country. Yours, Ms. Avery, is to protect thousands of years of world history, much of it which no doubt helped *shape* this great country. Staring at that Tower, it's honestly hard to know which of us has the more important job."

"Thank you, Mr. President."

"Is that all the Beinecke's books?" asked the president.

"Oh, no, sir. It's just the tip of the iceberg, honestly. The Beinecke has more than one million books, many millions of manuscript pages, tens of thousands of papyri, photographs, maps, posters, paintings, art objects, and a whole lot more."

"Impressive," replied the president. "Warren, Sue, let's do what we can to protect those books, okay?"

"Yes, sir," replied NSA Director Orson.

"Understood, Mr. President," responded General Covington, getting up to make a call on the wall-phone behind his chair to relay the instruction.

Director Orson added, "Mr. President, we have 15 soldiers in the building, 7 on the subterranean vault level accompanied by 4 Yale security guards to let them into the vault... and 8 more strewn throughout the Beinecke's research level and stacks on two underground floors beneath the main plaza. We're ready, sir."

"Thank you, Sue. Can you pull up the Beinecke's vault feed?" asked the president.

"Yes, sir," replied Director Orson. She pulled up on another monitor a new display of the subterranean vault, revealing several heavily protected book stacks enclosed in steel, and fire and impact resistant glass.

"What do you store in there?" asked the president.

Ms. Avery responded, "We keep our most significant works in there, and also, those that require more precise environmental controls. The vault is temperature and moisture regulated, and has individual manuscript pods for works that require their own special settings and conditions." She pointed to the screen. "There, you can see in the middle two of the manuscript pods, that's what we call them. The one on the right has the Voynich replica in it."

"What's in the manuscript pod to the left of the Voynich?" asked the president, worried that whatever was in that pod was at risk of being in harm's way.

"The Gutenberg Bible, Mr. President. The first Western book ever printed from movable type," replied Ms. Avery.

"Is that all," said the president sarcastically, suddenly wishing they had moved the Gutenberg Bible elsewhere. "Sue, Warren, remind your teams to aim carefully, if it comes to that."

"Yes, Mr. President," said General Covington, again returning to the phone.

"Thank you," mouthed Ms. Avery when the president looked her way.

President Barrett subtly nodded back. He wanted her to know he was doing what he could to address her worries, which he was beginning to share himself. "How secure are those manuscript pods? I guess what I'm asking is, how easily can the Russians get into them?"

Mr. Gibson replied, "They're locked but penetrable with the right tools, Mr. President, and normally, they're protected by an alarm, but I had security disable the alarm like your team requested. I still don't understand how you expect the intruders to get into the vault with all your soldiers surrounding it."

General Covington responded, "Mr. Gibson, I'm sure you understand that you are on a need-to-know basis only."

"Sure, of course. But as you know, those are my security cameras you are using, and Yale, as a private institution, has a right—"

"And I assure you, Mr. Gibson, that is why you are here," interjected Miles Garrison.

Mr. Gibson still wasn't satisfied. "The university president only agreed to cooperate with your Beinecke Operation based on complete transparency with our offices, and our ongoing involvement and oversight. We both signed all the NDA, confidentiality and national security documents you asked us to, so I think we're entitled to more of an explanation about what's going on."

At this point, President Barrett stepped in. "Mr. Gibson, we could not have coordinated this operation without your assistance, and I want you to know we appreciate everything you've done. And I promise, you will know what's really going on when you know. If it turns out nothing happens, then you will never know, and that'll just have to be good enough for you. Now, do you want to stay and help us out? The choice is yours, but national security owes you no explanation."

With his tail between his legs, Mr. Gibson replied, "Umm, yes, sir. Of course I'd like to stay. My apologies. I just thought I could be more helpful if I understood what was really going on."

"Believe me when I say, that makes all of us," responded the president.

There was an uptick of noise, chatter, and activity in the Situation Room. Something was happening...

"Mr. President, Dr. Bowling at NASA is reporting that Russia's Kosmos-14K046 optical reconnaissance satellite has repositioned itself over North America," announced Director Orson, reading from a computer screen in front of her.

"Can you be more specific?" asked General Covington.

"Yes. I was waiting for the details to come in. I can now confirm that Dr. Bowling's team has pinpointed the satellite's likely optical surveillance area over the northeastern seaboard, centering above Connecticut," replied Director Orson.

"Yale," stated Mr. Garrison.

"It's starting," said the president.

General Covington and Director Orson both picked up their respective phones to make sure all units were ready to go.

"What's happening?" asked Ms. Avery anxiously after hearing Director Orson say into her wall-phone, "Incursion incoming, all units prepare," and General Covington say into his phone, "Roscosmos is on the move. I repeat, Roscosmos is on the move."

As they were waiting for more to happen, the president could see Ms. Avery's concern for the Beinecke rising. He leaned over to talk to her while the general was away from his chair and the rest of the room was focused on their duties.

"I remember my first time in the Sit Room watching a covert military operation with soldiers running into a terrorist cell in Kabul that I sent them into. It took everything in me not to let everyone see how nervous I was that day, but I was. Everybody is the first time," commented the president.

"You?" responded Ms. Avery, somewhat surprised. "I know I've only seen you on TV and watched some of your speeches, but you always seem so calm, collected, like nothing rattles you."

"Trust me, the camera adds 10 lbs. of composure. But the truth is, I still get nervous, and I hope I never stop doing so because it helps to remind me of what's at stake and keeps my decision-making grounded. Listen, I know you're worried about the Beinecke…"

"It's my life, Mr. President. Ever since graduating from Yale, and pursuing a masters and Ph.D. at the university, all I've ever wanted to do was to be part of the history and culture that literally lives and breathes inside the Beinecke, to protect it and to help others to see it."

"Well, from what I understand, Yale couldn't have picked a more respected or qualified individual to serve as the Beinecke's youngest Executive Director in its history. You care, and that's why you're nervous, but that's a good thing. Caring about what you are protecting is the greatest gift you can give back to those who entrusted you to do so."

"Thank you, Mr. President," replied Ms. Avery appreciatively.

There was more beeping as a message was being received. Director Orson announced, "Mr. President, Lt. Col. Lain is reporting that the PAPA has picked up a z-particle signal over the Beinecke."

The president immediately straightened up in his chair and replied, "Do we know—"

"There's activity in the vault!" exclaimed Director Orson.

A bright white light splashed across the vault's live-feed monitor. Whatever was causing it was off to the side of the camera, although they knew what it was. They just couldn't see Russia's z-particle portal on-screen. But they could hear Russian voices.

"Damn, can we move the camera?" asked President Barrett.

"Trying, sir, but the video camera is not responding to our remote commands," replied Director Orson.

"That can't be right," blurted Mr. Gibson, mortified that his cameras weren't working properly. "You must be doing something wrong. Let me try..." Mr. Gibson stood up, but just as he did, four armed Russian operatives entered the video-feed, heading right for the Voynich.

"Sit down, Mr. Gibson, we don't have time!" snapped NSA Director Orson.

"Where did they come from?" yelped Mr. Gibson, falling back into his chair. Everyone ignored him.

"I don't see either Isa or Logan, sir," reported Director Orson.

The Russian operatives converged around the Voynich's manuscript pod and broke out tools. They began whispering to one another with some of the words loud enough to hear.

"Lt. Col. Borgarov, can you make out what they are saying?" General Covington asked the Russian intelligence specialist invited into the Situation Room to assist with the Beinecke Operation.

Lt. Col. Borgarov responded, "They are saying, 'We need to hurry. We have to get the book back to Russia fast before alarm sounds... Hand me a drill.' That's all I can make out, sir."

"Just like you predicted, Warren, they're taking it back to Russia," said the president.

"Yes, Mr. President. I recommend we stick to the plan," replied General Covington.

The Russian operatives on screen frantically worked to open the manuscript pod.

"Shall I have the troops outside the vault engage, sir?" asked Director Orson.

"No. We need to let them go back to Russia. That's where we'll find Isa and Logan," replied the president. "General Covington, have the soldiers at Pegasus West ready to launch upon receipt of the target's Russia-bound coordinates."

"Yes, sir." General Covington picked up the phone to speak to Pegasus West. "Col. Rodgers, the target is about to move. Stand by for coordinate transmission. Have your team ready to go."

"Copy that, general... standing by," replied Col. Rodgers, remaining on the phone, awaiting further instructions.

After a few more seconds, the Russians cracked open the manuscript pod and reached for the Voynich replica. Almost instantly, a high-pitched alarm started blaring, ringing loudly throughout the Beinecke.

"What's that?" asked General Covington.

"They tripped the alarm when they opened the pod," answered Ms. Avery.

"Gibson, I thought you disabled it!" exclaimed Director Orson.

"I did! I mean, they were supposed to have—"

The vault's doors crashed open, and in swarmed Yale's security guards, confused by the alarm and thinking that was their cue to engage. Left with no choice, the SEALS rushed in after them. The Russian operatives began shooting at the guards and SEALS, causing them all to seek cover behind the vault stacks.

One of the Russian operatives lifted the Voynich replica out of the pod and began running for the portal off screen. The remaining operatives covered his escape, rapidly shooting at the Yale security guards and SEALS to hold them off. Several SEALS fired back at the escaping operative, but it wasn't clear if they hit him. He disappeared from view quickly and presumably, had already reached the portal.

The other Russians began retreating, while the SEALS kept advancing, one stack at a time. The Russians continued to fire back, pounding the book stacks with bullets in order to keep the Americans at bay.

One of the SEALS shot a Russian intruder in the leg, causing the Russian to go down. Immediately, one of his comrades tossed a smoke bomb and something else toward the stacks while another fired his semi-automatic rifle to prevent the SEALs from getting closer. Smoke began filling the room and obscuring the video camera's view.

"Look out!" shouted a voice from the smoke. Everyone in the Situation Room heard an explosion, followed by a loud crashing sound and more gunfire.

"They're getting away!" yelled another invisible voice, and within seconds, the glowing light that was lighting the vault disappeared and everything went dark.

"Team Alpha, this is the NSA Director… report your status. I repeat, Team Alpha, report," requested Director Orson, putting her phone on speaker.

"This is Commander Andrews… all clear down here," responded a voice as the smoke began to dissipate.

"Commander Andrews, this is the president. What happened?"

"Whoever they were, they're gone, Mr. President. They escaped through some kind of light doorway, it's hard to explain, sir. There's a trail of blood from a bullet wound one of them sustained, but that's it."

"Is your team alright?" followed up the president.

"Yes, Mr. President. One of the stacks toppled over from a grenade blast, but we were all lucky to get out of the way. Fortunately, no serious injuries down here, sir, although two of the Yale security guards sustained minor bullet wounds to their extremities."

"Well done, Commander," replied the president, eyeing Mr. Gibson with extreme annoyance.

"Thank you, Mr. President," said Commander Andrews.

"The books…," Ms. Avery uttered, overflowing with worry.

Seeing the stress on her face, the president quickly asked, "Commander Andrews, are the books alright?"

"There's quite a mess down here, sir, but all the books actually look okay. The protective glass around them held up pretty well."

Ms. Avery fell back into her chair and exhaled, palpably relieved.

"Sue, contain the area," ordered the president.

Director Orson responded, "Yes, sir... Commander Andrews, coordinate with all teams and Yale security to lock down the Beinecke, and stand by for further instructions."

"Understood. Team Alpha out," replied Commander Andrews.

"How long do we have to wait for the tracker's signal?" asked the president.

"Shouldn't be long, Mr. President," replied General Covington. With the Beinecke-portion of the operation over, the general turned to Mr. Gibson and Ms. Avery and said, "At this point, we are going to have to ask you both to step outside." General Covington motioned with his hand for the Situation Room's officers to escort them out.

The president revised the general's order slightly. "Actually, Ms. Avery, I'd like you to stick around if that's alright. I know you're concerned about what happened at the Beinecke and we'll get you back there shortly, but depending on how the next phase of the operation goes, there may still be implications for the Voynich Manuscript."

"Oh, umm, sure, okay," replied Ms. Avery.

General Covington leaned in close to the president and whispered, "Are you sure about this?"

The president whispered back, "Yes. She signed everything. Besides, I'm convinced she can help us on the Pegasus Project. I want Gibson out of here."

"Yes, Mr. President." General Covington stood up to say goodbye to Mr. Gibson. "Alex, we'll let you know if we need anything further. As you can see, the situation remains fluid."

"Understood. Really though, I'm happy to stay and help if I can," responded Mr. Gibson, hoping to have a chance to redeem himself.

The president responded, "I'm sure you are, but you've helped enough already. Let's hope we don't have to bother you any further. They'll escort you out to the lobby. Stay close, just in case."

"Yes, of course, Mr. President."

Mr. Gibson jealously eyed Ms. Avery as the officers escorted him out.

A minute later, Director Orson announced, "Mr. President, Lt. Col. Lain reports that the PAPA has picked up the homing signal from the target. Coordinates acquired, sir. The PAPA places the tracker at 55.750556 N, 37.615556 E, 77 feet below ground."

General Covington said into the phone, "Col. Rodgers, can you confirm receipt of the target coordinates from the PAPA?"

"Affirmative, general. Confirming coordinates: 55.750556 N, 37.615556 E, 77' down," answered Col. Rodgers.

"Confirmed," replied Director Orson.

"Where do those coordinates put us?" asked Mr. Garrison.

"The Kremlin in Moscow," replied Director Orson.

"The Kremlin?" responded the president, shocked and wanting to make sure he heard her correctly.

"Yes, Mr. President. 77' beneath the Kremlin's Teremnoy Palace."

"Hmm, things just got a whole lot more complicated," stated the president. He paused to think for a moment.

While he did, all eyes remained fixed on him, wondering if he would actually send U.S. troops into the Kremlin, the fortified complex in the center of Moscow occupied by the Russian government. Translated, the name 'Kremlin' meant 'fortress inside a city,' and true to its name, tall defensive walls surrounded it. The 'fortress' itself consisted of five palaces, four cathedrals, the Kremlin towers, government buildings and the Grand Kremlin Palace which served as the official residence of the President of the Russian Federation. It was heavily guarded by the Russian military, both inside and out.

"Sir, send them into the Kremlin?" inquired Director Orson.

General Covington corrected her, slightly. "They wouldn't be going into the Kremlin as much as they would be going *below* it."

The president massaged his forehead while he contemplated what to do. He knew the ramifications of invading the Kremlin in Moscow were far greater than sending a team into a remote mountain base in Siberia. It was so quiet in the Situation Room that one could hear a pin drop.

"Mr. President, as you pointed out earlier this evening, time is of the essence," said General Covington.

"Go!" ordered the president. "Send them in!"

"Yes, sir." General Covington lifted the phone to his mouth and gave the final order: "Col. Rodgers, Operation Red Rescue is a go! I repeat, Operation Red Rescue is a go! Send in the soldiers!"

Chapter 31 – Operation Red Rescue

Prime Minister Menputyn stormed through the doors of the underground Russian science facility 77' below the Kremlin, followed closely by two guards carrying Isa. Because her arms were still tied behind her back, the guards carried her at the bend in her elbows, one on each side, holding her high off the floor so her short 11-year-old legs couldn't reach.

"Put me down!" shouted Isa, wiggling and kicking, unhappy with how the Russians were manhandling her.

Isa looked around at where her captors had brought her and saw a hangar-sized facility full of scientists, soldiers, and computer consoles, with numerous smaller bays off the main room. In one of the smaller bays, Russian soldiers were standing around a platform with a large book on it—which Isa presumed was the Voynich—while medics tended to injured soldiers nearby. And off to the side of that same bay, sitting in a chair, looking beat up and barely conscious, was Logan! His hands were handcuffed behind the chair with soldiers pointing guns at his slumping head. Logan's face was bloodied, black and blue, and his eyes were swollen.

"As you can see Issor, Mr. West's fate is up to you," said Menputyn, continuing, "If this turns out to be another one of your tricks, I will kill him. Or maybe I will just kill you both if you are no longer any use to me."

"Your Grand Master won't be too happy about that after all these centuries trying to capture me."

"I *am* the Grand Master, and I know what the ghosts of Grand Master's past didn't, that you are not the otherworldly power capable of bringing this world to its knees that they thought you were. But the Leyandermál is. And with it, we will finally have the power to rule the world. Even Supay will kneel to us."

"Are you crazy?! Have you heard anything Emma said? Supay will never kneel to you. He would rather destroy this entire planet than let you have the Leyandermál."

Menputyn wasn't dissuaded. "We will see. Power has a way of forcing unlikely alliances."

"You're insane. Supay doesn't care about alliances!"

Annoyed by Isa, Menputyn snapped, "Move!"

Menputyn's men carried Isa to the bay where the Voynich Manuscript was waiting. Her eyes widened when she saw it up close. It was the first time she had seen her manuscript in over 400 years, since the day the Christ's Templars dragged her away from Corte Del Milion and burned it to the ground. On the way to the center of the bay, they walked by two soldiers being treated for gunshot wounds.

"What happened?" Menputyn asked his men.

"The alarm sounded when we grabbed the manuscript, Prime Minister," responded one of them. "We faced enemy fire."

Menputyn wasn't surprised about the alarm, but he was surprised that ordinary library security guards could give his highly trained operatives so much trouble. "Who did this to you, Yale campus security guards?" he questioned derisively, having expected more from his operatives.

"No, Prime Minister. There were U.S. soldiers waiting for us also. They must have known we were coming."

"How is that possible?!" uttered Menputyn.

412

Isa immediately realized what had happened and began to laugh, amused by Menputyn's failure and the thought that Emma had escaped.

"Prime Minister, Roscosmos is reporting a muon signal projecting from our location," announced a scientist behind an operations console.

"What?!" shouted Menputyn. He suspiciously looked at the Voynich and rushed up to it. At first glance, it looked like he expected, unrecognizable text scribed on several hundred pages of parchment, bound together in a worn-down binding, although it didn't have that old book smell he was expecting. He began turning the pages, and then flipped it over. He spotted an opening on the bottom of the binding with something in it. He looked inside and saw the tracker. His face exploded in rage!

"Zachistite ob'yekt, vyklyuchite komp'yutery i otvedite zaklyuchennykh v bezopasnoye mesto!" [*Clear the facility, shut down the computers and take the prisoners to a secure location!*"] shouted Menputyn, giving sudden, unexpected orders to the scientists and soldiers in the subterranean facility, but it was already too late! Within seconds, a zeutyron portal appeared on the far side of the science facility and out of it poured dozens of U.S. soldiers from Pegasus West! The portal closed behind them, and shots were fired almost instantly!

Russian soldiers quickly ran for cover, while scientists ducked behind their computer consoles. Many of the scientists were armed themselves, but they were no match for the U.S. soldiers. Those who chose to pick up arms against the U.S. forces promptly found themselves dead on the ground beside the remaining scientists who weren't prepared to fight or die.

The soldiers who had been holding Isa, let go of her to cover Menputyn as the Prime Minister hurried back to the computer consoles. With bullets flying everywhere, Isa ran over to Logan, who was still sitting in a chair. Because her arms were restrained behind her back, she threw her body into him to knock him over, causing them both to crash onto the floor. It hurt but it was better than letting Logan sit upright in a chair with bullets whizzing by his head. After Logan hit the floor, he moderately woke up and opened his right eye as best he could. His left eye remained closed, swollen shut.

"What's happening?" he uttered weakly, lying on his side with the chair behind him.

"Your people are here to rescue us. Are you okay?" asked Isa, wanting to make sure she didn't injure him worse by knocking him over, although judging by his battered appearance, she wasn't sure if that was possible.

"Emma?" he replied, still somewhat dazed, after seeing the face of his 11-year-old best friend, Emma, a vision from his childhood that had never faded.

"I am Isa," she responded over the ongoing sound of gunfire.

"You look just like her," whispered Logan, still lost in the memory.

"We need to get out of here."

"I'm handcuffed to this chair," said Logan, growing more alert.

Isa had to do something. Now that Emma was safe and the others Menputyn had threatened to kill had presumably been warned, Isa knew it was time to escape. She closed her eyes to change form, stirring up the energy inside her until nothing remained of her but light. All of the chains around her arms and metal contraptions on her hands, dropped to the ground. She was free! She reconstituted her form, but when she did, she did not change back into a young version of Emma. Instead, she changed back to a face she hadn't worn in nearly 800 years: *her own.* Logan smiled upon seeing her small alien face with no nose, golden-white hair, silver-white skin, tiny mouth, and round white eyes with radiating blue pupils. Isa looked just like Emma had described, only slightly older. After all, 800-years had passed since Emma last saw Isa, who now looked like an older teenage or young adult version of her alien self.

"Come on," Isa said, standing up. She grabbed Logan's arm and pulled him, chair and all, behind some equipment, flinching from gunfire. She then generated a blast of energy from her hands to break apart the chair Logan was handcuffed to, freeing him although his hands remained handcuffed. "We have to get to the US soldiers. Can you walk?"

"I think so."

Isa looked at Logan's pants. His legs were battered and bloody at the shins. Isa helped him up and they began to move. They stayed low and close to the wall to avoid crossfire from the firefight...

Meanwhile, Menputyn was busy at the computer consoles, keeping his head down, working with a frightened Russian scientist to program the computer, yelling instructions. Soldiers flanked Menputyn and the scientist while they worked, firing back at the US soldiers to give them as much protection as possible. Near the end of whatever they were doing, a bullet struck the scientist in the chest. The scientist collapsed onto the console, dead. Menputyn sneered and callously shoved the scientist's body out of the way and onto the floor so he could finish the sequence.

When he was done, a new z-particle portal opened up in one of the adjacent bays, revealing 50 more Russian soldiers waiting to storm the room from a zeutyron base in the Siberian mountains. The reinforcements came rushing through the portal with guns blazing. Instantly, the US soldiers, who had been gaining ground, found themselves outnumbered. They began retreating from enemy fire, hiding behind equipment at the rear of the hangar and in one of the side bays.

While the additional Russian forces were running into the facility through the new portal, Menputyn, who had purposely left the portal open, planned to escape out of it. "Let's go!" he hollered to the soldiers guarding him. Menputyn and his guards began heading toward the portal, one step at a time, with his soldiers firing shots to protect him.

At the other end of the facility, a Russian soldier lobbed a grenade over equipment where U.S. soldiers were crouching. It landed, and a few seconds later, exploded, killing, or wounding numerous U.S. soldiers and blowing the equipment apart. The Russian forces advanced further while the U.S. soldiers who survived had nowhere to go.

The Russians tossed another grenade toward the U.S. soldiers, hoping to finish the job, but this time, a U.S. soldier daringly intercepted it mid-air and tossed it back in one fluid motion with an instant to spare. It detonated right over the heads of a dozen advancing Russian soldiers and knocked over a stack of computers. When the computers hit the ground, they sparked and lit on fire, causing something to go wrong with the Russians' z-particle portal. The portal out of which the 50 Russian soldiers had come and where Prime Minister Menputyn was headed, started spinning like a helicopter spiraling out of control.

The portal wasn't just spinning horizontally, it was spiraling vertically and diagonally in every possible direction like a gyroscope. Everything in its path disappeared within it and re-appeared in the Siberian base on the other side of Russia. That included not only equipment and soldiers, but the ceiling, ground, walls, *everything*! It was literally slicing, dicing, and transporting anything it touched as if the entire room had been thrown into a blender and the spinning portal was the blade.

Soldiers dove to escape it! Those standing in its way, where the portal spun into their upper torsos but their legs remained below its threshold, were killed because only the upper portions of their bodies were teleported to Siberia, leaving the rest of their body parts behind. Any portion of the soldiers' bodies not caught precisely within the portal's 20' by 10' dimensions didn't make it to Siberia.

Even those soldiers lucky enough to be scooped up whole by the spiraling portal encountered a painful ending on the other end. There, all the bodies, body parts, equipment, ground rock, earth, floor, walls, ceiling and debris transported from the Kremlin facility were flooding the small Siberian base, packing it to its breaking point. Soldiers who managed to survive the initial transport to

Siberia found themselves caught up in the middle of, and being bombarded by, bone-crushing levels of additional debris. There was no surviving it even on the other end.

The U.S. soldiers trapped in the far corner of the farthest bay, desperately called Pegasus West begging for an escape portal tracked to their location. Isa, who spied their thoughts, shouted, "We have to get over there!"

She put her arm around the injured Logan to help him move faster, keeping a close eye on the spiraling portal that was shredding up the subterranean facility. Crossfire had ceased as none of the soldiers, Russian or American, were shooting anymore. Everyone was scrambling for their lives, just trying to avoid the out-of-control portal.

"Duck!" yelled Isa when the portal spun their way. She and Logan dropped flat to the ground just as the portal grazed the air over their backs, narrowly missing them. But Viktor Menputyn was not so lucky...

In the moment Isa spent lying on her stomach, she saw Menputyn and his guards caught in the wrong place at the wrong time, directly in the portal's path. As the portal flew at him, Menputyn gazed helplessly at Isa, the witch he and his twisted order had spent centuries trying to capture. It was the first time he had ever seen Isa's real alien form, and in the split second he had left, he begged her to use her powers to save him, but there was nothing she could do. Her alien face, with its radiating blue eyes, was the last thing he saw before he died...

The portal spun into Menputyn's chest, transporting the upper portion of his body into the mix of debris in Siberia and leaving the rest of him on the floor. His guards faced the exact same fate. The portal cut through them with ease. Menputyn's reign of terror was over.

"Go!" shouted Isa after the portal shot to the other side of the science facility, or what was left of it. They ran toward the bay where the U.S. soldiers were taking cover, having to climb over or through rips in the ground caused by the rampaging portal eating up sections of the floor. And they had to hurry because the portal appeared to be gaining speed, rotating faster and faster.

Just in time, Pegasus West conjured up a new portal in the back bay where the U.S. soldiers were hunkered down.

"There's another portal!" Isa exclaimed, pulling Logan's hand to lead him to it.

Soldiers yelled, "Hurry!" to all who could hear it.

Even the Russian soldiers began running toward Pegasus West's escape portal, and the U.S. soldiers let them come. In a moment of shared humanity, the U.S. soldiers were waving the Russians in, trying to help everyone escape the zeutyron beast.

Isa and Logan reached the portal and Isa helped an ailing Logan limp through it, while a few remaining soldiers came sprinting in right behind them. Sadly, the last soldier didn't make it as the spiraling portal, seemingly intent on preventing as many humans as possible from escaping its wrath, swept through the soldier's lower half, killing him.

Dr. Ehringer and Ian Marcus, who, along with their teams, were watching the frightening scene in Russia from their side of the portal in Pegasus West, screamed at the same time, "Shut down the zeutyron field!"

The team at Pegasus West deactivated the zeutyron field and the portal vanished, closing the doorway to the hell taking place on the other side of the world. Doctors rushed into Pegasus West's hangar to help the wounded, while U.S. soldiers surrounded the Russians who had fled to safety through the portal, although none of the Russians put up a fight. Instead, they all laid down their weapons and put their hands up, just happy to be alive...

The Situation Room, which, with the benefit of Pegasus West's video feed, had also been watching the horror unfolding beneath the Kremlin on their wide-screen monitors, erupted in cheers when they saw Isa and Logan make it through the portal. The clapping and cheers only intensified once Ehringer and Marcus closed the portal to seal off the disaster unfolding in Russia.

"What was that?" asked Ms. Avery, who didn't remotely understand what she had just seen.

"*That* was what happens when scientists play with fire," replied President Barrett, continuing, "Sue, can we get some eyes on the Kremlin?"

"Yes, sir," replied NSA Director Orson, pulling up the PAPA's orbital surveillance of the Kremlin's surface.

An overhead view of the triangular complex just north of Moskva River popped up on screen. It was a clear early morning in Moscow so they had a good view of the Kremlin, The State Palace, the Kremlin's Terem Palace, Dormition Cathedral, the main square, numerous towers, and other government buildings.

"Anything?" asked the president.

Director Orson responded, "Lt. Col. Lain is reporting massive, fluctuating z-particle activity emanating from the Kremlin, sir. That runaway portal is still going strong, and it appears to be linked to a corresponding z-particle signal coming out of the Sayan Mountains in Siberia."

"Another Russian base?" inquired the president.

"Possibly, Mr. President."

For a moment, all seemed quiet, all seemed still, but then…

The ground around the Grand Kremlin Palace began collapsing, with a giant sinkhole opening up beneath it. The entire western section of the Kremlin fell into the hole, with buildings, towers and cathedrals caving in on top of one another. The Russian portal below the Kremlin had eaten up nearly everything under the surface and transported it into the base in Siberia. A plume of dust shot into the air, quickly obscuring visibility.

"Darn!" cursed the president, unable to clearly see what was happening.

"The CIA has just picked up a localized emergency broadcast signal coming out of Moscow, sir," announced Lt. Col. MacLeod, NSA Director Orson's CIA liaison.

"Are they asking for help?" inquired General Covington.

"No, they're warning everyone to stay away from the Kremlin," replied Lt. Col. MacLeod.

"Mr. President, if their zeutyron portal escapes Moscow, or continues to grow, who knows where it might go or what might happen next. We could be looking at a global catastrophe," said General Covington.

President Barrett agreed. "Whether they want our help or not, reach out to them to let them know we are standing by, ready to assist…"

"Wait!" shouted Director Orson. "Mr. President, Lt. Col. Lain is reporting that the z-particle signals coming from the Kremlin have stopped!"

"What does that mean?" asked President Barrett.

"It's over, Mr. President," responded Director Orson. "The PAPA is reading zero z-particle activity."

"What happened?"

Director Orson replied, "It looks like something happened to the Siberian base and that might have done the trick, Mr. President. Dr. Bowling at NASA is reporting a series of explosions and an avalanche in the Sayans at the same coordinates as the z-particle signal. Seems like their portal disaster destroyed two bases at once, and when the zeutyron link in Siberia terminated, like a flame deprived of oxygen, the portal below the Kremlin was extinguished, too. Perhaps they were feeding off one another."

The president took a look back at the video screen showing the damage at the Kremlin. Some of the dust had already started to dissipate. The western half of the Kremlin and numerous structures were submerged in a giant sinkhole in the ground.

"My god," uttered the president, standing up from his chair in shock.

Ms. Avery's jaw dropped, as well, aghast at what she was seeing. She wasn't alone. The entire Situation Room was stunned by the images.

"We play with technology we barely understand," said the president, humbled by the destructive power of the portal. "The only thing more dangerous than ignorance is arrogance."

"Mr. President… media reports are starting to come out of Moscow about some kind of accidental explosion in the armory beneath the Kremlin," stated Director Orson.

"I bet," replied the president.

"I doubt that will be the last speculative report coming out of Moscow," commented General Covington.

"How long until they start claiming it was a terrorist attack or they start pointing fingers at the U.S.?" asked Director Orson.

President Barrett agreed. "Sue, Warren, I want the Joint Chiefs assembled in the Sit Room in 30 minutes. In the meantime, let's get Logan and Isa brought back to D.C. as soon as possible."

"From the looks of it, Mr. West probably needs medical attention, Mr. President," said General Covington.

"I'll arrange to have him flown back to D.C. with Isa in a medical transport, Mr. President," proposed Director Orson.

"Very good," replied the president.

"So, what should I do now?" Ms. Avery whispered to Mr. Garrison, feeling like a fish out of water.

Director Orson, who overheard her, responded, "For starters, I think we're going to need you to sign a bigger NDA."

Chapter 32 – Reunion

When the elevator doors opened, Emma rushed out onto the 4th floor of Walter Reed National Military Medical Center in Bethesda, Maryland, anxious to see Logan. She hurried to find Room 454, passing doctors, nurses, nursing stations, and medical equipment, her heart pounding. She picked up her pace when she saw the room up ahead, guarded by two soldiers. She began running toward the door, while General Covington, Professor Quimbey, Dr. Arenot, and Captain Velasquez, all just happened to walk out of it.

Emma nearly plowed into Professor Quimbey for a hug. "Thank god you're okay!" exclaimed Emma. "I was so worried Menputyn was going to kill you all in France…" She let go and hugged Dr. Arenot next.

"He almost did," remarked General Covington, "but thanks to Captain Velasquez here, Evans and Stephenson, everyone's safe." General Covington put his arm proudly on Velasquez's shoulder.

Captain Velasquez responded, "It is what we are trained to do, sir."

"Oh, don't be so modest, Captain. It's okay to take a bow once in a while," rebutted the general. "Fortunately for everyone, Menputyn won't be a problem anymore."

Emma had seen the Kremlin disaster on the news on her way home from Egypt. While she didn't know precisely what had happened, she assumed the general's comment related to that.

"How's Logan?" asked Emma, wanting to know what to expect before walking through the door.

"Not great," replied Dr. Arenot.

Emma's eyes started tearing up.

"Oh, come here, dear," said Professor Quimbey, embracing her. Professor Quimbey gave Dr. Arenot a cross look for his poor bedside manner.

General Covington didn't do much better. He answered her question with even more blunt specificity. "According to the doctors, he's got several broken ribs, a punctured spleen, internal bleeding, bruised kidneys…" Emma covered her mouth and started crying. Professor Quimbey rolled her eyes, wondering whether anyone knew how to deliver bad news with a softer edge.

"I'm sorry, Ms. James, take your time," apologized the general, pausing to allow her to process the update.

"No, I'm fine," said Emma tearfully, wanting to be strong for Logan. "Really, it's okay,"

After a few more seconds, General Covington resumed, "He also suffered fractures in his cheekbones, shins, and kneecaps… his shoulders were dislocated, and he's recovering from a concussion. The good news is, doctors expect him to make a full recovery, and his sense of humor, such as it is, has returned."

Emma laughed slightly at General Covington's last comment, which he obviously intended to make her feel better. It did. She wiped her face.

"You okay, dear?" asked Professor Quimbey.

"Uh-huh," replied Emma, ready to go in. She turned to face the door, took a deep breath, and walked through it. What she saw on the other side, or more accurately, *who*, surprised her…

Standing by Logan's bedside was his mom, Loretta. Sitting on a couch in the corner under a daylight-filled window were two faces she didn't expect to see, Bryan and Allysa. And standing at the foot of the bed was a red-headed woman in her thirties who looked like *Annika*. Isa immediately let Emma know it was her. Emma smiled, finding Isa's choice to honor Annika a fitting one.

Emma's eyes locked with Logan's, and suddenly, to her, everyone else in the room vanished. She rushed up to hug him, tears pouring down her face. He did his best to reciprocate, but with all the medical equipment, tubes, and IV lines connected to him, it was difficult. Logan started to speak but Emma cut-him off…

"My answer is *yes!*" she exclaimed, laughing and crying at the same time.

"Yes?" replied Logan, not following.

Emma looked around and spotted a loose metal ring hanging from an upright IV unit next to Logan's bed. She unclipped the ring, which was there in case additional IV bags were needed, and handed it to Logan. "I don't want to waste another moment of my life, Logan. We almost ran out of time. We were that close. And all I could think when it was happening was, 'now it's too late,' and now that it isn't, I want you to know that I want to spend the rest of my life with you. I don't care what my dad or anyone else thinks. All I care about is you."

Now, Logan understood what she meant and his eyes watered up. He found the strength to sit upright, wincing a bit. "I know you've already said yes, but do you mind if I still ask the question?"

"No," laughed Emma, sniffling and wiping away tears of joy.

Logan pressed a button on his hospital bed to lower his mattress. It was dropping slowly.

"What are you doing?" asked Emma.

"Well, I can't get down on one knee, so I'm taking the hospital bed as low as it can go."

"Logan!" snapped Emma, bursting impatiently with excitement waiting for him to pop the question.

"Okay, okay." He held up the metal ring Emma had located and said, "You know, I had a much prettier ring the last time I planned to do this."

"So I've heard."

"Emma, from the moment I met you, I knew I loved you. I know that sounds corny..." Logan started coughing, and then, he grabbed his ribs due to the pain. "I'm sorry, I promise I had a much more romantic speech prepared before, too..." Logan paused, inhaled, held the makeshift ring up and in a weak voice asked, "Emma, will you marry me?"

Allysa grabbed Bryan's arm, anxiously awaiting Emma's response even though she already knew what it was going to be.

"Yes!" answered Emma, taking hold of Logan, kissing and squeezing him way beyond the limits of his pain medication. Logan winced and smiled simultaneously.

Logan slipped the metal IV ring onto her finger. "It's huge," he said with a chuckle.

"It's perfect!" countered Emma, giving Logan another kiss and then hugging Loretta, her thrilled-to-death future mother-in-law who had always loved Emma.

Bryan and Allysa popped up from the couch to congratulate them. Hearing increased noise in the room, Professor Quimbey, Dr. Arenot, Captain Velasquez and General Covington came in next.

Emma held up her hand to show Professor Quimbey. "Look, I'm engaged!" announced Emma in an extremely excited, high-pitched voice.

"Blimey! Would you look at that?!" blurted Professor Quimbey, closing in to congratulate the couple.

"Wow, congrats!" added Dr. Arenot, continuing, "You two are a match made in the heavens of multiple worlds."

Dr. Arenot's comment piqued Captain Velasquez's interest. "Multiple worlds?" he whispered to Dr. Arenot.

Dr. Arenot whispered back, "You know, because Isa's from Vanirya and Emma's related to Isa, so Emma is part Vaniryan, Logan is from Earth... two worlds... get it?"

"Oh, right, that makes sense," replied Velasquez.

Isa looked over at Captain Velasquez. She couldn't read his thoughts. His mind was guarded somehow. Velasquez glanced back at her as if he knew what she was trying to do. She didn't trust him, although Logan, Dr. Arenot and Professor Quimbey had told her she should because he had saved their lives multiple times. Still, she wondered...

The door to the hospital room opened, and in walked the President of the United States, followed by Miles Garrison and multiple Secret Service Agents. Seeing so many people in the room, the president said, "I didn't realize you were having a party in here. If I'd known, I would've had them put you in the presidential suite." Given how crowded Logan's hospital room already was, the president asked his Secret Service detail to wait outside. Looking back at Logan, he inquired, "How are you feeling, kid?"

"I've been better, Mr. President."

"I'm sure," replied President Barrett, glancing at Loretta and saying, "You see, I told you we'd get them home safe and nearly sound."

"You were right, Mr. President," replied Loretta, relieved and grinning.

"And how about you, Emma? How was your trip back?" Noticing Emma's ear-to-ear grin, the president followed up, "That good?"

Emma held up her finger to show him the IV ring. "Logan and I are engaged!"

"Well, finally some *great* news today," said the president. "I'm thrilled for you both." The president patted Logan lightly on the leg and added, "Well done, kid. Now, I don't want to hear anything about me not making it on to your guest list."

"You have nothing to worry about, Mr. President," replied Logan.

The president had an idea. "You know, I think I have the power to marry you both right now, if you want me to."

Logan politely shook his head. "I'm sure we're going to want to plan this out a bit more."

But it was too late. President Barrett was already running with the idea, and it was hard to tell if he was joking. "Miles, as president, I have the power to officiate over a wedding, don't I?"

"Not in Maryland, Mr. President," responded Mr. Garrison.

"Really? I didn't know that," replied the president, genuinely disappointed to learn that he didn't have the all-reaching-nuptial-power he thought he did.

"It's okay, Mr. President. I was hoping for a bigger party anyway," said Emma, letting him down gently. "And preferably, one with my parents in attendance."

The president laughed at himself. "Of course. Speaking of a bigger party, there's one face in here I don't recognize." The president was ready to meet the first known extraterrestrial to walk on the face of the planet: Isa. He turned to her and asked, "Are you Issor?"

"Yes, Mr. President."

He reached out to shake Isa's hand, astonished at the thought that he was making contact with an alien being, although it was hardly first contact given how many centuries Isa had lived on Earth. "It is truly an honor to meet you. And you go by Isa?"

"Yes."

"Loretta, I am sorry to do this, but would you mind stepping outside?" asked the president, preparing to discuss matters of national security.

"No, not at all, Mr. President." Loretta gave Logan and Emma one more ecstatic glance as she stepped out.

Once Loretta was out in the hallway, the president looked at Isa and asked, "Are you the one who left the clues behind in *The Final Journey of the Vanir* to help Mr. West and Dr. Arenot find Ms. James and Professor Quimbey on Vanirya?"

"Yes, Mr. President, with the help of Annika and my first Earth-father, Snorri Sturluson. He wrote the poem after we arrived on your world in the 13th century."

"Your message in that poem was brilliant. You saved their lives."

"I only wish I could have saved my planet, too, Mr. President."

"We all wish that," replied the president. "Was it you who helped Emma escape from the Great Pyramid?"

"No."

"Mr. President, I already told General Covington how I escaped," interjected Emma.

"I know you did, Emma, but… well, Warren, do you want to explain?"

"Yes, Mr. President," replied General Covington. "Egyptian intelligence is reporting that the hole blown in the upper section of their pyramid shows no bullet or fire damage, no shell casings, no shrapnel, no sign of an impact-based explosion. They don't know yet what happened, but based on the preliminary data coming back from Cairo, that hole you escaped out of, Ms. James, wasn't made by an AK-47 or a grenade."

The president jumped back in. "Emma, is there anything you want to tell us?"

It was obvious the president was aware that she had lied. She knew he deserved a better explanation, and quite frankly, she wasn't prepared to lie to the President of the United States a second time. "I'm sorry for lying, Mr. President, but something happened to me inside the Void that I didn't know how to explain at first, or maybe I was just afraid to, I don't know… There was a Vaniryan portal in there, and when I activated it, a holographic pyramid appeared that reminded me of the Vaniryan pyramid I visited 3½ years ago. I know everyone's heard stories about people suffering from memory loss who unexpectedly encounter something that triggers their memory to return, well, that's what happened to me. When I activated the portal and its energy moved through me, I suddenly recalled what the Vaniryans showed me 3½ years ago. I could see it all, Mr. President."

"All of what?"

"*Everything…* how all the electrons, protons, neutrons, atoms, molecules, and particles that make up energy, matter and life in the universe work, how it all interacts with space and time, how to manipulate the energy and how to use it. I blew that hole in the pyramid myself, Mr. President. That's how I escaped."

Velasquez's gaze fixed on Emma.

"Do you still remember what you saw or has it faded again?" asked the president.

"Yes. It's strange, but it's now more vivid than any memory I've ever had."

"Do you think you can help us defeat Supay?" asked the president.

"I don't know," replied Emma, doubt evident in her voice.

"Emma, there's more to you than you know. We have reason to believe that *you* are the Leyandermál."

"Me?"

"Yes. We believe the Leyandermál is written into your DNA, and that it is literally part of who you are," stated the president.

"Em, you're the Missing Remnant," said Logan, amazed. "It's always been you."

The door to the hospital room opened, and to General Covington's surprise, Captain Velasquez slipped out of the room. It was atypical for a military officer of Velasquez's rank and experience to leave a room full of superior officers without requesting permission to do so. Covington had to assume Velasquez had a good reason.

Emma was stunned by the president's revelation that she was the Leyandermál. "Mr. President, are you sure?"

The president responded, "Sure? No. How could we be? But based on what we saw in your DNA, and the story you just told us, it's all starting to make sense."

"Unfortunately, Emma, you're in danger," said the president. "Supay is going to want to find you when he learns who you really are."

Emma looked overwhelmed, suddenly feeling the weight of the whole universe on her shoulders.

"I know this is a lot to take in, but you may be the only one who can stop him," added the president.

Off to the side of the room, Mr. Garrison, who was talking on a cellphone, snapped, "What? Are you sure?" He hung up. "Mr. President, we have to get you back to the Situation Room immediately."

"Why? What's wrong?" asked the president.

"NASA and pretty much every major agency on Earth is reporting that more than 60 UOO's have entered our orbit and surrounded the planet."

"UOOs?" asked Logan.

"Unidentified Orbital Objects," replied Covington.

"Could it be Supay's fleet from Electra-1?" asked the president, looking for Captain Velasquez to ask his opinion. "Where's Velasquez?"

Before anyone could answer, they all heard a large boom and the hospital shook. It felt like a distant explosion.

"What was *that*?" asked Bryan, while everyone in the room steadied themselves.

In rushed the Secret Service. "Mr. President, we need to get you to the bunker immediately."

"What's happening?" demanded the president.

Mr. Garrison, who was again on the phone, had an answer. He had a look of dread on his face… "Sir, the Washington Monument and National Mall have just been destroyed by some kind of energy beam fired from orbit."

A bright light came from under the door and through the door jamb surrounding it. It was emanating from the hallway. Shortly after, they heard screams, and then, gunshots. The Secret Service ran back outside.

"Mom!" screamed Logan as loud as he could, given his condition.

From inside Logan's hospital room, they could hear screaming, and what sounded like laser fire and gunshots. More light flared under the door, and then, the door to Room 454 exploded inward, along with portions of the surrounding door jamb and wall. The incoming debris scraped the president's face but squarely struck Mr. Garrison, knocking him into the back wall of the hospital room, bloodied and unconscious.

Through the hole in the wall walked Captain Velasquez, accompanied by two hulking guards wearing all-black metallic suits with faceless, spiked helmets: they were Supay's Dokalfar warriors.

"Captain Velasquez, what are you doing?" questioned General Covington.

"I do not answer to your kind," responded Velasquez. His eyes flared brightly after he said it. He then stepped aside to make room for one more…

In walked a massive, otherworldly being standing over 8' tall, with a crooked white Vaniryan face, dressed in black armor. *It was Supay.*

Supay, after seeing several faces that he recognized, uttered, "What a nice little reunion." One face that he didn't see, however, was Emma's. "Where is she?!"

Logan looked around… Emma was gone! So was Isa! They had escaped during the commotion. Captain Velasquez, or whoever he was, charged at Logan, intending to find out from him where she went. Bryan and Dr. Arenot jumped in the way to protect Logan, but Velasquez knocked them aside with a swift swipe of his arm.

"Where is your girlfriend, West?" demanded Velasquez.

"She's not my girlfriend, she's my fiancé. And you can go to hell!"

"He does not know," said Supay. "No one in this room does." Supay turned to face the individual he understood was in charge of the planet: the president. He stepped toward President Barrett. General Covington tried to get in between them but Supay's Dokalfar easily threw him to the floor.

President Barrett, despite being the leader of the free world, had never been more frightened in his life. He tried to stand tall despite giving up several feet to Supay. "On behalf of the people of the United States of America and all of humanity, I demand that you leave this world at once. If you want to talk, I am happy to set up a dialogue—"

"There is no dialogue. There is only the Leyandermál. Deliver it to me or many will die."

The president wasn't about to sacrifice Emma's life, especially when he didn't believe the planet would be safe even if he did 'deliver' Emma. Trying to hold firm knowing Supay didn't yet have what he wanted, the president responded, "We do not negotiate with terrorists, from this world or any other."

Supay laughed in a sinister Vaniryan way, a multi-layered shrill sound that pained the ears. "This is not a negotiation." Supay said something in Vaniryan to one of his Dokalfar, who, in turn, relayed the message into a transmitter on his wrist. Supay glared at the president with disgust.

Fifteen seconds later, General Covington, who had stood back up, received a text message on his cellphone. He read it and reported, "Mr. President, New York City has just been struck by…

by what is also being described as an energy beam fired from the sky."

"How much was hit?" asked the president, stunned.

"All of it, Mr. President. The whole city has just been destroyed."

"There were millions of people living in that city! You didn't have to do that to make your point!" shouted President Barrett, furious.

Supay didn't care. "I will destroy five of your Earth cities every 20 of your minutes until you deliver the Leyandermál to me."

"Emma will *never* go to you! She would rather die!" yelled Logan.

"We will see about that," sneered Supay. He spun to face Velasquez. "Take them all back to my ship!" Supay next glared at the president. "And you will go back to your White House and find the Leyandermál for me."

Logan hollered, "Mr. President, he'll kill her! You can't do th—"

Velasquez smashed Logan in the head with his arm, knocking him out cold.

"And if I refuse?" challenged the president, after watching Logan get knocked out.

"You won't. Or you can explain to the rest of this world why their cities are dying and people suffering until none are left." Supay had humanity cornered and the president knew it. Although he kept trying to portray strength, the president's body language conveyed something else. Mockingly, Supay continued, "It is said you know the end when you see it, or so I am told. Yours, President, is a look I have seen on the faces of many on the worlds I have destroyed. Humanity is just another face. You will go to your White House and do what I ask. Do not attempt to leave or I will double the pace of your destruction. If you deliver the girl, I will spare Earth." Supay spun around and walked away. "Take the rest to the ship," he ordered Velasquez.

"Yes, Supay," replied Velasquez.

In short order, in swarmed more Dokalfar to collect the prisoners, dragging everyone out, leaving President Andrew Barrett alone.

Chapter 33 – The Wheels of Destiny

"**W**hat? Are you sure?" snapped Miles Garrison from the far side of the hospital room, hanging up his phone. "Mr. President, we have to get you back to the Situation Room immediately."

"Why? What's wrong?" asked the president.

"NASA and pretty much every major agency on Earth is reporting that more than 60 UOO's have entered our orbit and surrounded the planet."

Isa, worried, reached out for Emma's hand and pulled her in close. Telepathically, Isa said, *It's him!*

Emma nervously squeezed Isa's hand back and replied, *Everything's going to be okay.*

"UOOs?" Logan asked.

"Unidentified Orbital Objects," replied Covington.

"Could it be Supay's fleet from Electra-1?" asked the president, looking for Captain Velasquez. "Where's Velasquez?"

Like the president, Isa looked around for Velasquez but couldn't find him. Where'd he go, she wondered? Isa found the timing of his disappearance very suspicious, and suddenly, her concerns about his guarded mind seemed warranted. Before anyone could figure out where Velasquez went, the hospital shook from what felt like a distant explosion.

Emma and Isa grabbed each other to steady themselves.

The Hunt is coming, Isa said to Emma, even more anxious than before.

"What was that?" asked Bryan.

The Secret Service crashed through the door. "Mr. President, we need to get you to the bunker immediately."

"What's happening?" demanded the president.

Emma was wondering the same thing. They all were.

Mr. Garrison answered, "Sir, the Washington Monument and National Mall have just been destroyed by some kind of energy beam fired from orbit."

A bright light shined under the door and through the door jamb surrounding it. It was emanating from the hallway. Shortly after, they heard screams and then gunshots. The Secret Service ran back outside, closing the door behind them.

"Mom!" screamed Logan.

Emma, the Hunt has come! We have to get you out of here!

I can't abandon Logan! replied Emma, having just reunited with him and not ready to leave him behind again.

After hearing screaming, what sounded like laser fire and gunshots, Isa more forcefully insisted, *You have to go! If Supay captures you, he will destroy Earth.* Sensing Emma's internal struggle, Isa next spoke to Logan and Emma simultaneously... *Emma, we have to go now before it's too late! Logan, tell her she needs to go!*

Logan looked over at Emma, gave her one last reassuring glance to say, 'I'll be okay,' and threw his head in the direction of the window to indicate they should get out of there. Isa grabbed

438

Emma's hand and dragged her toward the outer wall while everyone else was focused on the commotion coming from the outer hallway.

Isa started turning her body into energy. Because Emma was holding her hand, Emma could feel Isa's energy changing and flowing into her. More than that, Emma, having gained a newfound understanding of the energy in her own body during her experience in the Giza pyramid, understood exactly what to do and matched Isa's energy as if she had always known how to do it. Once they had transformed, they slipped through the outer wall of the hospital room right before the door to Room 454 exploded inward.

They rematerialized inside Emma's nearby Georgetown apartment, having gotten there in a flash.

"I can't believe I just did that," uttered Emma, standing in her living room, stunned at herself.

"You are the Leyandermál. If you are what legend says, it is not all you can do. I have never been able to move like that before, but holding your hand, you enabled me to."

"I just knew once we got out of the hospital, we had to run. To me, it felt like we were running and this is where I thought to go."

"You move like the Tree Gates do, but without the tree roots," observed Isa.

They heard screaming outside and hurried to Emma's apartment window. People were standing in the street looking up. High in the sky, they could see a huge ship floating in orbit, easily visible from the ground.

Isa said, "I have seen ships like that before on Vanirya... it is a ship of the Hunt."

"What do we do now?" wondered Emma, pulling away from the window.

"We can't stay here. We have to get out of the city until we can figure out what to do next."

"Where will we go?" wondered Emma.

"I don't know, but somewhere where he can't find you."

They heard more yelling and screaming. They looked back outside and saw people running to their cars, and vehicles jamming the street, all trying to escape, creating instant gridlock. Emma quickly flipped on her TV to see what else she could find out about the alien ships. She did so just in time to see a breaking news report from a panicked male newscaster:

> *Alright, this just in... New York City has been hit by some kind of energy beam from what appears to be an aircraft or spaceship hovering in orbit! Reports are starting to come in that the city is in ruins... I repeat, something, maybe a UFO, we don't know at this point... but it apparently came out of nowhere and fired on the city! Wait, I'm being told we now have live footage...*

The screen switched from the newscaster to video being broadcast from a helicopter flying in the distance outside of New York City, showing a smokey, decimated Manhattan skyline full of broken or toppled buildings and skyscrapers...

> *Oh my God! People, what you are witnessing is aerial footage from our network's traffic helicopter just over the Hudson River in Jersey City. Manhattan is gone! ... It looks like a massive bomb went off! The beam came from...*

The helicopter's camera pointed up at the large ship hovering in orbit.

> *... from that ship high in the sky! It looks like a spaceship of some kind! We are also now being told that the National Mall in D.C. has been hit by a similar*

440

beam from another one of these ships. We are switching to that now...

The camera footage on screen changed to a helicopter flying near the destruction at the National Mall. The broadcaster continued...

You are looking at what is left of the National Mall, now the second confirmed attack on U.S. soil by these flying objects. You can see the White House in the distance, thankfully still standing... No news from the White House if anyone there was injured... Unconfirmed reports of these spaceships appearing around the globe are starting to come in... it seems whatever these things are, they're everywhere. So far, no other cities have been attacked as far as we know, but I recommend you take shelter if you can...

Again, no word yet from the White House or the Pentagon on what these ships might want... we can only hope to hear something soon... I am as scared as you are, but I think it's important right now that people remain calm, don't panic—

Emma switched off the TV. She felt sick to her stomach, devastated by the tragedy unfolding.

"Those were just warning shots," forewarned Isa. "That is the way of the Hunt. They will keep destroying cities until they get what they want, using suffering to extort your world into giving them—"

"Me."

"Yes, it is you that Supay wants."

Emma wanted to vomit, staring down the same impossible choice that she had faced in the Hidden City. "It's like Vanirya all over again," she whispered. Trying to pull herself out of the paralyzing feeling of shock and grief, Emma looked over at Isa and said, "We can't run. We have to stop him like we promised each other we would. We have to!"

"We will. You are the Leyandermál. It is legend. I have always believed it to be true."

Emma smiled at Isa's reassuring words and prepared to embrace her destiny. It all seemed so inevitable now. Suddenly overcome by a feeling of calm, she walked over to her balcony, opened the French doors, and stepped outside.

The midday sky was hazy from the smoke and dust caused by the destruction of the National Mall spreading over the D.C. area. Sirens from emergency vehicles were blaring in every direction. Panicking residents were hurrying to get to their cars. Others were running on foot just trying to get away. Isa joined Emma on the balcony.

"I've always loved the view from out here," said Emma. "The historic neighborhood, the brick buildings, trees, the buzz of city life... it's why I picked this apartment."

"It's nice," responded Isa, allowing Emma to have her momentary, perhaps final, grasp at tranquility.

"Logan and I used to sit out here, drinking coffee, people watching... God, that feels like so long ago... If only they knew there was nowhere to run," commented Emma, pitying her fleeing neighbors, several of whom were fellow Georgetown students. Now ready to do what needed to be done, although frightened, Emma said, "I have to kill him. I'm the only one who can get close enough to Supay to do it."

"I will help you," offered Isa.

"No, it's too dangerous."

"But Emma, you can't do this by yourself."

"I know, but there's something else I need you to do in case I fail."

"What?" questioned Isa. Emma looked at her. Isa's eyes widened. "Are you sure?" asked Isa.

"Yes."

Chapter 34 – The Price of Life

The Oval Office door slammed open and in rushed President Barrett while doctors and Secret Service agents attempted to keep up with him. Doctors were futilely trying to treat him for minor injuries he sustained from flying debris when Logan's hospital room door exploded, but amid an unprecedented global crisis, President Barrett wasn't slowing down for anyone. A number of people were already waiting inside including NSA Director Orson, high ranking military officers, senior White House staff, and Lt. Col. Lain from the Pentagon.

"Well, Sue," said the president as he briskly passed Director Orson on the way to his desk, "it seems your reconnaissance mission backfired." The president sat down and leaned his head to the side to allow doctors to clean a wound on his neck. His white shirt had blood on it.

"I don't understand, Mr. President," replied Director Orson.

"Velasquez…"

Orson, who didn't know about Velasquez yet, remained confused. "But he made it back and provided us vital intel—"

"He didn't make it back," interrupted the president.

Shocked, Director Orson responded, "What do you mean?"

"It may have looked like he made it back, but he didn't. It wasn't him. It was one of Supay's aliens posing as Velasquez, and we sent him right to Emma and Isa, and he led Supay right to them," explained the president. He suddenly felt bad. He couldn't possibly justify blaming the horrific events, or possibly the end of the world, on Director Orson, even if the recon mission was her idea. After all, he had greenlighted it. "I'm sorry, Sue, I apologize… let's figure this out, if we still can."

"Yes, Mr. President, I think we can."

"Good. Can I get the room cleared?" asked the president. "Josh, I need you to stick around with Director Orson," said the president to his Deputy-now-acting-Chief of Staff, Josh Simon. "You too, Lt. Col. Lain. Thank you everybody else."

"Mr. President, you still have some wounds that require attention," advised Dr. Alexander.

"Maybe, but we're done here. I've got other things to worry about right now."

"Very well, Mr. President. Let us know if your condition changes."

The president nodded, and then waited for the room to clear. Once everyone was gone, Director Orson asked, "Mr. President, are you okay?"

"I'm fine, just a few nicks from the attack at the hospital."

"Where are Miles and Warren?" asked Director Orson.

"Supay took them."

"And the others, did he kill—"

"No, he took them all back to his ship."

Stunned, Director Orson followed up, "Emma and Issor, too?"

"No, they escaped. Josh, how soon can I get on air? I need to speak to the country."

"I'm sorry, but not for a while, sir," Mr. Simon responded.

"Why not?"

Director Orson answered the president's question. "Because a few minutes ago, Supay's ships shot down all 2,000+ communications satellites orbiting the planet, disrupting pretty much everything. Took them barely over a minute to do it. We have no broadcast signal, and I doubt anyone's cellphones are working, either."

"There has to be another way!" insisted the president.

"There is, Mr. President," replied Mr. Simon, continuing, "The press is working on rerouting a national address through their fiber optic networks and non-satellite-based radio-broadcast partners, but it's going to take some time. I've given them 25 minutes. Maybe it's for the best because the remarks we're preparing for you aren't ready."

"For the best, Josh?" The president was dumbfounded by Josh's choice of words.

"I apologize, Mr. President. That came out wrong. All I meant was that we need these remarks to be perfect. We don't want to inadvertently cause mass panic."

"Has anyone looked up at the sky or at the National Mall or the gridlock in the streets? We are way beyond mass panic at this point. The longer we take, the worse it's going to get. Let me know when the press is ready. I'm going out there whether you have the remarks prepared or not."

"Am I the only one who thinks this is a bad idea?" asked Orson. "We need to get you as far away from the White House as possible, Mr. President."

The president shook his head. "If I leave, Supay will kill even more people. He wants Ms. James. As long as he thinks I'm looking for her, we're safe here."

"More people? They've already destroyed Shanghai, Dallas, Paris, Berlin, New York, and Miami!" exclaimed Director Orson. "With all due respect, sir, we need to hit back! We have the world's foremost nuclear arsenal… it's now or never! I have surveyed the nuclear readiness count and I think we can hit these ships with unprecedented force!"

The president began seriously considering Director Orson's recommendation until he noticed the grimace on Lt. Col. Lain's face. "You don't agree, Lt. Col. Lain?"

"No, sir."

"Why not?"

"Because 15 minutes before you returned to the White House, the Russians tried firing a nuclear load at the spacecraft above St. Petersburg. Their missiles all hit an energy shield surrounding the ship, causing them to detonate, resulting in a major nuclear incident above St. Petersburg. The city and pretty much everything within a 50-mile radius has been destroyed. They basically blew themselves up and the spacecraft relocated to Moscow, seemingly unaffected by the missiles."

The president glared at Director Orson. "Sue, did you know about this?"

"Yes, Mr. President, but—"

"Don't you think that's information I might've wanted to know?!"

"Mr. President, our arsenal is far more advanced than Russia's," replied Orson defensively. "Given the technology used in our warheads, I think—"

"No," stated the president bluntly.

"But Mr. President…"

"No. It's a last resort option only."

"Respectfully, Mr. President, we're there!" stated Orson emphatically.

"Sue, what I need you to do right now is figure out how to mobilize the entire U.S. military without the benefit of satellite communications. Contact the Admirals of all seven fleets and get our troops back home. Alert all aircraft carriers and Air Force bases to prepare every airborne asset we have for combat. Have all ground forces placed on active alert."

"Yes, Mr. President," replied Director Orson.

"And Josh, advise the State Governors that we will authorize the emergency funds necessary for full deployment of all local enforcement agencies 24/7. And activate the National Guard everywhere. I don't want mass chaos," ordered the president. "If we somehow get through this, we need a country to come back to. Also, suspend trading, freeze the markets. Get on the phone with the Federal Reserve Chair, if you can. People are going to make a run on the banks."

"Yes, Mr. President," replied Mr. Simon.

"Lt. Co. Lain, what can you tell us about these ships?" inquired the president.

"The data is preliminary right now, but what we do know is that the PAPA, before it was shot down, picked up a z-particle signal on the far side of the moon… a huge build-up of zeutyrons… possibly a massive portal on the other side of the lunar orbit. That's likely how they got here undetected using the moon to shield their entry into our solar system, and it's also why we didn't pick them up initially."

"Sue, what about the Vaniryan weapons we've been working on? I know General Covington and General Nemond were overseeing that, but do we have anything we can use?" asked the president.

"From my understanding, the prototype weapons Pegasus West has been working on are mostly handheld weapons and we only have four or five dozen of them, not nearly enough to make a difference. We do have two oversized laser cannon prototypes on the USS Roosevelt, but the Roosevelt's halfway across the Atlantic right now."

The red button on the president's phone rang. Rather than put it on speaker, he picked it up. "Yes? ... Alright, put him through... This is the president." President Barrett listened intently and closed his eyes. Eventually, he hung up. "Los Angeles, Nashville, Rome, Mexico City, Prague, gone," announced the president. He put his face in his hands, saddened beyond words.

"Mr. President, I hate to be the one to say this, but we need to do what Supay asks! We need to find the girl and turn her over!" insisted Director Orson.

"He'll kill her, Sue," replied the president.

"I'm sorry, sir, but she's *one* person. Compared to the hundreds of millions or billions of people who will die if we let this continue, it's a price worth paying."

"Even if we did, he might still destroy the world!" stated the president.

"He's already doing it!" countered Director Orson. "Maybe Supay will leave Earth alone if we give him what he wants. If he's going to blow us all up anyway, then I think we have no choice!"

"Sue, Emma might be the only one who can stop Supay!" declared the president. "We have to give her that chance while there's still hope."

"Hope? What hope, Mr. President?" responded Director Orson in a decidedly pessimistic tone.

"She's the Leyandermál. That has to mean something!"

"Mr. President, again, with all due respect, we don't even know what the Leyandermál is! Are you really now basing national security decisions on Vaniryan legends? On the chromosome count in Ms. James's DNA? I know you care about her, sir, but if General Covington were here, he'd tell you—"

"General Covington isn't here, god dammit!" screamed the president.

The red button on the president's phone buzzed again. The president answered, "Yes…" The president sighed, and again slumped his head. "Okay." He hung up.

The doors opened to the Oval Office and in walked Emma James. All eyes immediately turned to her. The room was dead silent while she nervously approached the president, fully aware of the ominous fate awaiting her. Before anyone could say a word, Emma said, "It's the only way, Mr. President."

"Sacrificing yourself can't be the only way, Emma," replied the president. "There has to be another."

"There isn't. Not after all those cities Supay's destroyed and the millions of people he's already killed. He won't stop, Mr. President. You know I'm right. I would never pretend to think that I'm more important than the millions more who will die if I don't. I'm not."

Director Orson nodded along, visibly whole-heartedly agreeing.

"Emma, if you go, he might kill you," warned the president.

"Might?" questioned Emma with a bittersweet laugh. "He'll *definitely* kill me, Mr. President… unless I kill him first."

"So, that's what hope sounds like," mumbled Lt. Col. Lain, after spending the last several minutes watching all hope get sucked out of the room. Lt. Col. Lain made eye contact with Emma and smiled to let her friend from the last three years working together at Pegasus East know that she cared about her and was there to support her in any way she could.

Concerned for Emma, the president stood up from behind his desk and walked over to her. "Are you sure about this?"

"I know what I need to do, Mr. President. I'm just a little scared," shared Emma.

The president, who, like everyone else, had grown very fond of Emma over the last few years, hugged her dearly and replied, "I know."

"Actually, I'm a lot scared," conceded Emma, squeezing the president back. After a few seconds, she let go and announced, "but I'm ready, Mr. President."

"Emma, you are one of the most courageous people I have ever met," said President Barrett. His eyes watering over from pride and sadness, the president turned to Director Orson and said, "Sue, can you please coordinate with Dr. Bowling at NASA to use one of our deep space arrays to get a message into orbit that we have Emma."

"Yes, sir."

ΔΔΔΔΔΔΔΔΔΔΔΔ

Emma stood with President Barrett on the Truman Balcony on the 3rd floor of the presidential Residence, overlooking the multi-acre South Lawn that stretched thousands of feet to what remained of the National Mall. She was extremely nervous waiting for the inevitable moment when Supay would swoop down in one of his ships or appear through a portal to grab her. It was only a matter of time…

The two of them were leaning over the balcony railing staring off in the distance at the ground where the Washington Monument used to be. It was a distressing sight, yet they knew it paled in comparison to the devastation at the other cities Supay had destroyed. A dozen soldiers stood on the balcony along with them, while hundreds more were positioned down below on the South Lawn and around the White House. The military had also transported and set up a significant collection of heavy artillery on the White House's north and south lawns, although Emma suspected their efforts were going to be futile given the aliens' superior technology. Still, the Department of Defense was doing its best to protect the president since he refused to leave the White House until Emma did.

The late afternoon sun had already started dropping in the sky. Watching the sun creep toward the horizon, Emma remarked, "I wonder if we're watching humanity's final sunset, or mine."

"You can't think like that," replied the president.

"I'm sorry, I know, but it's our reality now, isn't it? Whether we like it or not."

"I don't believe this is our end, or yours," remarked the president confidently.

"How can you be so certain at a time like this?" asked Emma.

"Because I don't believe in giving up... and I believe in you."

"I'm not giving up, Mr. President, but all those people in New York, Chicago, Miami, Dallas, Paris, and everywhere else, didn't give up either, and they died anyway. Optimism won't defeat Supay."

"No, but you will," replied the president. "Your name is written in the stars for a reason, and I believe Supay is about to find out why. If ever there was a time to believe in something bigger than ourselves, it's now."

452

"I like that," responded Emma, grinning, but her grin disappeared quickly when she spotted something in the sky. A ship was flying through the thin cloud layer above the White House on a controlled approach. It was flanked on its sides by five smaller triangular-shaped fighter ships like the ones from the battle in the Hidden City.

"It's happening," uttered Emma, tensing up.

The president looked to the sky. After seeing the incoming targets, the president called over to Colonel Thomas, the senior officer on the balcony, "Get ready, Colonel. Advise all units that the enemy is approaching."

The colonel sprang into action, alerting the troops and making calls on the comm unit. There was a discernible uptick in activity and chatter among the troops, all anxious to face the aliens after everything that had happened. With the ships descending, the president, well aware that it was probably already too late to change course, asked Emma one last time, "Are you positive about doing this?"

"Not absolutely, but I have to try."

"Right," replied the president, almost sounding disappointed she didn't change her mind.

Supay's ships gracefully descended to the South Lawn while hardly making any noise at all. The fighter ships came to rest several hundred feet away from the White House, stopping just above the grass like hovercrafts, while the larger ship set itself down on the lawn in between them. A ramp opened up onto the grass in front of the larger ship and out poured a legion of Dokalfar warriors wearing black metallic suits with faceless, spiked helmets, each carrying laser rifles.

"Hold your position!" shouted Colonel Thomas, sensing the tension rising among his soldiers, all of whom were catching their first glimpse of the alien life forms that had already destroyed cities around the world. "Focus!" the colonel yelled.

After a brief standoff, down the ramp walked the villain everyone was waiting for... *Supay*. Soldiers audibly gasped or gulped upon seeing the massive alien leader who, based on his size alone, looked like he could crush any one of them easily.

Supay gazed up at Emma standing next to the president on the balcony and hollered, "Come!" His eyes fixated on her and flared brightly.

"Colonel Thomas," stated President Barrett warily.

Colonel Thomas instructed two lieutenants to accompany Emma down to ground level.

The president looked over at Emma one final time and said, "I'm proud of you. Good luck."

"Thank you, sir."

Colonel Thomas' lieutenants escorted her from the Truman Balcony, guiding her down temporary steps erected by the military at the back of the balcony. Walking down the steps, Emma's legs started to get shaky.

"It's going to be fine... it's going to be fine...," she kept whispering to herself, trying to remain calm.

"Are you okay?" asked one of the lieutenants.

"Uh-huh," replied Emma unconvincingly.

When they reached ground level, Supay, who was still standing in front of his ship several hundred feet away, said in a booming voice that required no amplification, "Come here, girl, the Leyandermál's true destiny awaits!"

Emma turned toward the lieutenants and told them, "You guys have to let me go now."

They acknowledged her and pulled back to allow Emma to walk the rest of the way on her own. When she reached the grass, still far from Supay, the Dokalfar began converging around her, forming a wall behind and on her sides, so that the surrounding human soldiers couldn't clearly see her.

"What are they doing?" wondered the president, while the aliens closed in around Emma.

Emma slowed down. "How do I know you will spare Earth if I go with you?"

Supay scowled and replied, "Stop stalling, human." He motioned for his soldiers to push her forward, and they did, poking her with the tips of their laser rifles.

Supay's eyes began to glow as she drew nearer. That which he had spent every waking moment of his existence searching for was walking toward him, now only 75' away. His demented alien face showed visible glee. Control of the universe was almost in his grasp!

As Emma got closer, she could feel Supay trying to probe her mind. She couldn't let him, and so, she decided to deny him what he wanted…

Emma unleashed a fury-filled blast of energy from her hands at Supay, hoping to end this once and for all. Supay quickly put up an energy shield around himself to block Emma's attack while simultaneously firing back at her with a bolt of energy of his own.

When his counterstrike struck her, Emma collapsed to the ground, unconscious, and a frightened, panicked U.S. soldier discharged his gun at Supay, believing the battle had commenced. Immediately, other soldiers instinctively joined in and began firing, causing everyone to scatter and the Dokalfar to start shooting back themselves!

The president screamed "No!" when he saw Emma go down and the situation devolve into bloodshed. He knew that Emma was their best hope, and that any combat engagement with the aliens was one the Americans couldn't win.

The aliens' lasers picked off U.S. soldiers one after another, while the metallic suits they wore seemed impervious to ordinary bullets. It became obvious almost immediately that the fight wasn't a fair one, and it only got more lopsided when the fighter ships surrounding Supay's ship began firing their laser cannons at the U.S. troops. The additional firepower from the laser cannons took out multiple soldiers at a time given the width of the cannon beams and explosive discharge of energy upon impact.

Up on the Truman Balcony, Colonel Thomas and several Secret Service agents frantically ushered the president indoors to get him to safety in the bunker beneath the White House. They weren't exactly sure if they could protect him even down there, but what choice did they have? The president was long gone when Supay walked up to Emma's limp body and picked her up with his gigantic left hand.

"Foolish girl!" he shouted. "You have no idea what the Leyandermál can do!"

Carrying her unconscious body with ease in one hand, Supay calmly walked back to his ship, enveloping both Emma and himself in a protective shield of energy. Soldiers desperately fired at him, trying to stop him and save Emma, but there was nothing they could do. Supay sauntered up the ramp into his ship as coolly as if he was finishing up a midsummer's day stroll.

Meanwhile, soldiers off to the side of the South Lawn tried shooting rockets at the ships, but even the U.S's heavy artillery did absolutely no damage. If anything, their efforts gave Supay's ships more targets, resulting in additional losses. The worst blow was to the rocket launcher set up at the base of the Truman Balcony. After U.S. soldiers fired a missile at the main ship, Supay's ships fired back in retaliation, destroying the entire balcony. The back section of the White House collapsed to the ground, killing all the soldiers positioned underneath it.

With over one hundred U.S. soldiers dead, those who were still alive received orders from their superiors to fall back. Some made it to safety while others didn't, as Supay's Dokalfar continued to attack them even while they fled. Eventually, once most of the U.S. soldiers had retreated, Supay's forces returned to the main ship. When all the Dokalfar were aboard, the ramp closed and Supay's ships took off into the sky. The Battle of the South Lawn was over…

Chapter 35 – A Seat At the Table

When Emma awoke, her body and head ached from what Supay had done to her. She had no idea how long she had been unconscious, but at least he couldn't read her mind when she was asleep. So far, the plan had worked. She found herself strapped upright to a metal table in the middle of a circular room. The table wasn't smooth, but rather, bumpy and uncomfortable. It had lights on it that she couldn't study more closely because of the restraints holding her down. There was a low hum coming from the walls.

"So, the great Leyandermál has finally awoken," said a coarse voice from behind.

Emma strained to the left and then back to the right to catch a glimpse of who was speaking, but she couldn't see around the sides of the table. Emma could feel the alien trying to read her mind, but she wouldn't let him. "If you're going to talk to me, show yourself."

"Does it matter?"

"It does to me."

"What matters to you, no longer matters, human."

"If you serve Supay, then neither do you. You're dead just like me"

The face behind the voice stepped into view. It was the alien posing as Captain Velasquez, although why he still resembled Velasquez was unclear.

"I was right… your face looks like a dead man's," said Emma.

The alien snarled back at Emma. "What a shame to waste the Leyandermál on a human."

"I'm sorry to disappoint you."

"If you give it to me, I might help you escape before it is too late for you."

Emma laughed out loud. "After you've helped Supay kill billions, maybe trillions, around the universe, you actually believe I'm going to make a deal to give you the Leyandermál just to save myself?"

Agitated, Velasquez snapped, "Then, you will be the next human he kills!"

Emma chuckled again. "And you think I care about that? He's going to have to kill me because I will *never* give him the Leyandermál."

The alien responded in a malevolent tone, "Supay has his ways of getting information out of uncooperative lifeforms. He won't need to kill you."

Before Emma could respond, the curved metallic wall in front of her opened, revealing a corridor behind it. Dokalfar warriors came marching in and right behind them stormed Supay. Emma started squirming to break free even though it was useless. The Dokalfar surrounded her.

"Where are you trying to go, human?" inquired Supay, his Dokalfar cackling in the background.

"You should have killed me," uttered Emma, trying unconvincingly to appear brave.

Supay got close to her and replied, "Is that what you were hoping for when you fired upon me? Such a sad display of the power you possess."

"I guess I'm disappointing everyone today."

"Why don't we change that, hmm?" Supay began trying to read her mind. She resisted. Supay tried again but she continued to push back, stronger than he expected. He was surprised, although mildly amused. "Why do you continue to stall, human? Don't you know how this will end?"

"You're going to have to kill me—"

"No, I won't. The fate of the universe will not be undone by a stubborn human."

Supay twirled his massive left hand, giving his Dokalfar a signal. Moments later, the surrounding walls turned transparent and Emma could see holding cells behind them. Logan was in one cell lying on a bench, General Covington and Mr. Garrison in another, Bryan and Allysa in a third, and Dr. Arenot and Professor Quimbey in a fourth.

"Emma!" screamed Logan loudly despite his broken ribs. He leapt up, such as he could, and limped over to the translucent forcefield imprisoning him in the cell. He put his hands on it. It shocked him and knocked him to the floor. The professors approached their forcefield to see Emma, as well, but they stopped short of touching it.

"I suggest you don't be so careless with your courage this time around or they will all suffer," Supay warned Emma.

"I don't understand why you have to kill innocent people searching for the Leyandermál when you already possess the power to destroy stars and planets. What more do you need?"

Supay scoffed. "If only you knew what was out there in the universe, and how insignificant these weapons of power really are! Destroying a star is nothing! Now, stop stalling with your questions and give me the Leyandermál!" Supay again went into Emma's mind to find what the Vaniryans had given her. He got further than before, but still couldn't find the Leyandermál for some reason. "Where is it?!" he screamed. "Give me what I want, or I will kill everyone you have ever cared about and destroy your world."

"If you kill everyone I've ever cared about and destroy Earth, what possible incentive would I have left to cooperate?"

"Perhaps watching your friends suffer will change your mind. Who shall I kill first?" he questioned, pointing at the holding cells.

"You killing them isn't going to make me—"

"It will not be me killing them, but you!"

"Emma, don't do it!" shouted Bryan, reaching out for Allysa's hand. The professors also closed in toward one another, growing very anxious given what was happening.

Supay looked over at Bryan, who was encouraging Emma not to give up the Leyandermál. He walked over to Bryan and Allysa's cell and stared at them through the forcefield. "Everyone feigns bravery right before they die, but in the end, all are terrified." He spun to face Emma. "Will you still not tell me or do you prefer to watch them suffer?"

Emma's sad eyes revealed anguish for her friends but there was nothing she could do. Even if she wanted to, she couldn't give him the Leyandermál.

"Then you have chosen death for them."

"No!" screamed Logan and Emma at the same time.

Supay motioned with his hand and the top of Bryan and Allysa's holding cell retracted, opening it up to outer space. There were bars at the top of their cell to prevent them from getting sucked out completely. Bryan and Allysa let out terrifying screams as they got sucked up into the bars while their cell decompressed. Once decompression was complete, they began helplessly floating back down into their cell which was now filled with the empty vacuum of space. Within seconds, the water in their skin and blood vaporized, and shortly after that, their lungs collapsed. Soon after, they died of asphyxiation right as their bodies fully decompressed and froze. Their lifeless bodies bobbed in their cell like dead fish drifting upside down in a fishbowl.

Emma looked away, horrified. Professor Quimbey collapsed to her knees in despair, while Logan started yelling at Supay. "I'll kill you!" he screamed, finding strength in every uninjured inch of his body. "I'll kill you!" he repeated.

"Now, do you wish to watch death again?" questioned Supay, moving over to General Covington and Mr. Garrison's cell. "Or are you now ready to give me what I want?"

Emma cried. The Leyandermál always led to death, and it was a cycle that would only continue if she gave Supay what he wanted. She couldn't give in, and when Supay realized that she wouldn't, he gave the signal. His Dokalfar opened the airlock to General Covington and Mr. Garrison's cell and the two men suffered the same horrible death as Bryan and Allysa. Emma's head sunk, beginning to look defeated.

"Yes, I know it hurts watching those you care about die," taunted Supay. "It is okay, human. Pain is how you know you are the one still left alive." Supay walked over to Logan, getting ready to kill him next. "I suspect this one will hurt worse than the others."

Emma looked at Logan who, while scared, valiantly nodded that she had to see this through to the end. There was no half-way, otherwise, all their deaths would be in vain. The fate of the universe depended on her. She couldn't give in, no matter what! Not even for him.

"Still, will you not cooperate?"

Emma, her face drenched in tears, mouthed, "I'm sorry" to Logan and shook her head at Supay.

"Why do you delay what cannot be stopped?!" shouted Supay. Having watched Emma willingly sacrifice those she cared about to protect her secret, Supay realized that he had to try something different, so he signaled to his Dokalfar to flip a switch on the wall.

The table Emma was strapped to started glowing. Green energy quickly consumed it and enveloped Emma's body. Emma screamed and cried from the energy coursing through her, causing intense pain like she had never felt before. After a short pause, Supay, who seemed to be enjoying torturing her, had the energy turned up higher, drawing even more screams from Emma. "Do you still not see how this will end?!" he yelled.

"Stop!" shouted Logan, but Supay didn't care. He kept going. Emma looked like she was suffering.

In the shakiest of voices, she uttered, "I cannot give you what you want."

Supay could tell that her strength was waning. It wouldn't be much longer before he could try reading her mind again. His Dokalfar hit her with another jolt of energy, but this time, something happened that they didn't expect. Her physical form flickered for a split second, and in that instant, she didn't look like Emma, but rather, someone else.

"What?!" exclaimed Supay in Vaniryan, confused. He had the energy turned up to full power, tormenting Emma with the most possible pain. She screamed in agony until she finally lost control. She dematerialized into energy and melted away to the floor, whereafter she rematerialized in new form, her original form... it was *Isa*.

Logan, Dr. Arenot and Professor Quimbey each did a double-take when they saw Isa while Supay shrieked upon seeing the Vaniryan writhing on the ground in pain. He had been tricked!

Infuriated, Supay reached down to grab her. With what little strength she had left, and being as close to him as she was ever going to get again, she fired the fiercest blast of blue energy that her body could muster. Wrapped up in his own rage, Isa's attack actually caught Supay off guard and struck him, knocking him off his feet. He appeared hurt, with visible burn marks on his face. Supay's Dokalfar quickly shot her with the stun settings on their guns, incapacitating her. She laid on the floor in misery, barely able to move.

Supay stumbled back up, felt the wound on his face with extreme displeasure, and lifted Isa by her neck. He squeezed her throat hard to the point where she couldn't breathe, and raided her mind. Ailing badly, she couldn't resist anymore. Supay fully entered her thoughts, and after a few seconds, his expression stiffened. He finally saw the truth and understood why she had been stalling! *Emma was no longer on Earth! She had gone back in time to the battle in the Hidden City to kill him!*

Supay angrily threw Isa to the floor.

With a faint smirk that belied the agony she was in, Isa said, "You are too late. You are already dead."

Chapter 36 – Fire and Ice

The portal into the Hidden City opened, and through it strode Emma and nearly 100 soldiers from Area 51 who had agreed to go on a one-way mission to Vanirya to change human history, and perhaps, to save it, with the hope that in doing so, they would never have to go at all. It was a giant leap of existential faith forced upon them after watching Supay kill tens of millions of people and the rest of humanity facing the same fate, if they were unsuccessful. The mission objective was simple: find Supay 800-years in the past and kill him before he could ever come to Earth, while hoping that none of the temporal paradoxes of time travel that kept astrophysicists up at night came to pass.

They entered the frozen city just on the backside of a 20' tall wall of ice. The city built inside a giant glacier to hide Remnants from the Hunt looked just as Emma remembered: buildings, homes, towers, bridges, tunnels, and walkways all made of ice, with stone and metal mixed in for support, and a soft white luminescent glow emanating from the ice. There was no wind or weather inside the glacier, which was thousands of feet tall and many miles wide like the city. Rather, it was incredibly quiet and peaceful, although Emma knew that was about to change…

Soon, Supay's ships would blast through the ice ceiling and attack the Hidden City, marking Emma's return to a battle she had barely escaped the first time around. Whether she would survive the battle again remained to be seen, but regardless, she had to ensure that Supay didn't. Accompanied by trained soldiers, many armed with the Vaniryan laser-weapon prototypes that Pegasus West had been working on, they would try to stop Supay and prevent the massacre on Earth from ever happening. But their timing had to be perfect...

If they arrived too early and Supay got wind of their arrival, they would miss their window of opportunity to kill him while he was vulnerable. If they arrived too late, they risked being stranded on Vanirya when Supay destroyed the Vaniryan star, planet and them along with it, just as Emma had dreamt about in her nightmares. They had only one shot at this!

The portal deposited Emma and the soldiers right outside the walls of the compound occupied by Qelios, the Sentinel of the Hidden City, the traitor who had betrayed them all, including the Remnants he had swore to protect, by selling his loyalty to Supay. When they were trapped on Vanirya, Emma, Professor Quimbey and Captain Evans had gone to Qelios hoping he would help them return home. Instead, Qelios ambushed them, killed their Vaniryan friends, Lassar and Tamos, chased Isa and Annika to Iceland, and attempted to capture Emma for Supay. And he would have succeeded, too, had it not been for Supay killing him for his own failures, and the timely rescue efforts of Captain Velasquez, Logan, Dr. Arenot and others.

However, for one brief moment during the ambush inside Qelios' compound, they nearly defeated Supay and his Dokalfar, after a portion of ceiling in the compound's inner pyramid collapsed on top of them. Supay was vulnerable then, and that's when they should have finished him off, but they didn't. They used the opportunity to escape. Now that they had a chance to do it over again, Emma was determined to get it right this time, and she remembered the exact moment they needed to go back to do so...

ΔΔΔΔΔΔΔΔΔΔΔΔ

466

Captain Velasquez, Logan, Dr. Arenot, Commander Davis and Commander McGee burst into the massive pentagonal pyramid at the center of Qelios' compound where the ambush was taking place, just in time to find Supay dragging a helpless Emma toward the Vaniryan sphere where he planned to generate a portal to escape from.

"Emma!" screamed Logan upon seeing her. "Captain, they can't reach that sphere!" shouted Logan to Velasquez.

Captain Velasquez spotted Captain Evans firing futilely at Supay and his Dokalfar, who were protected within some kind of energy shield. Realizing that bullets were useless, he grabbed a grenade off his belt and threw it toward the sphere, trying to dislodge it or find some other way to stop them.

When Evans saw the grenade flying through the air and heard the clink on the ground, she pulled Professor Quimbey to the floor behind an ice statue. The grenade exploded, blowing the sphere off its base and knocking Supay and his Dokalfar over. Protected by their energy shields, the shrapnel didn't hurt them, or Emma who was enveloped within an extension of Supay's shielding, but with Supay on the ground, Emma was free, at least momentarily.

She jumped to her feet to run, but before she could get away, Supay leapt up himself and clutched her arm. Just then, Logan bowled into him to jar her loose again. Commander McGee crashed into Supay next, giving both Emma *and* Logan a chance to get away while he kept Supay occupied, grappling with the enemy as long as he could until Supay shot him in the stomach, killing him.

Meanwhile, Commander Davis, Captain Evans and Dr. Arenot were actively engaged in a fight of their own with the Dokalfar, firing everything they had at the enemy. Dr. Arenot spotted a large weapon on the ground near Qelios' dead body. Knowing that they needed something more powerful than their ineffective bullets, he went for the weapon! The Dokalfar spotted the professor and tried to stop him. Davis and Evans, aware their bullets were having no impact, shot the ice at the Dokalfar's feet instead, breaking up the ice and causing them to stumble slightly. It wasn't much but it was enough to make the Dokalfar miss!

After narrowly avoiding laser fire, Dr. Arenot grabbed the weapon and pulled the trigger. A red laser blast exploded from its tip and widened into a 20-foot-wide cone of laser fire that struck the Dokalfar and drove both of them back into the opposite wall. Dr. Arenot kept firing unrelentingly, hurting the Dokalfar, weakening their shields, and ultimately blowing a hole in the wall, causing ice and metal to fall on them.

Upon seeing the power of Dr. Arenot's weapon, Captain Velasquez shouted to the professor while pointing up at the ceiling above Supay, who had just killed Commander McGee, "Shoot up!" Dr. Arenot fired the potent weapon at the pyramid's ceiling several times and it came crashing down on Supay along with two side walls.

There was no way of knowing if Supay or his Dokalfar were dead, but with them covered in debris, that was their chance to escape. Logan, Emma, Evans, Quimbey, Arenot, Davis, and Velasquez ran out of the pyramid. When they reached the outside of the compound, the battle in the Hidden City was underway…

Supay's fighter ships were flying through the city shooting buildings and leveling structures. Remnants everywhere were scrambling for cover. Chunks of ice were falling from the glacial ceiling as the ships broke through, flattening houses, while Dokalfar were sweeping the streets on foot, firing upon Remnants.

As chaos reigned and explosions echoed, Velasquez led them all out of Qelios' compound to rendezvous with the other rescue team at the predetermined portal extraction point to return home…

ΔΔΔΔΔΔΔΔΔΔΔΔ

And *that* was when future Emma and the soldiers hiding off to the side of Qelios' compound, who were waiting for the past versions of Emma, Logan, Velasquez and the others to exit so as to not disrupt their timeline, made their move to go back in for Supay!

"Now!" screamed Emma to Commander Reynolds, the highest-ranking military officer in the group.

"Let's move!" ordered Reynolds to the soldiers under his command.

Guided by Emma, who knew the way, they stormed the compound all the way into the pentagonal pyramid with the soldiers carrying the Vaniryan prototype weapons charging in first. They found Supay and one of his Dokalfar slowly digging themselves out from the debris that had toppled down on top of them and began shooting immediately.

The majority of soldiers wielding the prototype weapons went for Supay, while a smaller group attacked the single Dokalfar emerging from the rubble. Another platoon of soldiers, mostly those without prototype weapons, stationed themselves outside the pyramid and throughout the compound, keeping an eye out for more enemy combatants. However, lacking prototype weapons, they stood little chance. Still, for the plan to work, they knew they needed to stand their ground.

The troops poured into the pyramid first, with Emma going in last. Just as they had hoped, the onslaught of soldiers caught Supay and his Dokalfar by surprise. The single remaining Dokalfar was unprepared for the incoming fire and U.S. forces swiftly overwhelmed him. With his protective shield already weakened from Dr. Arenot's previous attack, the Dokalfar fell back into the pile of debris, injured. The soldiers circled above him and finished him off, but not before he was able to send a signal calling for reinforcements.

When the rest of the soldiers attacked Supay, he immediately surrounded himself in a protective shield and fought back. He counter-attacked with multiple energy strikes, killing or incapacitating most of the soldiers, but they kept coming in waves, showing absolutely no concern for their own safety. They had only one thought: kill Supay in the past and prevent this suicide mission from ever happening!

Those soldiers fortunate enough to evade Supay's rapid-fire counterattacks shot back relentlessly, and they were making progress even at the expense of their own lives, as Supay seemed to be weakening. Although he continued to kill soldiers, he was badly outnumbered and, with U.S. forces using Vaniryan-based weapons not useless bullets, his protective shield was faltering. Even his energy discharges were slowing down. With the soldiers bearing down on him, Supay attempted to escape...

He began to change his form into energy so that he could exit through a wall. Soldiers' laser blasts began passing right through him. When Emma saw what he was doing, she sprinted forward and fired a blast of energy from her hands at his dematerializing form. When her energy struck his, it caused Supay's energy transformation to fluctuate and Supay to rematerialize back into himself. She had stopped him.

Supay, shocked, cackled when it was over, even while reeling in pain from her energy strike. "You are far more than the Missing Remnant," he uttered, realizing that he had underestimated her. A few minutes earlier, he had been dragging her helplessly on the ground, and suddenly, she had explosive power sufficient to overcome even his own. He tried to read her mind but couldn't! Emma's control over the power the Vaniryans had given her was increasing by the second, and her mind was no longer his to invade. Regardless, he taunted her, "Still, it will not be enough to save you!"

Supay stood tall. Everything he had ever wanted was standing right in front of him. He fired an energy strike at the wall behind the attacking soldiers, causing it to collapse. The wall and ceiling crashed down on many of them while the remaining soldiers scrambled to avoid falling debris. Emma herself had to dive out of harm's way.

Supay clearly knew what he was doing because waiting just outside the fallen wall were more Dokalfar! Worse, with the pyramid's interior now laid bare to the glacial sky with three of its five walls down, there were several fighter ships hovering above with a clear shot to fire in. The Dokalfar waiting outside charged in

470

while the fighter ships fired away at the U.S. troops, obliterating them in multiples.

Emma's heart sank. They had Supay badly outnumbered at a time when he was weak, and they had failed to kill him. Now, the tide was turning. Had they squandered the precious time Isa's gambit had given them? And just when she thought things couldn't get worse, she looked up out of the broken pyramid and saw a flash of bright light beneath the glacial ceiling. When it was over, dozens of new ships had appeared, having portaled into the Hidden City. Thinking back to the last battle, Emma knew *those ships weren't supposed to be there!* Almost immediately, transport vessels and fighter ships dropped out of bays from the bottoms of the larger ships and began heading their way. Emma's plan was failing.

"Look out!" screamed Commander Reynolds, shoving Emma to the side to save her from an incoming shot by a ship that had her in its sights. The attack narrowly missed her but resulted in an explosion that threw them both into the air and away from the impact. They landed on the far side of debris and took cover. Their faces were burned from the explosion and Reynolds had a deep cut on his cheek.

"That looks bad," remarked Emma.

"I'll live. We have to abort! There's no way we can—" Another explosion interrupted him mid-sentence.

"We can't let Supay get away!" objected Emma.

"I know, but look around, James! It's over! We've gotta get our team to that extraction portal your friends are headed to, the one you said brought you all home the last time you escaped this mess," insisted Commander Reynolds, ducking and returning fire.

"We won't make it!" replied Emma, a foreboding realization further reinforced when the transport vessels dropping from the ships reached the ground and more Dokalfar poured out of them, running in their direction. "We were never going to, I'm sorry," she said in a low voice barely audible over the screams of more dying soldiers.

By that point, Emma wasn't even sure how many soldiers were left alive.

Reynolds sighed. He knew she was right. The end was near. Ready to finish what they started, he said, "Okay. Now what?"

"We kill Supay."

"Which one?" he replied, pointing out of an open section of wall where *another* Supay and a horde of Dokalfar were walking toward the pyramid on foot. The future had come for her! Emma now knew Isa's gambit had failed and Isa and Logan were probably dead. With humanity's fate hanging in the balance, it was now or never!

Emma, with tears in her eyes, looked at Commander Reynolds and asked, "Are you ready?"

Realizing what she was suggesting, Reynolds replied, "You sure?"

She nodded with a tearful grin, and he nodded back honorably.

"Good... Cover me!"

Emma sprung up from behind the ice debris with Reynolds right behind her. She made a beeline toward the original Supay from the past, trying to get to him before the future Supay could reach what remained of the pyramid. The Dokalfar began firing at them. Reynolds ran behind Emma, keeping pace and firing rapidly to buy Emma time while she displayed additional mastery of her powers, dematerializing into energy so that the lasers would pass right through her. After doing so, she reached Supay almost instantaneously, while the Dokalfar eventually killed Reynolds, who had fulfilled his duty to the very end.

The speed with which Emma moved stunned Supay, who didn't expect it. Before he could even react, she exploded with energy, releasing every part of her heart and soul outward with a ferocity spurred by her desire to save the human race. The explosion killed almost everyone around her and leveled the last two remaining walls which, amazingly, were still supporting one another up to the peak of the once-pentagonal pyramid. The walls fell directly on top of her and Supay. There was nothing left but a pile of rubble when the other Supay from the future and his Dokalfar arrived, and they had prisoners in tow: Logan and Isa.

"Stupid girl, you have failed yet again," stated Supay in Vaniryan, well aware that if her desperate final act had succeeded in killing his prior self, he wouldn't be standing there with his past erased, but the fact that he was meant she hadn't. More Dokalfar from outside gathered around. Logan and Isa tried to break free but they weren't going anywhere. Logan was far too beat up to escape, and Isa broken to the point of powerlessness.

Supay looked over the remaining debris and saw movement. He spotted a hand clawing its way out from beneath the pile. The Dokalfar readied themselves for more bloodshed while Logan's and Isa's spirits lifted briefly, but soon, they all saw that it was Supay from the past, and not Emma, emerging from the rubble, looking battered. Logan closed his eyes and dipped his head when past Supay fully climbed his way out.

"You fool, you almost got us both killed," chided future Supay at his prior self.

The past Supay brushed himself off and responded, "She is the Leyandermál. None who succumb to her are fools, but it no longer matters. What was hers is now ours!"

"You have it?" asked the future Supay, his alien eyes enlarging.

"The universe is ours, brother!" shouted past Supay to his future self. With glee, and to Logan and Isa's horror, past Supay showed them all what he had obtained from Emma, making a sweeping hand movement that conjured up translucent images above their heads of the smallest fundamental particles in existence, quarks and electrons. The particles were so small that they consisted of nothing but themselves, like prime numbers.

"I can see creation!" crowed past Supay, twirling his hand to swirl the particles together. The quarks combined into protons and neutrons, and then, he mixed them with the electrons, forming a new combination of larger particles. He continued to build several more unique looking particles and then smashed them together, creating an explosion.

The explosion careened outward at light speed and they watched from within the middle of it all as the universe was formed. The exploding particles expanded, forming atoms. Those atoms joined with others until they formed balls of light that continued hurtling outward into empty space and replicating even more. The balls of light began forming stars, quickly multiplying into hundreds of billions of stars before turning into galaxies. And what started as a few galaxies soon became hundreds of billions of galaxies crashing through space away from the center of the universe at the speed of light until it all stopped right where they were standing.

With the future Supay salivating over the power, the past Supay said aloud, "I have seen the beginning of the universe, and now, I can see the end!" He moved his hands around again and formulated more combinations of quarks and electrons. He manipulated their shapes and merged them together to create new particles never before seen in existence, and started a chain reaction that he corralled in his hands like a fireball. He then flung it toward one of the visible galaxies and watched while the galaxy imploded in on its core and collapsed completely. The galaxy's destruction was nearly immediate.

"We *control* existence!" exclaimed the future Supay.

"No, brother, we *are* existence!" declared past Supay, much to the delight of the future Supay and their hooting army of Dokalfar. "The universe is ours to rule, ours to destroy, and ours to rebuild!"

An evil grin stretched across the future Supay's face, but then, he wondered, "If you possess the Leyandermál, then why do I not?"

"Because she still lives beneath the rubble and it remains her destiny to kill me when she emerges before what I possess can become yours."

The future Supay's eyes narrowed in consternation. "But it should be mine," he uttered, frustrated that the knowledge now known to his prior self was not also known to him.

"And it will be, once we intervene in her future and kill her before it is too late! Her power grows fast, brother. I can feel it. We must annihilate this pyramid and everything in it, from the sky! Destroy it!" The Dokalfar started to act upon the order.

"Hold!" hollered the future Supay. The Dokalfar looked at each other, uncertain who to listen to. Future Supay gestured to Logan and Isa, who were being held down by the Dokalfar, and asked, "And what about these two?"

"Destroy the pyramid! We don't have time to waste on the humans!" the past Supay shouted, worried about Emma re-emerging.

"And yet, you are," replied the future Supay.

The past Supay looked at Logan and Isa and said, "We have no more use for them." He stepped closer to the captives and stared into their helpless eyes. He glared at Logan, and after reading the boy's mind, yelled, "And no, human, love will never conquer all!"

"That is where you're wrong!" Logan snapped back, defiant until the very end.

The past Supay scowled and fired bolts of energy into Logan's and Isa's hearts, killing them both instantly and howling joyously while the Dokalfar reveled in their deaths. The past Supay turned and shouted, "Now, hurry, destroy the pyramid! We're running out of time!"

The future Supay, pleased with his prior self's choice to kill the prisoners, and ready to finally receive the power that was rightfully his, screamed, "Annihilate the pyramid and everything in it! And then, we will destroy *Earth*, and finish off these miserable humans once and for all!" The Dokalfar army cheered even louder.

They raced out of the center of the ruins where the pentagonal pyramid once stood, leaving Logan's and Isa's dead bodies behind. After they got far enough away, the future Supay gave the order to his ship in the sky. "Fire!"

The ship fired and obliterated the ground where the pyramid was while the Dokalfar continued to raucously hoot and howl. The pyramid was gone, disintegrated by the ship's beam.

"It is finally ours!" howled the future Supay.

"No, it isn't. What is mine will never be yours!" responded the past Supay.

The future Supay, initially puzzled by the comment, then watched as the past Supay's face and body melted away, dematerializing and re-forming into a new one: *Emma's*.

"No!" screamed future Supay, falling to one knee after realizing what he had just done.

Emma, with tears pouring down her face and her heart torn apart after having just shot and killed Logan and Isa, was still able to find satisfaction in Supay's mortified expression. "I may be stupid, but at least I still exist."

Supay wanted to attack her but couldn't. His arms and legs froze. He was suddenly unable to move. "This can't be!" he shrieked, gazing weakly at Emma.

Emma surveyed all the destruction and death around her and met Supay's gaze. "Get out of my universe!"

Supay screamed in anger as he began to wither away, with time itself coming to take back his very existence. Emma watched victoriously as he disintegrated into nothingness, and his irate screams dissipated into thin air, right about the same time as everything began to disappear for her, as well…

Chapter 37 – The Cityscape

Emma, Logan, Bryan, Allysa, Professor Quimbey, Dr. Arenot and Captain Evans sat around a circular table in a lavishly decorated private room in one of Manhattan's finest top-floor restaurants, *The Cityscape*, which was managed by Logan's mother. The room had floor to ceiling windows, a breathtaking view of the New York skyline, and fancy appetizers spread across the table, but all anyone was paying attention to, at the moment, was Emma.

"So, you're saying you shot Logan, just like that?" asked Bryan, astonished by Emma's story.

"Yep," responded Emma with a playful smile. "Isa, too."

"Just like that? No hesitation?" followed up Allysa, amazed.

"None at all?" asked Logan, hoping she hesitated even just a little.

"Nope," Emma replied, chuckling. "It was the only way to convince Supay."

"But what if you were wrong?" questioned Logan, flabbergasted.

"Well, in that case, I doubt any of us would be here today, anyway," replied Emma.

"I still can't believe you did it!" exclaimed Bryan.

"I can. James is bad ass. Always has been," said Captain Evans, who was recovering from wounds she suffered during the ambush in Falaise. The skirmish had transpired slightly differently in the new timeline with Captain Velasquez an ally, not an enemy.

"You're not going to get an argument from me," remarked Dr. Arenot. "Not when she saved the entire human race."

"Don't forget about the Vaniryans. She saved their whole planet, too," Professor Quimbey reminded him.

"Not bad for a cryptologist," teased Logan.

"Ha. Ha. Very funny," replied Emma.

Allysa, still trying to grasp the magnitude of it all, asked Emma while gesturing to herself, Bryan and Logan, "So, you're saying we all died…"

"Uh-huh."

"And Supay blew up Vanirya right after we escaped from the Hidden City… and then, he came to Earth and destroyed Los Angeles, Nashville, Rome, Mexico City, Prague, Shanghai, Dallas, Paris, Berlin, Miami, New York—"

"Yep… This restaurant was toast," interjected Emma.

"That's probably the only way to get my mom a few days off," joked Logan.

Allysa kept going. "And by killing Supay—"

"I didn't kill him," corrected Emma.

"Right, you tricked him into killing himself… and when he did that, it changed the past and stopped all that from happening?"

"Not bad, right?" Emma asked rhetorically.

"Not bad? It's the most incredible story I've ever heard!" exclaimed Allysa.

"You're, like, a comic book superhero!" declared Bryan.

"You know, Bryan," Emma started to say, "every single one of us has been to another planet and either fought an evil supervillain or his army; some of you even died in the fight and came back to life, so, I think it's fair to say we are *all* superheroes."

Bryan's face lit up when she said it. It might have been the greatest moment of his entire life.

Logan patted Bryan on the back. "You hear that, Bryan? You're a superhero."

"I wish Dewey was here. He would have been proud of us," said Bryan reminiscently, referring to his late friend and former owner of Dewey's Comic Books & Hobby Shop.

"He is," Logan assured him.

"Yeah," Bryan replied softly.

"So, how did the president and General Covington react when you told them about all this?" Professor Quimbey asked Emma. "I bet they were gobsmacked, and Orson probably threw a wobbly."

"Gobsmacked isn't the word I'd use, but let's just say, they've all had a lot of questions for me. I guess that's what happens when you're the only one who remembers saving the world."

"I feel like such an underachiever right now," said Allysa while laughing at herself. Bryan half hugged her.

Dr. Arenot was shaking his head in bewilderment. "I remember that fight in Qelios' compound like it was yesterday..."

"Professor, it was your shot in the past that buried Supay and gave us the opening we needed," stated Emma. "Had you not done that…"

"Well, working in the past is what us archeologists do best," joked Dr. Arenot. "It's funny though how differently I recall what happened in the Hidden City from how you described it. I remember escaping Qelios' compound after the wall collapsed on Supay and making it back to the rendezvous portal fairly easily."

"Trust me, it wasn't that easy the first time around. We barely made it to the extraction point and Supay nearly stopped us," said Emma, who was the only one who remembered the prior timeline, something she attributed to the Leyandermál and her ability to see and understand space and time in a way others didn't, or couldn't.

Dr. Arenot chuckled and continued, "Well, *this* time, Supay was nowhere to be found. I recall watching all the Dokalfar running toward Qelios' compound and thinking to myself, 'where are they all going?' Now, I know. They were off to defend Supay."

"I guess knowing what happened in the past helped save the universe," said Logan. "It's like Mr. Jackson always used to say… I mean, he's probably still saying it today: '*History is the greatest teacher, not me… It provides us with a rich compendium of information about the past, guiding us to learn from our mistakes and enabling us to make better choices in the future than our ancestors made…. so we better pay attention to our history.*' Wiser words have never been spoken."

"Hear! Hear!" uttered Dr. Arenot, wholeheartedly agreeing.

"By the way, where's Isa?" asked Professor Quimbey.

"She had somewhere else to be," Emma replied.

"Oh," Professor Quimbey responded, disappointed.

The double doors into the private dining room opened, and in walked Logan's mom.

"How's it going in here?" inquired Loretta.

"Ms. Richards, they've brought us so much food already that I don't know how I'm going to make it to the main course," said Bryan.

"Main course? I'm not even going to make it to the salad course," confessed Allysa.

"That's what leftovers are for," Loretta replied, winking at Logan, who practically grew up on them. "Emma, your mother texted to say they are on their way, just stuck in a little traffic."

"Oh, okay. Thank you," replied Emma, slightly disappointed that her parents weren't on-time.

Loretta responded, "I'm sure they'll be here soon, but in the meantime, there is someone else who wanted to stop by and say hello..."

In walked Emma's best friend, Chad Peters, along with Chad's boyfriend, Christopher. "Someone told me there's an engagement party going on in here!" said Chad exuberantly.

"Chad!" yelped Emma at the top of her lungs, leaping up from her chair and running over to hug him. "OMG! I can't believe you're here!"

After absorbing Emma's impact, Chad responded, "Are you kidding? I wouldn't miss this for anything! If my two favorite people in the world are getting engaged and having a party to celebrate, I'm coming to New York. End of discussion!"

Chad looked down at the engagement ring on Emma's hand, the one Logan had *originally* intended to give her, and his mouth fell open. He pulled her hand closer to get a better look. "Em, it's beautiful!"

"I know!" she blurted back, looking over at Logan with a huge smile.

Chad nodded approvingly at Logan, while Emma hugged Christopher next.

"Christopher, it's so great to finally meet you in person! I've heard so much about you," she said.

"Only good things, I hope,"

Emma shook her head. "Sorry. Chad only says *great* things about you."

Christopher laughed and put his hand on Chad, embarrassed and blushing. "Well, Chad only says great things about all of you, too."

Emma looked over at Logan. "Did you do this?"

Logan grinned. Emma hurried over to embrace him. "Thank you for inviting Chad!" she whispered in his ear. "I love you so much."

"I know."

Logan and the others went over to say hello to Chad and Christopher while Captain Evans, who wasn't quite mobile yet, remained seated.

"Wow, look at that spread!" uttered Chad, spotting the table full of appetizers. "I don't mind if I do." Chad moved over to help himself while Christopher continued to chat.

"Eat up everyone, there's a lot more on the way," announced Loretta.

"Bring it on, Ms. R!" encouraged Chad, happy to hear more food was coming. After all, as a former college football player standing 6' 3", he was a big boy and still had an immense appetite even though he wasn't playing anymore. He'd quit the team after sophomore year to focus on his studies in Comparative Literature, and according to Emma, he'd never been happier.

"Mom, seriously, how much more food do we need?"

"Enough for 16."

"16?" replied Logan.

"Well, don't forget, I'm joining you, Emma's parents, and, umm, we may have a few others coming, too…"

Right on time, the doors to the private room splashed open and in walked the Secret Service followed by the President of the United States, Andrew Barrett, First Lady Patricia Barrett, General Covington and Miles Garrison.

"Now, this is what a State Dinner should look like!" proclaimed the president, subsequently giving his Secret Service the okay to wait outside. They exited and closed the doors behind them.

"Mr. President!" blurted Emma, surprised to see him.

"Thank you for coming!" said Logan, walking over to shake the president's hand and greet the First Lady. Everyone did the same except for Chad and Christopher, who were frozen in awe, having never met the president before, and the injured Captain Evans.

Evans tried to snap to attention from her chair to salute President Barrett and General Covington, but the president quickly told her, "As you were, Captain. You've earned the right to stay put after everything you've done. It should be us saluting you." At that moment, both President Barrett and General Covington saluted *her*.

"Thank you, sir," replied Captain Evans, returning the salute with pride.

The president surveyed the room and said, "Look at that view! The Cityscape has always been one of my favorite restaurants. I can't remember the last time we were here. Pat, what's it been, 5, 10 years?"

"Quite a bit longer than that. Since long before you were anyone important," answered the First Lady.

"Are you sure? I honestly can't remember a time when I *wasn't* important," replied the president, only partially kidding.

"Oh, trust me dear," said the First Lady.

Loretta settled the debate. "Respectfully, sir, I'm going to side with the First Lady on this one. I've worked here for a long time. I'm sure I would've remembered you."

The president, amused, conceded. "I won't argue with either of you, especially since I make it a point not to argue with people when I'm wrong."

"So, when's the big day?" the First Lady asked Emma and Logan.

"Oh, we haven't even talked about that yet," responded Emma.

Sensing the opportunity, the president jumped in. "My offer still stands, you know. I am happy to marry you right now. The view is spectacular from up here. It's a perfect venue. Miles, can I marry them in New York?"

"Nope," responded Mr. Garrison coldly.

"Seriously? Not in New York, either?" questioned the president, thwarted yet again.

Mr. Garrison responded with an eye roll, "Mr. President, I knew you were going to ask because you're as predictable as a clock, so I had the staff look it up before we left. As far as marriage officiating goes, the 'most powerful man in the world,' you are not."

Emma giggled. "Thank you, Mr. President, but really, it's okay. I think we're good."

"How about your honeymoon? Any thoughts on where you'd like to go for that?" asked the president. "Because, on behalf of the people of the United States of America, who will never know what you did for this country because of some top-secret classifications and a whole lot of black ink, I'd like to thank you both by paying for your honeymoon. Anywhere you want to go."

"Mr. President, that is incredibly generous!" uttered Emma appreciatively.

"Thank you!" exclaimed Logan. "I guess we were thinking, maybe somewhere exotic so we can finally relax."

"Exotic, as in *out-of-this-world*-exotic or lay-around-and-do-nothing-exotic?" pried Bryan. "Because I don't picture Batman lying on a beach drinking Mai Tais. I always imagine superheroes vacationing in interesting places where stuff might go down."

"Bryan!" snapped Allysa. "It's their honeymoon, let them plan it!"

"I don't know… doing nothing sounds pretty good to me right about now," considered Logan.

Bryan snickered. "No way. You two? Relaxing and doing nothing? I don't see it. If you two were lying on a beach somewhere, one of you would dig something up or find a map on a rock that leads to a clue that leads to someplace interesting. You guys can't help yourselves."

"Bryan has a point," acknowledged Logan.

With a full-fledged grin, Emma informed the president, "Sir, we're still thinking about it, but if you're paying, I know for sure one place we want to go back to, is Italy… to, umm, visit Annika…"

General Covington's eyebrows raised, while the president chuckled to himself.

"Well, I think Italy sounds like a perfect honeymoon," said the First Lady, not remotely appreciating the significance of what Emma was actually proposing.

"And then, maybe, Delta Monocerotis," added Emma.

General Covington swallowed hard.

"Now that's interesting!" uttered Bryan. He looked at Allysa and said, "You see, I told you so."

The doors to the private room opened once again, and in came waiters to deliver champagne glasses with the Secret Service carefully watching their every move. Once they handed out all the glasses, the waiters left and the president clinked his glass. "I'd like to make a toast."

Everyone quieted down. The president had the floor…

"Now, you'll have to forgive me because I didn't have my speech writers work on this, but I'd like to say that I have never been happier to give a toast for two people I'm not related to in my life than I am for Logan and Emma. I met you both, what, 3½ or 4 years ago? And I was prepared to arrest you that day." The room laughed. "True story. For those of you who haven't heard it, they broke into the CIA Director's phone somehow, stole my phone number and finagled their way into my office to talk to me. And yes, Bryan, Chad, we've always known it was you two who helped them…"

Bryan's and Chad's faces went flush. "Are we in trouble?" asked Bryan, worried.

The president laughed. "Don't worry, I'm pretty sure we lost the files on the incident a few years ago. Anyway, Emma, Logan, you're both extraordinary. You truly are. I am constantly amazed by your commitment to decency, your pursuit of truth, your compassion for others, your brilliance, of course, and most importantly, your unbreakable love for one another. Over and over again, I have witnessed the lengths you two are willing to go for each other, I have seen the way you look at one another, and it's obvious to me that you belong together. You make each other better. You make the people around you better. You make our country better. And I am sure your marriage will make the universe better. So, let's everyone raise a glass to Logan and Emma! Congratulations!"

"To Logan and Emma!" said the room collectively, raising their champagne flutes and taking a sip.

Logan and Emma kissed one another celebratorily.

"And one more toast!" announced the president. He looked over at Loretta and asked, "That is, if it's okay with you?"

Loretta nodded.

"I would also like to congratulate Ms. Loretta Richards, the White House's newest Executive Banquet Coordinator. She'll be working with the White House Social Secretary, the White House Executive Chef, the White House Executive Pastry Chef and the White House Chief Floral Designer. And Logan, I promise the job will be far fewer hours than she's working now."

"Mom, really?!" asked Logan.

"Uh-huh," replied Loretta ecstatically.

Logan went over to hug his mom. "What about the restaurant?"

"I gave notice this morning. It's time. I'm moving to D.C. in two weeks."

"That's incredible!" stated Logan, looking over at the president and saying, "Thank you, Mr. President!"

The president replied, "No need to thank me. Miles let me know there was an opening and, well, I could think of no one more perfect for the job than someone with your mother's experience. She wowed everyone she interviewed with."

"Did you hear that? I wowed them," Loretta said to Logan, laughing.

"Mom, I'm really proud of you."

With a warm smile, Loretta replied back, "And I could not be any more proud of or happy for both of you." She waved Emma over for a three-way hug. Once she had them in her arms, she asked, "So, I assume you both plan to continue with your Pentagon internship?"

"Definitely," Logan replied, while Emma laughed before answering, "For sure."

"Just promise me you're both going to re-enroll in Georgetown next semester and finish your studies, okay?"

"Yes, mom," responded Logan, moderately embarrassed.

"Of course," Emma promised.

"Good."

Into the room came the waiters again, carrying more food.

Chad's eyes lit up. "Alright, let's eat!" he blurted.

Chapter 38 – Homecoming

Tassa was busy straightening up her small tree home from the mess of recently departed guests, pushing chairs back under the table and washing bowls, cups, and plates. Isa had been gone from Jaannos for a long time, roughly 68 sun cycles to be exact (or approximately 816 Earth years), and Tassa had counted every one of them, never giving up hope that Isa might one day return home. She had disappeared when the visitors from Earth left Jaannos with Lassar and Tamos to go find the Hidden City, and everyone had assumed Isa went with them, although no one really knew for sure.

What Tassa did know was that, shortly after Lassar and Tamos left Jaannos with the Earth visitors, anecdotes spoke of a group of Remnants, including a young Remnant girl, and off-worlders visiting the Hidden City on the day of the legendary battle that changed Vaniryan history forever. Stories recounted how the Remnants and off-worlders spearheaded a fight against Supay and his Hunt that resulted in Supay's defeat and the scattering of the Dokalfar. Tales told by Remnants who survived described great explosions, ships blasting away at the city, Dokalfar attacking Remnants on foot, off-worlders fighting back, falling chunks of ice from the glacial ceiling smashing homes, mystical portals appearing and disappearing in the sky and on the ground, and the obliteration of Qelios' compound and most of the Hidden City.

The stories had spread throughout the land and Tassa had always believed that Isa, Lassar, and Tamos had played a part in what had happened, and for that, she was grateful. Still, she missed Isa terribly. While she presumed Isa, Lassar and Tamos were dead after 68 sun cycles passing without their return, a small part of her held out hope that they might have escaped through one of the portals described in the stories. But if they did, why hadn't they returned to Jaannos? Tassa knew it was because they were most likely dead, but then again, their bodies had never been found, which, given the devastation left behind in the now-defunct Hidden City, was neither surprising nor definitive.

And so, every double-full-moon, Isa's friends would gather in Tassa's home to celebrate Isa, just as they had tonight. They would share their favorite memories of her and hang new keepsakes or remembrances of her on notches carved in the tree branch that poked through the middle of Tassa's floor and disappeared into the ceiling. After 68 sun cycles, there were a *lot* of trinkets and knick-knacks hanging on the tree limb.

With Supay now nothing more than a distant memory, Jaannos had thinned out. No longer needing to hide from the Hunt, many Remnants had returned to bigger cities or more populated areas. Others, like Tassa, had remained in Jaannos, having grown used to the simplicity of life in the tree village. But those weren't the only reasons Tassa had stayed behind. She had remained in case Isa ever came walking through the door again. She wasn't ready to give up. She wasn't sure if she ever would be.

Tassa was scooping water from a bucket to wash dishes when the door behind her slowly opened. Tassa often dreamt of the day when she would finally hear the sound of Isa's little feet coming through the door again, and regularly imagined it even while awake. So when it first happened, she didn't turn around, assuming that she was imagining things or that it was another friend from Jaannos. But then, she heard a familiar voice call out her name...

"Tassa..."

Tassa dropped the dishes in her hands, and they crashed into the bucket. She trepidatiously turned around, afraid to find that her imagination was mocking her, as it had before. When she saw Isa standing there, albeit wearing strange clothes, and not a little girl but a young adult-looking-version of the child she remembered, she fell to her knees, overcome with emotion. She couldn't believe her eyes! Before the tears even had time to run down her face, she bounced back up, screamed "Issor!" and rushed over to hug her.

Isa, who was holding a bag full of books and keepsakes that she had brought back from Earth, set it down on the floor and met Tassa halfway. "I've missed you so much!" exclaimed Isa, wearing clothing borrowed from Emma's closet.

"I can't believe you're alive!" cried Tassa.

"I know. I'm so sorry!" apologized Isa, her guilt from stowing away on Emma's Hidden City-bound adventure with Lassar and Tamos without telling anyone, having weighed heavily on her mind for the last 816 years.

"It's okay," Tassa reassured her, having let go of any resentment she felt for that decision, long ago.

"But it's not. I should have told you," responded Isa, unwilling to let herself off the hook so easily just because Tassa was willing to.

"Shh. You're here now. That's all that matters to me," replied Tassa, refusing to dwell and hugging Isa even tighter.

Isa was incredibly relieved. She squeezed Tassa back while tears ran down her cheeks. Pure joy set in.

Their hug lasted for as long as any hug could last. Neither wanted to let go. While they embraced, Isa gazed at the tree branch growing out of the floor. She had always loved that branch, the trinkets and keepsakes hanging from it, the glowing floral bulbs blossoming up and down it, everything! The branch was quintessential Jaannos, and it was one of her fondest memories of a home that, until she walked through the door, she wasn't sure she would ever see again. After more than 800-years away on an adventure that she had so desperately craved to have, she was finally home.

Looking around, everything seemed pretty much the same as when she left, and that was just fine with her, and truthfully, exactly what she would have expected. In Jaannos, things rarely changed, which was what had spurred her decision to sneak off on Emma's adventure in the first place, not that she regretted it. On Earth, she had lived dozens of different lives, each more unique than the next, an experience she never could have had in Jaannos. She had truly *lived*, seen amazing things, fallen in love, had a family, and been loved. And she would cherish it all for the rest of her life.

"Look at all the trinkets hanging from the branch," remarked Isa, wiping away tears. "The tree is so full."

"It is full of you, Issor, of memories of you from everyone who has ever loved you," replied Tassa.

"It's incredible," said Isa, approaching the tree with astonishment. And that's when Isa saw it, halfway up the branch, something shiny dangling at eye level. It was a heart-shaped pendant necklace. Isa gravitated to it immediately and lifted it off the branch.

Tassa said, "It belonged to the Earth-girl who came to Jaannos right before you disappeared."

"Her name was Emma. She's family," replied Isa.

Her response surprised Tassa, who suddenly had more questions on top of the mountain of questions she already had, but for now, Tassa was content to reply, "She left it for you. She said you would enjoy it."

"She was right," Isa responded, with as big a smile as her tiny Vaniryan mouth would allow. After a momentary pause, Isa turned to Tassa and said, "Tassa, I have a lot to tell you. You're going to be gobsmacked!"

The End...

Audiobooks

If you enjoyed reading *The Coordinate, The Hidden Coordinate* and *The Final Coordinate,* perhaps you would enjoy listening to the series performed by the amazing audio narrator, MacLeod Andrews! Produced by Podium Audio and available on Audible, MacLeod's narration will take you on a whole new journey to the stars…

THE COORDINATE (Book 1 in *The Coordinate* Series)

THE HIDDEN COORDINATE (Book 2 in *The Coordinate* Series)

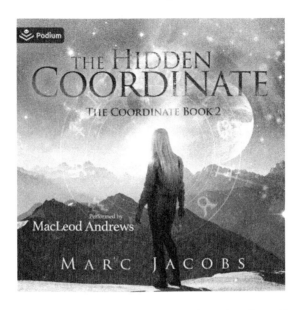

THE FINAL COORDINATE (Book 3 in *The Coordinate* Series)

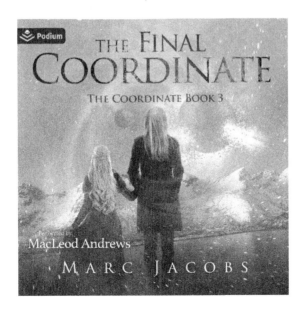

More...

Please Leave A Review

Thank you for buying THE FINAL COORDINATE, Book 3 in THE COORDINATE Series. I truly hope that you enjoyed it, and if you did, please consider leaving a review and/or rating it so that others can discover THE COORDINATE Series and join in on the adventures of Emma James and Logan West. I would love to hear your feedback. Leaving a review anywhere would be great, but also, please consider leaving a review on Amazon or Goodreads too! And of course, email me directly if you would like! I'd love to hear from you.

Receive Updates

Receive updates for new books and audiobook releases by signing up for the Updates Mailing List at **www.marcjacobsauthor.com**.

Contact Me

If you would like to contact me, I would love to hear from you. Please visit my website at **www.marcjacobsauthor.com** or shoot me an email at **marc@marcjacobsauthor.com**.

Thank you!

Marc

Credits

Book Cover: Alexandre Rito / Podium Audio

Voynich Manuscript Cover and All Interior Images depicting the Voynich Manuscript, in whole or in part - Beinecke Rare Book & Manuscript Library, Yale University

World Map Image: shutterstock1249221784 by Andrei Minsk

Interior Images of the Stars: shutterstock 1202146780 by Matsumoto

Snorralaug Photo, credit TommyBee, 2007 (https://en.wikipedia.org/wiki/File:Snorralaug10.JPG)

Arco_romanico_e_porticato_del_teatro_Corte_seconda_del_Milion_Venezia, credit Wolfgang Moroder, 2015 (https://commons.wikimedia.org/wiki/File:Arco_romanico_e_porticato_del_teatro_Corte_seconda_del_Milion_Venezia.jpg)

Marco Polo Plaque, credit Sailko, 2014 (https://commons.wikimedia.org/wiki/File:Venezia,_casa_di_marco_polo_della_corte_del_milion_vista_dal_canale,_targa.JPG)

Royal Coat of Arms of the United Kingdom, Artist, credit Sodacan, 2010 (https://commons.wikimedia.org/wiki/File:Royal_Coat_of_Arms_of_the_United_Kingdom.svg)

Painting, Nicolas_Poussin, Et in Arcadia ego, 1628 (https://commons.wikimedia.org/wiki/File:Nicolas_Poussin_-_Et_in_Arcadia_ego_(deuxi%C3%A8me_version).jpg)

Beinecke Rare Book & Manuscript Library Interior (34254026911).jpg, credit Gunnar Klack, 2014 (https://commons.wikimedia.org/wiki/File:Beinecke_Rare_Book_%26_Manuscript_Library_Interior_(34254026911).jpg)

Printed in Great Britain
by Amazon

78236188R00285